dial M for mascara

Kyle Wallace

mousetrap press

First published in Great Britain in 2009 by
mousetrap press
33 Latham House
London
E1 0RB

This novel is entirely a work of fiction. The names, characters, events and localities are of the author's creation and any resemblance to actual persons alive or dead is purely coincidental.

Copyright © Kyle Wallace 2009

The moral right of the author has been asserted.

All rights reserved. No part of this publication may be reproduced, stored in a retrieval system, or transmitted, in any form or by any means, electronic, mechanical, photocopying, recording or otherwise, without the prior permission of the publishers. This book is sold subject to the condition that it shall not, by way of trade or, be lent, re-sold, hired or otherwise circulated without the publisher's prior consent in any form of binding or cover other than that in which it is published and without a similar condition including this condition being imposed on the subsequent purchaser.

ISBN 978-0-9563588-0-6

Photography and cover design by Jonathan Dredge.

A catalogue record of this book is available from the British Library.

Typeset in Adobe Garamond by Chandler Design
Printed by Ashford Press

www.dialmformascara.co.uk

With thanks to:

*Kevin Collins (just for being Kevin),
Jonathan Dredge (for being the coolest photographer),
Paula Bedoya (because everyone should have a Paula in their lives),
Gavin Belton, Gary Caughey, Peter White and Vanessa Bell*

A siren shrieked from somewhere, ripping Spencer from unconsciousness like a wax-strip from a sunburnt nipple.

"Can you hear me?" a man asked.

An avalanche of pain rushed Spencer as he struggled to open his eyes. He wanted to scream, but the only sound that escaped his throat was a congealed gurgle.

"Stay still," the man said. "You're in an ambulance. You're on your way to hospital."

At first Spencer couldn't make sense of it all and in those few blissful moments the events of the past three months hadn't happened. Then he remembered; he remembered every moment with resounding clarity.

He closed his eyes and prayed it would all end here.

With his surroundings beginning to evaporate around him, Spencer's thoughts were drawn towards religion and final retribution. Unfortunately, if memory of Sunday school served him correctly, repentance would rely on confessing to all his sins, and he still wasn't sure how many people he had actually killed. He was fairly confident, however, that last night's three in a row would preclude him from any welcoming cocktails at the Pearly Gates.

A pinpoint of light opened in the distance.

It struck Spencer that his only hope was that Heaven ran on a rotational basis: Allah gets it one year, Jehovah the next, Buddha the year after, that sort of thing. If he was lucky it might be the turn of some Hindu god of twisted karma, but if his recent run of luck was anything to go by it would be run by the evangelists, in which case he had been destined to be the Devil's piñata before he'd even poisoned his first drag queen.

CHAPTER 1
THREE MONTHS EARLIER

The harsh lights around the dressing table mirror left nowhere on Bette's face for imperfections to hide. Throwing herself into a pout, she stood up and tossed her hair over one shoulder, challenging the mirror for brutal honesty. The reflection confirmed what she already knew: she looked fabulous, and anyone who disagreed was clearly in need of attention to cataracts or sense of style. Clinging to her in bespoke perfection, her dress's sequin-glittering thigh splits revealed the kind of legs most women would secretly give their first born to possess, and scattering light to the furthest corners of the room, her bling of necklaces, bracelets and rings sparkled like a deconstructed glitterball against her dark skin; there were lighthouses that didn't have Bette's reflective output.

A quick glance at her ladies fauxlex told her it was fifteen minutes to opening. She checked her teeth one last time for lipstick and ran her tongue across them just to be sure. Once satisfied, she headed out into the maze of cold corridors, her every step demonstrating immaculate and calculated deportment. When Bette had her heels on, everywhere was a catwalk.

Bette had always considered posture to be one of the many defining points that separated her from the others in her field. Collectively termed as drag, Bette felt her profession lay somewhere in between drag (a man dressing up as a woman for purposes of humorous entertainment) and transvestite (a man dressing up to *be* a woman because of deep-rooted psychological needs and a dodgy wardrobe). Spencer - and woe betide anyone who used that name when she was working - didn't need to wear women's clothes; there was no sensual thrill involved. And although wit was an essential part of her job, it was not solely for humour. This was a serious career. Bette was a female impersonator.

On arriving in the foyer she let out a squeal of glee; despite having spent the afternoon putting up all the posters, seeing them still made her feel like a child on Christmas morning discovering a gift-wrapped pony at the foot of her bed.

She spotted a poster's corner that had come away from its Blu Tack and took a moment to reattach it and admire the artwork's glossy headline: *Bette Noir's Opus Gay: The Club You've All Been Praying For*. She wondered if this could be the happiest moment of her life; she was Halle Berry at the Oscars, she was Jennifer Hudson on the set of Dreamgirls, she was Whitney before a mound of white powder. She was Bette Noir, London's very own cross-dressed, black diva, at the opening of her new club night.

Dinner-suited bouncers stood either side of the main doors. Beyond them, through the club's glass frontage, Bette could see people outside. Queuing. Flushed with love from her fans, she suppressed the desire to dangle a baby over a balcony at them.

Danny, Bette's favourite bouncer, pecs like widescreen TVs, arms like waistlines and a carved expression on his face that suggested he could easily forget his name, but never his purpose, nodded in readiness.

Bette's head began to spin. She clutched at her diamante necklace as if it were the ripcord of a parachute. It was here, minutes away, her arrival into London's clubbing hall of fame.

Euphoria aside, Bette had no illusions as to how important tonight was. Having reinvented herself enough times to warrant being registered with the patent office, tonight wasn't just another ambition to tick off her list. Tonight, she had decided, was when her luck changed. And not before time. In the last five years, since turning thirty, Bette had seen her modelling work getting eating disorder-thin on the ground and decidedly quirkier; there was only so many times you could convince yourself that modelling inflatable, latex bras for tranny catalogues was as a favour to your agent. Even her status as one of London's clubbing 'it' people was diminishing; a fact subtly telegraphed when doormen started to check if she was actually on a guest list or not. She knew if she had any hope of salvaging what dubious minor celebrity and career she had, the club needed to be a success. Besides, she wasn't ready yet to ask the question, 'what becomes of a female impersonator when there's no one to impersonate for?'

Bette also knew it could be argued that now was not the best time to be opening a new club night. Having employed nearly every friend and every penny she had into Opus Gay, and having watched everything from Woolies to her beloved fabric supplier go bust in the past couple of years, it wasn't just her social status at risk. But the state of Global economics aside, there were other matters that might have steered a less focused mind away from club promoting. All across the capitol the police were clamping down on clubs in a desperate attempt to stem the flow of a new recreational drug that was hitting the scene; a drug that had seen eight fatalities to its name in its first two months on the circuit, two of which in the very club Bette now stood. All over London, door security were having to almost strip-search customers in an attempt to keep out drugs if a venue was to have any hope of retaining its licence. But the chance to open her night here, at The Tumble Dryer, was one Bette could not turn down.

Easily North London's most fashionable nightclub, Bette had always loved The Tumble Dryer's over-the-top grandeur. A lavish and outrageously converted, Victorian music hall, one of its many attractions was its VIP room, better known as The Lint Tray. Over the years it had become a haunt for celebrities from C to A-list, and it was Bette's firm belief that if you hadn't been found face down and unconscious in a mound of white powder here, then you just didn't have what it takes for the music business or kids' TV. Here she was, nonetheless, the prestigious first Saturday of every month was hers. The fact the previous promoter had been stabbed to death as he left here one night for nothing more than his *iPhone* should have troubled her more, but, as she'd been doing for weeks, Bette reminded herself that one man's body parts spattered across the pavement was another woman's red carpet.

Her heels clicked excitedly on the marble floor as she headed across the foyer to the ticket booth. Sitting behind the glass was

Mandy, Bette's closest friend, and the greatest friend anyone in Bette's line of work could ever have. An absolute genius with a sewing machine and a dress pattern, Mandy had been running up Bette's costumes for years. If ever asked what luxury item she would take with her if stranded on a deserted island, without hesitation Bette would have said Mandy.

"Remember not to let them in too fast," said Bette. "I want anticipation arching from that queue."

Mandy, who had been called Mandy Warhol for years on account of his ever-present, short-cropped, bleached blonde hair, looked up and nodded before continuing to adjust an overly-padded cleavage. The cleavage, which resembled a builder's crack about to light its own fart, was making another attempt to escape the bounds of a hideous, leopard print dress. When Mandy had hugged Bette earlier, the combination of ample belly and excessive bust left Bette feeling like she had been attacked by a bouncy castle.

Bette tried not to sigh; being Mandy's first time in drag, Bette felt she owed some support. Normally, once the giggling was done, it was a bonding moment between two friends, each standing exposed and naked of any macho. Unfortunately, when Mandy stepped from the dressing room with a *ta-daah*, a field promotion had quickly been made and Mandy's backless dress - which exposed a back as spotless as Jeffrey Archer's character - was sent to the confines of the ticket booth.

The sound of a throat being cleared made Bette turn. Danny was pointing at his watch. It was time.

CHAPTER 2

A chorus of meowing and scratching at the bedroom window woke Spencer. The cats, Dolce and Gabbana, belonged to his neighbour, Lucy, and despite living on the top floor of a three-storey red-brick, they regularly strolled the ledge between the two flats. Spencer tried to ignore them, along with the pounding headache and arid tongue sticking to the roof of his mouth. Pulling a pillow over his head he promised his body he would never drink that much again; hoping, in turn, his body would forget all his past broken promises and let him off with a warning.

Throat crackling with dehydration he reached into the darkness towards the bedside table for a glass of water. The back of his hand caught the glass and knocked it to the floor; he wasn't going to be able to sleep this off. He sat up and switched on the bedside lamp. The fauvist remnants of Bette's makeup stared back at him from the pillowcase. Panic flashed through his hangover. He grabbed his hips.

Relief surged from his fingertips as he found sequinless flesh; the dress had been taken off, even if the face hadn't. A quick scan of the room further quelled his fears as he spotted the dress suspended on a hanger on the back of the door. Someone must have undressed him; he would *never* have used *that* hanger.

With Bette having her own room just across the hall, it was strange to see drag in the bedroom; it felt as if his personal space had been invaded somehow. From couture to cosmetics, everything was kept in Bette's room. Over the years, he had developed a strict rule: makeup and dresses were never put on or removed in the bedroom. It was a successful apartheid, allowing him and Bette to comfortably co-exist under the same roof.

Moving as if wearing nitro glycerine earrings and fearful any sudden movement might spray the room with cranial debris, Spencer pulled himself from the bed and shuffled over to the dresser. A reflection came into focus in the mirror. He slapped both hands over his mouth to stifle a scream; the makeup-smeared, crimson-eyed offspring of Don King and Medusa stared back.

Having always felt more at ease with Bette's reflection, the occasional, drunken, morning-after hybrid was always unsettling. As a man, Spencer felt his face was disproportionate, plain and lacking masculinity. During puberty his features had remained much the same, it was the gaps in between that had grown out of proportion. With makeup, however, those same features seemed to corralle into an aesthetic sense and beauty, eradicating the banality of the face with which he had been given to trudge through the rest of his daily life.

He heard laughter coming from the other room.

Straightening to confront his demon he lifted a hairbrush from on top of the dresser. Halfway down, on the first stroke, the brush stuck fast.

The lounge's post-party odour of tobacco and alcohol churned Spencer's stomach. He stood in the doorway with the brush sticking from his hair in right-angled defiance, lipstick smeared up the side of his face in an involuntary Batman-villain grin and a white, towelling bathrobe tied round his waist, and waited for the room's two occupants to spot him. First to notice was Jason, the man whose title for the past two and a half years Spencer regularly alternated between partner and thorn-in-the-side. He looked up from the sofa where he was tying his boots and flicked his mop of blonde hair back to get a better look at the manachronism that stood in the doorway.

He flashed a smile at Spencer. "Love the new look, Spence. What you calling it, bag lady chic?"

"Who put my dress on a wire hanger?" said Spencer.

"Not me," Mandy said from the other side of the breakfast bar as he dabbed at a stain on his tee-shirt.

"It was me." Jason's face turned from floppy-haired cute to its more familiar scowl. "Now back off, *Mommie Queerest.*" He pulled on a tiny, tight tee-shirt. The tee-shirt snagged momentarily on a nipple ring before being pulled down to his waist, leaving a hint of taught flesh visible.

The view distracted Spencer. It was one of his 'things', that little strip of hair which ran from the bellybutton down to the pubes. He'd once heard it called a crab ladder and thought it the most vulgar name for something so beautiful.

"I thought you were staying here tonight," Spencer whined. "It's Sunday..." He turned to Mandy. "It is still Sunday, *isn't it?*"

Mandy nodded. "A bit left of it."

"You've been unconscious for hours," said Jason. "So gimme a break. I need to get home." He pulled on a leather jacket and lifted a motorbike helmet before heading along the hall for the front door.

"Can't you stay for a bit?" Spencer held out his arms. "How's about a celebratory hug?"

Something was muffled as the helmet was pulled on. Moments later the front door slammed.

Spencer's arms drooped to his sides. "I swear to God, Mandy, the day they invent homo replacement therapy I'm slapping a patch on my ass and packing his bags." He sunk into the armchair across from the sofa.

"So how you feeling?"

"My brain hurts, my body aches and my mouth tastes like the litterbox of an agoraphobic cat. I'm also thinking about shaving my head." He pointed at the insubordinate brush sticking from his hair. "And I had that dream again where I was being chased by Simon Cowell. He was naked this time." Spencer held up his hand and curled his pinkie back and forth.

"Coffee?"

Spencer smiled.

"Jason tells me he's thinking about going freelance," Mandy said over the topography of spent bottles and cans that had been piled onto the partitioning breakfast bar. "So isn't it working out with Lancôme?"

"Yes, it's working out with Lancôme. It's working out the same as it's done with every other make-up company he's worked for: He's about to get fired."

"Oh. So do you think the freelance thing is going to work?"

Spencer shrugged. "I dunno. I do know I'm fed up bankrolling him in between jobs. This'll be the fourth make-up company he's left, or been asked to leave, in under two years. Mean and moody might work as a sexual stimulus, but it's doing sod all for his career prospects and my bank balance. And you know I've not seen a penny of that money I leant him after the last stuff-your-job storm out."

Mandy's sudden fascination with the instructions on the side of the coffee jar said everything Spencer needed to know about his desire to take the conversation further.

Spencer scanned his surroundings. The detritus of the post-club drinks doo was still evident in the ashtrays that lay scattered about the room in a carcinogenic landmine formation.

"How come you're here, Mandy? Did you crash here?"

"No. I said I'd come back later and give you a hand to tidy up. I've done most of it. What's left won't take long."

Spencer moved an overflowing ashtray with his foot. "How bad was it?"

"I managed to get the puke off the shower curtain and__" The doorbell rang.

"What fresh Hell is this?" said Spencer, sinking deeper into the armchair.

"Stay where you are." Mandy delivered the cup of coffee before heading for the front door.

Spencer wanted to be swallowed whole by the armchair when he saw Lucy, his neighbour; she was as appropriate a treatment for hangovers as amputation was for hangnails.

"Like the new hair?" Lucy breezed into the room flicking at an auburn bob with shampoo ad enthusiasm. "Yesterday was the tenth anniversary of my divorce and I fancied doing something to celebrate. It was either this or a Brazilian."

Spencer's stomach offered a warning spasm.

Lucy turned to him with the kind of look usually reserved for fungus-growing mugs found under beds.

"Any comments," said Spencer, "keep to yourself."

"I wasn't going to say a thing…other than to mention I just passed the Grim Reaper on the stairs, and she says she'll be back for you in an hour." Lucy sat on the sofa. "So, tell me, how was it? You know how I love to hear how the other tenth live."

"It was great." Mandy positioned himself at the other end of the sofa. "Everybody loved it."

"Talking of 'everyone'," said Spencer, "when did 'everyone' leave here?"

"When you passed out just after three p.m., apparently. So why didn't you come to the club last night, Lucy? You'd have loved it."

"Why? Because I'm female on my birth certificate and my idea of makeup isn't to induce tinnitus or frighten small children. Besides, my bitch sister set me up on another blind date. I had to get blind drunk just to get through it. It could never have worked. He was only five foot six and I'm *gnomeophobic*. So, your tranny club?"

"I've told you," snarled Spencer, "it's not a tranny club. It's a fusion club. It's all about getting back to the days when clubbing was fun and people made an effort. It's a move away from the clubbing apartheid we've all got stuck in. It's for outrageous people. Eccentric people. Kinky people. Beautifu__"

"Yeah, yeah, yeah." Lucy waved her hand dismissively. "We get it. How many more times do we have to listen to your ad? So dish the dirt: who looked crap, who looked fab, who picked up and who split up? And don't tell me that's not what it's all about. You queens live for this shit."

Spencer and Mandy nodded at each other in agreement.

"It was fabulous," said Spencer. "I nearly broke even."

"*Nearly!?*" said Mandy. "But it was packed."

"I'm not looking at making anything in the first four months. It's all going back in to advertising and PA's. After that, and the punters still love it, I've got them. Job done."

"Did I see Drucilla last night?" said Mandy.

Like the brass and percussion section of a special-needs school band, the memory of last night's uninvited guest pounded in agonising dissonance with Spencer's headache. "Yes, like syphilis at an orgy, she turned up."

"Who's Drucilla?" said Lucy.

"My arch-nemesissy." He tugged at the brush sticking from his hair. "She runs a couple of nights at the same club and is so far up the owners ass it would take worming tablets to get her out." He continued to tug at the brush. "One of her friends wanted my night. It was going to be another tacky red-and-green-lit-camouflage-netted affairs. All I've done is save London from another venue that gets hosed down at the end of the night instead of swept up."

"So what's the big deal?" said Lucy. "Why didn't you just tell her to naff off?"

"She does a gossip column for one of the clubbing magazines." He pulled furiously at the brush. "She turned up with the club reviewer and a photographer. And I can't prove it, but…" He yanked at the brush one last time, managing to rip it free along with enough hair to stuff a small cushion. Mandy and Lucy winced. "I'm sure it was her who got into my dressing room and superglued the lock on my makeup case. Security wouldn't have let anyone else backstage." He pointed the hairbrush at Lucy. "And a big box of the chocolate liqueurs we give out went, too."

Lucy took the brush from him. "Hon, you need to forget about her while you've still got hair."

"Jason tells me he's going to some restaurant opening tomorrow," said Mandy, throwing a much appreciated change of subject. "So where is it?"

"In Soho," said Spencer. "It's François' place."

"Doesn't he own a brothel?"

Spencer nodded. "The night will be vile and I'll probably run into Drucilla, but there'll be photographers, and the next couple of months is all about promotion."

Spencer felt his hangover throb at the very thought of it.

CHAPTER 3

Bette adjusted her white, rippled silk dress as the black cab crawled through traffic. Across from her sat Bo and The Grand Duchess Anaesthesia. Bo sat tilting her head back, and to the side, so her tower of candyfloss pink wig didn't attach itself like Velcro to Anaesthesia's mass of afro, which filled most of the cab's airspace.

"Bette, *dahling*," said Bo, fluffing her bright pink ballgown, "your dress is simply stunning. If I were still capable of jealousy at my age, I'd be tearing out what little hair I had left." She took a small compact from her clutch.

Bette was always intrigued when Bo made veiled reference to her age; it was a better-kept secret than the Coca Cola recipe. Not the first Etonian to wear a dress, but certainly the first to have made a career out of it, Bo was hailed as a cult TV star. Having skinny dipped with Fidel Castro and snorted coke with Royalty, she now hosted a hugely popular cable chat show called *Bo Talks*.

"Mandy's a genius, girl," said Anaesthesia, whose vastly 'fuller figure' was festooned in Westwood faux fur. "I could just eat that boy up sometimes."

"If you like this," said Bette, "you'll love the dress Mandy's working on for my appearance at the BAHTI's."

"I'm not sure if I'll be going this year." Bo peered into her compact mirror as she dusted her face in an unnecessary attempt to make herself paler than she naturally was.

Bette took a sharp intake of breath; having twice hosted the BAHTI's (British Academy of Homosexual Triumphs over Ignorance), and then being dropped from its line-up two years ago, Bette was usually ready to slate their name at the drop of a Philip Tracey. However, a ceasefire of hostilities had been called this year when they invited her to present an award. "You have to, Bo. They're a vital part of the PR machine that recycles stereotyping and ignorance into acceptance and understanding. It's like racism." Anaesthesia pointed her lipgloss at Bo and nodded in agreement. "You can't take your eye off the ball. The days of 'they're okay so long as I don't have to live next to one' weren't that long ago. We have a duty to continue making ourselves seen, and the BAHTI's do just that."

Bo looked doubtful. "So, *dahling*, in pursuit of doing your bit for the cause and our fallen sisters, what award are you presenting?"

"It's for the-celebrity-whose-face-you'd-most-like-to-spend-a-weekend-on. Did I mention it's televised this year?"

"Oh, Lordy!" Anaesthesia pointed her lipgloss at a trail of phlegm sliding down the passenger window. "That differently-abled man just spat at me." Outside, a man in a motorised wheelchair was daredevil riding with one hand as the other flicked Anaesthesia the finger. "You work it, girl!" Anaesthesia cheered. "Awww, bless him, and so modern using one finger. His generation usually prefer to use the two."

As the cab turned from the bumper-to-bumper traffic, Anaesthesia blew the wheelchair Evil Kenevel a kiss. He went ballistic. In his determination to vent his disgust and disapproval, the man let go his steering and V signed with both hands. The last Bette saw of him was his four fingers stabbing in the air as his wheelchair veered into the middle of the road. Everyone flinched as they heard the screech and crunch.

"Someone just got themselves twenty bonus points," said Anaesthesia, pursing her lips in readiness for the gloss.

The cab soon pulled up outside a restaurant with the name *Whore's D'ouvres* emblazoned on its canopy. Bette's flesh came out in sympathetic goosebumps when she saw the two muscle-boys meeting and greeting out front. Naked for all but boots and underwear, the evening's chill was making itself evident in their baggy g-strings.

Once through the doors and past the photographers, the

restaurant's theme soon became apparent in the Roman orgy mural that ran along the walls. Surprised to see the place void of tables, Bette watched as semi-naked waiters trawled the assembled guests with trays of drinks and nibbles, each waiter wearing little more than a change purse of garment and an implied price tag.

Bette spotted one of the raised balcony areas being vacated so they made their way through the crowd to secure the vantage point. From this position they could get a good look at who was here and who was here could get a good look at them. Posing with the strained indifference of supermodels in a cake shop, they scanned the room for any interesting faces: there was a couple of singers, an author, a Times columnist, a game show host, several drag queens, a high smattering of clubbing 'it' people and the obligatory camp, Big Brother contestant.

"So where's Jason?" said Anaesthesia. "I thought your little stud muffin was gonna be joining us."

"He said he couldn't face another night going out with me as Bette. He says he's starting to feel like a bi-sexual."

Bo raised her trademark eyebrow. "Oh." She rubbed Bette's shoulder "Well, never mind, we've been long overdue a girls' night out."

"So how's the show going?" said Bette.

"Frightfully well," Bo said. "There's talk of doing a couple of specials from L.A. I rather like the idea of conquering the States. I bet Robbie Williams £50 I'd do it before him." She stopped a waiter and took an orange juice for herself and champagne for Bette and Anaesthesia. "I have a new producer, though, and we're not hitting it off. He used to work in current affairs and I think he sees my show as a little beneath him."

On reflection, Bette decided she didn't feel up to discussing Bo's ever more successful career as her own lay so precariously in the balance. "So did you enjoy yourself at Opus Gay on Saturday?"

Before Bo could respond, their attention was drawn towards the entrance. Two photographers were throwing themselves from the path of a gargantuan armour-clad drag queen, one bouncing off her warrior's shield. Bette watched, transfixed, as the behemoth tossed her blonde hair from beneath a horned helmet and away from an armoured cleavage.

"Is that who I think it is?" said Bette.

"Yes, *dahling*, that's Valkeyre Te Kanawa."

"Didn't she get sent down for dealing and ABH?" said Anaesthesia.

"Got out a few months ago. She organised an operatic society in Wandsworth prison and got several months off for good behaviour. She's back on the drag circuit. We had her as an audience warm-up for the show a few weeks ago. Sticky fingers. She left our green room rattling like an aircraft drinks trolley in turbulence."

"So she's not working for Mad Mickey anymore?" said Anaesthesia.

"*Dahling*, she didn't just work for Mickey. They were much more *intimate* than that. You know Mickey, girls, he likes them strange."

Everyone who worked in London clubs knew Mad Mickey, and his name wasn't ironic. His notorious temper aside, he was the Starbucks of drug dealing: he had outlets everywhere. So far, Bette had managed to avoid him and any conversations about him supplying Opus Gay, and she wanted to keep it that way.

Bette tore her gaze away from Valkeyre and over to a clique near the window. "There's Sherry Amontillado, the one who looks like Pee Wee Herman in a puff-ball dress. I knew I was getting a whiff of formaldehyde from somewhere."

"And that's Sue Nami she's with," said Anaesthesia.

"Looks like Sue's had some work done." Bo squinted in an apparent attempt to focus.

"How can you tell from here?" Bette said.

"Look at the hair. That's not a widow's peak, *dahling*, that's eyebrows."

Bette knew better than to question Bo's eye for 'work'; having had enough cosmetic surgery over the years to be on first name terms with half of Harley Street, Bo could spot the tiniest scar behind an ear at twenty paces in thick fog.

"Bo, Duchess, Ms Noir," came a voice from behind them, "I'm so glad you could make it."

They turned slowly, allowing their drinks to arrive before them, to find Francois, the owner, perma-tan 'popping' in violent contrast with his sharply cut, white linen suit. Next to him was a recently killed-off soap star.

"*Mwah, mwah,*" went Bette from a safe distance, shortly followed by Bo and Anaesthesia.

"Girl, where's the food?" said Anaesthesia. "You don't keep a figure like mine on vol au vents and sausage on sticks."

"Indeed," said Bo. "We were under the misconception we were going to be fed."

Bette almost choked on her champagne; beneath the acres of Bo's pink ballgown lay the physique of a scaffolding tower.

"It's a party," said Francois. "We're here to celebrate the opening of the restaurant. If people want to come and bitch the food they can pay. Anyway, most of this lot are too coked to waste good food on."

Anaesthesia grabbed a loin-clothed waiter who was carrying a tray of canapés. "Ooooh, I don't know what to sink my teeth into first. So what's your name?"

"Simon," said the waiter.

"I was actually talking to the platter, but now we've got the intros out of the way – Hi, I'm Anaesthesia, and I'm going to be your letching customer for tonight." She turned to Bette and Bo. "I'll catch up with you folks later." She hooked her arm through the waiters arm and led him off. "Come on, white boy, feed me that smoked salmon."

"I promised my friend here," Francois turned to the killed-off soap star, "that I'd introduce him. He's a *huuuge* fan of yours, Bo. He'd love a minute of your time. And I'd like to steal Bette here for a quick gossip, if that's okay?"

Before she knew it, Bette was being spun away by the elbow, leaving the killed-off soap star to launch himself at Bo.

"Once a pimp, always a pimp," said Bette.

Francois smiled. "The poor lad isn't taking unemployment well. An interview on Bo's show would do him the world of good. It could save him from the humiliation of Aladdin at the Scunthorpe Palladium. You know me, Bette. I like to think of myself as one of life's Dolly Levi's."

Bette sipped her champagne to stop herself rising to the bait of the Dolly Levi comment.

"So what do you think of the place?" Francois said.

"The murals are interesting." Bette's eyes came to rest on a centurion 'tending' to a couple of slaves. "Who did them?"

"Very talented young artist. Rick." Francois pulled a card from his pocket and handed it to Bette. "Just starting out, so very reasonable. Worked at the agency till he put on weight."

Bette took the card and slipped it into her cleavage; she needed someone to do backdrops for the stage at the club.

"So what's the training ground for what, Francois? Do the hookers train in the restaurant for the brothel, or the other way round? I can see where the hygiene issues overlap, and essentially they're both just mincing about for tips, but surely this lot have more experience inserting food than serving it."

"Times got hard all round. Credit crunch, recession, call it what you like, but paying for cock was the first thing to go. Business is slow at the agency, not like when you were there."

Francois' words wrapped around Bette like a cold, wet shower curtain. It had been years ago, and only as a receptionist, but of all the skeletons in her closet the three months working for Francois was the one she would happily have ground down into china plates and donated to a Greek wedding.

"So why a restaurant?" Bette tried to pull herself back from the conversational cliff edge.

"It was a logical step. There's too many amateurs offering cock delivery from classified ads now. And as for the Internet, well, anyone who knows their way round Photoshop can have a six-pack and a donkey dick. It looked like I was going to have to let some of the boys go part-time, which would simply have meant they would have done their own classifieds and ended up competing with me full-time. So, I thought I'd try my hand at something new. I'm a caring employer, you know."

Bette remembered just how 'caring' an employer Francois had once tried to be. "I still don't see why you think it's a logical step."

"Half of them have been to catering college and the rest have worked tables at some point. It'll never be Michelin Star but it doesn't need to be if you've got bodies like that *grrrinding* your pepper... And you can order your waiter for dessert and take him to one of the private rooms upstairs." Francois eyes followed a waiter who was carrying a tray of canapés.

"Too many cooks spoiling the brothel?"

A photographer stepped in front of them, gesticulating for permission to take a photo. Bette embraced Francois for the camera and in an instant their faces illuminated 'best friend' smiles, which evaporated the moment the flash died.

"So what you been up to, Bette, anything new happening?"

The question horrified her. She had worked tirelessly to make sure the club had been as well publicised as a celebrity adoption. "You don't club much these days, Francois, do you?"

"Don't need to." Francois' grin almost left a slime trail in the air as he followed the bare ass of another waiter.

"Well, if you did, you would have heard that__"

"A moment please." Francois grabbed the arm of a peacock head-dressed, drag queen as she tried to teeter past in cheap heels and a badly made-up face.

"Bette, I'd like you to meet Divine Inspiration. She's going to be one of the drag stars of the future."

Only if the future is a nuclear wasteland where people eat their young, thought Bette. "Pleased to meet you."

"Pleasure's mine," Divine said, offering a hand so limp it felt as if it had been filleted of bone. "I'm such a fan of yours. I watch your show all the time."

"No, you stupid bitch," said Francois. "That one's over there." He pointed towards Bo. "The one in the pink ball gown...who's white!"

"I'm so sorry," Divine said. "Out without my contacts."

"That would explain the outfit," said Bette, as Francois shooed Divine in Bo's direction. "I'm getting the feeling you're moving into some, and I use the word loosely, '*talent*' management, Francois."

"Just another little project I have on the go. I like to keep a lookout for all kinds of young talent."

They both watched as Divine went wig over sling backs as she missed a crouched waiter who was trying to hide from Valkeyre. Divine's headdress, which separated from the mothership mid-fall, came to land in a tray of prawn tempura.

"They had a lookout like you on the Titanic, you know."

Francois turned his back on Divine as she started plucking prawns from her millinery. "Anyway, what about you, Bette? I was just saying to Drucilla this afternoon that__"

Bette's chest tightened. "Is it here?"

"She'll be here shortly."

Bette knocked back her champagne and grabbed another from a passing waiter.

"So, what have you been up to, Bette?"

"Well, if you had opened a magazine in the last couple of months you would know that I've__"

Francois waved at a couple coming in the door. "Tony, Guy, so glad you could make it."

"Toni and Guy the hairdressers?" said Bette.

"Tony and Guy the undertakers. They run a chain of gay funeral directors called His 'n' Hearse." Francois beckoned them over and waved to a big-haired woman behind them. "Shar, delighted you could come." He turned back to Bette. "That's Sharon D'enfroid, the restaurant critic. Complete bitch. Once I've introduced you to Tony and Guy I'll have to go speak to her."

Left to endure small talk so small it was measured in microns, Bette had been about to take her leave of Tony and Guy when Guy pulled a tiny brown bottle from his shirt pocket.

"A line?" said Guy, waving the bottle in front of Bette.

"Oh, I don't mind if I do." Not a big fan of class A's as a whole, Bette thought it rude to turn down a free line when offered. She gently inhaled to clear her sinuses. "Coke?"

"No," said Guy, "blu."

Bette's excited pre-rush crashed; she hated blu. Blu was the very drug that had been causing all the problems on the scene, leaving a trail of devastation in its wake that made crystal meth look like a health food supplement. Bette had tried it once. It had been an amazing high: you were Cher before going on stage to yet another final farewell tour, you were Streisand laughing in the face of rhinoplasty, you were the most fabulous superstar with the most perfect life…until, it either reacted with alcohol or some other substance and your body tried to expel your stomach through your face, or you came down with a bang so hard you longed for the cheery surroundings of a Romanian orphanage. Rumoured to be at the heart of the most recent drug-turf war, Bette wanted to keep it as far away from her and her punters as possible. A task she feared was not going to be easy.

"I'll pass, thanks."

"Okay," said Guy, "if you're sure." Guy inhaled the faintly blue powder from the plastic spoon that hinged from the side of the bottle top then passed the bottle to Tony.

About to take her leave of Tony and Guy's company for the second time, Bette froze. Making a grand entrance through the photographers was a hippo-sized drag queen in a three-quarter-length dress of electric blue sequins. Flicking her platinum bob wig, she dismissed the photographers with a smile and headed for Bette like a tidal wave to an Indonesian beach.

"Tony, Guy, sweethearts," she said, the oesophageal blancmange of her triple chins undulating with every plumy word. She turned cold, blue eyes to Bette and stared, scrutinising Bette's face as if searching for a flaw with which she could launch an attack. "Bette."

Bette returned the scrutiny, giving an obvious once-over as she collected ample ammunition for a counter attack. "Drucilla."

Drucilla's makeup, which had been applied with her usual igneous rock formation layering, seemed to strain as the tectonic plates of her features fought against each other to suppress an expression.

Tony wiped his nose and offered the bottle. "A line?"

"No, you naughty boy," said Drucilla. "You know I never touch the stuff. Now, sweeties, do you think I could have a quick word with Bette in private. I won't be long."

"Sure," said Tony, "we'll catch up in a bit."

"I look forward to it." Drucilla's glowing smile was devoured by a scowl the moment Tony and Guy turned their backs and moved on. "My editor at the magazine tells me you've bought a block of ads. You sure that's a good idea?"

Bette took a deep breath; she could feel the grip on her glass tighten. "It's just good business sense."

Drucilla smiled and nodded at a passing couple before returning her stare to Bette. "Good business sense would have been to accept Stella's offer to take your club elsewhere."

"Listen here, you family-sized bucket, no amount of threats from you or your skanky, rancid friends will move me. The reason you want me out isn't because any friend of yours wants it. It's because you know my club will show yours up as the tired, dated crap that it is and that means your days at The Tumble Dryer will soon be as popular as Gary Glitter tribute bands at Children in Need fundraisers."

Drucilla's eyes darted back and forth across Bette's face as if searching for something she'd missed. "Stella has made you a good offer. I'd take it before it's too late."

"Next time you're having your industrial strength lipo done, why don't you get them to syringe your ears? I'm going nowhere. Deal with it!" Bette clicked her fingers back and forth in the air to emphasise the closing point.

A cold smile asserted itself on Drucilla's face. "Okay, sweetheart, if that's the way you want it. But don't say I didn't try to be civilised about this." She turned and launched herself into the crowd.

Bette snatched another champagne from a passing muscle mary. There was something unsettling in Drucilla's smile. Bette waited for the pulse in her neck to stop throbbing before going in search of Bo.

After several air kisses, a few more empty conversations and promising to put half a dozen of the waiters on the guest list for the next Opus Gay, she found Bo holding court amidst a gaggle of rapt hangers-on.

"...*Dahlings*, I told him I didn't care if he was a Republican Senator, a grown man in a nappy just isn't seemly. Of course, they call them diapers over there." She turned to Bette. "*Dahling*, come join us. You must know Apollo, surely?" Bo waved her orange juice at a Versace clad 'it' person next to her. The few remaining unanalysed muscles on Bo's face seemed to be struggling to semaphore 'get me out of here'.

"Hi," said Apollo. "I think we've met before."

Bette offered a constipated grin. "Apollo...yes, you're faces seem familiar." Bette remembered all too well the last time she met Apollo; he had refused her entry into the VIP room of the club he worked at.

"Do excuse us, *dahlings*," said Bo, taking Bette's arm and moving her away from Apollo and the assembled fans.

As they clutched each other's arms, suppressing girly giggles, Bette's drink was almost knocked from her hand. The photographers were rushing towards the entrance, a lightening storm of camera flashes erupting as the latest guest made her way in. Male, female, straight, gay, it didn't seem to matter, the entire restaurant's attention was drawn irresistibly to the new arrival. Standing amidst the photographers, she worked the moment with professional ease, flicking her raven hair whilst offering a devastatingly white smile for the cameras.

"Oh, great," said Bette, curling her lip. "Look who it is: *Maaaaaah leeeeee.*"

"Don't torture your vowels, *dahling*. It's so unattractive. What is it you have against Malee?"

"Let's start with the pretentious name."

"There's nothing pretentious about her name, *dahling*. It's Thai for flower, or something. It was her grandmother's name, apparently. My new producer wants her as a guest on the show."

Bette watched as Drucilla attached herself to Malee's arm

and insisted on another round of camera flashes. "What's the big deal with her at the moment? She's plastered all over every magazine. I'm fed up seeing her face. And if I have to see that picture of her dancing with Prince Harry once more I'll puke."

"She's young, beautiful, connected and is being hailed as the tranny Kate Moss. And she has a figure to simply die for."

"A size zero on a man is sick."

Bo's eyebrow rose. "Am I detecting a little jealousy?"

"Of that *thinvalid*?"

Bo took Bette's arm and turned her away from Malee. "I saw Francois sticking you with Tony and Guy earlier. Dull, aren't they?"

"They should come with a warning not to operate heavy machinery near them."

"Threw a wonderful '*party*' once upon a time, if you know what I mean. Quite the A list hosts. Tony's a bit of a shameless chubby chaser, and as for Guy, well, he could snort the pattern from a Formica table." Bo scanned the room. "Do we know what happened to Anaesthesia?"

"She's being given a tour of the private rooms upstairs." Bette spotted Drucilla sneering over. "Did you notice Drucilla's arrival?"

"In that dress, *dahling*, noticing is hardly optional."

"She made another veiled threat for me to give up the Tumble Dryer. Do you think she'll cause trouble?"

Bo's eyebrow rose as she sipped her orange juice. "She has a legendary vicious streak, *dahling*, I'd watch my back."

Bo's words haunted Bette for the rest of the evening. Could everything she had heard about Drucilla be true? Could she really be as hideous as her word of mouth press-pack suggested? Did she really have a legendary vicious streak?

Bette tried her best to put Bo's warning out of her mind, but by the time she got home it had built into a fully formed paranoia. Then she spotted the two missed calls on her phone, both from a 'M. Mickey'.

CHAPTER 4

It was the Thursday after Opus Gay and Spencer could hardly bear the suspense any longer. Beginning to feel like a West End starlet awaiting the reviews for his first leading role, the anticipation of Jason's arrival with the clubbing magazines was torturous. The weekly clubbing magazines were distributed free from bars, shops and clubs across the capitol and were a bizarre mixture of news, events, club reviews, classifieds and 'personal services'. Spencer, however, saw them as the gay scene's very own *Tattler*, *Hello!* and *Okay*. This was upheld by the ubiquitous nature of their photographers, for it was they who gave the clubbing crowd a weekly stab at their fifteen minutes of fame. Each week, clubbers tore open their pages, flicking past the rare news items about AIDS or homophobic lynch mobs in South London, to find out if their sweaty, pupil-dilated picture had made it into the weekly glossies. It seemed you hadn't officially 'arrived' in London until your gurning pout had been displayed in their pages.

In the meantime, hoping to rekindle what little romance his and Jason's relationship had left, Spencer had decided to prepare a celebratory meal. With sexual frustration at a level he knew must be dangerous for his blood pressure, and the fact he had begun to notice a marked difference in the muscle tone of his right forearm, anything seemed worth a try.

Once everything was ready in the kitchen, and to stop himself clock watching, he tied his hair back with a scrunchie, tucked it into the back of his sweatshirt and went in search of another job to keep himself busy. Heading along the hall to Bette's room he had to sidestep Gabbana as he made a quick dash for the kitchen window with one of Bette's makeup brushes in his mouth. Bette had very few makeup brushes that didn't have cat's teeth in them now and was convinced Gabbana had been a bitter drag queen in a previous life.

Spencer had relegated everything in the past month unrelated to Bette or the club to essential maintenance only. The laundry pile in Bette's room was starting to smell like designer compost. The heap's position in front of the floor-to-ceiling mirror now gave the intimidating effect of doubling its mass, and the rails of drag reflected from the other side of the room made it all look like an Elton John, charity jumble sale.

First things first, thought Spencer. A figurine sat amongst the rows of crèmes, powders and cosmetics on Bette's dressing table. It was of a man with bulging eyes, waving his arms in the air. At its base it had the words 'World's Greatest Clubber'. Spencer had accepted the gift with warmth and gratitude, but had promised himself it would be hidden from view after a suitable period of display. The week was up.

He opened the door of the room's large cupboard. The cupboard was a repository of souvenirs, mistakes and junk that would most likely never be used or seen again. Somewhere in amongst the boxes, bags and shelves were a George Foreman grill, a soda stream, a breadmaker, a facial steamer, a vegetable steamer, a smoothie maker - or was it a juicer? He could never remember - and an ice cream maker, to name but a few.

He pulled a shoebox down from one of the shelves, careful not to unbalance the precarious nature of the storage system. The box was full of apparently random pieces of junk, but Spencer saw them for what they really were: memories. He sat the figurine in beside the giant thermometer he had nicked from a swimming pool he worked at for a day and a half (apparently the ability to scream really loud didn't count as a lifesaving skill). Amongst the box's other contents were a ticket stub from the Empire State building; a Tina Turner signed programme; the order of service from his mother's funeral - he had kept hold of this in the hope he could collect the set, but his father hadn't been seen since Spencer was five; a sleep mask from Virgin Upper Class - the only time he had ever been upgraded, and it was worth the blow job he had to give the cabin steward; a magic wand from when Bette had worked as a magician's assistant; various wrist bands from various clubs and a host of other tat. He closed the lid and put the box back on the shelf.

Before attacking the washing he went over and switched on the computer. Once the washing was on he intended to upload some pictures from Saturday night onto the Opus Gay website. Being a member of the homo-techno-incompetus gene pool, Spencer was still having problems navigating the site.

His hand hovered over the mouse, contemplating looking up the club reviews online. *What if they hate me,* he wondered? *What if they thought Opus Gay sucked? What if my career's over?* He decided to wait for Jason; he couldn't face this alone. He also decided to stick to his new resolution of not acting needy and resisted the urge to phone Jason to find out where he was.

A couple of hours later, after accidentally deleting half of the pictures already on the website, leaving a navy blue sock in with a white wash, discovering Cillit Bang couldn't be used on aluminium and still no sign of Jason and the club reviews, Spencer's nerves were as frayed as a pair of 80's denim shorts. Spotting the potential for further destruction if his nervous energy wasn't harnessed, he went back to the cupboard in Bette's room for his Innovation catalogue, floor-polishing slippers. At least this way his pacing would do some good.

He was on his fourth circuit of the lounge when the mobile rang from the kitchen.

A starting pistol announcing the commencement of the rest of his life fired in his head. A torrent of pent up frustration exploded in his limbs and he catapulted himself at the phone.

Skidding across the kitchen, realising too late the slippers were not designed for traction, he grabbed the phone from the work surface as he sped past. His trajectory ended with a thump, a squeal and a splash as his groin slammed against a knob on the cooker and the mobile fell from his grasp, landing in a pot of boiling potatoes. The ringing stopped.

He turned the gas off, leaving the phone to stew, and with

one hand on his crotch, limped back to the lounge.

He suppressed the urge to call Jason to make sure the previous phone call wasn't the police looking for someone to identify his body and lay down on the sofa with a damp cloth over his forehead until, sometime later, the doorbell rang. He kicked off the floor-polishers and ran for the door.

"Where have you been?" he shrieked, almost tearing the door from its hinges. "I've been worried si__"

"Sorry I'm late," said Mandy, looking like a two-year-old who'd just heard his first balloon go pop.

"Sorry, I thought you were Jason." He waved Mandy in and closed the door.

"Something smells good," said Mandy.

"It's a special dinner for me and Jason… Hold on, what do you mean 'late'? I wasn't expecting you."

"Jason asked me to drop the magazines off. Didn't he call?"

Spencer glanced towards the pot with the potato and Ericsson soup. "No."

"He said something had come up, so couldn't make it over tonight and wanted me to make sure you got the reviews."

"But I'd bought him a new tee-shirt…and we were…I…"

"I haven't looked yet." Before settling on the sofa, Mandy pulled two magazines from inside his denim jacket.

Spencer put crap boyfriend drama to one side. With trembling hands he took the magazines. Ignoring the 'Three more deaths from blu' headlines, he flicked straight to the club reviews. He licked sweat from his upper lip and read: "'The famous Tumble Dryer, which has seen falling numbers over the last couple of years, has been given a long overdue shot of dragged-up adrenaline for its first Saturday of the month spot in the form of Opus Gay. A triumph of fusion clubbing, Opus Gay gave us a hormone and heels packed night, coming up with the goods all the other clubs promise and often fail to provide. Billing itself as a 'religious experience' and 'the club we had all been praying for', it had great music, class entertainment, plenty freebies and an atmosphere kickin' with high heels and gorgeous bods.'" *So far so good*, though Spencer.

"'The Grand Duchess Anaesthesia, whose famous gargantuan afro filled the DJ box to capacity, kept the upstairs dancefloor busier than it's been in years. Meantime, for Bette's Fourth of July theme, on the main stage was the American Drag Rock band, Katy Mean and the Powder Poofs. Katy treated the crowd to camp, catchy, rock-cock-in-a-frock fun. The whole night was Fire Island meets Ascot on acid. The fabulous Bette Noir,'" Spencer smiled as much with relief as by compliment, "'packed the place out, and if all goes well can look forward to an enthusiastic following in the months to come. Drucilla, The Tumble Dryer's very own resident fluff cycle, told our reporter that she had done everything she could to make sure Bette got the coveted spot at…'" Spencer held the magazine out at arm's length. "WHAT!?" Scanning the photos, he noticed the one they used of Bette had Mandy, in his animal print fiasco, standing closed-eyed next to her.

Spencer threw the magazine to one side and snatched the other one. This was the magazine Drucilla worked for. Malee was on the cover, dressed in a leopard print bikini and flanked by a couple of tattooed hunks. Spencer turned to the reviews and scanned to the punchline. "'Managing to pack the crowds in on a fabulous night, Bette Noir's Opus Gay was a huge success. But where would it all be without London's favourite, Drucilla?'" Spencer's voice hissed into a rasping exhalation of hate. "'When you've been running clubs as long as I have', said Drucilla, 'it's a pleasure to pass on your wisdom.'"

Spencer sank onto the sofa.

"You okay?" said Mandy.

"She's never run a decent club in her life. Christ, if you've ever stood near enough her you'd know she can't even run a bath." He scanned through the photos. There was only one of Bette, compared to the three of Drucilla. In one of them Drucilla was clinging to a half-naked go-go boy, a terrified look on his face as though a gun were pointing at him from just off camera.

"It's not that bad," said Mandy. "They loved Opus Gay."

"How can you say that? Didn't you just hear what I read?

I'm relegated to best supporting actor in a non-specific gender role in my own movie." Then Spencer noticed something else. "That's not the Tumble Dryer. That's a picture they've pulled from their library." He pointed at one of the photos next to Drucilla's. "I'd never have let Christopher Biggins in. Where's the pictures of the real celebrities? My VIP room was a Liza Minnelli wedding rehearsal of faces. I've *sooo* been stitched up. She's publicity hijacked me."

"What do you care? They're good reviews."

Spencer looked Mandy up and down in the way a Royal dignitary would look at a sewage pump operator who'd come straight from work to accept his OBE. "The whole point of Opus Gay was to offer something new. With Drucilla's name attached to it it's going to look like old hat calling itself new millinery. I've got to put those magazines straight."

"Spencer, remember what Bo said when one of the tabloids said she was addicted to cosmetic surgery."

"But she is addicted to cosmetic surgery."

"That's not the point. Bo said the only thing you should put straight is unattractive bi-sexuals."

Spencer considered the words and, strangely for Mandy, they made sense; there was little point trying to take on Drucilla in her own publication. He closed the magazine and looked at Malee on the cover before turning the magazine face down.

"Have you spoken to Anaesthesia today? I had a weird text message from her earlier saying she had some ripe gossip."

Mandy's shoulders sagged. "We spoke earlier."

"So what's the gossip? Is she in love again?"

Mandy shook his head. "Apparently the club reviewer for Drucilla's magazine, was found naked in Kensington High Street firing a potato gun at passing cars. He'd OD'd on blu."

"God, I hate that stuff. So what happened to him?"

"He bit the ear off a policewoman. He's been sectioned."

"Messy. I wonder who they'll get to replace him."

Mandy's shoulders sagged even further. "Drucilla."

"WHAT?"

CHAPTER 5

Bette checked the time as she took off her watch. It was 2.25pm. Since 4.30am she had felt the atmosphere between her and Jason gathering electrical energy like a storm at sea. A long weekend of clubbing was beginning to take its toll and her professional smile, in a striking similarity to the gold plate on the jewellery Jason had bought her for their first anniversary, had long since worn off.

She stared into the dressing table mirror and sighed. Her ideal man, she believed, was one who would open doors for her, and not just cubicle ones, and one who wanted her for her glamour, but not her dresses. Unfortunately, at the very mention of what she did for a living most men ran like a pair of cheap tights. She hated being single, but hated the bitter compromises that populated the minefield of relationships just as much. All too often she felt her entire collected wisdom on the subject of relationships was similar to that of her experience of flying: check you know where the exits are before getting comfortable.

Jason stomped past the dressing room door in an I'm-not-speaking-to-you-therefore-I'm-going-to-make-as-much-noise-as-possible-to-draw-attention-to-it huff. Bette tied her hair back.

"So, you calmed down yet?" Jason said from the doorway.

"I have no idea what you're talking about." She grabbed a tub of makeup remover. It was empty.

Jason grunted and moved away.

"I'm all for you going freelance, but I still can't believe you would have that vile queen as a client." Bette searched for another tub. "She just loved rubbing my nose in it last night with her news about Madonna Kebab. And as for telling her you would put her on the guest list for Opus Gay, were you trying to humiliate me? You know we're going to have to see her at the BAHTI's on

Friday?" Bette scanned the room behind her for a tub. She needed to get her face off before continuing this argument: Jason always took things more seriously if speaking to Spencer.

"No, I didn't know that," he called from the other room. "But I'm sure if you tell me a *sixteenth* time I'll remember... He's a client. It's just business. Get over it."

"You know she's Drucilla's best friend?"

"I think I got that one on the tenth telling."

Bette stormed through to the kitchen, ignoring Jason on the sofa, tore open the cutlery drawer and pulled out a knife. "I know the term loyalty is as appealing to you as 'vaginal dryness'," she waved the knife at Jason from across the breakfast bar, "but a little__"

"Aw, give the Drucilla shit a rest, will you?" Jason's voice had all the compassion of an evangelist preacher at a gay wedding. "*She's trying to stop me getting the club, she's superglued the lock on my makeup case, she's lied to the press, she's stolen my PA.* Have you listened to yourself?"

"Drucilla did steal my PA. I can't have Madonna Kebab singing at my night a week after she's appeared at Drucilla's. It'll look like I'm taking her seconds."

"So why didn't you have a clause in Madonna's contract to make sure she couldn't do that?"

The question sliced straight through Bette's fury to the heart of the matter: she was learning the club promoting business as she went along, and Columbian drug dealing and armed robbery were starting to look like the more stress free career choices.

"I...I..." she shook the knife in the air.

"If you're that bothered, I won't go to the BAHTI's."

The line made Bette gulp so hard she felt as if she had swallowed her Adam's apple. She stomped back to the dressing room.

She took her frustration out on the superglued lock of her Lois Vuitton makeup case. Stabbing in a frenzied attack, she gouged at it until it snapped open. She snatched the tub of makeup remover from inside and kicked the case under a clothes rail so she couldn't see what she had done.

She unscrewed the lid from the makeup remover, fuming at Jason's poker hand; she couldn't turn up at the BAHTI's unescorted, and Jason knew it.

"Okay, then," she called to the other room, "how's about a compromise?" She scooped out a handful of crème. "I'll shut up about Drucilla if you show a little understanding?" She slapped the crème onto her face and rubbed it in. It tingled in an exhilarating chill.

"Sure," called Jason. "I understand…I understand you're a drama queen and can't help yourself."

Massaging the crème vigorously into her face, Bette came to the conclusion that Jason was the kind of guy that if you told him you loved him, he would have asked why. And it would have been a valid question. His only redeeming feature was the fact the drag didn't bother him, but even Hallmark would have found difficulty marketing 'you don't thoroughly disgust me' as a term of endearment.

Her eye makeup smeared into a horror-movie melting face as she continued her cleansing ritual. Feeling her pores prickle in harmony with her mood, she was sure the crème seemed colder than usual against her skin. She had a horrible feeling she was at the birth of a stress line.

"Let's not argue," she called to the other room, hoping to calm the situation so there might be a remote chance of some post-clubbing coital.

"Whatever. I'm gonna crash for a few hours."

Bette fumed. What was the point? If she bit through her tongue any more, sex was going to be out of the question.

As the last remnants of Bette were removed from his skin, Spencer calmed. He wondered if he was expecting too much of Jason? It couldn't be easy having a time-share relationship with Spencer while Bette waits in the wings to come out. Anyway, what else was out there? At least he wasn't spending the night alone, and that had to count for something.

He wondered if celibacy might make life a whole lot easier.

At best, sex had always been fraught with problems. Asides the tedious negotiations of who does what to whom and with what inserted where, just securing a sexual partner for the night had always been traumatic enough to make him want to marry the first man who didn't run for the hills the moment they discovered what he did for a living. There were few professions Spencer could think of that had the same turn-off value as drag, and yet, as most drag queens would tell you, there is no shortage of hunky hangers-on or gleeful entourage when you're out clubbing in a frock. But ask any of them back for the euphemistic coffee and they sober up fast: kiss, kiss, bye, bye and they're gone.

Climbing into bed to the *Gaydrian's* wall of Jason's back, Spencer realised there was to be no kiss and make-up shag. With light bullying its way through the curtains, he reached over to the bedside cabinet and opened the drawer in search of a temazapam; he had no desire to lie awake listening to his teeth grinding in frustration as Jason snored.

Spencer woke to a dark room with a start, having dreamt he was being eaten alive by ants as Jason watched on. Eyes now wide open, the excruciating sensation of being eaten alive persisted; his face felt as if it were on fire. He clawed at himself, trying to gain some temporary relief. It made things worse; his face burned from the inside out. He tore at his cheeks in a desperate attempt to remove the burning flesh. He grabbed the glass of water from beside the bed and threw it over himself. Splashes hit Jason's back.

Jason switched on the bedside lamp.

"What the fuck are you doing, you mad__" Jason froze, his bleary eyes focused on Spencer's face.

CHAPTER 6

Spencer arrived home from Accident and Emergency just after 10am. As he came through the front door he took a deep breath in preparation for his reflection in the hall mirror. Red sores and blisters, glistening with painkilling and anti-histamine crèmes, covered his face. His eyes were puffed and swollen and his lips had a distinctly Lesley Ash/Pete Burns quality. If it wasn't for the puffy weeping already coming from the corners of his eyes, he would have burst into tears.

He touched his cheek cautiously. It felt as raw as it looked.

This was a disaster of epic proportions, thought Spencer. He had a job tomorrow and unless they were looking for a recent convert to Islam - which would be highly unlikely for an underwear company employing a drag queen - there was no way he could get away with wearing a veil. A thick veil.

The doorbell rang; he wasn't in the mood for visitors.

He opened the door to find Lucy, a look of thunder on her face.

"I'm being sued!" she said, and stomped past.

Having heard this statement from Lucy many times over the years, it had all the revelatory impact of hearing a supermodel had an eating disorder or drug problem. Spencer knew of few people who loved their jobs as much as Lucy. The owner of an Internet company called *Vitriolics' Anonymous*, her company's web site allowed you to order any one of a number of 'gifts' to be sent to the person of your choice. Inspired by her hobby of tormenting her ex-husband and his new spouse, Clifford, whom Lucy still referred to as the homo-wrecker, *Vitriolics' Anonymous'* list of gifts and possibilities was endless: bouquets of dead flowers for divorce anniversaries, cream cakes to people on diets, wreaths inscribed with the message 'In Deepest Anticipation', stuffed rabbits in broilers, boxes of laxative chocolates etc. Lucy sold acrimony at a price, including post and packing.

"Work?" Spencer closed the door.

"Yes. This time it's serious, though." Lucy sat down. "You know our best line is the plastic dog turd in a box...well, one of my shit-packers wasn't putting in plastic ones. Bad enough some kid took a bite out of one thinking mummy had been sent chocolate, but the psycho-shit-packer sent one to a bloody magistrate who'd just done him for possession."

Spencer could feel a grin pulling at his raw flesh.

"If you laugh," said Lucy, "so help me, God, I'll tear out your intestines and box them for our 'I hate your guts' range."

"Have you spoken to your solicitor?"

"That's where I've just been. He shook his head, scratched himself with a pen in a place where only a Mont *Bloke* would go, and asked me how my insurance was...You could train a bloody monkey to do that."

"What about the guy who did all this?"

"He's gone Lord Lucan. This could ruin me." Lucy looked as if someone had just told her they didn't make the batteries for her favourite vibrator anymore. "All I want to do is bring a little balance into otherwise unjust lives. I just want to earn a living, provide some jobs for the community and pay my taxes. What's so wrong with that?"

Spencer couldn't believe what he was hearing, and he was a bit pissed off she hadn't even noticed his ravaged complexion. "Lucy, you send Visa charged venom to heartbroken people, your workforce is mainly cash-in-hand and you're a qualified accountant – your job is spreading misery, employing people on the dole and cheating the Chancellor. If that makes you a pillar of the community then Samson's strapped to the other pillar and his hair's grown back real thick and shiny."

"You know something, with friends like you Prozac is going to remain a brand leader."

Spencer sat down beside her. "So what's your solicitor going to do?"

"Other than scratch himself, pick wax from his ears and bill me for it as if it was after dinner theatre? Nothing. Says I've got to wait and see if any others turn up."

At a loss for anything to say, and unable to contain himself any longer, Spencer ploughed in. "Aren't you going to aks me what happened to my face?"

Lucy shrugged. "I'm assuming it's chemical peel time again. Bit close to that award ceremony thing."

"Oh shit, the BAHTIs! I'd forgotten about them. I can't go looking like this."

"So if it's not a peel, what happened?"

"I was poisoned. The night my makeup case had its lock glued someone put caustic soda and fibreglass shavings into my makeup remover first."

Lucy sucked in air. "You gals sure play rough."

"I'm sure it's Drucilla. I was warned she could be like this. It makes sense now. She was looking at me funny when we met the other night. This..." he pointed to his face, "could just be the start. And the BAHTI's are televised."

"I'd get there early and grease the lenses with Vaseline."

"Is it really that bad?"

"It should look much better by the weekend."

"What about tomorrow afternoon?"

Lucy took a closer look. "You're screwed for that."

"What if I do my own makeup before going to the shoot, do you think they'll notice?"

"You'd put makeup on *that*?"

"A bit heavier than usual, naturally."

"Put makeup on there and you'd keel over with toxic shock, you mad bitch. When a nurse says they're going to dress your wounds they don't mean in something by Versace with matching accessories and a heavier foundation."

"But I can't afford to lose the work."

"Maybe Jason will be able to do something with it. You might be able to hide it with some professional help."

"That bastard. He only came with me because he thought it

might be something contagious. Then he legged it."

At the slightest whiff of a bitch at Jason, Lucy perked up like a lioness spotting limping prey on the horizon. "You know how I feel about him. It's tradition for the hag to loathe her fag's boyfriend. And certain traditions, like that and dwarf throwing, I'm all for keeping."

"So do you think I'll be able to get away with tomorrow's job?"

"Only if they don't get too close or take pictures."

CHAPTER 7

Spencer considered Lucy's wisdom of the day before as he sat on the sofa before a pile of bills he had been avoiding. He touched his cheek. It still felt raw. He began opening the mail.

The invoices were merciless; the zero's just kept coming. Then came the bill for the Drag Up and Boogey Down banner. The newest of the summer dance festivals, Drag Up and Boogey Down was designed to be Britain's very own Wigstock. Opening in Brockwell Park in South London, Bette had been asked to compere the main stage. Spencer had then seized the opportunity for great publicity and negotiated Opus Gay into the dance tent line-up. Carried along on a wave of PR enthusiasm, he designed and ordered a huge Opus Gay banner for the tent. Holding the bill for just over £1200, he wondered what he had been drinking when he placed the order. He left the bank statement unopened and called Jason to get him to come over earlier; he had to do the job and was going to need professional help with the makeup.

"You fucking mad?" said Jason, taking one look at Spencer's face as he came through the front door. "I'm not touching that and neither should you."

"But, babe," Spencer followed him through to the lounge, "I can't afford to blow this job out. Is there nothing you can do to hide the worst of it?"

"Listen to yourself, Spencer, 'hide the worst of it'. Your face is peeling off and the last thing you need to be doing is putting makeup near it." He went through to the kitchen and opened the fridge. "Now I might be able to do something for the BAHTI's at the weekend if you leave it to heal for a few days, but not if you put any crap near it. Is there no milk?"

"But I__"

"You can't put makeup near that." He shut the fridge door.

"Okay. I hear what you're saying, but can't we just try to put some on to see how it looks and play it by ear?"

"Do what you like. I'm going to get milk."

Spencer took the bills through to Bette's room. He sat down at the dressing table and flicked through them one last time. He looked up at his reflection. The bills were bad, but the face was worse. Much as it pained him to admit it, Jason was right: it would be madness putting slap on. He picked up the phone to call his agent; she could make his excuses to cancel.

The line was engaged.

He opened the bank statement.

Just over an hour later, after having applied makeup with the delicacy and care of shaving round a haemorrhoid, Bette tied the belt round her trench coat and headed for her front door. Mandy had buzzed up a short while before and Jason had leapt at the chance to go down and wait in the car; he wanted a lift home.

Mrs Chapori, who lived on the ground floor, was out sweeping the landing as Bette locked the door.

"Hi, Mrs C."

Mrs Chapori raised her broom. "Oh, Bette…" She lowered her weapon. "I not hear you coming."

"Sorry, Mrs C." Bette thought it highly unlikely Mrs Chapori hadn't heard her coming. For as long as Bette could remember, Mrs Chapori had taken it upon herself to maintain the stair landings. This meant that if voices rose anywhere in the building, you were almost guaranteed to find Mrs Chapori brushing away just outside your front door, sometimes in a hairnet and dressing gown.

"So, you is modelling again?"

"Yes, Mrs C."

"You lead such glamorous life. When I was young girl back in Poland, I used to__" Mrs Chapori grabbed Bette's arm as she tried to go past. Setting the broom to one side, she adjusted her spectacles to get a better look at Bette's face. "You need to get yourself good man."

Bette cringed; Mrs Chapori believed Bette and Spencer were a couple. She had once told Lucy she wasn't keen on the black man in the flat upstairs and further confided that she thought Bette was too good for him. Lucy being Lucy agreed and went on to tell her that she thought Spencer had been raising his hand to Bette and she suspected he also dealt drugs. It had all been a bit of a giggle at first, but now Bette didn't have the heart to tell her the truth. "I've got to go, Mrs C. People are waiting for me outside."

"Busy, you young people are always so busy. If you would just take time to let Jesus into your life you might find you…"

Mandy was finishing a bag of crisps as Bette got into the car. His look of shock when he saw her said it all. Jason sat in the back with an I-told-you-so smugness.

"What happened to…?" Mandy pointed at Bette's face.

"Didn't he tell you?" Bette glowered at Jason.

"No, we were talking about the BAHTIs."

"Is it bad?" said Bette.

"No, not really…it's just…well, it's…"

"Just what?"

"Well…it's__"

"Scary, disgusting, repellent, what?"

"Weeping."

Bette pulled down the vanity mirror to see a damp patch on her nose where something was seeping through. She screamed.

"It might be okay if you__"

"Shut-up, Mandy. The day I take style and grooming tips from you is the day Vogue announces Amy Winehouse as the new face of Gucci and flab is the new size zero." She got out the car. "I'm cancelling the job. Satisfied, Jason?"

Jason just smiled.

"I can still borrow the car?" said Mandy.

"Just take the thing." Bette slammed the car door and stormed back into the building.

CHAPTER 8

Walking up the steps to Mandy's front door with a bunch of yellow lilies in one hand, Spencer remembered all too well the estate agent's blurb from when Mandy bought the place: A compactly designed studio flat with North facing aspect and easy access to public transport.

He waited for the noise of the train going past to die down before buzzing the intercom.

"Hello," came a crackly, unidentifiable voice.

"Hi, it's Spencer."

"Oh, hi, Spence. When I buzz you in you'll have to push the door hard. It's sticking."

The door buzzed and after getting nowhere with a few hard shoves, he applied pressure with his shoulder. The door burst open, catapulting Spencer half way along the hall and smacking the flowers against a wall in the process.

Mandy opened his front door.

"Hi." Spencer straighted himself up. "I was a total bitch yesterday." He offered the now bashed lilies. "I'm really sorry."

Mandy smiled and took the flowers. "Oh, don't be daft. It's okay. I just ignore Bette when she gets like that."

Following Mandy into his grown-up bedsit, Spencer thought the Bette comment was a strange thing to say, but with grovelling to do decided to ignore it.

"So how's the face feeling?" said Mandy, searching in a kitchen cupboard for a vase.

"I'm not shaving until the BAHTI's. Jason says it might be workable by then." Spencer looked around for somewhere to sit. There was nowhere. Navy blue curtain fabric poured out across the room from the sewing machine on the makeshift workbench by the window.

"Just shove the material to the other end of the sofa," said Mandy.

Spencer lifted an end of material to see if a sofa lay beneath it. "How big are the windows these are supposed to cover?"

"It's for a couple in Soho. They've got one of those loft apartment places with huge great windows. The material was what I needed the car for."

"About yesterday, Mandy, I really am sorry. I don't know what got into me. It was crap behaviour, especially taking it out on you."

If Spencer wasn't mistaken, Mandy was blushing as he sat the vase of flowers on his tiny coffee table.

"Once the curtains are out of the way," said Mandy, "I can put them over on my workbench where I can see them when I'm working."

"Sorry they're a bit bashed." Strangled into Mandy's only vase, Spencer thought the flowers looked like they had been removed from a dented roadside railing, the kind you see next to big yellow police signs asking for witnesses.

Mandy smiled, once again looking as if he was blushing. "They're the first time anyone has ever bought me flowers. They look fabulous to me."

Feeling they both needed it, Spencer gave Mandy a hug.

"Seeing as you're here," said Mandy, parting from their embrace, "you can take your BAHTI dress home with you. I finished it last night." He lifted curtain material from one end of the workbench to reveal a sparkling pale green and silver sequined dress, its lizard-like train doubling back onto the bench.

"Wow." Spencer took a moment to catch his breath. It was spectacular. It was everything he had wanted, and more.

"The train's just over six foot. I'd rehearse flicking it before the night. Get it just right and it'll look amazing under the lights."

Spencer felt tearful, and guilty; having made Bette's dresses for years, Mandy had never taken a penny for anything other than the material.

"Oh, and before I forget," said Mandy, "I've had new business cards done." He lifted some more material and handed Spencer a box of cards. "If you could give these out as usual if anyone asks about the dress. I could really do with the work. I've not much on."

Unable to tear his eyes away from the dress, Spencer took the cards. He stared at it for a few seconds more before taking a piece of paper from his wallet. "Here, it's my agent's number. His wife needs someone to make a couple of dresses. I said how amazing you were. She's waiting for your call."

"This is great, thanks." Mandy looked chuffed. "Oh, and you'll never guess who called me the other day offering me work...Drucilla."

"You are kidding me."

"Yeah, I was shocked, too. I told her I wasn't interested."

Something in the pit of Spencer's stomach told him Drucilla was up to something.

CHAPTER 9

By the night of the BAHTI's Bette's healing hadn't been up there with Lazarus, but Jason had worked wonders with concealers and the flesh seemed to be staying put on the bone. Her nerves were finally beginning to abate until the hate seeking missile of Drucilla's voice targeted her from across the room.

"Oh...my...God," Drucilla shrieked through the crowd of backstage well-wishers, "it's true: you're finally sloughing your human form."

Jason squeezed Bette's hand. "Don't let her get to you. Not tonight."

Drucilla was covered from chins to fat ankles in feathers. Not a thread of garment could be seen beneath the accumulation of white plumage.

"Drucilla," said Bette, "don't you look fowl."

Drucilla's feathers bristled as she marched through the backstage crowd with her henchwomen, Sherry Amontillado and Stella Stairlift. Bette recognised Sherry's puff-ball dress as the one she had worn to Whore's D'Ouvres, whereas Stella, on the other hand, was in the most ridiculous spiky, skin-tight PVC number with a tower of black hair.

"*Mwah, mwah.*" They air kissed as far away from each other as was possible without retreating to separate rooms.

"I'm so sorry to hear about your unfortunate reaction to makeup remover," said Drucilla.

"How do you know what caused it?"

A hush descended upon the other cocktail swillers as they craned like attic-reared cannabis to a light source in their attempts to eavesdrop the conversation.

"I'm not sure, but everyone is talking about it. At least,

everyone I've been talking to is talking about it *now*."

Bette felt a vein in her neck throb. "Shouldn't you and the ugly sisters be out front?"

"Well, yes, actually. Oh, of course, they've given you the consolation prize of handing out an award this year." Drucilla's eyes ran over Bette's silver and green sequined dress. "If that's all I had to do, I wouldn't have made the effort, either."

Sherry and Stella giggled.

"Out with mother are we?" Bette glared at the sniggering henchwomen. "One day you really should let Cinders come to the ball."

Drucilla waved her finger at Bette. "Now, now, now, we mustn't get all worked up. Stay calm for your big moment. What if you're presenting your little award to me? We don't want you illuminating with jealousy." She turned to her two companions. "We can all see green *isn't* your colour."

Drucilla…nominated for an award. Bette added that to her list of reasons to die. "I'm doing the award for the celebrity-whose-face-you'd-most-like-to-spend-a-weekend-on. Not the person-whose-face-you'd-most-like-to-put-a-pillow-over."

"Sweetheart, if you had a pillow right now it would be best employed by cutting a couple of eye holes in it and wearing it on stage."

"A trick you've no doubt used to get yourself a shag."

Stella stepped around Drucilla's plumage, her outfit creaking as she moved. "Hi," she said in her thick, Valleys' accent. "Thanks again for the other night, Jason. The publicity shots turned out lush."

As Bette tried to move forward she felt Jason's foot on the train of her dress, nailing her in place and crushing sequins.

"Oh yes, I've heard what a talented young man you are," Drucilla said, winking one of her floorbrush-sized eyelashes at Jason. "You really must give me your card."

"He's not you're type," said Bette. "He's not inflatable."

A smile manoeuvred itself onto Drucilla's lips, leaving the rest of her face to convey contempt.

"Could everyone who's not presenting, please move front of house," called the assistant stage manager.

"Well, Bette," said Drucilla, turning to follow the crowd, "don't you worry about your face. I'm sure you'll be backlit."

Once Drucilla was gone Bette turned to Jason. "I can't do it. I'm a mess. I'll be a laughing stock. This'll ruin me."

"You look great," Jason said. "She's just jealous."

Bette thought his reassurances had the hollow ring of someone telling Oprah her bum didn't look big in a bikini. "What award could she possibly be up for? If the police had a warrant to search her for talent they'd come up clean."

"Ignore her. She'd love to think she'd got to you." He pecked her on the cheek. "I'd better get out front."

Jason turned on his heels and vanished without so much as a look back. Bette felt as supported as a bra-less double H. She was beginning to wish she had brought Lucy. It would have taken several armed men with no fear of losing their testicles to get Lucy to leave her side.

Music sounded from the stage.

"Bette?" said the assistant stage manager. He thrust a shiny pink envelope into her hand. "This is yours. Nominations come up on the autocue. It's real easy. Deep breath and read slow. I'll let you know when you're on."

"I've done this before, you know. I used to__" The assistant stage manager was already talking to someone else.

Bette looked at the envelope. She considered running from the building, but her heels weren't designed for quick getaways.

"Nervous?" Coming up to just past her nipples, a brightly tanned man stood grinning at Bette.

It took a moment before she recognised the Oompa Loompa. It was Romero Striker, the original Italian stallion from countless porn movies. There could be no gay man over the age of thirty who hadn't at some point cracked one off to one of Striker's movies, but looking down from her heels onto his badly dyed hair, she wondered how old those films were.

Bette felt his hand on her ass, massaging slowly.

"I'm presenting award for *best porn star turned actor/poet*. And yes..." he looked up with a full-fat cheesy grin, "I am who you think I am."

"Well I'm not who you think I am." Bette moved away from his hand. "I'm not someone who's interested."

"Don't kid yourself, babe." He slapped her left buttock.

Bette, who was in no mood to turn the other cheek, was not as playful when she slapped his face in a cathartic release of tension.

"I like my boys feisty," said Romero, getting up from the floor and rubbing his jaw. "I'll catch up with you later."

Romero winked and aimed himself at a Victoria Beckham-drag look-a-like who was filling her face with complimentary tequila. Bette couldn't believe Striker's opening line: "So what's a Spice Girl like you doing in a place like this?"

So many freaks and not enough circuses, thought Bette and moved to the wings to watch Malee, the show's new host, whom even Bette had to admit was looking stunning tonight, kick-off the proceedings: biggest-religious-bigot went to Pope Benedict XVI and was accepted on his behalf by the head of the Gay Buddhist Association, the Dolly Lama; in-your-face homo-hero went to a gay traffic warden who had bitten 'the finger' off a homophobic white-van-man (there was a live link-up with Wormwood Scrubs for that) and best stand-up comedy went to a lesbian double act from Australia called Mel 'n' Oma.

"Okay," the assistant stage manager thrust a Perspex BAHTI into Bette's hand, "you're next."

The words exploded in Bette's head. Stomach acid leeched onto her tongue.

"And to present the award for the celebrity-whose-face-you'd-most-like-to-spend-a-weekend-on," Malee said from the stage, "...the dark Goddess of temptation herself, the beautiful, the breathtaking, the one and only, Miss Bette Noir."

Bette clutched the envelope as if it were her last will and testament and sashayed her way to the podium, smiling graciously to Malee and her faultless, blemish-free, perfect skin, whilst resisting the impulse to twat her on the side of the head with the Perspex BAHTI as she went past.

The crowd applauded and whistled as she positioned herself at the lectern. Thousands of sequins scattered light from her dress. She milked the applause with a quick, but well rehearsed, flick of the dress train. As Mandy had assured her, they loved it. The cameras all turned on her, and then, to her horror, she saw her face on the giant screens either side of the stage. Bette was reminded of the first time she saw Jessica Tandy in HD. She gripped the BAHTI in one hand and the envelope in the other and tried to focus her attention away from the giant screens. Smiling out at the audience she spotted Romero Striker sitting at the front. His hand was on a waiter's butt.

The autocue rolled.

Fuck that, she thought, anger still stoked from her earlier encounter with Romero: "Friends, *short Romans*, provincial queens..." A television camera zoomed in on Striker to get his reaction. Instantly his image replaced Bette's on-screen. It took Striker a few seconds before he realised his trademark butt massage technique was up there for all to see. The crowd peeled with laughter as he blushed through his perma-tan.

No doubt deafened by the director's screams in their headphones, the cameramen quickly returned their lenses to Bette. With her confidence now buoyed by Striker's humiliation, she blew him a kiss when her face came back on screen. The crowd roared with laughter again. A man in a pair of oversized headphones, resembling a Borg assimilated Mickey Mouse, started waving his arms in protest of her adlibbing. Much to the audience's delight, Bette blew him a kiss, too.

The Disney droid didn't look happy.

With wistful resignation Bette turned to the autocue and read: "Sex appeal is a difficult category to define. Not since the leather clad Brando straddled his Triumph in *The Wild One*..." Reading through her cheesy spiel, Bette began to wonder what award Drucilla could possibly be up for. There was no award for talentless drag; there was nothing for backstabbing ho. "... So, this year's nominations for the celebrity-whose-face-you'd-most-like-to-spend-a-weekend-on are: Carlos Acosta…Wentworth Miller…David Tennant…and…" Bette paused as her heart hit the back of her tonsils and missed several beats before relocating itself back behind her ribcage. "…Calvin Pryce."

Having long since forgone the juvenile joys of posters in bedrooms, if ever there was a man Bette would have Blu-Tac'd to the wall above her bed it would been him, Calvin Pryce. Lead singer of the gay rap band, The Arse Bandits, Bette thought Calvin was a gay icon in a league of his own. Having made his name as a kids' TV presenter, his career had come crashing down in a tabloid Sodom and Gomorra. Caught by paparazzi leaving an East London leather bar, bare-assed in a pair of chaps with a man's finger up his ass, the resulting tabloid feeding frenzy that followed could have been narrated by David Attenborough. Refusing to follow the time-honoured showbiz tradition of hiding out in Australia, he persevered, setting up The Arse Bandits and surfing the tidal wave of his own publicity into a hugely successful music career. He even went so far as to use the offending picture of himself for their first album, 'Pull Yo' Finga Out, Brotha'. Bette adored him.

Squinting through the lights in search of Calvin, she spotted Jason. He was sandwiched between Drucilla and Stella. Bette's blood boiled; she could hear hissing coming from her ears (somewhere at the back of her mind she took a mental note to watch this on TV to see if steam really did come out). She had been about to sear Jason with an I'll-get-you-for-this stare when behind him she spotted Calvin. He was smiling directly at her.

The technician threw his headphones to the floor in exasperation and mouthed, 'AND THE AWARD GOES TO…'

Fuck, thought Bette, *the envelope.* "And the award goes to…" She tore open the envelope, picturing it to be Jason's scrotum. "…Calvin Pryce."

The scrotal substitute was thrown over her shoulder as she started waving the Perspex BAHTI in a Pro-Plus addicted five-year-old frenzy. The audience cheered, apparently caught up in Bette's elation, as Calvin made his way to the stage.

The temper-fuelled hissing in her ears faded to the drone of a Scottish pipe band. *Welling up with matrimonial pride, Bette clutched her bouquet. Calvin was coming towards her through the congregation, smiling his famous dirty grin.*

He was coming up the aisle towards her now, lust and adoration in his haunting dark eyes. She was moments away from being Mrs Calvin Pryce. She wondered about adoption; Calvin would no doubt make a wonderful father.

A loud burst of *Slapper, She's Gettin' Hysterical*, Calvin's first single, roared out across the stage. Bette was propelled from her wedding day fantasy as if by the ejector seat of the bride's limo. In a fluster of self-awareness she realised it hadn't been a moment too soon; she had been about to throw her wedding bouquet of solid Perspex BAHTI over her shoulder, no doubt killing a cameraman in the process. Calvin's hand being placed on the small of her back cushioned her landing.

She presented the award, which still had a heady scent of gardenias, and returned the peck on his cheek whilst reminding herself, every millimetre of the way to his face, no tongues. Knowing that professional grace dictated that she now took the customary four steps back and to the side, Bette eagerly got into place for a good letch. Her eyes ran up and down his Armani tux, lingering briefly at his broad shoulders before moving down to muse on whether he was going combat or not.

Her game of one-handed strip poker came to an end as Calvin finished his thank you's. He turned to Bette and whispered: "I hear you're supposed to come and sit with me at my table now."

Fingers entwined, she gripped Calvin's hand and brandished it for the audience. Thinking it was another cue to applaud, they responded. The fact the crowd wanted to join in with her moment of 'up yours' glory was neither here nor there; the hand waving was for Drucilla and Jason.

Walking through the tables back to where Calvin had been sitting, Bette realised it might take a team of dedicated surgeons to make her let go of his hand. Then, just as they passed Drucilla and Jason's table, Bette's entire body electrified as Calvin spun her round and planted a kiss on her lips. It felt like snagging a kite on a national grid pylon. Every hair on her body arched with excitement.

"Sorry about that," whispered Calvin. "I'll explain in a minute."

Screw adoption, thought Bette, *we'll steal a baby and go live in Mexico.*

Once they were settled with a drink at the table, Calvin turned to Bette and smiled. "I hope I didn't freak you back there. It's just I saw the cameras about to point at someone I hate."

"Well, if you want to freak me some more," said Bette, who was now so high she couldn't even see cloud nine below her, "just remember: I'm shockable, but never judgemental."

Calvin smiled again and clinked their glasses.

Still savouring the taste of his breath mint on her tongue, Bette nodded acknowledgements around the table to the rest of the band as they took it in turn to examine the BAHTI. They were an eclectic bunch, and with names like Farley, Miles and Hugo, Bette thought they seemed a little more RADA than rap.

"That's the one." Calvin leant over and pointed his glass at Drucilla, who was stroking Jason's shoulder. "I can't stand that vicious queen."

Ding, ding, ding, jackpot! Tonight's paying out like a faulty fruit machine. "Me too." Bette wondered if Mr Right had just become Mr Too-Fucking-Right. "I'd piss on her if she was on fire, but only if I was passing lighter fuel."

"I'm glad it's not just me."

"Oh, don't worry, we who loathe are legion." She saw Calvin's jaw flex. "So what's the story? Even I don't grind my teeth when I see her."

Calvin leant forward and put his hand on Bette's knee. Her feet tingled as the sexual charge earthed through her toes.

"Remember the picture of me in the red bands a couple of years' back, the one of me snorting a line from a table in The Lint Tray?" Bette nodded. "I recently found out it was her that sold it. And all because I wouldn't do some crappy charity thing she was doing. It's not that I don't do charity stuff, it's just this thing was all about promoting her and not the charity."

"I had my tyres slashed three times just because I dared to go for the Saturday night spot at the Tumble Dryer."

Calvin tore his eyes away from Drucilla. "Someone should do something about that queen."

"Hey, dude," said Otis, handing the BAHTI to Calvin, "wouldn't Bette be wicked for the new video?"

A smile erupted across Calvin's face. "Oh my God. You're right. She'd be wild. I don't know why we didn't think of this before. Tonight must be fate." He grasped Bette's hand, launching her heart into tachycardic euphoria. "We're doing a cover of that old Ram Jam number, Black Betty. It'd be so cool if you could do the video. Oh, God, it would be just so cool – Bette Noir as Black Betty. Fuck me it'd be wicked."

Bette couldn't believe her ears; she was going to be in her very own signature tune video.

Their excitement came to an abrupt halt when the killed-off soap star from the other night announced the winner of the most popular charity. The award had gone to a gay youth charity called DICK (Drugs' Ignorance Can Kill), and was being picked up on behalf of the trustees by someone who had apparently worked tirelessly to raise funds for the charity: Drucilla.

The killed-off soap star rubbed his nose and sniffed as he waited for Drucilla to make her way through the crowd. Bette noticed a momentary grimace on Calvin's face as he began his applause.

"Calvin," Bette pulled his perfectly nibbleable ear towards her, "do you really want to get right up her nose?"

"Like a finely chopped gram of anthrax."

Bette smiled. "I may have an idea if you're interested."

CHAPTER 10

Bette slammed her front door and followed Jason into the lounge.

"I told you," said Jason, who'd made full use of the BAHTI's open bar, "the witches of fucking Eastwick hijacked me as the lights went down. I didn't know where I was sitting."

"Hijacked?" Bette said. "So your hand down near Big Bird's giblets, then, what was that, Stockholm syndrome?"

"Gimme a break. She grabbed my hand when the nomination came up and wouldn't let go." Jason threw himself onto the sofa, denting the cushion with his temper as much as his butt. "What was I supposed to do?"

"So did she 'hijack' your wallet and force her card in there?"

"What card?"

Bette felt her eyes go wide with gotcha; she had expected a lie. "I saw it when you put *my* change from the cab away."

Jason shrugged. "She says she can put work my way."

Bette was shocked. She had anticipated a more protracted denial. This was new territory. "You wouldn't dare."

"What am I supposed to do? She's offered me work on the Tumble Dryer's calendar."

Bette thought this was going too far. The Tumble Dryer's twenty-fifth anniversary was coming up later in the year and the owner had come up with the idea of doing a commemorative calendar. The task of organising it had gone to Drucilla. "Don't you see? She's just doing this to get at me."

Jason struggled to his feet. "It's always about you, isn't it? Couldn't she be doing this because I'm good at what I do?"

"Depends what you're doing for her."

"You'd hate it if I started earning good money, wouldn't you? You'd prefer it if I was kept grateful of your handouts."

"I'd prefer it if you were grateful of anything."

"Grateful of what, living in a threesome with a neurotic cross-dresser and a man who smells like Cocoa-butter Chanel?" There was something in Jason's smug delivery that suggested he'd been saving that particular line for just such an occasion. "When was the last time we went out as a two men?"

From somewhere at the back of Bette's mind, Spencer empathised with Jason. But this wasn't about Spencer, she told herself, this was about Bette, and she didn't take to having her position threatened.

"I'm taking the job," said Jason. "I'm having lunch with her Tuesday to discuss it. As you've said in the past, I've got a future to think of. Anyway," he tapped the side of his temple, "it's all in your head. It wouldn't do you any harm to try and get on with Drucilla."

Bette heard a campanologist's chorus of warning bells. "You ungrateful, fucked-up, little shit."

Jason laughed. "Of course I'm fucked-up. If I wasn't fucked-up do you think you'd be gettin' any?"

"Getting any! There are lesbians who're getting more cock than I am."

"Spare the self-pity crap. Everyone you get involved with is fucked-up. It's part of the deal to be able to *fuck you*. If you've shagged with a sane man in the past ten years it was only till he sobered up. Look at yourself, you freak."

Bette took a deep breath to fuel the rage that was now ablaze in her gut. "Typical. It doesn't bother you when this..." she pulled at her dress train, "gets you into clubs free, gets you free drinks and gets you just about every one of your new clients. Oh, no, then it's okay. But ask you to show the person behind it all a little respect, a little affection, a little loyalty, and suddenly it's all too much for you. Suddenly it's all a bit freaky.

"So tell me, Jason, who's worse, the freak or the loser who lives off the freak? Just you remember, without all this..." she threw her dress train back to the floor, "you'd be pushing lipgloss and eyeliner from behind a counter in Boots. Do you actually think

I want to spend my life prancing about like this?"

Jason staggered to within inches of Bette's face. "Yes, *actually*, I do. You love it. This isn't just a job for you. You've hidden beneath *this* for so long..." he stabbed hard at Bette's shoulder with his finger, "that it's Spencer who's the work - pathetic Spencer, who's incapable of holding a conversation about anything other than Bette. Well this might be okay for you, but I don't want to live this 24/7. You need to chose who you want a relationship with, me or the drag."

"What relationship? I buy you clothes, I pay your bills, I cook you meals. I even do your laundry. With the total absence of sex this isn't a relationship: I'm your bloody mother!"

Jason's face lit up, clearly pleased with whatever he was about to say next. "Well, isn't that a great coincidence, *mom*. You think I'm a fucked-up, ungrateful, freak shagger. I'm also a huge disappointment to you and you can't stand the sight of me. Kinda what your own mother felt about you."

Bette saw red. Jungle Red. Before she knew what she was doing it was all over. In a flash of distilled temper, she swung her fist at Jason, smacking him square in the face and sending him back onto the sofa with a bleeding nose where her 'big' ring had hit him. She straightened her dress, spotting the crushed sequins on her train from earlier. "And by the way, *no one* damages my threads."

Jason grabbed the sofa either side of him as if he'd just woken up on a rollercoaster to discover he wasn't strapped in.

Bette continued. "How stupid am I, huh? How utterly pathetic have I been, tiptoeing round your moods, bribing you for affection, praying you might still be interested in me, so desperate for physical contact I'd wait till you were asleep before I'd even hug you? You've kept me begging at the table for emotional scraps, waiting for whatever feeble affection you were willing to throw down to me. Well, enough's enough. Take the job with Drucilla. See how far it gets you. But don't come crawling back to me when it all goes tits up. 'Cos it will."

"Look, Spence," Jason's voice dropped to a placating croon as he let go the sofa, "I didn't mean to___"

"Too late, Jason, this gravy train has derailed."

"Okay, babe, I was out of order. No. Way out of order. I'm pissed. We're both a bit pissed. Let's not argue. Let's not, huh?"

"Oh, don't worry." Where a few moments ago temper had raged through Bette's head in a dizzying furore, there was now calm. "This wasn't an argument, Jason." She pointed at the front door. "*This* was a break-up."

Jason waited. Bette's hand stayed pointing at the door.

He got to his feet. "Aw, fuck you."

"Not since September seventeenth you haven't."

Wiping blood from his nose onto the sofa, Jason left without another sound. He didn't even close the front door.

Bette was motionless, still staring at the sofa, when moments later she heard the door close and footsteps come along the hall. Half expecting to see Jason's apologetic face, she was about to slip off a stiletto and throw it when she saw Lucy.

"Need any help?" Lucy said, a baseball bat in her hand and her dressing gown tied tight at the waist in preparation for action. "I couldn't help overhear. You can probably still see the ring marks from the glass." She circled around her ear with the baseball bat. "Do we need mixers or is this a straight up job?"

"Straight up." Bette sank into the armchair.

Lucy propped the bat against the wall and went to the kitchen.

Bette watched the dent of her now ex-lover's butt slowly erase as the sofa's cushions pulled back into shape. He was gone by the time Lucy arrived with a couple of very large JD's.

"Am I a freak, Lucy?"

"Course you are, hon. It's the sane ones you gotta look out for. They've got 'agendas'."

Bette felt her face try to grin, but nothing happened. *This must be how Anne Robinson feels all the time*, she thought.

"I hit him." Bette said. "I can't believe I hit him."

"Tony hit me once."

Bette was shocked by Lucy's confession, and the suicidal lunacy of any man who would consciously incur her wrath. "What did you do?"

"I went out next day, bought five bars of laxative chocolate and grated them onto a chocolate gateau. He loved chocolate gateau." She swilled the JD in her glass and smiled. "It's what gave me the idea for our laxative chocolate range."

"You fed him poisoned Gateau?"

"Nope. I just left it in the fridge and let the greedy pig do it himself. The fun part was the loo roll." Lucy's smile stretched further across her face. "I unwound it and rubbed it with scotch bonnet peppers, then rewound it and put it back on the holder. By the end of the week he was in so much pain he thought he had bowel cancer." She raised her glass. "Here's to freaks."

"To freaks." They clinked their glasses.

"So what happened?" said Lucy.

"Let's just say I decided being a doormat was *soooo* last season. Why didn't you tell me he was a complete bastard?"

"I did. Regularly. Almost daily."

"Okay, yes, you did, but why didn't you make me listen?"

Lucy rubbed Bette's knee. "You're right, hon, it's my fault. I'm a bad hag. Bad, bad hag."

Bette's shoulders sagged, she felt like a contestant on one of those endurance game shows the Japanese do so well; left to scratch at her rat bites and piranha scars as the titles went up, wondering if it had all been worthwhile.

"Did I ever tell you about my mother, Lucy?"

"The bible bashing, homophobic, racist loon?"

"Stick 'is dead' on the end of that and it could be the opening line of my eulogy."

"You've mentioned her. Why?"

"Oh nothing." Bette took a slug from her glass in a manner she felt offended the femininity of the dress, so, in an act of recompense, took a second, daintier sip.

"You want a refill?"

Bette looked at the tumbler of straight JD and knew better.

"If it's okay, I'm going to get all this off," she gestured to her face and dress, "have a bath and wash that man right outa..."

"You sure, hon?"

Bette nodded.

"Well, if you change your mind and you need to talk, bitch or burn effigies, I'll be up for a bit." Lucy got up and kissed Bette on the forehead. "Just remember, being with a guy who's wrong is stopping you from being with the one who's right."

She retrieved her bat and blew a kiss from the hall. Just as the door was closing Bette heard Lucy speaking. "Yes, the skirting boards were looking a bit grubby. Goodnight, Mrs C."

Bette ran a bath.

Spencer lay for a while with just his head sticking out from the bubbles. Michael, his first boyfriend, came to mind as he rubbed the broken skin on his knuckles. Spencer had been convinced Michael manufactured arguments just to have an excuse to lash out. It had been whilst with Michael that Spencer created Bette. Originally a way of making a few quid at amateur talent nights, Bette was soon making more money than the crappy telesales job he was in. He had never felt pathetic on stage as Bette; he felt adored, and for the first time in his life people noticed him.

It had also been thanks to Bette that Spencer found the strength to finish the relationship. Michael hated Bette. After lashing out at her one night he had made the mistake of issuing an ultimatum: either Bette went or he did. Bette then wiped the blood from her mouth and calmly smacked Michael on the side of the head with a Lecruset frying pan. She thought she'd killed him at first. When he regained consciousness he ran from the flat and was never seen again.

As the bubbles thinned, it occurred to Spencer that every boyfriend he had ever split up with he had done so while dressed as Bette. A sudden wave of cold despair hit him; it was as if God had whispered into his ear that he would never be happy again.

A tear slid down his face into the bubbles. They were still running down his face long after the bubbles had gone.

CHAPTER 11

Spencer was dealing with relationship bereavement the only way he knew how: by Tuesday he had gone through denial and anger, and by Wednesday he was going through backrooms and a bottle of Jack Daniels a day.

Staring up at an unfamiliar ceiling, he wondered what had happened to Mandy. He thought he had probably mislaid him somewhere between the second and third bar they had gone to; the night was proving difficult to piece together. He stopped trying. Instead he turned his thoughts to the advantages of going back to someone else's place as opposed to your own: if it got wild there was no post-coital tidying up to do - especially if you did an 'oh shit, is that the time'; there was the little designer tips you could steal from their recessed lighting; there was no need to worry about what state you left your place in; and with no drag around you could avoid the what-do-you-do-for-a-living trauma.

A phone rang from somewhere in the room, spinning Spencer's pick-up encounter to stage six: the morning-after who-the-fuck-are-you?

Please don't wake, Spencer prayed, *not yet*.

The disadvantages of going back with someone came flooding into focus: you can't remember where you are; you can't remember anything you might have said, done or promised and you can't remember his name.

Spencer turned away from the waking stranger and onto his side, trying to buy some time to remember his name or what he looked like.

The body next to him moved.

"Hi, there," said a sleepy voice.

Still looking away, Spencer had been about to reply before

he realised his bedmate was talking to someone on the phone.

"...Yep, I'll be going in late. I've paperwork to do here."

Sounds under forty, thought Spencer.

"...No, I'm playing squash tonight."

Fit, looks after himself. Not bad.

"...Do we have to? I hate the Ivy. What about Quag's?"

Got taste, a bit of class. Liking the sound of this.

"...If you want, but we've got to meet the financiers later."

Good job, probably got dosh. Where have you been all my life?

"...Love you, too, babe. See you tonight..."

And a cheating bastard. Oh shit, is that the time?

A handful of paracetamol and a hair of the dog later and Spencer's spirits were riding as high as the new boxers he was premiering. Sitting with Mandy at the window of Compton's bar in Soho, watching with morbid fascination as a group of screeching, Japanese fashion students from St. Martin's Lane minced past in a peripatetic audition for a gay manga cartoon, they waited for Bernice.

"They should really get in touch with fashion victim support," said Spencer, as one of the students twirled his electric pink, fur fabric kilt.

Mandy craned his ear at Spencer's chest. "What's that?"

A small, tinny voice could be heard coming from Spencer's pocket. He pulled out his phone.

"BETTE, YOU DUMB BITCH, CAN YOU HEAR ME?" It was Anaesthesia, shouting at the top of her voice.

"Sorry, Anaesthesia," Spencer said into the phone.

"Girl, you need to get yourself a new phone. That's the third time this week I've had to listen to conversations via your sweat glands. Either get it sorted or put your phone on the table so I can hear the gossip properly. It's like being at a lesbian nudist camp: all I'm getting is snatches... So did you get the flyers from the printers?"

"Just picked them up." Spencer tapped his shoe against one of the four boxes at his feet.

"Fabulous. Speak later. Say hi to Mandy."

Spencer made sure the phone was switched off. The quizzical

look on Mandy's face said an explanation was expected.

"It's my new phone," said Spencer. "Apparently it can play music in full Dolby surround, walk the dog and on vibrate can do a full deep tissue massage with guaranteed sexual satisfaction. It also comes with a money-off voucher for a six month Open University course on how to work it. I can barely make calls on it and it keeps ringing Anaesthesia. And you don't want to get her when she's still wearing her sleep mask. The upside is I keep missing Jason's calls...so it's not all bad."

"I never understood Jason. He always seemed so angry."

"Hairdresser syndrome."

"But he was a makeup artist."

"Doesn't matter. It's an affliction men in the camp professions suffer from. Jobs like hairdressers, trolley dollies, makeup artists, that kind of thing. They either go with the cliché and become all out screamers, or try to fight it and forge themselves a macho alter-ego with steroids, piercings or tattoos. Trust me, Mandy, every other overly tattooed man you see on the scene is a hairdresser."

"What if they've got loads of tattoos and piercings?"

"Web designers."

"So has Jason picked all his stuff up from yours yet?"

"If by *stuff* you mean his clean washing, a bulb douche and a CD of Snoop Doggy Dog. Then yes. And at long last I can get rid of those naff second-hand motorbike leathers he bought me."

"So what about anything you had at his place?"

"Like nature, Jason abhorred a vacuum - and a duster, and cleaning products in general. I hated his place. It was all skanky bed sheets and rap music to fuck to: interior design by Tracy Eminem. He's welcome to anything I've left there."

"So what happened to you last night? One minute you were snogging that guy with the beard, and then when I came back from the loo you were gone."

Spencer was as confused as Mandy now; the guy he woke up with was clean-shaven. Spencer's phone rang. Mad Mickey's name came on screen.

"Is that..." Mandy nodded at the phone, "from the club?"

Spencer slipped the phone back in his shirt pocket. "I don't know how long I can keep avoiding him before he comes looking for me. It's just the longer I can keep him and his boys out of the club the better."

"Haven't they just set up shop already?"

Spencer shook his head, uncomfortable talking about Mickey while the phone was still ringing. "I think he's a bit 'old school' and likes to get unofficial 'permission' first."

"Be careful, Spence. I don't think he's the patient type."

"I know. I think he's more familiar with creating patients for the local A and E, but the club's owner wants the place a drug free zone, or else I'm out."

"That's a bit like wanting pubs to be a drunk free zone."

"I know," Spencer fought with the desire to whisper as the phone continued to ring, "but Drucilla's managing to keep her nights totally clean, apparently."

The phone stopped.

"So, can I see the flyers?" said Mandy.

Spencer bent down and opened a box. He handed a glossy, post-card flyer to Mandy.

"I still can't believe you managed this." Mandy stroked the card. "This is going to be amazing."

Spencer took a flyer. The lettering of Opus Gay was in fronds of red flame. Below that was a semi-naked picture of Calvin Pryce. Licking at his feet were cold, blue flames that read: 'Bette Noir Presents, the only London club appearance of The Arse Bandits'.

"Can you afford them?" said Mandy.

"It's biting into my budget for next month's act, but it should draw in extra crowds this month and with the money I'm getting for doing the video. It should just be manageable." Spencer grasped Mandy's hand. "I still can't believe it. I start rehearsals next week. I'm going to have my own signature tune: Bette Noir's Black Betty."

"Won't it be Arse Bandit's Black Betty?"

Letting go Mandy's hand, Spencer dismissed the technicality with a flick of the wrist.

"I couldn't buy this kind of publicity for Bette, or the club. Drucilla being a vile bitch is actually starting to pay off for me."

"Did you manage to get the advertising changed from Madonna Kebab to the Arse Bandits?"

"Most of them. Drucilla's mag said they couldn't change it at such short notice but offered not to run it for me if I wanted. I called their bluff and cancelled the ad."

"What other stuff did you get?"

Spencer smiled. "I've got a couple of fire jugglers to entertain the queue. There was three of them, but there's only two now... I didn't aks. And I've got a team of strippers called the Donkey Sanctuary doing the cages above the dancefloor. This is going to be *the* best night The Tumble Dryer has ever seen. It's costing me a fortune, but it'll put Opus Gay on the map and Drucilla in her place." Spencer stopped as everyone in the bar turned to the door.

"Bernice is here," said Mandy.

Many of the bar's occupants continued to stare, slack jawed, at Bernice. Standing in a bright orange boiler suit with scarlet tutu, and a full armoury of facial piercings that made her look as if she had just snogged a landmine, Bernice waved over to Spencer and Mandy.

Spencer waved back, thinking Bernice's outfit made her look like a member of Guantanamo's corps de ballet.

"*Th*orry I'm a bit late, *Th*pence," said Bernice.

"You want a drink, Bernice?" said Mandy.

"Nothing for me." Bernice stuck out her tongue and pointed to a painfully swollen piercing. One of three.

"Tongue still bad?" said Spencer.

Bernice nodded. "*It'th* an infection. I'm on *antibioticthth*." Courtesy of Bernice's fascination for collecting ever more piercings, Spencer now knew the names of body parts that he had until recently been blissfully unaware even necessitated naming. Her full metal jacket aside, though, what really got Bernice noticed was her hair, or rather her total lack of, technically. To successfully carry off drag, or tranny, Spencer felt the hair was important. So the brave step of shaving one's head might have been a foolhardy one, if you hadn't had a brunette bob tattooed onto your scalp as Bernice had. "You got the flyer*th*? I'm meeting the girl*th* in fifteen minute*th* in *Th*oho *Th*quare."

Spencer pointed Bernice to the boxes at his feet; Bernice was in charge of the Lusherettes, whose job it was to patrol the club with usherette trays selling bottled water and poppers, whilst also giving away free condoms, lube, glow sticks, chocolate liqueurs and other freebies. For the next few days, however, Spencer was paying them to wander the streets of Soho in an Ibiza style promenade show, thrusting flyers into the hands of the terrified and unsuspecting.

"That's all of them for now," said Spencer. "I'm picking up another three boxes in a few days so you can do a final blitz next Thursday and Friday. And one of the boxes is the money off flyers. Don't give them to any dogs."

Bernice took two boxes under each arm and headed off. Spencer watched her amble along Compton Street and, for the first time, felt a sense of confidence about Opus Gay. It looked like even Drucilla couldn't stop Saturday being a success.

"Oh no, look," said Mandy, flicking through a copy of Boyz, "there's been another two deaths from blu."

CHAPTER 12

Bette knew, as any club promoter did, that a club could burn and die on its first night like a solo album from an unattractive boyband member. The second and third nights, if you were lucky, were when you got your punters hooked.

From the moment the doors opened just under an hour ago, the crowds had been coursing through. After putting Pavlova on guest list duty - her well-insulated, dessert-themed dress made her the best person to withstand the evening's unseasonable chill - Bette slipped into the quiet of an empty Lint Tray with Bo.

Before sitting, Bette did a twirl in her little black, crushed velvet dress, letting the lights scatter off her best silver and diamante jewellery.

"And you'll never guess what," said Bette. "Calvin's asked if I'd like to go to a party with him Sunday night."

"As Bette?" said Bo.

"What do you mean?"

"Well, if he asked Bette, it might just be work. If he asked Spencer, on the other hand, it might be interesting."

Bette hadn't considered the difference. She had been done up for a rehearsal of their video when he asked, but she assumed he was asking Spencer. She quickly realised she didn't give a damn: she was going out with Calvin Pryce!

"Time Out wants to do an interview with the two of us next week. My agent has leaked that there is absolutely no romantic interest between us and that we're just good friends."

"Oooh, well done, *dahling*. That'll have the press bidding for your wedding pictures by the end of the month."

"I know. I couldn't buy this publicity. I just couldn't."

Bo pulled a tiny, silver topped bottle from inside her glove.

The gloves, one black and one white, were the finishing touches to her sixties, panelled, black and white dress.

"I think tonight's the night where my luck changes, Bo. I think things are finally on the up for me. The whole thing with Calvin's video could save my career, and his appearance tonight means Opus Gay will be safe."

Bo unscrewed the top from the bottle and dipped the tiny silver spoon that hinged from it into the bottle then offered it, coke-laden, to Bette's already positioned nostril. Once Bette was finished, Bo reloaded the spoon and took it to her nose, inhaling the powder as if sampling a delicate scent. She then reattached the top and handed the bottle to Bette and curled Bette's fingers around it. "A little gift. You might need it before the night's out. The bottle was a present from Heath Ledger. Poor *dahling*."

"I can't accept this, Bo."

"Of course you can. Think of it as a good luck charm."

Bette smiled and slipped the bottle into her clutch bag.

"I recorded an interview with Calvin for the show last week." Bo raised her eyebrow, signalling there was more. "You know he's single? Split up with the boyfriend six months ago."

Bette's heart fluttered; she had avoided asking Calvin if he was single. But she knew now. "Did you find out if he likes drag queens?"

"I don't know about that, *dahling*, but he mentioned you a few times when we were chatting later."

Unsure whether it was the coke or hormones, a rush hit Bette that would have knocked her from her heels if she hadn't been sitting down. She struggled to catch her breath. "Bo, do you think…nah…is there…nah…I'd never be his type…never…"

Bo raised an eyebrow. "I'd be careful. He works in the music business. Those people have to throw concerts for the starving of Africa to convince themselves they have a sincere bone in their bodies." She took a sip of her orange juice. "Now, I won't be able to stay too long tonight, *dahling*. I'm sorry. But I've had a hectic week and I really can't face a long night."

"S'okay. Thanks for coming. Just make sure one of the

photographers gets a snap of you enjoying yourself before leaving. I need all the celebrity endorsements I can get."

"*Dahling*, I'll tell them you throw a better doo than Elton."

"So, Calvin, what else did he say about__"

"Forget him for a bit. Come and meet my ATM. I left him in front of a mirror, so he won't have moved."

"Your ATM?"

"My actor turned model. He's half Turkish, half Italian and half my age. Enough brains to walk and chew gum but not enough to talk during sex."

After having her picture taken with Bo, Bette left her holding court in the upstairs bar with her ATM and an entourage of fans. Bette then went into hostess walkabout mode, weaving through the swarms of wide-eyed well-wishers, occasionally stopping to air kiss and accept compliments. She felt indestructible.

Someone grabbed her arm as she tried to make her way towards the bar for a quick Jack Daniels. About to sear them with a how-dare-you-touch-me glare, she looked up from the shovel sized hand that was wrapped around her arm to see Mad Mickey's steroid mass taking up the space of three people.

"I NEED TO HAVE A WORD WITH YOU, BETTE," he shouted in her ear - a necessary trick to be heard over the music.

Bette felt so tiny next to Mickey. Her mouth went dry. This had been the moment she had dreaded. "MICKEY, HI. LISTEN, SORRY I'VE NOT GOT BACK TO YOU BUT__"

Gavin, one of the DJs, appeared beside Mickey.

"BETTE, WE'VE GOT A PROBLEM," said Gavin.

There was something in his tone that made Bette feel she had intercepted a call to Houston. She looked down at Mickey's hand on her arm and he let go. She turned to Gavin.

"WHAT'S UP?"

"ANTHONY, THE LIGHTING ENGINEER, SOMETHING'S REALLY WRONG WITH HIM."

Bette grabbed the bat phone in her head. They couldn't do without the lighting engineer. "WHERE IS HE?"

Gavin gestured for Bette to follow and headed off at a pace only someone who had spent their life in 'flats' would have attempted.

"I'LL CATCH UP WITH YOU LATER, MICKEY."

Relieved to have a drama to deal with, Bette chased through the crowd after Gavin, but she knew Mickey wouldn't leave it there. Following Gavin upstairs to one of the small offices they used for cashing up, she knew it was going to be almost impossible to avoid Mickey all night.

Sitting on the floor of the office was Anthony, hugging a waste bin as he tried to fill it with frothing vomit. Bette took a deep breath and bent down to face his bulging eyes.

"Are you okay, hon?" she asked in her best nursie voice.

"*Bllllleauuuck*," went Anthony into the bin.

"Get rid of him," Bette said as she stood up. "Throw him in the bloody wheelies out back." She pointed to the faintly blue snot streaming from Anthony's nose. "He's been snorting blu."

"What we gonna do?" said Gavin, stepping back from Anthony as the bin echoed with his retching. "I start my set in ten minutes and I can't do the lights as well."

Bette rapped her nails against her thigh as she glared at Anthony. The Tumble Dryer's laser and lighting system was famous, and complicated.

"This is probably going to cost me, so you'd better have children to sell." She turned for the door.

"What will I do about him?" said Gavin.

"Get him another bin and a bottle of water."

Heels clattering along the warren of backstage corridors, Bette was beginning to think that club promoting was a bit like being a wedding planner: to the assembled guests it's just a few hours that glide seamlessly together, but what if the groom doesn't show, or the bride's stuck in traffic? What if the florist mixes up orders and you get the 'In Deepest Sympathy' wreaths whilst a funeral gets your 'Congratulations On Your Happy Day' arrangements? What if a rhino sized drug dealer is on the hunt for you and your lighting engineer is vomiting so hard his toe nails are beginning to retract?

She brought herself to a halt and hugged the wall as the curdling tones of Drucilla's fake, plumy accent echoed from up ahead. Bette straightened her dress and gave a self-comforting flick to her hair before continuing round the stairwell.

"Drucilla," Bette said in mock surprise, "don't you look swollen. I mean swell. Now what the fuck are you doing back here?"

Drucilla was clutching a dinky little muscle mary to her arm. A look of terror burned in the muscle mary's dilated pupils like the screaming heroine caught between Kong and the T-Rex.

"I was taking Pablo to meet Calvin. He's a big fan."

Big Nancy, more like, thought Bette, as Pablo took a half step behind the giant barber's pole that was Drucilla's sequin striped dress. "I don't care. It's staff only backstage."

"Norman won't mind, sweetie. He likes me to keep an eye on things."

Bette knew she didn't have time for their usual vitriolic banter, but the attempt to undermine her by wielding the owner's name couldn't go unchallenged. "Drucilla, how much longer do you think Norman Daniels is going to put the creeping sensation of your ass kissing down to a yeast infection?"

Drucilla stepped forward, leaving Pablo trembling behind. "You're looking a little flushed, sweetie. Everything okay?"

Careful, Bette thought, *this old trout has shark in the family; she can probably smell a single drop of trouble across an ocean of calm.* "Everything's fine. In fact, it looks like being the busiest night the place has seen in years. I think after tonight *Norman* might have to re-evaluate some of the dead wood this place is carrying."

Drucilla's face puckered up as if she'd just been offered a warty cock to suck on. She grabbed Pablo's arm and stormed past without another word.

Bette had no time to gloat. As soon as Drucilla was out of sight she tore on up the stairs, cursing Nike for not making a stiletto. By the time she got to Calvin's dressing room, her calf muscles were bulging as if her knees had swallowed melons. She knocked on the door.

"I said no thanks," came Calvin's voice from the other side

of the door.

"It's Bette."

"Yo," his tone changed instantly. "Come in."

Bette did a quick straighten of the dress and a hair flick for some false sense of composure and opened the door.

"Bette, wha's up?" Calvin was lying on a threadbare sofa in nothing but his underwear. Bette thought she might faint.

When she got back down to the main dancefloor, after an expensive negotiation with Calvin's lighting man, the club was heaving. As the smoke machines pumped disco smog over the mass of writhing bodies, Bette's facial muscles began to relax from serial killer smile to hostess cheer. A drink was called for.

"*Blllleauuuuck!*"

Someone next to Bette threw up, just avoiding her shoes and his subsequent decapitation. She stepped around him and smiled at his friends, who seemed to be handling the situation quite ably by ignoring it.

Nodding hellos, Bette pushed on towards the bar. A single JD wouldn't suffice now; she needed a large one.

Mary Poppers, one of the Lusherettes, grabbed Bette's shoulder as she tried to fight her way through the crowd. Bette turned to face Mary's usherette tray, which courtesy of Mary's platform shoes came almost to eye level.

"CAN I NIP TO THE UPSTAIRS FIRE ESCAPE FOR A FAG BREAK, BETTE?"

"SURE," said Bette, thinking Mary looked a bit peaky - which was quite an achievement for someone whose idea of makeup fell into the less is pointless school of thought.

Mary smiled and turned on her platforms, cracking the back of someone's head with her usherette tray as she went.

Bette was about to make her final lunge for the bar when she spotted Mandy. He was trying to get her attention by waving his arms about in the style of grand prix starting flags. Bette sighed and waded her way towards him.

"BETTE, SOMETHING AWFUL'S HAPPENED," said Mandy. "PAVLOVA'S GONE UP IN FLAMES."

CHAPTER 13

Nodding greetings and distributing air kisses with the urgency of a diarrhoea-troubled star at a movie premier, Bette followed Mandy's lead through to the club's foyer. Flashing blue lights could be seen reflected along the corridor before she got to the entrance. They arrived as Pavlova was being lifted into an ambulance. Her blackened and melted dress flopped at her side.

Bette smiled calmly to two drag queens as security ushered them through, apparently incapable of knowing where to begin a search of their attire. Bette thought she recognised one of them so smiled and handed them a couple of drinks' tokens.

"What happened?" Bette whispered to Mandy.

"One of the fire jugglers dropped his torch. It rolled under Pavlova's dress, and whoosh!" He threw his hands into the air demonstrating a mushroom cloud. "Fortunately Danny put it out before her wig caught."

"Was anyone else hurt?"

"No. Danny's had to go change his shirt, but he's okay."

"Excuse me," said the paramedic, "is anyone coming with..." he seemed to be struggling to find an appropriate pronoun, "...him?"

Bette checked her watch. "Mandy, you go with her."

Mandy nodded. "I put Bernice on the front desk while I went to find you. She can't do it for long, though - she's having trouble with a new piercing." He pointed to under his crotch. "I think it's called a guiche."

"Don't worry. I'll get Mary to take over. Call me as soon as you know how Pavlova is."

"How will you hear your phone?"

"I'll have it in my knickers on vibrate...let it ring for a bit. It'll probably be the high point of my night."

Bette caught up with Mary Poppers in the upstairs staff toilets. Her platforms were sticking out of a cubicle as she bear-hugged a toilet bowl in an attempt not to be thrown down the U-bend by the force of her retching.

Bette sat her clutch bag next to the wash hand basin and checked her makeup in the mirror. "I'm guessing you'll be needing a longer fag break, Mary."

Mary looked round from the pan, the sheen of lip-gloss replaced by the glisten of stomach acid. "I don't know what's wrong with me, Bette. I think it might be swine flu."

"Bollocks. You've been snorting blu, that's what's wrong with you."

"Bette, all I've had is__" Mary returned to the Armitage Shanks logo as her stomach tried to escape through her face.

Bette fought the desire to pull the flush as Mary spasmed over the pan, only stopping herself as she realised the time: the Arse Bandits were due to go on soon.

"Get yourself down to the front desk, Mary." And with that Bette ran from the room.

The quickest way to get across to the stage entrance at the side of the dancefloor was to head through the mass of spinning butts and waving arms. Two of The Donkey Sanctuary strippers were dicks-a-swinging in the cages above the crowd while at the front of the stage the other two writhed over each other in what looked like a lubricated game of Twister. Suddenly Bette found herself face first in a wall of white cotton.

"I NEED YOU TO COME WITH ME," said Danny, looking down the IMAX screen of his chest.

"I CAN'T, I'VE GOT TO BE BACKSTAGE."

"IT CAN WAIT."

"NO, DANNY, I NEED TO INTRODUCE THE__"

"COME WITH ME."

The crowd parted ahead of Danny as he ploughed through. Bette sighed and followed in his slipstream, once again chasing someone who had no idea of the fine balance that had to be struck between weight distribution and momentum to walk at speed in heels.

Just in front of the double doors up ahead, someone was puking on the floor. Bette threw him her best disapproving stare.

"You noticed folk chucking up?" said Danny, stopping outside the office where Bette had last seen the lighting engineer with his head in a bucket.

"Well, yeah." She checked her shoes for splashes. "The days of GHB when they just passed out seem strangely preferable now. Tidier, at least."

"Someone's been selling blu."

"Is it Mickey's guys?"

"No. Mickey won't let his guys sell blu."

"But I just saw Mickey. If Daniels finds out you've let___"

"He's in here." Danny flicked his salami-sized thumb at the locked door. "I searched him real good when he came in, and he had nothin' on him. Honest. Absolutely nothin'. If Daniels finds out I've let someone in dealing blu."

"I know. I know." Alarm bells started to ring in Bette's head as if someone had set light to a polyester blouse under a smoke alarm. "I don't have time for this, Danny. If you've___"

"And then there's what Mickey'll do if he thinks you've let someone else deal?"

Bette took the point. She nodded for him to open the door.

"You!" she screeched, instantly recognising the mangy dreadlocks and shell suit of Mildew, one of the gay scene's most pathetic small-time dealers. Bette loathed Mildew, thus named after the rancid smelling coke he used to sell, and had barred him from every club she had ever worked in due to, amongst other things, his predilection for stealing unattended drinks. But worst of all Bette hated his 'brotha' routine. As pale a white man as was possible to be without pink eyes, Mildew could have given Michael Jackson tips on racial self-delusion. "How many times have I said I never want to see your face again, Mildew?"

"Yo, Bette, you lookin' wicked, sister." Mildew tried, and failed, to flick his fingers into a snap.

"Save the slime for your trail home." Bette turned to Danny. "What did you find on him?"

"Pills and blu." Danny pulled three clear plastic bags from his pocket. One contained what appeared to be several hundred pills and the other two had dozens of small paper wraps.

"If I go get Mickey," said Bette, "and ask if you're working for him, what's he going to say, Mildew?"

"Woooow, hold on, gorgeous. Why don't we just keep it cool and you just give me my stuff back and I'll get outta here? No trouble, ye nah wha' am sayin'?"

"Mildew, here's what we're going to do. Danny's going to flush your *'stuff'* and you're going to get your skinny ass as far away from me and this club as possible. Capiche?"

As Mildew was about to reply, Bette raised her hand for silence; the music in the club had stopped. Calvin was about to go on stage without anyone to introduce him.

Bette turned for the door. "Chuck him out back and make sure none of Drucilla's cronies see him."

She charged, arm outstretched, towards the doors to the main bar. With her entire momentum anchored to earth by the tinniest amount of shoe leather, she slammed through the doors.

For a brief second she saw the stage over the heads of the crowd, and then it was gone. Her head hit the floor with a crack and her limbs splayed out beside her in a blow-up doll formation, leaving a similar expression of shock on her face.

"Welcome one and all, my dear, dear fans," boomed Drucilla's unmistakable voice from the sound system. "It's so good to see so many of you here tonight. And I'll be expecting to see you all here again in a couple of weeks at Muscle Hustle. I've got some treats in store for you all then with…"

Bette pulled herself from the sticky floor, ignoring Drucilla's voice droning over the PA. If Bette had been a Bond villain, this was the point she would have set the club to self-destruct and jumped into her escape pod.

A numbing sensation crept along her thighs as the small of her back turned cold. She thought she was having a stroke.

Calculating if she had enough time to tear through the crowd and rip off Drucilla's head before paralysis stripped away the last of her mobility, she realised the cold on her back was from the puddle of vomit she had slipped and fallen in and the numbing sensation was her phone, vibrating in her knickers.

"... So, without further ado," said Drucilla, "I'd like you to welcome onto the Tumble Dryer's stage, a dear, dear old friend of mine...Calvin Pryce. Calvin, get your Arse Bandits out here."

The crowd roared and cheered as the vibrating continued from its place of hiding. She went back through the doors and retrieved her phone, ignoring the twinkling mass of phone screen lights above heads of the audience as they all captured Drucilla on stage with Calvin.

"Just tell me if she's alive," Bette said into her phone.

"She's just seen a doctor," said Mandy. "I think she's going to be okay, but her dress is ruined."

"I know how she feels." Bette pulled damp, crushed velvet away from her back. "Mandy, I'll call you later."

She headed back up the stairs to the office. Mildew was gone. She pulled off the dress and laid it on the desk. It was then she realised she had left her clutch in the loo where she found Mary Poppers. It had her emergency makeup, hankies and perfume, from which a few sprits right now would have done her dress the world of good. Flicking her hair back, she also discovered a lump of chewing gum clinging to its mass. It could wait. As for the dress, there was only one thing for it: she removed her tights and took off her knickers to use them to scrub.

The vomit proved harder to remove than a Korean dictator. It just seemed to embed itself further into the pile. She picked off the 'bits' and slipped the dress back on; she'd change into something else once she'd dealt with Drucilla.

Stealthing her way back through the club, Bette headed for the guarded doors that led backstage. All eyes were on Calvin as she nodded to security and slipped backstage. She sprinted along to the stage wings, trying not to think about the vomit-soaked, chewing-gum-haired, knickerless mess she had deteriorated into.

Drucilla was standing just off-stage, microphone in hand, poised at the ready to throw her bulk back into the spotlight.

"No you don't." Bette lunged for the mike.

Drucilla turned just in time to swipe the microphone away.

"No one knew where you were," Drucilla said. "Someone had to introduce them. And in the interest of professional continuity, I think I should be the one who goes on now."

"By all means." Bette positioned herself between Drucilla and the stage. "But you'd better have a big white stick up that big white ass, 'cos I'll tear your friggin' eyes out if you try."

Standing within the lights of the stage, but not visible to the crowd, Bette prepared herself for showdown. Drucilla stepped back, apparently sizing up how far Bette would go.

"You bin great," came Calvin's voice. "Stay cool."

"Go!" Drucilla smiled and thrust the mike into Bette's hand and shoved her towards the stage.

Dazed by the sudden capitulation, and suppressing the desire to check her back for blades, Bette launched herself at centre stage before Calvin could leave.

"Come on, give it up for The Arse Bandits," she roared into the mike, egging the audience on to louder applause "Come on, I want to hear the screamers in all of you."

"Don't even talk to me," said Calvin as he pushed past.

The rest of the band followed in a similar sulk, exiting the stage with their noses in the air in a very un-rap band hissy fit.

The audience didn't seem to notice their abrupt departure, however. In fact, roars of laughter erupted from them as people pointed at Bette. She looked to see if there was something behind her. What was so funny?

It was like one of those dreams where you turn up to school without your trousers on. Then she looked down. Under the UV light of the stage, the front of her dress looked as if it was covered in something. Something very un-ladylike. Her dress looked as if it had been picked off the floor of a busy orgy; it look as if it was covered in spunk. Even over the noise of the crowd, Bette could hear the roar of Drucilla's laughter coming from off-stage.

CHAPTER 14

In the week following Opus Gay, Spencer's desire to curl up under a duvet and let his muscles retract and waste was made all the worse after several dozen unreturned phone calls to Calvin, who was refusing to forgive being photographed as Drucilla's 'dear, dear old friend'. Spencer's injury was further compounded by a call from his agent telling him the video job with the Arse Bandits had been cancelled, along with the interview in *Time Out*. The feeling that it was all about to get worse, however, came late Thursday afternoon when he was summoned to Norman Daniels' office.

Sitting in the office, waiting for Daniels to finish on the phone, Spencer could feel the staged tension building like the onset of a cold sore he knew was going to get ugly. Daniels unsettled Spencer. A sartorial elegance that could only be described as 'vegan Christian' and a haircut that would have had the RSPCA hammering down your door if given to a family pet, Spencer couldn't think of a single reason how someone with all his money could look this bad. He was the Donatella Versace of clubbing.

Daniels took a bite of a chocolate Hob Nob, letting crumbs fall and nestle into his chequered tank top before taking a slug from a mug of coffee. The fact Spencer had been offered no refreshments when he arrived had left little doubt as to the upcoming tempo of the meeting.

Daniels finished his call and turned to Spencer. "So have you seen this?" He slapped a copy of the magazine Drucilla worked for onto the desk.

"No," said Spencer. "I was going to pick them up later."

Daniels opened it and threw it across the desk. "Well, let's have a look together, then, shall we?"

It was open at a picture of Bette with a working-girl-caught-in-police-headlights-as-her-punter-fled expression on her face.

"Not one of my better poses."

Daniels' pale blue eyes focused on Spencer with all the compassion of a hungry bull shark with PMT (pre-mauling tension). "No, not one of your better ones. What the fuck happened? You disappear for half the night then turn up looking like you'd just collected everyone's donations for a charity spunk-a-thon. And then you go threatening the only person who showed some professional consideration."

"The pictures aren't all bad, are they?" As the words were out of his mouth Spencer remembered what Lucy had told him that barristers and lawyers try never to do in court: ask a question to which they don't already know the answer.

"Fortunately not." Daniels flicked the page to a picture Spencer would rather have bathed in a pool of his own vomit than see: Drucilla and Calvin on stage, beaming 'professional' smiles at each other. Next to that picture was one of Drucilla with a sweaty muscle troupe; and another of her with some ex-boy-band member sandwiched between her and Stella Stairlift. "You're lucky Drucilla's working as club reviewer for her magazine at the moment. She said nothing about your club this week. Not to mention pulling a few strings with the other mags and hushing up what happened to the flaming flamer who was carted away in the ambulance."

Spencer could just imagine Drucilla's joy at the opportunity not to even mention Opus Gay; she knew slagging it off would be indirectly attacking Daniels' club, and she couldn't do that, but omitting it completely could be seen as a favour.

"I want you to make an effort to get on with Drucilla," said Daniels, smiling in the way a social worker tells a parent it's for the best their children are taken into care. "She's worked here a long time and knows how I like the place run. You owe her big-time for keeping all that crap out of the press."

Spencer sat in silence for a moment, scanning the only article that mentioned Opus Gay. It was a fabulous review of the night. It called Opus Gay 'the most buzzin' club in London'.

"The review's great, Norman. What's the problem? Okay, I

ended up looking like a Jerry Springer slapper. And yes, maybe fire-eaters and flammable drag queens weren't the best pairing since Take That and Lulu, but the club was the busiest it's been in years."

"You are, of course, right. And that's how I want it to stay... whoever is in charge of the night."

"Look, the dress isn't what you think. It was pollen. My stupid dressmaker left the dress sitting under a vase of lilies." Spencer felt his jaw tighten at the thought of Mandy's fuck up. He could have slapped Mandy when he told him he had spent an afternoon trying to scrub pollen out of the dress's pile. He was just as furious with himself, however, knowing it was the very flowers he had given him. "And the reason I was late getting to the stage was__"

Daniels waved his hand for silence. "One more thing before you go." He opened a drawer in his desk. "I believe this is yours."

Bette's missing clutch bag was deposited onto the desk.

Spencer lifted the bag and looked in. His heart sank; the silver-topped coke bottle and joints were still there. This must have been Drucilla; she was the only person who would hand something like this back with all the drugs still in it. Some lucky charm that bottle turned out to be.

"I've warned you, Spencer. Two clubs in South London have already lost their licences because of this whole blu thing. I'm spending a fortune having the upstairs bar and dancefloor renovated next month and our licence review is coming up in November - I need the place spotless until then. And I mean spotless. Not a hint of dealers. You understand?"

Spencer nodded, deciding to keep the Mildew incident to himself.

Returning home from his encounter with Daniels, Spencer had gone straight to Lucy's for a much needed bitch and sympathy. Lucy, who was always in the mood for a bitch, had obliged, and when the alcohol ran out they decanted to the pub on the corner. Come chucking out time, the world had been put to rights and it had been decided, once and for all, that all men were indeed bastards.

On their way back from the pub their slurred rendition of Mamma Mia came to an abrupt halt when Spencer saw what was sitting on the steps of their building. Jason lay fast asleep, sprawled across the doorway, inebriate drool glistening on his sweatshirt. All the scene lacked was a dog on a rope and a piece of cardboard saying 'hungry and homeless, please help'.

Spencer swayed as JD and fresh air fizzled in the brain. "What does he want, Lucy?"

"Oh, I don't know, hon. Maybe he was in the area and thought he'd return some CDs." She slapped the back of Spencer's head. "Get real. He probably had a stiffy a couple of hours ago and headed off like a homo pigeon to the roost." She kicked Jason's leg. "Oi, dick breath, you've missed the last bus to sad. You're gonna have to walk home."

Jason stirred and pulled himself into a seated position, obviously struggling to remember where he was.

"What you doing here?" Spencer said.

Jason scrunched his face as he tried to focus. "I really need to talk to you, Spence."

"You really need a shower and a breath mint," said Lucy, stepping in front of Spencer. "But you're getting neither of them here. Now shift before I throw a match on your meths soaked carcass."

Ignoring Lucy, and abandoning a flawed attempt to get up from the step, Jason persevered. "Please, can we just talk? I've missed you so much. I've been such an ass."

Feeling alcohol and commonsense battle for control of his decision-making process, Spencer tried to sober up. The cute little fop of blonde hair that always fell across Jason's eye when he was tipsy dangled there adoringly. It made him look so vulnerable. *Would it do any harm to let him come upstairs and talk?* Spencer wondered. But if he did, he knew they would probably end up staying the night, and he'd only just managed to get Jason's hair gel out of his white pillowcases. *But I can't just leave him out here in this state? He could get attacked, or something.* He remembered Jason's verbal attack after the BAHTI's; maybe leaving him out here would be a good lesson. *But it was quite romantic, really, coming over here and camping out on the step. It's so Romeo and Juliet. It would have taken a lot of guts.* A lot of alcohol, more like.

Lucy took out her keys and moved towards the door. "Come on, leave him."

Jason tried to get up. He slipped, hitting the back of his head against the wall with a pitiful clunk.

"Drucilla's fucked me over," he said. It got Spencer's attention. "You were right. She never had any work for me. At least not the kind she promised. She was just using me to get at you." Pulling himself from the step like a tangle-stringed marionette, he held out his arms and added: "I hate her now, too, babe."

Spencer felt his eyes widen in a look he knew all too well as one of Bette's. He pushed his forefinger against Jason's chest. Jason fell backwards, hitting the ground with little more than a sigh.

"Ignore him," said Lucy, shoving Spencer through the door. Spencer glanced back as Jason floundered to coordinate an apparent surplus of limbs.

"Be careful of Drucilla," Jason shouted from his crumpled position. "She really wants you out."

Spencer's ear, which was tightly gripped between Lucy's thumb and forefinger, started its journey upstairs.

CHAPTER 15

Bette lifted her mail as she and Mandy came through the door.

"I'm so looking forward to going out," said Mandy. "I bought a new shirt for tonight and I'm feeling lucky."

Bette's mobile rang. She checked the caller's name on the screen. It was Mad Mickey. She sat the phone on the breakfast bar. "Pour us a couple of JDs, Mandy. Let's have a quick drink before I take my face off."

"So, the photo shoot you just did, who was it for?"

"A crappy drinks company. They're *rebranding*." Bette curled her fingers in the air around 'rebranding'. "The drink used to be called Plastered."

"I remember that. Didn't the handyman from one of those decorating programmes advertise it?"

"That's the one." Bette threw her estimated gas bill to one side and sat down. "He's why they're rebranding. He's on his third celebrity retreat with no mini-bar privileges. I'm tellin' you, if my modelling career was a cancer patient you'd tell it to stop treatment, get their affairs in order and go swim with dolphins."

Mandy arrived with the drinks. "It's not that bad, surely?"

"I don't have another job for two months."

Bette watched Mandy's brow furrow with concentration as he seemed to scramble for something positive to say. "Ooh, that looks interesting." He pointed at a bright blue envelope.

Bette accepted the change of subject and opened the letter. "It's just an invitation to Fran's book launch. Wanna come?"

"I'd love to. I thought Fran made porn movies."

"He does. This is his autobiography." She read the invite properly. "It's called *Huge dicks have feelings too*." Choosing another envelope on the grounds no good news came in brown envelopes, she tore open a white one.

"I think I've got one of his films. Was he in Tuff, Rough, Sleazeball, Locker-Room Donkey, Sexpig Marathon II?"

"Crap!" Bette threw the contents of the envelope onto the table. "Pavlova's invoiced me for her burnt dress. I'm haemorrhaging money like a crack addicted city trader with four mistresses." She grabbed another envelope and tore it open.

"I've got an idea. Why don't I make her a new one? You get me the material and I can__"

A rasping gargle was coming from Bette. Words log-jammed at the back of her throat.

"Bette, are you okay?"

"I...don't...fucking...believe...it..." Her eyes widened in a hyperthyroid stare. She thrust a card into Mandy's hand.

Mandy read the card aloud. "'Drucilla's turning the big five O and is cordially inviting you to the birthday bash of the year. So forget everything else and get yourself down to the Tumble Dryer'. Big deal. Let her celebrate cheating death for another year. What odds does it make to you?"

"*This* came with it."

Bette's hand was flailing about so much Mandy had to grab her wrist to secure the piece of paper. He read again: "'Dear Bette, as you can see, my birthday falls on the same night as your little club venture. I would have had my party a couple of weeks later at my own night, but the upstairs dancefloor and bar are closed all that week for renovations. Anyway, Norman says you owe me for keeping the Pavlova thing quiet and not letting those unfortunate pictures get published, and when I asked him he said you would be only too happy to let me have the upstairs for a private function. I hope that doesn't cause too much inconvenience. The invitations went out today. Drucilla.'"

"I...I..." Bette hissed out the last air in her lungs and her eyes bulged as if being pushed out of their sockets from behind.

"Bette, now would be a good time to breathe."

"I...I...I..." Bette could see stars in her peripheral vision.

"Bette, breathe!"

It had taken little persuasion to convince Mandy to go out on his own. Almost leaving a Mandy shaped hole in the door in his haste to leave, he had been like a Sellafield employee who had overheard the word 'meltdown'. Bette was quite pleased; she needed the time to seethe in private.

She could feel a writhing mass of frown lines gathering on her face. If any of those lines stayed she was going to sue Drucilla.

After finishing over half the bottle of JD she nodded off: *Before long she was at a celebrity-studded funeral: everyone in black Gucci or Versace. The coffin, which had the words 'WIDE LOAD' painted in large yellow letters down its side and an impressive finger buffet laid out on top, had a discarded newspaper on the floor beside it. The headlines read: 'Peace at Last. Palestine and Israel find common ground: they both hated Drucilla.'*

Bette reached down to pick up the newspaper and as she did she could hear a faint scratching coming from inside the coffin.

Bette woke to the scratching sound in the room - a chilling moment until she realised it was only Gabbana at the window.

She swayed into the kitchen and let him in. Gabbana strolled past and nudged the bowl on the floor that was kept there for him and Dolce. Bette filled it with water before taking a tuna steak from the fridge and slapping it onto a saucer for him. The cat rubbed against her leg in a perfunctory thanks.

She refilled her glass and took the bottle to the dressing room.

Feeling Spencer gnawing to be let out, Bette slugged her JD and ignored the makeup remover. She sat at the computer and downed her drink, sitting the bottle on top of the small filing cabinet next to the desk. She checked her emails. Amongst the numerous spam for Viagra and other pharmaceuticals there were two advertising invoices. She closed the screen.

Had it all been a mistake, she wondered? Should she have taken Bo's advice all those months ago and looked at other venues for Opus Gay? Bo had told her not to go up against Drucilla. But it was too late now; Bette's survival and the club's success were now inexorably linked. Especially now, after being so publicly dumped from Calvin's video. She poured another drink and thought about the pile of bills sitting in the lounge. She was going under. The club had to succeed. It had to.

A cloud of dark thoughts rolled in on a weather front of hate. What would she be willing to do to keep Bette and the club? What would she be willing to do to stop Drucilla? She thought about the email invoices. This was an every woman for herself situation. Drucilla was out to ruin Bette and she wasn't going to stop until she had. She had done it to people before; Bette had heard the stories. A line had to be drawn. Enough was enough.

Several hours and a bottle of JD later, Bette switched off the computer. Holding on to the desk, she pulled herself up from the chair. She steadied herself then lifted a small stack of papers from the desk and took them through to the bedroom. She flopped onto the bed and held the papers to her chest, grinning. She lay there for a moment, debating what to do with the papers. Should she shred them before this went any further? Should she shred them and forget this had ever happened? She sat up and spread the papers out across the bed in front of her.

The thirty or so pages were a recipe book of murderous intent. Amongst the information on deadly poisons were little scribbled notes in the margins suggesting uses and administering techniques. Asterisks were next to particularly gruesome toxins and fluorescent markers underlined especially fast acting ones.

Bette stared down at the papers. She knew Drucilla wouldn't stop until she had ruined Bette, but did Bette have what it took for this?

She got up and went back through to the dressing room. She swung open the door of the storage cupboard. There was something in there she needed.

CHAPTER 16

Bette was enjoying the calm of purpose in which she had found herself after deciding to remove Drucilla. Everything made much more sense: it was all about how much you wanted something; it was all about how determined you were in the pursuit of your career goals; it was all about doing whatever it took. And whatever it took had presented itself when Drucilla phoned a few days earlier demanding a dressing room for the night of Opus Gay, claiming she would need it for her no doubt numerous birthday gifts. It was here the plan had formed; Drucilla had presented a deliciously poetic opportunity for Bette to be rid of her troubles.

Opus Gay was in full flow. Bette introduced the night's act and kicked off her heels as soon as she left the stage. With both shoes in one hand, she pressed the stopwatch facility on her diamante Swatch and shot off in the direction of her dressing room, tearing through backstage corridors at a pace she knew no one would have thought odd for someone doing a costume change.

She pressed stop as she got to her dressing room door. It had taken her 32 seconds. She opened the door. Mandy was waiting. Draped over the back of a chair to Mandy's left was a padded leather, body harness, its numerous buckles and straps looking more like an outfit you would wear to one of London's more 'exotic' clubs.

She turned her back to Mandy, who undid the dress zip. The dress slipped to her feet. She stepped out of it. In one movement Mandy swiped it from the floor, strung it on a hangar and hooked it onto the rails behind him. As his hand swung back from hanging the dress he grabbed the harness from the chair. Bette turned to face him. Mandy pulled the straps apart. Bette stepped into its mass. She turned around and braced herself against the grey metal wardrobe. Mandy pulled the harness's top straps up over her shoulders.

"Damn!" said Bette. "I don't have the headset mike."

Mandy stopped. "Crap, we need to attach the battery pack to the harness. Where is it?"

"I've left it sitting on the table offstage where the bottled water is. I was doing sound checks earlier. We need it. When I take the act off they don't want me using the hand mike."

Mandy looked at his watch. "We've got time. I'll go get it. See if you can get some of the straps on the harness tightened meantime and then I'll strap you in properly."

As soon as the door clicked shut behind Mandy, Bette could feel her heart thumping as if it was trying to escape her chest. She clicked the timer on her watch again. If it had taken 32 seconds to get here using the shortcut of the backstairs – which Mandy not being as familiar with backstage won't use – and the radio mike being hidden down behind the table, and then the return trip, Bette calculated she had just over 4 minutes before Mandy got back. She let the harness drop from her shoulders and pulled a brand new holdall out from under the dress rail. Like so many in her profession, Bette arrived at a gig with the kind of luggage and makeup cases the likes of which were last seen being carried into staterooms on the Titanic. Amongst all this, another bag's presence or absence would never be noticed.

She unzipped the holdall and slipped on a pair of rubber gloves before lifting out a large, gift-wrapped box - that cupboard full of unwanted tat at home had finally come in handy. Sitting the gift to one side, she folded up the bag and crammed it into the side pocket of another holdall.

After checking the coast was clear, and with every nerve-ending in her body raw with adrenaline, she clutched the gift and headed off in the direction of Drucilla's dressing room.

Excitement rippled through her as, in nothing more than tights, bra and knickers, she tore along the corridor and up two flights of stairs to the second floor dressing rooms. With everyone out on stage, this was the only point of the evening when the area was quiet.

She stopped and listened at Drucilla's door before opening it. Coast seemed clear. She went in.

Like the cover of an Argos Christmas catalogue, the room was littered with gaudily wrapped tat. Bette was surprised how many gifts there were, almost appalled, but she consoled herself with the reassurance this made it easier for hers to go unnoticed.

She sat her gift next to an unimaginatively wrapped dildo and removed several gift tags from neighbouring gifts. This would add to the later confusion of who gave what.

The sight of Drucilla's makeup table creaking under the weight of her industrial-accident-strength slap made Bette shiver. A quick glance at her watch told her she had less than two minutes to get back to her dressing room. Pulling off and balling her rubber gloves, she checked once again to see if the coast was clear. She ran off down the corridor.

She skidded to a halt at the top of the stairs. Someone was coming. She stuffed the balled-up gloves into her knickers and ducked into the nearest dressing room.

"Nah, we've gotta do regular checks backstage now," Bette could hear someone saying as they passed her door. "Some tranny got stuff nicked from her dressing room a few weeks back. Means I get a break from the queers to call you... So what ya wearin'?"

Bette pulled the door open a crack and watched the security guard stroll along the corridor. His attention was firmly on his dirty phone call. Bette checked her watch; if Mandy got back to the dressing room before her the game would be up. With the security guard's back to her only until he reached the end of the corridor, Bette knew she only had seconds to escape. She slipped out the room and ran without looking back. Thankful of her stockinged feet, she tore down the stairs three at a time.

Once her dressing room door was closed behind her she checked her watch again. By her estimations she had less than fourteen seconds. She stepped into the leather harness, pulling its shoulder straps up and into place. Her body writhed and twisted amongst the numerous straps and buckles that now encased her body from crotch to shoulder. When working as a magician's assistant, harness equipment and elaborate costume changes had to be done at breakneck speed; this was all second nature. A fact she had kept to herself. By the time the door opened she looked as if she'd spent the entire time wrestling with the harness's straps.

"Found it," said Mandy, waving the headset mike and battery pack. "It had fallen down behind the table."

"I've managed to get this thing adjusted, but it was a nightmare." Bette turned to face Mandy just as he placed the mike down on the table, and just as she noticed her crotch: the straps around her groin were accentuating the rolled-up gloves and gift tags tucked in her knickers, creating a gargantuan man bulge. She quickly turned round. "Start with the back." She dug the gloves out as Mandy began tightening the straps.

Mandy tugged and yanked at the harness, further restricting Bette's movement with every tightened strap. Once done, he tapped her on the back. Bette turned to face him, throwing the balled-up gloves over his shoulder as he dipped to the straps at her groin. She had to stifle a 'bullseye' as it dropped perfectly into the wastebin on the other side of the room. After more strapping, tightening and readjusting of crotch support, Bette squatted a few times to stretch everything into positions of bearable discomfort.

She put on the headset mike and attached the battery pack to the harness as Mandy took an outfit from the rails. Climbing into the dress proved difficult, but once it was all in place its icicles of pale blue, sequined strips hung from her in breathtaking perfection.

She did a quick spin.

"Fab," said Mandy, stepping back to admire their work. "You can't see the harness at all. Even with the side splits."

Bette took a moment for a quick touch-up and hair tidy, aware of the fact when she reapplied her lipstick she was looking into the eyes of a murderer.

They got to the stage wings just in time. Four drag queens were spinning out above the heads of the crowd, costume changing mid-air to the sound of Divine's 'Make me a Man', before gently floating down to centre stage in full French/Canadian lumberjack outfits.

Bette took her cue and launched herself forward. "Come on, Tumble Dryer, I wanna hear a high-flyin' scream of applause for the amazing talents of Cirque Du So Gay!"

As the crowd roared and stamped their feet, the four lumberjacks surrounded Bette in a formation they had spent a day and a half rehearsing. She felt the click of her harness being attached as the heavily made-up lumberjacks lifted her onto their shoulders. The theme to *An Officer and a Gentleman* filled the club and slowly, as the music built, they began to float up into the air and away from the audience.

The crowd loved it. They screamed their appreciation and stamped their applause. Tiles on the roof must have shaken loose with the noise thundering from the dancefloor. Bette looked down at the sea of bug-eyed, E'd up, sweaty faced, adoring clubbers and knew tonight was a success.

Understanding now why they wanted her to use a headset mike, she embedded her nails into the shoulders of two lumberjacks as she worked the crowd, camping it up about whose hands were where. Then she saw Mad Mickey, his huge mass easily recognisable from above. Their eyes met. He pointed at her as he mimed making a phone call. His face showed no expression.

With a terrifying judder they swung up past the proscenium. Moments later, the stage lights darkened and dance music flooded the club once again. Out of sight of the audience they came to ground in the stage wings. Bette struggled to catch her breath as the lumberjacks extricated themselves from various harnesses and pulleys like Village People marionettes. She felt someone unhook her and pat her on the back.

The noise of backstage began to spin around her as the bitter taste of adrenaline overpowered her taste buds. Her heart was now hammering more beats per minute than the music. She felt unsteady. Her vision blurred; everything stretched into the distance as if looking through the wrong end of binoculars. A vicious spasm in her stomach announced the imminent arrival of its contents. She threw herself at the nearest fire bucket with such force she almost buried her head ostrich-like into the sand. Gripping its sides, her stomach somersaulted and wretched.

"Get a grip of yourself!" she shouted into the bucket.

"Do not *worree*," someone said from beside the bucket. "*Eet* can do *zis* to some people. You are on *zee* ground now."

As Bette turned her head to see the lumberjack she realised he was holding her hair back, away from the sand.

Once her stomach had emptied itself of everything but its lining, Bette thanked the lumberjack and took receipt of her hair. She suspected it wasn't the onstage acrobatics her stomach was rebelling against, but she wasn't prepared to let her conscience and constitution battle it out here.

"Come wis me and let's get you out of ze *arness*."

Bette nodded passively and followed.

"Tonight was amazing," said Mandy. "Everyone was blow away by the show."

"The girl's not wrong," said Anaesthesia, beaming so enthusiastically she could have got a job at Disneyland - not Paris; the excessive warmth and cheer in her smile would have had her sacked on the spot. "Apparently it's the busiest the place has been for years. You're really putting the Dryer back on the map, girl. *Cirque Du So Gay* was a mega idea. I hadn't a clue how you were going to follow The Arse Bandits, but you did."

Bette poured Anaesthesia and Mandy a vodka and smiled wanly from the other side of the bar. The crowds had left and the club was echoing with the sound of rigging being dismantled from above the stage, but she could see little consolation in knowing the place had been creaking under her success.

"Yeah, it was great, but I've lost a fortune."

"What…?" said Mandy.

"How?" said Anaesthesia.

"There are two things every London household got this year: a council tax bill and an invite to Drucilla's birthday.

She'd done a bigger print run than the last Harry Potter novel. We were turning paying customers away because the place was filled with *her* freeloaders."

"I don't get it," said Mandy. "What are you saying?"

Bette resented having to spell it out. "Her 'guests' were going upstairs and then security, who I think got a backhander from Drucilla, were letting them all down to the main club. I got screwed good. Most of what would have been my paying customers marched through the doors on a freebie."

Walking through the hatch to Anaesthesia and Mandy's side of the bar, Bette noticed a bottle of Drambuie tucked down next to the last fridge. *That might do it*, she thought, *nothing else has been able to get rid of the taste of vomit*. She pulled the Drambuie out and poured herself a glass.

"Careful," said Tim, one of the barmen, who was counting his tips. "That's Drucilla's. That's all she drinks and she doesn't like anyone touching it. I'd piss in it, but I think it'd improve the taste."

Bette smiled and winked at Tim before knocking it back in one. Tim was right; it tasted worse than the vomit, but Bette felt a point had to be made: Drucilla had sipped her last Drambuie.

CHAPTER 17

Spencer rolled over and hit the radio button on his alarm clock. An eager presenter, who Spencer thought altogether too pleased with himself, was handing over to traffic: it was eight thirty, Monday morning, apparently, and the Hangar Lane gyratory was in gridlock.

Flopping back onto the bed, he realised his plan of necking several temazepam and vallium with a bottle and a half of JD hadn't worked. His cunning attempt to destroy enough of his short-term memory so he had no recollection of what he had done had been a disaster: he remembered everything.

He had replayed it over and over again and had come to the conclusion that despite there being no love lost between him and Drucilla, their dislike for each other didn't warrant murder. An innocent, albeit vile, drag queen was going to die because of what he had done.

Maybe he could buy a real gift and say there had been a mix-up; tell Drucilla the one she had was really for someone else. This, he realised, would have been as believable as someone going to an ambulance chaser and saying it wasn't about the money. Or what about breaking in to her home and stealing it back. That way he could reduce his charge sheet to attempted murder and burglary. He put a pillow over his face and screamed.

When eventually hoarse he threw the pillow away. It landed on the chair at the foot of the bed. Draped over the back of the chair was Saturday night's blue dress. He got out of bed, head still spinning from the temazepam and vallium, and took it through to Bette's room along with the shoes he found on the floor.

Unsteady on his feet, he sat the shoes on their shelf and put the blue dress on a hanger. He buried it amongst the others so he couldn't see it. He felt a sobering chill run down his spine as he looked at the rows of costumes. They hung before him like the sloughed skins of a monster he knew to be lurking nearby.

Aware of standing naked before his full-length mirror, he felt the need for clothing; he was in no mood to see any more of himself than was absolutely necessary right now. He took a sarong from a drawer and wrapped it round his waist, giving the mirror one less eye with which to follow him around the room.

The balled-up rubber gloves he had rescued from the wastebin were sitting on the dressing table. He sat down and unwound them, unravelling the stolen gifts tags from inside. One by one he took the tags and shredded them into tiny, confetti-sized pieces and threw them next to the broken, swimming pool thermometer in the bin at his feet. When he came to the last two he stopped, and froze. He read the cards several times, disbelief ricocheting around his senses.

"Oh shit...!"

CHAPTER 18

The satisfying glare from the newly waxed parquet floor made Gary smile as he flicked the plasma screen's remote. The room filled with the sound of *Emmerdale's* theme tune. Calculating he had a half hour before Corrie, he took a small tub of ice cream from the freezer and left it on the counter to temper before heading for the bathroom.

He ran a bath and poured some lavender and tea tree oil in with the bubble bath before turning his attention to the engraved glass and chrome of the bathroom's new décor. He hadn't bonded straight away with the room's design. For a while he felt it had a youth and vitality that was deeply unfair; he had spent almost as much on his hair plugs as he had on the bathroom, and only one of them looked the better for it.

He looked at his reflection in the mirror. The man who stared back was old, ancient, decrepit. At least that's how he felt. He bent his head forward. With his chin touching his chest and his eyes straining towards the mirror, he examined his follicular field of dreams. Cropping the sides had done little to draw attention from the small clumps of hair that dotted the barren landscape of his scalp. Sprouting pitifully in a drought-stricken paddy field formation, his hair plugs advertised rather than disguised his baldness. Much to his relief, the room filled with steam and his reflection began to fade.

He slipped out of his clothes and added some more lavender oil to the water. He stepped in and slid down so his chin touched the scented bubbles. His muscles began to relax. It was bliss.

The phone rang from the lounge, jarring and persistent. *Fuck that*, he thought.

"Stella," came a shrill voice from the answer machine,

"pick up the phone if you're there. Stella, you'd better not be screening…Stella…Stella, you there…? Stella…Call me when you get this. I've heard on the grape vine that the black bitch is in financial shit. Already. Our birthday thing worked. At this rate the cow should be out of the Dryer in a couple of months."

A smile tugged the corners of Gary's lips as the answer machine clicked off. He hated the black bitch; she was so full of herself. He wished he could have seen her face as its flesh started to peel after her caustic soda facial. He and Drucilla had almost wet themselves laughing after they'd done it. He had to admit, Drucilla's idea for a joint birthday party had been brilliant; his birthday wasn't for another four weeks. Telling Norman Daniels they had the same birthday had been an inspired deal clincher. The gifts, on the other hand, were a bonus. Even though he suspected Drucilla had gone through them first and pulled some of the choice ones for herself, claiming there were missing gift tags.

He closed his eyes and let himself drift.

The Corrie theme tune woke him some time later. He got out the bath and did a perfunctory towelling of his hair, wrapped himself in a bathrobe and went to the kitchen. Dripping on the kitchen floor, he decided on a cup of camomile tea.

The new smoothie maker he got for his birthday was plugged in where the kettle usually sat. Promising himself he was going to make good use of it he decided that, meantime, it was best to keep it in the cupboard. He dried his hands on his bathrobe and went to unplug it. His mobile rang. He ran through to the lounge and grabbed the phone from where he had left it on the sofa. He checked the name on the screen whilst unconsciously running his fingers through damp hair plugs. It was Drucilla again. He switched off the phone.

Returning to the kitchen to make his tea, he gripped the plug of the smoothie maker and pulled.

He let out a scream as the plug cover came away in his wet hand. He had narrowly missed touching exposed wires. Head and heart pounding, he sat the plug cover on the worktop. He could have killed himself.

could have killed himself.

He went to the fridge for some juice instead. What cheap crap had someone bought him? It was going in the bin.

He took his glass of juice through to the lounge as he heard it kicking off in the Rovers. He sat the juice on a coaster on one of the side tables next to the sofa and picked up a small plastic bag from beside him. Inside the bag was a glass bottle, about the size of a bottle of poppers, and a leaflet of instructions. He took out the leaflet and scanned its promises again. It was called Miracle Glow and it guaranteed to take years off tired, mature skin. The bottle's contents were an infusion of rare Himalayan spices and minerals; the latest skin treatment from Hollywood, it rejuvenated the upper epidermis by means of a natural, non-abrasive exfoliation action whilst clarifying the subcutis with its patented deep pore formulation of stratum corneum lipids. And according to the leaflet Angelina Jolie and Nicole Kidman swore by it.

The adverts came on TV. He went to the kitchen for the tub he had taken out of the freezer earlier. He pulled off its top and tested the contents with a spoon; it was the first ice cream he had made with his new ice cream maker. He took it through to the lounge to sample it. It was strawberry and peach. He dug his spoon in for a generous scoop. The ice cream maker had been one of the gifts whose tag had been missing; he figured Drucilla must have one already. He shovelled the strawberry and peach into his mouth and savoured, swirling it around his taste buds and letting it melt on his tongue.

He was unconvinced by its strawberry and peachy goodness. When he had taken the ice cream maker out of the box it had had a strange smell. He had put it down to being new plastic and had run it through the dishwasher, but something wasn't quite right. He swallowed and took another spoonful. No, it definitely wasn't right. He took a third, smaller spoonful to make sure. He spat it back into the tub.

So much for his crappy birthday presents, he thought. He took the tub through to the kitchen and emptied its contents into the bin.

Corrie was back on. It was all kicking off between Ken and Deirdre now. Seeing Deirdre in close-up, Gary decided now was as good a time as any to test the claims of his new miracle facial treatment. He plugged in the facial steamer that had been sitting under the lamp table and read the instructions on the bottle's leaflet. It was all simple enough: shake the bottle vigorously and pour into the steamer's well, then position face onto steamer and breathe deep for twenty to thirty minutes.

He shook the Miracle Glow and poured it into the well. He read its list of ingredients. Amongst them were Himalayan orchid extract, kernel oil, aloe, barbadensis leaf extract, kaolin, Himalayan Mountain silver and bergamot. It sounded so exotic. He looked at the bubbling liquid in the facial steamer's small well and could tell they weren't lying about the Himalayan Mountain silver. As he brought his face down to seal in the steam and inhale he wondered how much it was to buy this stuff. If the free sample that came with the facial steamer worked he might think about getting some. He inhaled deep. At least this birthday present worked.

CHAPTER 19

The news that Stella had been rushed to hospital came while Bette was putting the finishing touches to her mascara. The brush skidded into her hairline.

"It happened a couple of days ago," Mandy said from the other end of the phone. "Anaesthesia says it was Monday night."

"Do they know how it happened?"

"I'm not sure of how much is true, but the rumour is she asphyxiated during a facial. She'd been inhaling mercury."

Himalayan Mountain silver, Bette almost corrected. "But she survived. She's okay?"

"She's in intensive care. It doesn't look good."

"Stella never looked good." Bette turned back to the mirror and tried to dab out the trench of white mascara that had been drawn across her face.

"That's not funny. She could die."

Bette brandished her mascara brush at the mirror as if the reflection was Mandy. "That bitch would have walked over you if you lay bleeding in the road. She wouldn't give a damn if *you* were the one in hospital. Why does everyone become a better person the moment they get ill or die? Would Osama Bin Laden become an ambassador for peace if he dropped dead of swine flu? Would Mugabe have become a humanitarian visionary if he died of cancer? No. So why are you so bothered about Stella?"

Mandy didn't answer right away. "What are you wearing?"

"What?"

"You heard me."

"Mandy, I swear to God, if you're getting fruity on me."

"You're in Bette's room right now, aren't you?"

Bette put down the mascara. "No," she lied.

There was silence again from the other end of the phone before Mandy eventually said, "I'll see you at six thirty for Fran's book launch, then. And is it okay if I borrow the car tomorrow? I've still got the spare keys."

"Sure." Bette sneered at the phone and hung up.

She picked up the mascara again. The brush slipped from her fingers. Her hands started to shake. She grabbed the sides of the dressing table. Bottles and jars rattled on its surface as if the room were being hit by the first wave of an earthquake.

"Casualties of war," she hissed through gritted teeth.

The table stopped shaking.

After a few deep breaths she released her grip on the table and returned to the makeup job at hand. Sleeping for a day and a half and then being wide awake for two had left her with the body clock of a long haul, trolley dolly and bags under the eyes like cabin luggage. Now feeling retrospective empathy, she would never again point fingers and giggle at the sedimentary layering of an air stewardess's makeup.

She was not happy with the final result. The usual smooth strokes of foundation and gentle brushes of powder that were the oils to the canvas of her face had been applied in stabs and smears; Devine Brown looked back from the mirror.

Bette threw the mascara across the room. Stella was going to be okay, she told herself. She was in good hands now, and would probably come out of all this with better skin. Drucilla, on the other hand, was still breathing. Bette realised she had to finish the job she started, or she might never sleep again. She dismissed her reflection as a work in progress and went to her filing cabinet.

She opened the drawer and flicked to the file marked 'unpaid bills'. She reached in and took out the papers she had printed off a few nights ago and sat them on the desk. Smiling at the celebrity endorsements she had put on the fake instruction leaflet for the Miracle Glow, she checked the time. It was quarter past one. She was going to have to call Anaesthesia and tell her she couldn't make it to the prostate cancer awareness lunch. Of the many charity fundraisers Anaesthesia had conscripted Bette into over the years, she thought this was a rather inappropriate subject to be having lunch over, anyway.

She looked through the papers for something appropriate.

Off all the jobs Bette had done, her time as a magician's assistant was definitely her least favourite - of the ones she could put on a CV, that is. Nine months of being crammed into boxes, sawn apart, stabbed at and shot at had left her feeling like a roadie for So Solid Crew. But here she was, years later, glad to bear the scars of a magician's sword box.

Until working for the Great Spondulli, Bette had always assumed magicians built their own magic props and stitched together their own silk hankies. She had never dreamt that shops existed for them. Discreetly hidden away, and usually run by the kind of people who weren't cool enough to be members of chess clubs or play Dungeons and Dragons, these shops sold everything the budding David Copperfield could ever want. So long as you knew what an Elmsley pass, a Devano deck and a goose-neck levitation were, they had no problem selling you some of the more 'secretive' items: a magic shop was a surprising apothecary for lethal chemicals, and as it was all under-the-counter there was no poison registers to sign.

Using every ounce of her skills as a faux femme fatale, Bette waited patiently in the dim light of the magic store for her eager sales assistant to rummage about in the back shop to find what she wanted. Behind Bette, giving off a dim and insubstantial light, were display cabinets filled with various equipment for chopping off arms, impaling bodies and vanishing rabbits. The only other source of illumination was the three small spotlights shining down onto the counter. In one of the pools of light, the other assistant's hands worked seamlessly, demonstrating to the only other customer the ease with which he could make a cigarette pass straight through a pound coin.

The sales assistant returned with a small, brown paper bag and sat it on the counter away from the nearest spotlight. "You know one of these needs to be kept in the fridge and the other in the freezer?" he said in a hushed voice, talking to his hands as he strained not to stare at Bette's cleavage again.

Bette stroked the back of his forefinger. His entire body shivered with the pent-up, explosive energy of a twenty-something virgin.

"Yes," said Bette, "I'm quite experienced."

He buckled at the knee slightly. Bette handed him the cash and smiled, leaving him to deal with the scout's tent forming in his navy blue slacks.

Once inside the safety of her car she hid the bag containing her purchases in the glove compartment. She had been about to turn the key in the ignition when her phone rang. She let out a squeal and clutched at an imaginary string of pearls.

Her agent's name shone in the small screen. She took a few deep breaths before answering. "Malcolm, hi." Bette fumbled with the red scarf tied around her neck and braced herself for what passed as conversation with Malcolm.

"Glad I caught you. I've got a job for you. It's for a company called Boy Brides. You heard of them?"

"I think so. Did they__"

"They do tranny couture for the wannabe bride and her maids."

"Oh, yes, they__"

"Anyway, they're going national and there's talk of stores opening in Amsterdam and Paris. Thing is, they don't want any pictures of the frumpy trannies that'll be buying the dresses in their catalogue. So they're looking for types like you, not traffic wardens in taffeta. They start shooting next week for the new catalogue and it's turned out one of the models has just had her OP brought forward so they need someone to replace her and they need the answer by tomorrow."

Bette didn't know if she could face another tranny catalogue shoot, but she desperately needed the money. "I'm on my way to a charity lunch, Malcolm. Can I call you later?"

"Sure."

The phone went dead. Pleasantries over.

With her first purchase from the magic shop stored safely in the freezer, Bette unwrapped a bunch of red roses onto the kitchen worktop. Next to the roses were three plastic pots the size of £2 coins, a tub of Q-tips and a packet of dressmaking needles.

She opened one of the plastic pots and stared at the clear gel inside. The first time the Great Spondulli had shown her this stuff in use it had terrified her; she was convinced he could control her mind. He had torn a strip of tin foil and scrunched it into a ball before handing it to Bette, asking her to clench her fist around it. Taking another strip of foil he then held it up to a candle flame, telling Bette the heat would transfer from his piece of foil to hers. She had been about to tell him where to stick his tin foil when she felt the foil in her hand getting warm. Then warmer still, until it was so hot she had to drop it.

Fortunately for Bette, like the hooker with the *News of the World's* number on speed dial, the Great Spondulli did reveal his tricks. Before scrunching the foil into a ball to give to someone, he would discreetly smear the gel onto the inside of the foil. The gel reacted with the aluminium, instantly corroding it from the centre of the ball and generating surprising heat. The heat quickly worked its way through the foil to the person's hand, scaring the bejesus out of them in the process. Bette had never forgotten Spondulli's golden rule, however: the gel could never be handled with even the slightest nick in your skin. A pep talk Bette remembered as she put down the pot and pulled on a pair of Marigold gloves to handle the mercuric cyanide gel.

She spread the red roses evenly along the worktop. Having chosen the roses stem-by-stem for their profusion of vicious barbs, she stripped the stems of some leaves to give better access to the thorns. But just to be sure, she inserted dressmaking needles through the stems to the tips of every other thorn to maximize their efficiency. Once the needles were done, she coated a Q-tip with mercuric cyanide and began to paint the thorns with the gel.

Two tubs of gel did just under three coats. She put the remaining tub into the fridge and, keeping the gloves on, wrapped the flowers in a cone of clear plastic wrapping, around which she further wrapped tissue paper and sticky taped it secure. The final touch was a big red bow.

Once the car was parked, Bette pulled down the vanity mirror.

"Aw shit," she said to her reflection. In her rush to get into the second-hand biker's leathers Jason had bought Spencer for their second anniversary, she had forgotten to take her face off. There was nothing she could do about it now.

She tucked her hair into the back of the leathers, then from beside the flowers on the passenger seat she lifted the helmet and squeezed her head into it. The play-dough face that squashed into the helmet's window had her cheeks and eyelids almost touching. She was quite unrecognisable, but decided the visor down might be a good idea to hide the tell-tale white mascara.

Feeling quite butch and Hollywood-villain, she pulled on leather gloves and lifted the bouquet. The moment was soon ruined by a girly squeal echoing from the helmet as she thumped her head on the door as she got out.

Beginning to question the wisdom of having parked a couple streets away, Bette chafed and sweated more and more with every step towards Drucilla's flat. She lived at number 14, a large garden flat of a canalside development. Wisteria trailed around the door-facing and along the wall towards an ornate glass sculpture of a scaled-down Easter Island head. Bette was rather impressed; she had expected something much more basic. With sweat running into the crack of her butt, she rang the bell.

Almost immediately the door opened.

Drucilla stood in full drag, red leather skirt and jacket with a matching scarlet pillbox hat perched jauntily on her platinum wig. She was holding a mobile phone against her ear. Bette wondered if she dressed like this all the time.

"On Friday, sweetie, and I'll..." Drucilla stopped and eyed Bette with an oleaginous leer. "Talking of deliveries, a leather-clad man has just arrived on my doorstep. Let's hope he's a late birthday present. Don't go away." She sat the phone down next to a red shoulder bag on a small table near the door and pointed to the flowers. "They for me?"

Bette tried to butch-up the voice, but the husky echo from within the helmet was less Darth and more Dorothy Vader. "You Drucilla?"

"The one and only."

"Then these are for you." Protected by her biker's gloves, Bette offered the flowers.

Drucilla stared at them for a moment. "Is there a card?"

"Um… Don't think so…umm…anonymous admirer." Bette almost gagged.

Drucilla turned to the table and reached behind the shoulder bag for a pair of matching leather gloves. She pulled on the gloves, slung the bag over her shoulder and lifted the phone. "You still there, sweetie? Good." She gestured for the flowers to be handed to her and flicked her wrist to dismiss Bette.

Seeing her holding the flowers in a gloved hand made Bette want to tear them from her and beat her across the head with them.

"Is there something else?" Drucilla said.

Bette shook her head and turned to leave.

"Sorry about that, sweetie," Drucilla continued into the phone. "I'm just on my way out. I'm done up to show my face at Fran's book launch for an hour…" *Shit, the book launch,* thought Bette, *I'm supposed to be taking Mandy to that.* "…but I'm popping in to the hospital to see Stella first. I'm taking her in some flowers…"

Bette felt salty drips scoring down her face as she headed back to the car. They could just as easily have been tears of frustration; she knew she had to head the flowers off, somehow.

CHAPTER 20

Samuel hated the smell of hospital disinfectant; it was as if the building was trying to hide the fact it stank of old people piss. And he hated old people.

He spotted a tear in his tracksuit.

"Fuck!" It was his favourite tracksuit, a genuine Tommy Hilfiger copy.

A passing nurse gave a disapproving glance.

"You got a fucking problem?"

The nurse ignored him and picked up pace.

His mobile rang while he was checking his tracksuit for any other damage. He pulled the phone from his pocket.

"What?" It was Chantelle. She wanted to know where he was. "I'm in the fucking hospital. Okay? It's a fucking maze. What ward did you say you were in?"

Chantelle told him the building and the ward again and he compared the information to the floor listing beside the lift. He was on the wrong floor of the wrong building.

"I'm on my way." He flipped the phone closed.

Chantelle had been in hospital for two days now, and Samuel felt she was getting too pushy by far. He couldn't help notice that every time you got a bird up the duff she suddenly thought she owned you. "Complications," the doctor had said. Samuel had to agree, women were just one long list of fucking complications.

The phone rang again, this time it was Caroline. The way his day was going she was probably calling to tell him she's got one in the oven, too. Although, he wouldn't have minded that so much; her old man was loaded, and Caroline getting up the duff would really piss him off. He had called Samuel 'reprehensible, white trash', and even though he didn't know what reprehensible meant, he was fairly sure it wasn't Latin for 'welcome to the fucking family'. If she was up the duff he could definitely get them on Trisha.

He pressed cancel on the phone and pushed the lift button.

When the lift came he didn't get in. He slipped to the side and hid in the stairwell, flipping open his phone again as he did.

"I understand, doctor," said Drucilla, wiping a tear from her eye. "And thank you for everything you've done." She dropped a bunch of flowers into a waste bin before saying goodbye and getting into the lift.

"You'll never guess who I've just seen at the hospital," Samuel said into the phone as the lift doors closed. "...Yeah. In the full drag shit. It's got no fucking shame." He was thrown against the wall as a leather-clad biker thumped his shoulder in his rush to get up the stairs. The biker wheezed an apology through a dripping visor and ran along the corridor. It was the strangest run Samuel had ever seen, it looked like he was wearing a plaster cast under his leathers and was bursting for a shit. "Yeah, I'm tellin' you," he turned his attention back to the phone, "it's just left." He went over to the waste bin and pulled one of the roses out by its bud; if he took the whole bunch to Chantelle she'd know they were nicked, and he wasn't up for the earache. "Okay, mate, call you laters."

Another lift arrived. Samuel got in and pressed the ground floor button repeatedly. He saw the weird biker reappear and grab the flowers from the waste bin. As the doors began to close he saw him stuffing them into an empty holdall.

What the fuck's he on? Samuel wondered.

After getting lost a second time, he eventually found the right building and ward, but one of the four pints he'd downed in the pub needed setting free before he saw Chantelle.

The graffiti-free walls of the toilet cubicle had him mentally kicking himself as he closed and locked the door; he had no marker pen on him, and these walls were just crying out for some comment on the amount of Paki doctors the place had.

He needed another pick-me-up before facing Chantelle; she

would start yapping the second she saw him. Sitting the rose down on the cubicle's window ledge he took a small plastic bag of white powder from his wallet. He took out a bunch of keys and dipped one into the bag, scooping out some of its contents. He snorted from the key. He dipped the key in again and took another, smaller amount, before returning the bag to his wallet.

He had picked up the rose and unlocked the door when his bladder reminded him why he had come into the cubicle in the first place. Turning back to the toilet, he put the rose between his teeth and pulled himself free of his underwear.

He had been mid-slash, running through a quick rehearsal of the bullshit he was about to give Chantelle, when someone pushed the cubicle door. It hit him in the back, causing him to miss the toilet, piss on his shoe and bite into the rose. He spun on the door, slamming it shut, and bit deeper into the rose stem, snapping it in two places. Thorns impaled his tongue and lips. It felt like nails being driven through the roof of his mouth.

He spat the broken rose into the toilet. "Fuck off, faggot!"

The person on the other side of the door made what sounded like a quick exit. *Just as well for him*, Samuel thought, glaring at the mashed rose floating in the toilet.

Drops of blood rained into the bowl from his mouth as he stuffed himself back into his underwear. He sucked in blood, swallowing so as not to get any on his tracksuit, and grabbed a stream of toilet roll from the dispenser. Still sucking in blood, he bent down and dabbed piss from his Reebok.

His mouth was bleeding heavily. A drop of blood went onto his shoe. He pulled another stream of toilet paper and applied pressure to his mouth. Once the blood-soaked tissue was saturated he threw it into the toilet. It landed on top of the broken rose. He took another stream of tissue and held it to his mouth again.

Putting the feeling of light-headedness down to a rush from the coke he had just taken, he pulled yet more tissue from the dispenser. Careful not to get any blood on his tracksuit, he lifted his foot onto the toilet seat to clean the blood from his Reebok. With one hand at his mouth and the other at his foot, a sudden spasm in his stomach almost made him loose his balance. He steadied himself with a hand against the cubicle wall.

"What the fu__" He started to feel tight around the chest, like how he imagined asthma would feel. He tried to suck in air. He couldn't get enough into his lungs. He could feel his pulse in his tongue. He started to wheeze. Stars began dancing in his vision. The cubicle suddenly felt very small.

With the second, more violent spasm, he did lose his footing on the wet floor. He was thrown forward against the cistern, smacking his head with unsurvivable ferocity against a metal panel engraved 'push'.

Samuel's face slid down to its resting place on the wet seat as the rose vanished in a vortex of pink disinfectant.

CHAPTER 21

Spencer could feel his eyes closing as he wiped the last of Bette from his face. He slouched over the table and let his head rest on his arms; he felt as if he hadn't slept in weeks.

The doorbell rang, sending him bolt upright.

"Mandy! Fran's book launch! Shit!"

He leapt over the damp motorbike leathers and was halfway to the front door before the slapping sensation at his groin and the breeze around his nipples told him he was naked. He ran back to the bedroom and pulled on a pair of joggers.

The doorbell rang again. And again. He got to the door and pulled it open just as the bell rang for a fourth time.

"I'm sorry, Mandy, I..."

"He left ages ago," said Lucy, "and he was pissed off." She pushed past. "Have you seen Gabbana? I can't find him."

"I haven't seen him since yesterday afternoon." Spencer followed Lucy into the lounge. "When did you last see him?"

"This afternoon. I don't know how he could have got out."

"Have you looked out front?"

"Yeah, but it's not like him to leave the building. The only time he ever got out there he just sat and wailed."

"He was in here earlier, but..." Spencer looked behind him to check if he had left the kitchen window open and spotted the Marigolds and the saucer of mercuric cyanide-coated Q-tips still sitting beside the toaster. He threw a tea towel over them. It was then he spotted Gabbana lying on the kitchen floor, very still, with a Q-tip sticking out the side of his mouth.

Spencer darted to Lucy's side. "We should go out and look for him. You know, now, before he gets too far."

"He's been gone hours. I'd rather be here if he comes___."

"But you're not here, are you? I mean there. I mean your place. I mean shouldn't we wait downstairs?"

"Calm down. He's a cat, not a virgin on the Pitcan Isles."

"How can you be so calm?" Spencer could hear hysteria in his voice. He wanted to slap himself. "You love those cats."

"I know, but I'm thinking everything comes in three's."

"What?"

"Last night my sister set me up with a man that was as pleasant on the eye as a cracked contact lens, this morning I got my court date for the cat-crap-caper and this afternoon Gabbana, like every other shit of a man in my life, walked out on me." Lucy waved her hand dismissively. "You can't fight fate, hon. You can fight dehydration, though. Any chance of a cuppa?"

"Sure, of course. That's a good idea. Something sweet. We don't want you getting hysterical. That'd be a bad. A drink." He walked towards the kitchen then straight away turned back. "No, Lucy, I'd feel better if we went and had a look for him."

"Just get me a bloody coffee."

Spencer leapt to the kitchen. "Okay, you stay where you are. Relax. Take it easy. Don't think about Gabbana."

Gabbana lay rigid on the kitchen floor, his back legs splayed and his crotch pointing to the ceiling. Spencer grabbed a bottle of JD and with his bare foot slid the cat over towards the ironing board cupboard. Gabbana was cold.

"Why don't you look out the window and see if he's there?" said Spencer, taking two glasses from the shelf.

Lucy rolled her eyes and went over to the window. Spencer seized the moment to open the cupboard and kick the cat in. Gabbana slid across the floor with remarkable speed and ease, hitting the bottom of the ironing board and sending it clattering towards Spencer. The ironing board's legs came at him. He tried to slam the door. It wouldn't shut. He tried again, slamming it harder. It still wouldn't shut. He had been about to give the door one last hinge-shattering thump when he noticed Gabbana's tail sticking out, now grotesquely bent and fractured.

"You okay?" said Lucy, moving away from the window.

"Yes. Fine. Stay where you are, I'll bring the drinks." He kicked the tail into the cupboard and sloshed Jack Daniels into the two glasses before snatching them from the worktop, leaving most of their contents behind. He ran to Lucy and thrust a drink into her hand. "Cheers."

Lucy stared quizzically at her glass for a moment. "You been sprinkling coke on your moccachinos again? It didn't work for Kate Moss and it ain't gonna work for you. It's not called a mad mocca for nothing, hon." She downed her drink and handed him the empty glass. "I'm going to make up some flyers with his picture. If he's not back by the morning will you help me to hand them out and stick them up?"

Spencer followed suit and knocked his drink back. "Great idea. Of course I'll help. We'll do all over. Everywhere. But I'm sure he'll be back. Probably got himself a girlfriend."

"He's been done."

Spencer led the way to his front door. "Well, he's probably got himself a nice little eunuch soulmate, then." He opened the door. "Speak later." He closed the door on Lucy's bemused expression and ran to the kitchen.

He opened the cupboard door to find Gabbana's head bent up the side of the mop bucket and his tail zigzagging at macabre angles. He slid him out with the mop. He had no idea how he was going to get rid of him. Lucy had once told him the cats were chipped; he wasn't entirely sure what that was, but he was fairly certain it meant he couldn't just chuck Gabbana in a skip. If she got him back she might want an autopsy, and he was fairly sure cyanide wasn't on the list of ingredients in Whiskas.

Spencer pulled on his Marigolds and hid Gabbana away from view in a leather holdall. After a while he came to the conclusion there was only one place where a man carrying a large holdall in the middle of the night wouldn't arouse suspicion.

CHAPTER 22

Spencer parked the car and turned off the engine. He tied his hair back and tucked it behind the collar of his denim jacket and waited for the coast to clear.

Trying not to think about the holdall sitting on the passenger seat, he watched with dry, painful eyes as two men skulked down a dirt track path to the Heath. After a few minutes Spencer felt himself nod off. He slapped his face and grabbed the bag; he couldn't trust himself to wait any longer.

Relieved it hadn't rained in weeks, the trek down the rocky path was a lot easier than the last time he had come here. On that occasion he had slipped at the top of the hill and careered to the bottom over rocks and mud, arriving on the heath with a sore ass when all he had been looking for was a blowjob. At the bottom of the hill he stopped. The lights from the road were far behind him now and he needed to acclimatise to the near total darkness of a cloudless night. He waited, paranoid spectres dancing in the peripheral vision of his tired eyes, until he had enough night-vision not to walk into a pond or tree.

Two men walked past, more interested in each other to notice Spencer.

"Got any interesting toys in there?" asked a man who had appeared from nowhere like the shopkeeper from Mr Ben.

"I'm only into small cocks," said Spencer, knowing it was a line guaranteed to confuse most gay men and a remit to which no man would admit to filling.

It worked. The man shrugged and vanished back into the undergrowth to continue his search for Mr Right-now.

Moving on carefully, Spencer headed into the bushes near one of the larger ponds. He could hear snapping of twigs, squeals and grunts coming from the other side of the water.

He glanced over his shoulder into the darkness and sat the bag down next to the fence that ran round the pond. The ground was dry and hard, fine for not ruining your trainers, but no good for digging a cat grave with a window box trowel.

He unzipped the bag and pulled on his Marigolds. The slapping and wailing from the other side of the pond was beginning to pick up pace. He knelt down and reached into the bag for the trowel, trying not to touch Gabbana. His hand came across the little, fluffy mouse toy he'd brought to bury with him. He felt himself welling up. He had to hold it together.

He sat the mouse on the ground and reached in for the trowel, grabbing Gabbana's tail by mistake. It was at that point, he would later convince himself, that his heart stopped momentarily.

Someone lunged towards him, a glint of metal in their hand aiming at Spencer's throat. His light-starved eyes had up until now only registered the man as part of a tree, but this tree was now coming at him with a knife. It all happened so fast. With Gabbana's tail still in his grip, Spencer swung the cat at his attacker. Gabbana smacked the side of the man's head with a thud and a crack, sending the assailant backwards.

There was a better view of the weapon the man was wielding as he landed in a pool of moonlight. *Oooh, nice knob,* thought Spencer, as the man floundered to cram it back behind the safety of his trousers, his stiffy's metal piercing glinting in the light of the half moon as he kicked the ground to get away. He let out a scream as his tool stuck in his zipper, then scrambled to his feet and ran off through the trees.

Spencer's legs shook and buckled beneath him. He dropped Gabbana and staggered over to a tree for support, prodding it first to make sure it was indeed a tree. Was it time for another eye test, he wondered? Reading glasses, at least.

He slid down the tree, gasping for breath. *What's the matter with me*, he asked himself? *I'm on Hampstead Heath in a pair of Marigolds, with a dead cat at my side and aggravated assault added to my rapidly-increasing list of crimes. I need help.* He looked at

Gabbana's broken silhouette, limbs now pointing in different directions, and realised he also needed a bigger shovel.

Pulling himself from the tree, he decided on a plan 'B'. He lifted Gabbana back into the bag and started looking for rocks: he could sink him in the pond.

He only had six rocks in the bag when he heard the sound of pitchfork wielding villagers charging through the undergrowth towards him.

"He was over here," one of them shouted. "I'm telling you, he hit me with a club, or something."

"Aww gimme a friggin' break," Spencer whispered. He grabbed the bag, zipped it up and swung it over his shoulder. He stopped himself just in time from throwing it into the pond, wondering why he would be so stupid as to think his luck would choose this moment to turn from shit to favour.

Tearing through the woods in what he prayed was the right direction for the car, twigs gored and scratched at his scalp, pulling his hair from the protection of his jacket. He could feel the rocks thump and squelch against Gabbana in the bag.

A branch hit him in the mouth as he picked up pace. It knocked him from his feet. He hit the ground back of the head first and the bag flew from his hands. In his dazed state he lay there for a moment before hearing a voice cry, "Over this way."

Spencer scrambled to his feet and searched for the bag. He couldn't find it. His first reaction was to run, leave the bag, get as far away as he could from the vigilante hoard that was chasing through the bushes after him, then he spotted it nestled in a bush. He reached in to grab it. Thorns ripped their way through his Marigolds into flesh. He stifled a scream.

With the bag slung back over his shoulder and rocks squelching against the cat, he continued to run through the undergrowth towards where he hoped he had parked the car. Wasting no time, he pulled the keys from his pocket and began flicking the lock sensor in desperation. The doors bleeped moments before he crashed through the bushes.

"I heard someone run up here," came a voice from the

undergrowth behind him.

Spencer wrenched open the door and threw the bag onto the floor in front of the passenger seat. He stabbed the key at the ignition before he had even closed the door. It missed. He pulled the door closed and tried again. He missed again. His bladder almost emptied with relief as the engine chugged to life on the fourth attempt. The car skidded away from the pavement.

He drove home without once glancing at the bag; he had no desire to know the answer to the question: what would a dead cat, you'd used as a club, look like if you put it into a bag of rocks and it shook vigorously?

He pulled into his street just as the petrol gauge flashed empty. He knew how it felt. He spotted a parking space right in front of his building and almost burst into tears: it was his first lucky break all day.

Fortune quickly delivered a swift kick to the balls when he spotted Lucy through the glass of the building's front door. He shot a glance at the bag. He was going to have to leave it in the car and come down for it once she was gone; he couldn't face her with the pummelled remains of her beloved pet draped over his shoulder and act casual.

He pulled on the handbrake and turned off the engine before lifting the bag and shoving it behind the passenger's seat. *Just keep calm,* he told himself. *There's no reason for her to suspect anything.* Lucy was tying her dressing gown as she opened the front door.

"What in the name of Christ happened to you?" she said, just as Spencer closed the car door and spotted the Marigolds he was still wearing.

He pulled off the gloves, catching his reflection in the driver's window as he did. Sticking from his hair was a topiary of twigs and leaves, a trickle of dried blood ran down the side of his face and the collar of his shirt was torn.

"I've…" he pulled the largest twig from his hair, "…been out. Hampstead Heath, actually." He knew simplicity was the best bet if his brain had any chance of formulating a lie.

Lucy's lip curled. "Had a good night, then?"

Spencer shrugged and yanked another twig from his hair. "I've had better."

"There's still no sign of Gabbana."

He put his arm around her and moved them upstairs. "I'm sure he's not far."

Spencer woke on the sofa in the same position in which he had sat down several hours before. Twigs were still sticking from his hair like a primary school nativity player who had landed the consolation role of 'second tree on the left'. He took himself for a much needed shower.

He was dressed and drying his hair when he remembered the cat. Dreading what lay squashed in the holdall, he dressed and went outside. Mrs Chapori was sweeping the front steps.

"Morning, Mrs C," he said.

"Morning," said Mrs Chapori, in the usual clipped tone she reserved for her dealings with Spencer.

Spencer looked up and down the street for the car. He was sure he had parked it across from the building. His stomach tightened. It wasn't there. He replayed last night in his mind, thinking maybe he hadn't parked it where he thought.

"You look for car?" said Mrs Chapori.

Spencer nodded, incapable of speaking.

"Your friend with strange hair take it. He just left."

"Mandy!" Spencer yelped.

CHAPTER 23

Feeling the need for a paper bag to breathe into, Spencer felt his world closing in around him. Then he remembered the petrol gauge: last night it was on empty.

Leaving Mrs Chapori looking up at him whilst simultaneously trying to look down her nose at him, he took off at a pelt for the garage at the end of the road.

Darting across oncoming traffic, he spotted his car sitting in the garage's forecourt. Mandy was walking towards it with a family sized bag of crisps.

"Mandy," Spencer screamed. "Mandy. MANDY."

Mandy got into the car as Spencer dodged a Citroen Dolly.

"MANDY." Spencer jumped the knee-high wall at the garage's forecourt.

Mandy started the car.

"Mandy." Spencer slammed his hand down on the car's bonnet and caught his breath.

The crisps went everywhere.

Mandy buzzed the window down. "Hi." He managed to convey frosty in a single syllable.

Spencer gulped in air and tried to sound casual. "Hi... So... off anywhere interesting?" He cast a quick glance to the floor in front of the passenger seat. The bag was still there.

Mandy didn't look up. "I'm going home to pick up some stuff then I'm doing deliveries." He put crisps from his lap back into the bag and popped the last one into his mouth. "So if this is about the book launch, I don't have time." He started the car.

A white van man waiting behind tooted his horn. Spencer moved round to the passenger side and got in. Mandy drove off. "Look, about that, I'm really sorry. I forgot my phone, then

I got held up, and I got back after you had left, and it was too late, and..." The car was heading back into Spencer's street. Lucy was out front talking to Mrs Chapori. "You delivering those huge curtains?"

"Yes."

"Well let me give you a hand. Come on. Please."

Mandy sighed and turned the car.

Asides a brief conversation about there being a strange smell in the car, they had made it all the way to Mandy's and then on into Soho with Spencer doing all the talking. They pulled up outside one of Soho's trendy loft apartment blocks.

"I'll take the curtains up," said Mandy, a chill still evident in his voice, "if you stay with the car in case of traffic wardens."

"Whatever I can do to help." Even Spencer thought he was beginning to sound desperate.

Mandy loaded himself up with as much curtain material he could carry and scowled his way to the burnished metal doors of the apartment block.

Once Mandy had gone inside, Spencer pulled the bag onto his lap. Driven by morbid and ill-advised curiosity, he undid the zip. The smell of rock-mulched cat hit him. His stomach heaved. He zipped it back up and sat it at his feet again.

Mandy arrived back a few minutes later for the rest of the curtains. He didn't acknowledge Spencer. By the time he sat back in the driver's seat some time later, he had two envelopes in his hand. The fact he waited until sitting in the driver's seat before putting them somewhat theatrically in his jacket pocket left Spencer with little doubt Mandy wanted them noticed.

"So what's the envelopes?" said Spencer.

"Just my payment..." Mandy pulled the car into gear, "and an invite to a party they're having. I'm not the only one who gets invited places, it seems."

Driving south, Mandy's mood seemed to have lightened and the tension let up a bit when they turned to each other and cried, "Chavalanche!" as two buggies and their Burberry-clad parents took to the road before them at a crossing.

"So where we going next?" said Spencer.

"Malcolm's."

"Malcolm, my agent?"

Mandy nodded to the back seat. "The two dresses are for his wife and daughter."

"I've never been to his house. You mind if I come in with you? I'd like to see how my pimp lives."

"Sure."

The meter they bought the parking sticker from guzzled the last of their pound coins, letting them the road space at an hourly rate that would have been cheaper to get the car a hotel room.

Spencer had noticed Mandy didn't tell his customers that delivery was part of the service; in doing so it meant he got payment in full when he needed it without the goods sitting around waiting to be collected, and usually got him a nice tip for going out of his way. Spencer thought it all surprisingly business savvy for Mandy.

Carrying a dress each, they aimed for a front door festooned in brightly coloured balloons. Children's screams could be heard from inside as Mandy pressed the bell.

"Delivery for Bedlam," Spencer said, regretting the jest when he saw the expression of tethered rage on Malcolm's face as he opened the door.

Malcolm grabbed Spencer's and Mandy's shoulders and pulled them in. "Thank God. I thought it was another sprog."

Malcolm's oleaginous comb-over, which he usually kept scraped from ear to ear via the top of his head, dangled across his face like a threadbare hula skirt. He swept it back over, once again recreating the flawless illusion of a hirsute scalp. He took a step out the door and breathed in deep.

Josie, Malcolm's wife, popped her head round a doorway from along the hall. "If you disappear out that door, I'll shoot you dead in the street. I swear. Hi, Mandy. Hi, Spencer."

They nodded hello.

Malcolm stepped back inside and closed the door. "I wouldn't do anything without running it past the escape committee first, darling."

Josie smiled at the dresses. "Is that my new__" She turned back to the room. "Royston, no, not the Versace cushions." She darted out of sight.

"I'll get rid of these upstairs," said Malcolm, taking the dresses. "Wait there and I'll get your money. And don't let any of the little ones touch you: they're covered in germs and jam."

"Olivia," came Josie's shriek, "what did your mummy say about putting things up other people's noses?"

Spencer and Mandy couldn't resist. They crept along the hall and peered in. Josie was in a tug of war for a cushion with two chocolate covered six-year olds whilst also trying to stop a little girl dressed as a witch from sticking her wand up a boy's nose. Behind her was a rather spent looking clown, whose curly, blue wig was being brandished trophy-like by a boy bouncing up and down on the sofa. The clown seemed oblivious to his missing wig as he struggled to catch his escaped rabbit before the masses tore it limb from furry limb. Attached to one of the clown's legs was a child, or, more specifically, a child's teeth. And in the middle of it all was two of the cutest little fairy princesses, all dressed up in their party finery, holding a boy down whilst stuffing slabs of birthday cake into his mouth.

"You just know Hieronymus Bosch must have had children," said Malcolm, coming back down the stairs.

"Shouldn't we help the clown?" said Mandy. "I think he's bleeding."

"Don't worry. It's just jam. He wears protective clothing under the clown suit. He used to train attack dogs. Although why anyone would give up the calm of being set upon by police Alsatians for this is beyond me." He gave Mandy an envelope. "There's a few quid extra in there. Thanks for dropping them off." He turned to Spencer. "You didn't get back to me about the Boy Brides job so I just put you down to do it."

"Oh," said Spencer, unable to disagree. "Thanks, I think."

"MALCOLM!" came Josie's shriek.

"I'll let you see yourself out." Malcolm took a deep breath

and headed back into the throng.

As they headed back to the car, Spencer had a renewed appreciation of the get-out-of-jail-free card afforded to him by the gay gene. The occasional homophobic abuse, job prejudice and Islamic fatwa's seemed a small price to pay for never having to lose sleep over teething tots, good schools and MMR jabs.

His mobile phone rang as he got into the car. It was Mickey. He let it ring.

Mandy's mood seemed to return as they drove back to North London and he insisted on getting out and making his way home by tube. Spencer suspected it was partly the smell of dead cat, which was now so bad he had the air conditioning on *and* all the windows open.

He was met by Lucy when he eventually pulled into his street. She was knocking on the driver's window before he had even pulled on the handbrake

"Where have you been? Gabbana's still not back."

After an hour and a half of handing out flyers Lucy perked up.

"I've got some more for you," said Lucy, as she thrust a 'missing cat' flyer into the hand of a woman who was juggling two kids and an armful of shopping. "What do you call a lesbian with a waistline...? Bulimic. What do you call an Irish lesbian...? Gaelick."

"Lucy, you're outside McDonald's in Stoke Newington making lesbian jokes," said Spencer. "What you got on after this, BNP flyers in Brixton?"

"Oh, I hadn't thought of that," said Lucy. Spencer wondered if he was witnessing Lucy's first ever revelation of sensitivity to others. "They like their cats, don't they? Maybe we should 'dyke' the flyers up a bit and say it's a missing 'pussy'."

Spencer scanned the immediate vicinity for any signs of lesbians that might be 'packing' and moved away from Lucy.

"What's the matter with you?" said Lucy. "You've been twitching since we came out."

Spencer bolted for conversational safety. "So how come your sister is back trying to set you up with a man again?"

"I know," she thrust a leaflet into a passer-by's hand, "you'd think she'd know better by now. I've told her I'm not interested. I'm better without a man." Spencer envied her resolve. "Courtesy of my sister, I've been on enough blind dates to claim my free dating-guide dog. She used to think that if you don't have a man in your life you turn lesbian after a while."

"Somehow I can't see you sitting at home listening to K.D. Lang and staring up at your poster of Lindsay Lohan."

Lucy stabbed a leaflet at a startled hoodie. "My sister's latest thing is this book called *Single Friends: the conduit through which the charge of divorce is transmitted*. According to this book, being single is like having dodgy wiring, so it's better to have everyone you know earthed. I blame Jeremy Kyle and Trisha. It's all that 'my sister slept with my fiancé', 'my best friend cheated with my husband' crap."

"So no chemistry with the last guy?"

"Oh there was chemistry, but it was easily sorted with some Pepto Bismol. And he finished every sentence with one of those two syllable laughs." Lucy demonstrated the laugh as she handed a leaflet to a rather bemused elderly couple.

The leaflets in Lucy's hand were almost spent. Seizing the opportunity to save the North London lesbian community from any further abuse, and to avoid the possibility of getting any blood on his tee-shirt, when Lucy wasn't looking Spencer dumped the remainder of his leaflets in a bin.

"Finished?" said Spencer, over-playing the innocent empty hands by clapping them several times.

A woman with a bleached mullet got Lucy's final leaflet.

Walking back towards their building, and the car, Spencer's palms became clammy and his lip started dripping with sweat. He needed a drink. He would wait it out in the flat till dark and the coast was clear from Lucy's constant checking of the front door. He had to get rid of the cat tonight, somehow.

CHAPTER 24

Each minute dragged round the clock in a belligerent determination to draw out every moment before dark. Spencer watched from his window as the last of the sun beat down on the car. He could only imagine the effect it must be having on the boil-in-the-bag cat behind the passenger seat.

Sitting at the window the penny had finally dropped like a carpet bomb on an Afghan mountain: he had killed someone. Stella was an awful drag queen, but if you killed all the bad drag that was out there the hen night circuit would collapse and gay amateur nights would be fifteen minutes long. He now realised that the needle on his moral compass had come spinning off and embedded itself in the wall.

By quarter past ten he was stir crazy. He had to go now.

The smell of slow-cooked meat rushed him as he opened the driver's door. He retched. Pulling the bag onto the passenger seat he sprayed it with air freshener. Once the air was thick with Alpine scented chemicals, he turned the air-conditioning on full and remained outside for the air to filter.

"Is there a problem, sir?" came a voice from the other side of the car.

As if his heart was demanding the right to stop there and then, the jar of an authoritative voice caused Spencer's chest to tighten so much it hurt. Glancing furtively and uncontrollably at the bag on the passenger seat, the first thing his terrified eyes saw as he looked up from the bag was a policeman's hat. He almost screamed. The second thing he saw, and the fraction of a second it took to register seemed like hours, was Mandy's face.

Spencer looked down at his feet to check if there was indeed a pile of skin he'd jumped out of.

"Mandy, you scared the fucking shit out of me."

"Sorry," said Mandy, removing the hat. "You off somewhere?"

"No...no...going nowhere." Spencer opened the door and turned off the engine. "What you doing here?"

"I had to pick up a couple of policeman costumes from a kiss-o-gram company on the other side of the park today. They want me to sew badges onto the hats and Velcro the sides of the jackets and trousers so they can be ripped off easily." He pulled a rucksack from his shoulder and put the hat inside. "I was too busy being a bitch to you today I forgot to go pick them up. Sorry. For being a bitch, I mean. Not the costumes...cos they're my fault, really. And they're nothing you could have, I mean me, well__"

"Let's call it quits, then, shall we?"

Mandy smiled. "You going upstairs?"

Spencer glanced at the bag. "Yes. Yes, I'm going upstairs. Fancy a drink?"

"Love one. Don't forget this." Mandy opened the passenger door and pulled out the holdall. "Leave this in here and it'll get nicked. You'll lose it."

Chance would be a fine bloody thing, thought Spencer.

"I really am sorry about today," Mandy said once they were upstairs. "It's just I was really looking forward to going to that book launch. Everything else in my life at the moment is just such a disaster."

A faint whiff of dead cat hit Spencer's nostrils. "Let me put this bag away and I'll get us a drink."

He took the bag through to the bedroom and sat it next to the open window. He shook his head in exasperation; what hope did he ever have of getting rid of Drucilla when he couldn't even dispose of a dead cat? He had turned and was almost out the door when he heard a meow.

A liquid nitrogen chill ran down his spine. Had the walls of his reality broken down and he'd just stepped onto the set of a Stephen King movie? He turned to face the bag, half expecting a zombie Gabbana to be staring back at him, murderous intent and brain food lust in its milky white, dead eyes.

Dolce was sitting on the windowsill, meowing affectionately at Spencer.

"No, Dolce, go home." Spencer waved his arms. "Shoo!"

Dolce meowed and swished his tail.

"Shoo! Go home."

The cat leapt through the window and landed on the bag. Spencer clamped his hands over his mouth to stifle a horrified guilty scream.

Dolce sniffed the bag. His claws unsheathed from the fur of his paws. His teeth bared and he started to hiss and spit like a pressure cooker. His back arched and his tail shot bolt upright. He began to spin round and round on the bag, letting out a tortured wail as he went.

Spencer moved towards him in a let-me-explain gesture, unsure how to communicate repentance to a bereft cat. Dolce flipped in mid-air to get away from him, jumping at the window.

He went straight out and over the ledge.

The agonising squeal was short and Spencer could just make out the dull thud of his landing.

"So you going to Stella's funeral?" Mandy asked from the other room.

Spencer stood in silence, mouth agape like a ventriloquist's dummy expressing shock.

CHAPTER 25

"Do we know if Stella had a will?" whispered Anaesthesia.

Bette threw her a reproachful stare and slapped the back of Anaesthesia's hand with a hymnbook. "This isn't the time."

Anaesthesia rearranged the ruffles on her black dress and fluffed her mass of afro. "I'm just saying what everyone else is thinkin'. That girl had a *fearsome* collection of bags."

"It's true, *dahling*," said Bo, the single, black ostrich feather on her hat vibrating to emphasise her agreement. "She didn't have a stitch of clothing you would have given to a charity shop, but she had an Hermes Berken."

Bette pulled her Jackie O glasses down and glowered over the rim. "Could we please not mention Drucilla's name today?"

"Don't need to tell me, girl," said Anaesthesia. "I haven't had a chance to tell you, but I got a phone call from her last night."

The brim of Bette's Dynasty-styled, funeral millinery prodded Anaesthesia's afro as she spun to face her.

"What about?"

"She wants me to DJ at both her clubs. But on the condition I quit Opus Gay."

The feather of Bo's hat craned forward. "She didn't?"

"I swear," said Anaesthesia. "She says we have such a lot in common and we could really work well together. I was mortified. I said to her, 'you use Mac lipgloss, girl?' she tells me yes. So I told her that was the only thing we had in common and I don't expect to be exploring any further avenues of our similarities any time soon. So long as there's Venezuelan clinics looking for spare organs, girl, I'll never be desperate enough for cash to work for that witch."

"Well done, *dahling*, but I'd watch my back if I were you. I had my car covered in paint stripper after a spat with her a few years back and__"

"Shhh," said Bette. "Here comes the coffin."

Knowing it was her fault there was a body in that coffin, Bette braced herself and pulled her glasses tight to her face.

"I've done some freaky shit for you in my time, girl," said Anaesthesia, "but this…"

A few feet away from them Mandy pressed play on the ghetto blaster and Elaine Page's rendition of Memory, from *Cats*, filled the garden. Lucy carried a cardboard box draped in a Dolce and Gabbana blouse and Mrs Chapori, who had provided the hymnbooks, walked beside her, a black headscarf framing her weathered complexion.

Lucy placed the 'coffin' into the prepared hole and adjusted the blouse before stepping back. Anaesthesia removed a hanky from her cleavage, pointed at the coffin and sobbed.

Mrs Chapori introduced the first hymn, *All Creatures Great and Small*. Anaesthesia wept throughout most of it. Even Mrs Chapori's prayer to St. Gertrude (the patron Saint of cats, apparently) was punctuated by nose-blowing sobs. By the time Lucy had finished her rather tender tribute, Anaesthesia seemed ready to throw herself onto the coffin like a Beirut housewife.

"It's not fair, Lucy," sobbed Anaesthesia. "To be cut down in your prime like this. It's just not right."

Bette pulled her glasses down so there was no mistaking her disapproving stare, but Anaesthesia's afro was waving back and forth with her sobs so much she couldn't see her face. Bette nodded to Mandy to take her away. Mandy jumped to attention and pressed play, escorting Anaesthesia off to the sound of 'Everybody Wants To Be A Cat' from Disney's *Aristocats*.

"We all bow heads now," said Mrs Chapori, "and offer prayer for Gabboner."

"But, Mandy, that blouse is *this* season's," wailed Anaesthesia from the other end of the garden. "You can't bury drag like that, girl, it's just not right."

After sedating Anaesthesia with a large vodka, Mandy arrived beside the grave just as they finished their prayers. He had a shovel.

"Where'd you get that?" said Bette.

"It was in the bike cupboard across from Mrs Chapori's flat. I think it's hers. Why?"

The memory of trying to dig a hole on Hampstead Heath with a trowel mocked Bette as they moved away from the graveside.

Bette put an arm around Lucy's shoulder. "How you holding up?"

"Okay I suppose. Somehow, I think Dolce knew his brother was dead. I'm going to plant two rose bushes there." Lucy pointed at Dolce's grave. "One for each of them."

Bette hugged Lucy and looked over her shoulder at Mandy shovelling dirt into the hole. She had an idea.

"I need a drink," said Lucy.

"I've got another bottle of JD upstairs," said Bette. "I'll be back in a mo."

"There's plenty here."

"You can never have too much."

Bette had a fully formed plan by the time she was raking through her bedside table for the bottle of sleeping pills. She poured half a dozen into her hand and took them to the kitchen where she crushed them down in a saucer with a spoon.

She looked over at the fridge and cringed. Last night, after telling Lucy the bad news about her cat, Mandy had stayed over on the sofa. His attempt to be supportive, however, had left the problem of a dead cat rotting in the bedroom. Once a spare toothbrush had been found for Mandy and he was safely out of sight doing his bedtime ablutions, Spencer packed Gabbana into a plastic bin bag and stuffed him into the freezer compartment of the fridge. But he wouldn't be in there for much longer, Bette thought. She couldn't have buried Gabbana in the garden before; Mrs Chapori tended the block's small communal garden as if it was her own, and the freshly dug soil would have been noticed. But now, with Dolce's grave, he could be buried with his brother unnoticed. Bette also liked the poetic sentiment.

She folded a piece of paper into a tiny envelope and tipped

just over half of the crushed powder into it. Once it was dark the only problem would be the pathologically sleepless Mrs Chapori, and with her bedroom window facing out into the garden, Bette couldn't take the chance. She tipped more of the powder into the envelope and discarded the rest.

When she returned to the garden everyone had moved into the shade near the house. Lucy had laid out drinks and food. Bette was handed a glass to toast Dolce and Gabbana.

"To fashionable pets," said Lucy, a slight quiver in her voice. She knocked back her drink and poured another.

"Lucy, *dahling*, I'm afraid I'm going to have to make a move," said Bo. "I'm doing an interview for *TV Quick*, then I've a gift to buy for a wedding I'm going to in Windsor tomorrow."

"Someone you know doing an Elton-Furnish at the registry office?" said Lucy.

"If only, *dahling*. They're a couple of dishwater-dull architects who think they're being frightfully witty and ironic by having it at Legoland."

Lucy pulled on Bo's hand as a cue for her to hydraulically lower herself so she could peck her on the cheek. "Thanks for coming. You guys really cheered me up."

Bo took Bette's hand. "Oh, thank Bette here for rallying the troupes. We all know how much you loved those cats. And it was rather refreshing to go to a funeral where the deceased's porn collection wasn't an issue."

Bette nodded in agreement.

"Now, *dahling*, I'm away for a few days in Milan, but my network's sponsoring the VIP tent at Drag Up and Boogey Down next weekend. Why don't you come?"

Lucy smiled. "Thanks, but I think I'll give it a pass. I wouldn't know whether to deliberately butch up so everyone would think I was a man dressing convincingly as a woman, or femme up so no one mistook me for a man and then me having to smack them in the mouth for the insult."

Bo seemed to take the point.

After Bo left they proceeded to honour Dolce and Gabbana's

memory in the time honoured bereavement tradition of getting respectfully paralytic. The sun set on the garden with Mandy judging the finals of 'Crock Idol'. Bette and Lucy's version of Ike and Tina Turner doing *D.I.V.O.R.C.E.* being pipped at the post by Anaesthesia and Mrs Chapori, who had spent most of the afternoon 'bonding' in their joint loathing of all things German (ever since Günter, Anaesthesia's last boyfriend, left, even the sight of a frankfurter was enough to set her off). Anaesthesia and Mrs Chapori won with an impressive rendition of Sonny and Cher's 'I Got You Babe', in Polish.

After Anaesthesia had been poured into a cab and Mandy and Lucy were talking at the far end of the garden near the grave, Bette poured the powder into a glass of orange juice and took it to Mrs Chapori, who was sitting on the grass singing what sounded like the Polish equivalent of *Danny Boy*.

"Here you are, Mr C," said Bette. "Some vitamin C so we don't get hangovers tomorrow."

Mrs Chapori took the glass and smiled. "You nice girl. You need nice man. Get rid of Spincir. He not good for you."

Bette nodded and pointed at the glass. "Drink up."

"You like daughter to me…if I had black husband, not useless Polish dead one. I always wanted to try black man. That Obama, he sexy man. I would have vote him. I would have done much more than vote him if I was young girl."

Lucy and Mandy arrived beside them. Mrs Chapori grabbed Mandy and pulled him down beside her.

"Manfred," Mrs Chapori said, "you strange little man, but I think you good heart. You ever try black man?"

"Don't forget your vitamin C, Mrs C," said Bette just as Lucy grabbed her wrist.

"Listen," Lucy said, "I've not had a chance to thank you."

"Aww, shush, it was nothing."

"No. It was really thoughtful. And I utterly appreciate it." She pulled Bette's face so they were looking into each other's eyes. "You know when I say I don't need a man in my life, and that I'd be a happier person if I never had to deal with another relationship, well, you're the best relationship I've ever had with a man. I can't imagine my life without you." Lucy kissed Bette on the cheek. "If my sister could see and hear me right now she'd be convinced she was right and I'd turned." Lucy looked round at Mrs Chapori. "Let's get the old bag to bed."

Bette went over and took the glass of orange juice from Mrs Chapori and held it up to her lips. "Come on, Mrs C, drink up." Unable to refuse, she slugged the orange juice. Bette continued to push the glass to her lips whilst ruminating on Lucy's tender words. It was at times like this, when Lucy's hard exterior cracked, that Bette loved Lucy all the more. But how would Lucy feel about her if she knew the truth? How would Lucy feel if__

Mrs Chapori was choking. The glass was empty.

"Sorry Mrs C," said Bette, patting her gently on the back.

"Hangover not matter if I drown," coughed Mrs Chapori.

"I think we need to get her to bed," said Lucy. "I'll do that if you two tidy up out here."

Mrs Chapori got to her feet. "I not bloody invalid." She slipped back onto the grass. "I bloody drunk as Yeltsin." She started to laugh to herself and mutter in Polish as Lucy pulled her from the grass and guided her to her flat.

"There's something we need to talk about," said Mandy, sometime later when he and Bette were alone upstairs. Bette looked up from tidying the contents of Anaesthesia's makeup bag. Its contents were scattered across the kitchen worktop from when Anaesthesia mascara-tinted Mrs Chapori's moustache for her performance as Sonny. "I don't want us to fall out over it."

Bette stopped gathering the makeup. "What's the matter?"

"Drucilla's offered me work again."

"You what!?" A lip-gloss flew out of Bette's hand and over her shoulder.

"I know what you think. I__"

"Are you telling me you're considering whatever crappy little job she throws your way? You heard what she did to Bo."

"I know, but it's not like that. Daniels is paying for a twentieth anniversary stage show at the club and Drucilla wants me to make the costumes. It's great money. I'll be working for Daniels, not her. They want me to let them know by the weekend. Thing is, it'll take up most of my time for the next couple of months if I take it."

"You can't do it. She's come between me and my work, my friends, my partner, but coming between a drag queen and her dressmaker is just too far."

"But I really need the money."

"I'll lend you some money."

"You can't afford to."

"I'll pay you more for supervising the Lusherettes."

"I need to make some real money."

Bette knew she was on dangerous ground. "This is about loyalty, Mandy. Doing business with her is dealing with the devil. It's like those guest actors who used to get into business with J.R. in Dallas: you just knew they would only be in the series for a couple of episodes before they got ripped off or killed." She folded her arms in drunken petulance.

"But, Bette…"

Bette swished her hair and started shoving Anaesthesia's discarded makeup back into its bag again.

"Okay," Mandy sighed. "I'll turn it down if you want."

"I do."

"But I need a new central heating boiler."

"It's summer. Why do you need central heating?"

"I need hot water."

"Shower here." As the words were out, Bette knew how ridiculous they sounded.

Mandy remained silent, staring at his feet.

"Can't you see what she's doing, Mandy? She's using you to get at me."

"I can't refuse work from everyone you don't get on with. I'd never work again."

"Who have I ever asked you not to do work for?"

"Priscilla."

"She's a slimy tramp. She'd just rip you off."

"What about Lola Lovehandles?"

"Two-faced cow."

"Okay, what about Consuela or Wynonna Bego?"

Bette could feel the situation slipping away from her. She pushed Anaesthesia's makeup bag to one side. "What am I doing? I'm being a complete bitch...again. All I ever do is focus on my career and my work. It's all me, me, me. You deserve a break too. In fact, you deserve a break more than most. Maybe you should go work for Drucilla. So long as you get something down in writing, to protect yourself."

"Like I said, it'd be Daniels I'm working for."

"Even better, then. So long as you can protect yourself. I mean..." Bette put a deliberate quiver in her voice, "I don't want to hold you back. You're so talented and you deserve it. You don't think I'm holding you back, do you?"

"Of course I don't think that. I'd__"

Bette cut in; her performance was just getting going. "I'm an awful friend sometimes, Mandy. I know that. I'd hate to see Drucilla do anything to hurt you. I know I could be a better friend sometimes and I... It's just..." if Bette had been having an MRI scan right now, doctors would have been able to spot the Machiavellian drama queen section of the brain as it lit up like Times Square, "...it's just, after Jason..."

"No, no, no," Mandy reached out and took Bette's hand, "you're a great friend."

Bette looked at him and smiled softly. "It's just after Jason, I couldn't bear it if Drucilla got between me and...and my best friend."

"She won't," Mandy smiled and squeezed Bette's hand. "Trust me. I'll tell her there's no way I can work for her... I'll tell her I'm way too busy making a whole new range of outfits for you."

"No Mandy. You need the work. You've already said so. What about your boiler? I can't let you do this. You have to take the job. Just make sure she__"

"No. I've made my decision. I'm not doing the job. I'll get a bank loan, or something. You're right. She's just trying to cause trouble between us."

"You're the best, Mandy." Bette gave him a peck on the cheek. Mandy blushed. "I am right, you know. You have to believe me. I know I sound like a paranoid bitch sometimes, but that doesn't mean Drucilla's not an evil cow who's out to get me. Look at Jason. She promised him work and all he ended up with was some dubious offer from Francois."

"He got what from Francois?"

"I don't know exactly, I just delete messages when I hear Jason's voice, but suffice to say he never saw any of the work Drucilla promised him." She rubbed Mandy's shoulder affectionately. "I'll make sure I hand out as many of your new business cards as I can over the next few weeks. I've already given out all your last ones and several people have been asking me about the dress you made for the BAHTI's. Who knows, you might start getting calls from them. I've been bigging you up everywhere. And Malcolm's wife thinks you're a genius. I've told him to spread the word. He might be a slimeball of an agent, but his missus has good taste."

"Thanks." Mandy slouched against the worktop.

"I have an idea. Why don't you come to Drag Up and Boogey Down at the weekend? A dressmaker in a park full of trannies and drag queens is like having a ten inch dick at an orgy: everyone will want a piece of you."

"I don't want to go on my own," Mandy seemed to sway slightly, "and you'll be compering most of the day."

"Bo's going. Didn't you hear? Her network is sponsoring the VIP tent. Go on, it'll be fun."

Mandy shrugged and moved over to the sofa. "I'll think about it." He sat down.

Bette looked at her watch; she had a cat to get out of the freezer. "I'm going to get my face off. I've an early shoot for Boy Brides tomorrow. You want a cab?"

"To be honest I'm feeling a bit funny." He slumped onto his side. "I think I might have had too much to drink. Is it okay if...?" He seemed to be struggling to keep his eyes open.

"Mandy, what was the last thing you drank?"

"Some orange juice."

"You pour it yourself?"

"Yes. I mean no. I mean Mrs Chapori gave it me. She swapped it for my vodka and orange. Why?"

He keeled over on the sofa.

Bette rolled her eyes, realising her chances of ever being a criminal mastermind were as likely as Rosemary West getting a mother of the year award.

After carrying Mandy through to bed, Bette poured herself a large JD; the cat was going to have to wait.

She took a slug from her glass and began tidying the last of Anaesthesia's makeup into her bag. The last thing to go in was a stick of lipgloss. It was new, still sealed. She sat it to one side and opened the fridge. The pot with the remains of the mercuric cyanide was behind a tub of low fat spread. She took it out.

Bette remembered Anaesthesia saying the only thing she had in common with Drucilla was her lipgloss. She opened the pot and scrutinized the gel inside. Its consistency was almost identical to lipgloss. Bette felt her face lift into a triumphant smile. Why hadn't she thought of this before? There probably hadn't been enough cyanide on the rose stems to kill Drucilla, anyway, but this might work.

CHAPTER 26

An altercation yesterday at the Boy Brides job had the shoot overrunning. Ordinarily Bette would have been only too happy to get in another morning's work – she desperately needed the money - but with the Tumble Dryer's calendar shoot that afternoon, it had her running late. The problem had arisen with a disagreement over a certain outfit. Or, more specifically, who wore a certain outfit. It was stunning. It was a copy of Carrie Bradshaw's wedding dress from the *Sex and the City* movie (without the hideous dead parrot headdress, naturally). Everyone wanted to wear it. Bette would have happily gouged someone's eyes out for it herself, but after much 'debate' and a little name calling, the effete stylist and hissing designer minced away from the building drama and let the model with the don't-fuck-with-me-biceps wear it - literally, the words 'don't fuck with me' were tattooed in gothic font on her upper arm.

Stuck in traffic watching the minutes tick past, Bette could imagine Drucilla rushing everyone into place to start early so she could legitimately exclude Bette from the shoot.

"I think we've met before, you know," said Bette's passenger, who had been her 'groom' for most of the morning. He was also one of the Tumble Dryer's new go-go boys, so he, too, was taking part in the calendar shoot. "Got it!" he squealed. "You were at the opening night of Whores D'Ouvres. I used to work for Francois, but then I got the job at the Tumble Dryer through Drucilla. She's great. A real laugh. You know him?"

"Yes," said Bette, tersely.

"Yeah, I do a bit of modelling work now, too. You might have seen the poster campaign I did for gonorrhoea." (Bette had been under the misconception gonorrhoea hadn't needed any ad campaigns to maintain its brand leadership.) "My landlord's a drag queen like you. Carmen Monoxide. You know him?"

Bette's grip on the steering wheel tightened. She knew Carmen, a hen night act of the old school: costumes as threadbare as brothel bed sheets and breath as toxic as her tongue. Bette had seen her act, and if the words *arse, cunt, cock, fuck, fanny, minge, snatch, spunk* and *dildo* were removed from her vocabulary, it would have been a mime act. Being compared to Carmen was like comparing Halle Berry to Devine Brown.

"What did you say your name was?" Bette said, in a need to put a name to the face she was loathing.

"Troy."

"Popular name in Bradford, is it?"

"It's my real name, honest. My sister's called Paris."

"Like in Greek mythology?"

Troy pouted in vacant confusion.

"Troy, Paris, Ancient Greece." Still nothing registered on Troy's face. "The wooden horse?"

"Oh, the film with Brad Pitt. No, I was born way before that was made. How young do you think I am?"

The rest of the journey, which showcased Troy's full conversational repertoire of from 'I' to 'me', was relatively painless once Bette realised she wasn't expected to participate. They arrived at the Tumble Dryer just before three, where Troy fulfilled the unspoken part of his transport contract by carrying Bette's large makeup case for her. Troy was waxing lyrical about his upcoming job in L.A. (*Lengths 'n' Arses*, the porn mag) as they pushed through the Tumble Dryer's main doors.

Standing in front of them before the ticket desk was Drucilla, festooned in red and white and crowned with a large, peaked Santa hat. Bette thought she looked ho, ho horrendous.

Drucilla glared at the makeup case in Troy's hand. "Is that yours?"

"No," Troy said.

"You shouldn't go picking stuff up off the street, Troy. You don't know where it's been."

"I didn't." Troy looked down at the case. "It's Bette's."

"It's *her* I'm talking about, sweetheart."

"I see the poor little children will be getting nothing for Christmas this year," said Bette. "Unless the reindeers are fitted with Lear jet engines the sleigh's got no chance of getting off the ground with your excess baggage."

Drucilla's eyes narrowed to hateful slits. "I take it you've put talent and a personality on your Christmas wish list?"

"If you're willing to lend me one of your stockings to hang up, I'll put a fifty two inch plasma screen and the French rugby team on my list."

"What are you doing with this tragi-tranny, Troy?"

"She was my bride today on a modelling job." Troy dropped Bette's makeup case at her feet. "But in real life I wouldn't marry her even if I needed a passport. I did need a lift, though. Sorry I'm late." Troy flashed a cold smile at Bette and minced off into the club with his nose in the air.

Bette pictured his go-go gonads on the end of a hot-hot skewer.

"He knows where his loyalties need to be, Bette. He also knows he won't last long here without my say so. Something you'd do well to remember."

"I could never forget how much I owe you, Drucilla. If ever I need a reminder of the dangers of over eating, you're the first person I think of." Bette lifted the makeup case in one hand and slung the straps of her holdall across her shoulder.

Heading through the club towards the stage, Bette was greeted by Sherry Amontillado, Drucilla's spare drag henchwoman if anything ever happened to Stella; which, of course, it had. Sherry's face was her usual Romford-grandmother-on-the-pull makeover, its violent blend of greens, reds, blues and glitter hardly noticeable atop her multi-coloured stars, stripes and chevrons outfit. If Mary Shelly had been a drag queen, this is how Frankenstein would have looked.

Without uttering a word or offering any assistance, Sherry led the way to Bette's dressing room. Like a tranny butler in an Edgar Alan Poe novel, without a word she pointed at the door of what Bette had always assumed was a cupboard.

Bette swung her bags in and closed the door. A bare light bulb illuminated the tiny room. Its only furniture was a camping table and a stool. There was a dirty outline on the wall where a mirror had once been, no doubt removed earlier today. This was the hospitality equivalent of an asbestos-lined Winnebago. Bette smiled at their petty games.

She checked for the poisoned lipgloss in the case. It was safely in its sealed plastic bag. She would wait until later to put it in place. The swap needed to be done once Drucilla was out of drag; Bette couldn't take the risk of her poisoning herself whilst she and Bette had any proximity that would draw suspicion.

After changing into her lucky red dress and heels, she used a compact mirror to do some minor repairs; Bette knew she could go up on stage with a double pushchair and skid marks on her chin and still look classy next to Drucilla's collection of sad-drag, but that didn't mean she shouldn't look fabulous.

The shoot was for the December picture in The Tumble Dryer's commemorative calendar. For this the stage was backdroped with an Alpine landscape and decorated with tall, cardboard icicles. Three rows of chairs sat centre stage, each row slightly higher than the one in front. Front centre was a padded throne edifice, of which Bette had no doubt was intended for Drucilla.

"I'm fucking telling you, Bette," said Carmen Monoxide, as she and Bette secretly shared a joint at the side of the stage near a fire exit, "I thought I had fucking thrush. My arse was screaming like a fucking banshee."

"So what was it, then?" Bette said, as anxious to know as she was to experience chemotherapy.

"Cunt of a doctor tells me it was friction burns. Fucking friction burns!" Carmen slipped a hand under her skirt for a good scratch. The red skirt was part of an outfit that Bette could only imagine had been made from the Von Tramp family's dining room curtains. "I told him it must be off public fucking transport, because there's been no fucker up my coit since New Year. And even then there wasn't enough fucking friction to get a spark out of nylon bloody sheets."

On the scale of too much information, Bette felt this was up there with knowing whether your mother liked to spit or swallow. She passed the joint back to Carmen, who took it with the same hand she had just removed from her itching gusset.

"Everybody out front, please," said Drucilla.

"That queen gets right on my fucking tits." Carmen took a couple of puffs. "I'd love to__"

"NOW, everyone." Drucilla clapped her hands. Then, glaring at Carmen: "And put out that cigarette."

Carmen rolled her eyes and offered Bette the last of the spliff. A pubic hair stuck proud and erect from one of her nails.

"I'm okay, Carmen."

The stage started to clutter with drag queens, over two dozen in all, each trying to fill the space in a pathological need to be louder, funnier and camper than the one beside them. Bette despaired for their collective tedium and reassured herself they were but a distant, redneck cousin of her profession.

As Drucilla pointed everyone into position the go-go boys arrived in their elf hats and furry, red jockstraps. She directed them to kneel in a sycophantic row in front of her throne. With Santa's little hookers in place, Drucilla began rearranging everyone else in an attempt to accommodate hair and costume. She didn't even acknowledge Bette.

Anaesthesia came on from the other side of the stage and waved at Bette. Drucilla looked furious; Anaesthesia, as always, had thrown herself headlong into the spirit. A mini Christmas tree, complete with flashing lights, crowned her mass of afro, which was strewn with red and silver ribbons. Beneath the hair, which Bette was sure seemed larger than usual, was a cleavage like a pair of Volkswagen Beetles revving to escape the confines of her pillar-box red with sequined mistletoe dress. Finishing it all off were two Christmas tree fairies perched on each shoulder as if parrots on a gay pirate.

Drucilla pointed to a seat in the middle of the back row and continued to scowl as Valkeyre Te Kanawa marched on. Two

Christmas baubles dangled from the horns of Valkeyre's helmet in a reluctant, festive compromise with her armour. Bette thought Drucilla's look said it all: Valkeyre was another one she didn't want in the picture.

"Come and sit in front of me, Bette," cried Anaesthesia. "You'll look fabulous under my mistletoe."

"Don't move," Drucilla said. "*I'll* tell you where to sit."

Anaesthesia put her finger over her lips and mouthed 'oops'.

Sherry minced on and took the seat next to the throne. She sneered over at Bette. Bette was reminded of years of PE at school; all those freezing mornings on the football pitch, waiting for the humiliating consolation of being picked last. But this time the skinny black kid was going to get the last laugh.

"You go there." Drucilla pointed Bette towards the last seat on the top row.

The seat in front of Bette was occupied by a peacock head-dressed drag queen. It would have taken Bill Oddie to have been able to spot her through the plumage.

"Hi there. Bette, isn't it?" said the peacock, poking feathers into Bette's eyes as she craned back to say hello.

The lack of recognition or gives-a-damn on Bette's face must have spurred the peacock on for a second attempt. "Devine Inspiration...We met at Whores d'Ouvres."

"Oh, yeah, hi." Bette vaguely remembered.

"This is my stage partner, Heavenly Desires." Hitting Bette in the face with a second swish of plumage, Devine nodded to the feather boa-clad oddity next to her.

Bette smiled politely.

"Where's Manthrax?" said Drucilla, an impatient tone rising in her voice. "Is she here yet?"

At the mention of Manthrax's name, Bette seethed. The last time she saw Manthrax she had threatened to glass Bette; Manthrax had not taken the news well that Bette's club proposal for Opus Gay had been accepted.

"I'm here queers." Manthrax appeared at the side of the stage. She was wearing a giant sequined, red and silver, sleeveless dress.

The sleeveless look was her stock in trade. It allowed a better view of the tattoos that had no doubt been a status symbol during her formative years in borstal. She was the kind of drag queen Bette thought should be illegal; she was an insult to the profession; much to Bette's unending horror, Manthrax had made a career out of looking like she had just been to a needle exchange prom night and been voted 'most likely to be killed by their pimp'.

Manthrax took the seat on the other side of the throne and whispered something across to Sherry. It was an almost unheard of act of subtlety and discretion.

With Drucilla in place, and Bette only in the frame in spirit, the photographer started snapping. The stage erupted with versions of 'say cheese'; everyone thinking they were simply hilarious as they cried out 'gorgonzola', 'brie', 'stilton', etc. The exception to this was Carmen, whose voice could be heard through the cacophony shouting, "Cheesy cock. Cheesy cock."

Bette pulled apart the feathers of the headdress in front of her and stuck her face through in an attempt not to be erased altogether. The grimace as a feather twanged up her nose was not a good look, however, so she sat back and recited the full range of Philadelphia low fat products until it was all over.

Once the shoot was finished Bette tried to keep Anaesthesia talking on stage as long as possible; she needed things to quieten down backstage before she made her move. Unfortunately, their conversation came to an abrupt halt when smoke started coming from Anaesthesia's hair as her tree lights overheated.

Back in her cupboard, Bette was anxious to get started. She pulled on a pair of latex gloves, took the poisoned lipgloss from her makeup case and removed it from its sealed plastic bag. She felt strangely devoid of emotion and wondered if this was how vets felt when they had to put down mangy dogs.

When she could hear nothing from Drucilla's room next door, Bette psychologically coiled herself in readiness for the sound of her door. As she waited, she became more aware of her sense of calm; there were no butterflies. No nerves at all, in fact.

Drucilla's door slammed. Bette waited a minute before

cracking open her own door to see if the coast was clear. The supercilious cackle of the self-fascinated still echoed through the corridors, but from a safe distance. Bette crept the three steps to Drucilla's dressing room and let herself in.

Ignoring the fetid stench of bad taste and cheap drag, Bette went straight for the makeup case. It was locked. This was as confusing a discovery as it was infuriating; why Drucilla would think anyone would want to steal her slap when you could get it by the bucket load from any DIY store was beyond Bette.

"I left it in my dressing room," came Drucilla's voice from the other side of the door.

Shit! Bette darted glances around the room in panic as if expecting to spot a door she had never noticed before. There was only one place to hide. She climbed into the metal wardrobe.

She could hear the dressing room door open.

"Is black bitch still next door?" It was Manthrax.

"Yeah," said Drucilla, "you don't think taking *that* slap off is a quick job, do you?"

Manthrax's laugh was hollow and spiteful.

Bette felt her breathing go shallow as she held the door closed and pushed her face against its metal grilles. The grilles angled downwards, so all she could see was Drucilla's unmistakable fat ankles and Manthrax's scuffed DMs.

"So how's Troy working out?" said Manthrax.

"He's okay. Not the brightest bulb in the chandelier, but he can tie his own laces and knows how to fill a jockstrap."

"Dick of death on him, I hear. Any chances of borrowing him for some *overtime*?"

"I've told you before, don't complicate things."

Drucilla's feet turned away from Manthrax. Bette pushed her face right against the grille, but still couldn't see further than their calves.

"Have you spoken to black bitch's mate again?" said Manthrax. Bette's attention was seized by the short and curlies.

"Yes." Drucilla did a short, cold laugh. "Not as thick as it seems. Asked for more money."

"Really? Didn't think you'd have been able to buy that one. So what you gonna do?"

"I agreed to it."

"You what?"

With her face pushed right up against the grille, Bette could see Drucilla's feet turn towards Manthrax.

"The job won't last for long - just long enough to fuck with black bitch's head. So it's not going to cost me, is it?"

Mandy, Bette fumed, *the double-crossing little shit*. She wanted to throw open the doors and stab Drucilla in the eye with the lipgloss. She wanted to tear her a new… Every hair on Bette's body stood to attention. She had left the lipgloss out there. It was still sitting on the table.

A gaggle of queens screeched past the dressing room door.

"Give this to…" Bette couldn't hear what Drucilla was saying over the commotion outside. "…and keep an eye…if I can help it."

By the time the noise outside had stopped, Bette was concentrating so hard she thought she could hear her heartbeat echo inside the metal box of the wardrobe.

"Did you hear about slimeball Samuel?" said Manthrax.

"Yes," Drucilla's tone was clipped. "It was in the next building to Stella."

"What happened?"

Drucilla's feet angled from each other and she made a grunting noise. She seemed to be lifting something onto the table. "Well, it's a bit weird. Come on, I'll tell you downstairs. Let's have a drink."

Bette watched as Drucilla's water-retaining ankles and Manthrax's scuffed boots left the room.

Rigid with fury, Bette waited for silence before opening the wardrobe door. If the door hadn't been metal, her nails would have been embedded into it by now. She couldn't believe Mandy was being so two-faced; he deserved to get ripped off.

Bette noticed the makeup case had been moved onto the table just as she heard someone else at the door. Like a Hollywood lesbian, Bette threw herself back in the closet. Heart pounding, she pressed her face against the grille again and watched for whose feet appeared. A pair of Timberlands stepped into the room. *Timberlands. Great*, thought Bette, *that narrows it down to two out of every three gay men in London.* The door closed. She watched as the Timberlands turned to face the table. The boots moved about the room. Bette could hear stuff being moved around, but carefully. The boots eventually turned and left.

Bette opened the metal door. The makeup case was still sitting on the table. She got out and moved over to the table to look for the lipgloss. It was gone. Drucilla must have put it in her makeup box thinking she had left it out. Bette smiled and returned to her broom cupboard.

Satisfied her target had been hit, Bette decided to leave taking her face off until she got home. All she had to get rid of now was a dead cat in a freezer.

CHAPTER 27

Bette's mood had turned dark on the drive home after the shoot as she let two calls from Mandy go through to voicemail. She fumed at the thought of him negotiating with the enemy, haggling for another bag of silver. A call from Mad Mickey had her turning off the phone altogether. His persistence was getting scary, and earlier in the day, at the Boy Brides shoot, Bette had heard a rumour about Mickey that had done little to put her mind at ease. Struggling with a new crew on the clubbing scene, Mickey was apparently tightening up on his ongoing concerns. Bette wondered if that was going to include her.

Once indoors she poured a drink and knocked it back in one. She opened the fridge and pulled down the door on the ice compartment. The ice compartment's mouth had over the past six months reduced in size. Getting Gabbana in had been a difficult enough task, but looking at the torn plastic bag round his rigid, twisted, iced-in limbs that now filled the space, Bette knew getting him back out was going to be problematic. She bent down and tore away the plastic around his face. He was now missing an eye. She slipped on a new pair of Marigolds, grabbed his back legs and pulled. He didn't budge. She adjusted her grip and pulled again. Still no movement. She could feel her mood barometer swing from stormy weather to city-wide evacuation. She tried pushing him in further to see if that would loosen him. Still he didn't move. In desperation, she grabbed a leg and shook.

With a gruesome snap, Gabbana's leg tore off in Bette's hand. She crashed backwards, slamming her head against the floor. She lay there for a few seconds, still clutching Gabbana's leg, before getting up and pulling a bread knife from a drawer.

She stood with the blade poised, ready to hack at ice, cat,

or anything that defied her or got in the way. What was left of Gabbana's face peered one-eyed out at her.

Bette stabbed the knife into a wooden chopping board and pulled off the Marigolds. She poured another straight JD. Gabbana's leg lay on the floor. She threw it into the ice compartment and slammed the fridge door. The whole thing was going to have to be defrosted, and that wasn't happening tonight. She went to get her face off.

Feet aching from two days in new stillies, Spencer filled a basin with warm water and took it through to the lounge. With his jeans rolled up to the knees, he sat back and let the warm water engulf his feet. The blissful release of tension only lasted a few seconds. He looked down at the basin and wiggled his toes, wondering if he had given up the right to appreciate the smaller pleasures in life. After all, he had a dead cat in the kitchen, a dead drag queen to his name with another on the way, and here he was soaking his feet like a Roman Emperor. What was happening to him? Deeply unsettled in his own skin, it was as if he was becoming a different person, and one he didn't like.

The doorbell rang. Water splashed over the floor as he leapt from the basin. The bell rang again, more insistent.

It was the police, he knew it. They had come for him.

The bell rang again.

With dripping feet he tip-toed to the door and peered through the spy hole. Lucy was about to press the bell with her nose. She was clutching two anorexic, bald kittens.

Curiosity got the better of him. He opened the door.

"Here, grab him." Lucy thrust one of the kittens into Spencer's hands. "He was using my tit as a scratching post." She walked past into the lounge, holding her cat at arm's length. Spencer followed, brandishing his charge in a similar fashion.

"Meet Hirohito and Chairman Meow," said Lucy. "They're Siamese. Brother and sister, so Siamese twins, really." She stuck hers to the side of her head to demonstrate the Siamese point but it just took the opportunity to try and claw at her scalp.

"They're hideous." Spencer pulled the cat from an attempt to draw blood from his arm and sat it on the floor, stepping away from it as if it were an over-filled nappy. "They look like a couple of old men's willies with teeth."

Lucy let the other cat loose on the floor. It sniffed around the basin.

"They're designer, hon," she said. "These are the Rei Kawabuko of the cat world." Spencer did notice the resemblance. "They've got a better pedigree than the Windsors."

The two cats hissed at each other from either side of a puddle on the floor.

"They're not exactly cuddly, are they?"

"They're adjusting."

"Don't you think this is a bit soon?" Spencer's eyes flicked guiltily towards the kitchen.

"The house just seemed so empty without Dolce and Gabbana." She pulled one of the cats from her shoe as it sunk its teeth into the leather at her heel.

"They're quite...*playful*."

"They'll be okay once they've__"

Both cats threw themselves at each other, morphing into a hissing ball of skin and teeth. Lucy cupped water from the basin and threw it over them. They separated in an instant and darted for the kitchen.

"What you going to do when there's no water handy?"

"I'm going to buy a water pistol." Lucy followed them into the kitchen. "Spencer, come and see this. *Awww*, it's so cute."

Spencer froze. The two cats sat staring at the fridge.

"It must be the buzz of your cooling element," said Lucy.

"Must be." Spencer moved towards them to coax them out of the kitchen.

The cats turned their cold, blue eyes on him. Spencer stopped. They started sniffing the lino where Gabbana's leg had hit the floor.

"I think they're warming to you," said Lucy, in a tone that sounded desperate for reassurance.

In the blink of a cat's eye, the twins threw themselves at Spencer's naked ankles, embedding their teeth and claws into his flesh. He shrieked his best girly scream and shook his feet to get them off but they just dug deeper.

"Don't move." Lucy dropped to her knees and tried to remove them from Spencer's legs. "They're just showing how much they like you." They gouged and tore at his flesh, tearing lumps away with them as Lucy pulled them free. Holding them as far away from herself as she could, they hissed and spat in a fit of rage. "They're a bit excited."

Spencer saw blood dripping from his ankles. "Then get them on bloody Ritalin!"

Lucy smiled apologetically. "I'll take them back next door. Wave bye, bye to Auntie Spencer." She shook the hissing balls of skin and razor like a couple of demonically possessed glove puppets. "Get the door, hon. I don't want to risk putting them back down." She winced as one sunk its teeth into her hand.

Spencer kept as much distance between them as his narrow hall would permit. The cats writhed and spat at him from Lucy's now bleeding hands. He quickly checked the mirror before they left; he needed to know if they cast reflections.

Spencer suppressed the desire to burn sage and spray the room with holy water and settled down with cotton wool and antiseptic lotion to dab at his ankles. Skin peeled away from his shins in tattered layers. He grimaced with every touch of the lotion and decided the first thing he was going to do once the flow of blood had stopped was to make sure the back windows were all shut; he didn't want Hirohito or Chairman Meow climbing in at night and finding him asleep. He reckoned his chances of surviving a gun-toting, crackhead burglar would be better.

Several crimson, cotton wool pads later, Spencer surveyed the ravaged flesh before him. It was Drag Up and Boogey Down tomorrow and he looked like he had just been given a pedicure by Freddie Kruger. Heels were going to be torture.

CHAPTER 28

Troy struggled to shove a semi through his lucky cockring. He sat down again on the toilet and tried thinking about Drucilla naked. The blood started to drain from his swollen piece almost immediately.

He was glad to be getting out of this business, there was just too much to remember: the constant shaving of pits, sack and crack; dancing to music and smiling at the same time; the complicated costume changes.

With his dick soft again he forced it through the cockring and put it away. He checked to see if he had everything before leaving the cubicle: boots were on, cockring was on and jockstrap was in place. He was good to go.

Tonight's job was to bring on stage the contestants in an amateur talent competition. He had worked these things before and knew that amateur talent in a gay bar was a cross between an X Factor blooper tape and a tranny self-help group. But it was helping pay the rent and he didn't have to remember any names.

Valkeyre was snorting a heaped spoonful of coke from her little brown bottle when Troy got back to the dressing room. He would have loved a line, but even the old trick of asking someone to help you into your cockring hadn't worked; the resulting erection that had him seeking out a private cubicle was for the possibility of coke, not Valkeyre. At least that's what he hoped. She had shovelled four lines into her face in front of him without so much as acknowledging she was doing it, let alone offering any, and try as he did, the only thing his continuous nose rubbing and twitching had got him was the offer of a tissue. He thought he'd try one last charm offensive.

"So are you going to Drag Up and Boogey Down tomorrow,

Valkeyre?"

Valkeyre's lip curled. "Do you really think I wear this shit for fun?" She gestured to her armoured drag and flicked one of the blonde ponytails that draped from her helmet.

Troy could see this one slipping away from him; he wasn't used to this happening. "I thought you might be headlining in one of the cabaret tents."

Valkeyre, apparently seeing through the line like a wet tee-shirt, shoved her coke bottle into her Lois Vuitton bum bag and did some final adjustments to her makeup.

"Could you offer me any tips? I'm going for a laugh with some mates and I've never done drag before."

"You've never done drag?" Valkeyre's face lit up as she smiled at Troy in the mirror. "You're going to have the most wonderful time. There's nothing more uplifting than men coming together through their love of the freedom of frocks."

Troy relaxed. He knew he would crack the old boot eventually. There wasn't a gay man born he couldn't charm with a smile and a flash of his cock. He smiled and moved closer, hooking his thumb over the top of his jockstrap. "Really?"

"No, you stupid queen! It's a park full of nancies and deviants, all trawling about with faces painted happier than the people behind them. Gay men dressing up in frocks is a pathetic cliché." Valkeyre stroked her eyelashes with mascara. "And straight men doing it are just a lippy and a camisole away from divorce and a lifetime of therapy and alimony."

Now confused, Troy had no point of reference to deal with this kind of weirdo rejection. "But...but, you do it."

Valkeyre resheathed her mascara and turned to face Troy. "If you tell a joke, does it make you a comedian? No. If you piss on your ex-boyfriend when he's on fire, does it make you a fireman? 'Course it doesn't. But if a queen buys a dress from a charity shop, sticks on some lippy and gives himself a stupid fucking name like Desiré Dickwad, he thinks he's a friggin' drag queen. It's a bloody insult."

That reminded Troy, he needed to get some lippy.

"Ten minutes, Valkeyre," came a voice from outside the dressing room door. "And watch out for the four lesbians in the front. They wouldn't take plastic glasses."

Valkeyre finished touching-up and zipped everything into her bum bag. The untrusting glance she cast Troy as she tucked the bum bag into another bag was enough to tell him that a line had never been on the cards.

Valkeyre got up and lifted her shield. "Once you've brought them on stage to me I don't want you mincing about flashing you ass. If you wanna sell it, get an ad in *QX*."

"Okay." Troy smiled. "Break a leg." He hoped it would be in at least four places.

Valkeyre's signature tune started up from the stage. Troy thought she said it was by someone called Vagnir. It was quite a famous piece of music, apparently. He headed for the dust-thick curtain that passed for stage wings and waited for his cue. Peering round the curtain at the crowd, Troy could see it wasn't a very busy night. The only man he could see who looked remotely attractive was sitting with the lesbians. He counted the lesbians: one...two...three... It seemed there were no attractive men in tonight.

A loud clatter came from the stage. Troy jumped, hitting the curtain and getting dust all over his oiled torso. He looked around for something to wipe himself with. He didn't want to get dirt streaks on his tits if he sweated; it would look like fake tan running.

There was an even louder crash from the stage. Someone in the audience screamed. The floor started to rumble and vibrate and more dust shook from the curtains onto Troy. It was getting in his hair now. This was really pissing him off.

The rumbling got worse. Metallic clattering of what sounded like pots and pans came from the stage. He thought it was an earthquake at first and was about to run for the dressing room doorway when he saw Valkeyre. She was flat on her back, arms and legs thrashing against the stage floor. Sparks were flying from her costume as it crashed against itself. Mesmerised, Troy just watched, thinking it was the oddest opening routine of any act he had ever seen. Valkeyre was a weird fucker.

With a final thundering judder, Valkeyre came to a halt. Her limbs clattered to the floor. Troy began to think this might not be part of the show.

Steve, the club's manager, rushed to pull a flimsy, glitter curtain across the stage. Valkeyre's boots still stuck out towards the audience. Steve started pulling at Valkeyre's armour in an apparent attempt to find flesh from which to take a pulse.

"Call an ambulance, you dip-shit!" Steve shouted at Troy.

Troy ran the five steps to the dressing room and grabbed his phone. Switching it on, he pulled Valkeyre's bum bag from its place of hiding.

He pressed 999.

Before shoving the bum bag into his duffel he looked inside. He stifled a *'Jackpot!'*. Asides the bottle of coke there was a bag with three wraps in it. And the lipgloss and mascara would save him a trip to Boots.

"Hi, yes, I need an ambulance…"

CHAPTER 29

The air over Brixton was thick in hairspray, no doubt providing it with its very own hole in the ozone layer after today, and from Bette's vantage point on the main stage she could see enough of the park to wonder if every man from across Europe who had ever hankered for the feel of nylons and lippy had pilgrimaged here. She had never seen so many drag queens, trannies and dressing-up box tragedies all in one place. Asides the dressing-up, the event had all the usual stuff for such an occasion: dance tents, cabaret tents, headliner stage, stalls and a fairground, but it all seemed to have been done with tongue placed firmly in pinched and blushed cheek. Even the hawkers, whose range of poppers, glow sticks and whistles, had lipgloss and waterproof mascara added to their stock.

Bette introduced Chlamydia de la Douche onto the stage and quickly climbed the stairs down to the park to head for the VIP tent for a quick glass of complementary champers and some peace and quiet, but before she had got as far as the last step a strangulated note jarred her and the crowd into a spontaneous grimace that travelled across the park in a facial Mexican wave; Chlamydia was brutalising her way through her first song, *I am what I am*. Chlamydia was the drag circuit's very own Ethel Merman. No musical note got past her vocal chords without being mutilated into a nails-down-chalkboard screech. Chlamydia was blissfully unaware of her breathtaking lack of musical talent and her unchallenged status as high priestess of the delusional, and for years had been accepting applause from her laughter-teared audiences in the name of her angelic voice. Singing lessons would have ended her career, and Bette would have gladly paid for them.

Every pitch-defying note Chlamydia tortured upon her audience seemed to vibrate the straps of Bette's shoes so they dug deeper into the cat-ravaged flesh of her ankles, but she strutted through the pain; in fact, there was a spring in her step just knowing that somewhere, maybe even at this very moment, Drucilla could be glossing her lips with cyanide. She held her face up to the sun as she went and smiled.

Up ahead, she could see the white picket fence that ran around the VIP tent. A breathtaking, shaven-headed, hunk of man meat gestured for her to come through as he opened the little gate in the fence for her. Her need to stare at him and feast on his aesthetic almost hurt. Feeling quite light-headed by her proximity to him, she wondered if it was possible to get high from simply looking at someone. She sashayed through, giving a playful smile as she slipped past. He winked back. Today was turning out to be such fun. Nothing could dampen Bette's spirits.

The VIP tent was much smaller in size than the others and had an altogether more sedate atmosphere. Smart waiters offered complementary drinks and at one end of the tent a dozen or so small tables sat before a well-catered finger buffet. The tables hosted a collection of barely C list celebrities and their friends whilst the rest of the tent was the usual networking media whores. A waiter thrust a tray of plastic champagne flutes at Bette. She took one.

With only a handful of people in drag, Bo was easy to spot in her fabulous fuchsia dress.

Bo waved over and took leave of the group she was talking to and weaved effortlessly through the crowd towards Bette. "*Dahling*, I'm so glad you could get away for a bit." She looked back at the crowd she had just left. A large, tearful drag queen with Shrek sized fingers was trying to extract a hanky from a tiny sequined purse. "And I simply had to get away from Janice."

"It's true, then," said Bette, "her place lost its licence?"

Bo nodded. "She tried everything she could to stop them dealing in there, but somehow the dealers still got the stuff in."

"I'm having a similar problem at The Dryer. I have no idea how it's getting in."

"Of course, Janice's bar manager keeling over dead of an overdose in the cottage didn't help her case."

Bette gestured her glass at the tent. "An odd mix."

"Yes," Bo said in a hushed voice, "industry voyeurs and reality TV contestants. It's all so frightfully dull. Where did all the talent go?" Bo sighed as she spotted a sharply dressed silver fox coming towards them. "Oh, talk of the devil, a man with the kind of talent one used to have to pay peanuts for."

"Hi," said the silver fox in a creamy transatlantic accent. He thrust his hand at Bette and eyed her up and down in the way straight men do when their dicks are arguing with their brains over why they shouldn't be attracted to her. He lingered for a moment along her legs, caressing them with his eyes where Bette knew all too well his hands wanted to be. "I'm Christian, Rob's new producer. You must be Spencer."

Bette seethed at his inappropriate use of name. "Pleasure's mine." She shook his perfectly manicured hand. "I've heard so many wonderful things about you."

Bo smiled and raised her glass at him.

"I wonder if we could do a bit with you backstage later, Spencer? You've just missed our camera crew here, they're off filming around the park now, but I'd really like to get some of you on film. Rob's been singing your praises. I feel as if I know you already..." his eyes strayed to her legs again, "and Rob doesn't do you justice."

"I'd love to."

"Okay, then." He looked up. "Say in an hour?"

Bette nodded casually, as if this sort of thing happened to her with tiresome regularity, whilst in her head she screamed with glee.

"I'm really looking forward to seeing the rushes for today," said Christian. "There's some utterly outrageous characters wandering about out there. You know there are nine camera crews in the park from six different countries. You've not agreed to be interviewed by anyone else, have you?"

"No," said Bette, stroking a seductive finger along Christian's forearm in a gentle warning shot of pronoun boundaries, "I'm all yours." She could feel him tense, thrill and shiver all at the same time. *That ought do it*, she thought.

"So why aren't you *out there* taking it all in, Christian, *dahling*?"

"I'm keeping out of the crew's way. You know them, Rob. The director prefers me low profile."

"Really...? Well, why don't Bette and I take you on a little wander through the park and introduce you to some of the community's more..." Bo paused for effect, her trademark raised eyebrow peaking to emphasise her inevitable punchline, "...*colourful* characters?" Bette noticed Bo's eyebrow seemed to twitch and stammer back into place.

"I'm fine here, Rob. I should really wait for the__"

"Scares you, *dahling*, doesn't it?"

Bo moved closer to Christian so their height differential became sharply apparent. They locked in a stare. Bette had no idea what was going on, but she was loving the front row seats.

Christian knocked back his champagne. The muscles on the side of his face clenched and unclenched. "Okay, okay, it scares the living crap out of me. I thought this was just going to be a cutesy, camp, dress up for a laugh sort of thing. Just coming in here I saw a huge transsexual pulling three guys in rubber shorts along by a chain attached to their nipples."

Bo and Bette looked at each other and chorused: "*Dame Judy.*" Bette noticed Bo's eyebrow stammering again.

"Who?" said Christian.

"Dame Judy Drench," said Bette. "High class dominatrix who specialises in training watersports slaves."

"For gay men?"

"Goodness no, *dahling*. Contrary to popular opinion, gay men are a lot more discerning that their straight counterparts."

"There can't be much call for that sort of thing. The heterosexual/transsexual/watersports/dominatrix thing, I mean. Must be a very small market."

"She has a two year waiting list to see her, *dahling*."

Christian paled.

Bette noticed Bo's eyebrow twitching. "You've had more work done, haven't you?"

"How charming of you to notice. It was a little impulse purchase when I was in Milan."

"Shoes are an impulse purchase, Bo."

"*Dahling*, I have more than enough shoes. It's youth that's in short supply."

"I dunno," smirked Christian, "I hear *he's* keeping you in good supply of youth." He nodded triumphantly over at Bo's actor turned model. The ATM stood rigid with fear as Ursula Muffcross (the famous transsexual, sword-swallowing contortionist) stroked his ear with her big toe. "Seems like you're getting enough *youth* in you not to need surgeons."

Bo looked down on Christian with an icy glare. "Consider yourself lucky I'm not claiming on expenses - the word around the office is that you think I'm looking 'tired'."

Bette jumped in before Christian could respond. "So what did you have done?"

"It's a new treatment pioneered by the wonderful Dr Gaspard Fontaine. The man's a genius. He's known by the Hollywood A-list as the Fontaine of Youth. It's a course of injections, no surgery, and it's guaranteed to take off ten years. And before you get all huffy," she turned on Christian, "it hasn't been tested on animals."

"What has it been tested on, then?" said Bette.

"The Kurds I should imagine. It's a nerve toxin Dr Fontaine came across whilst working in Iraq. He's treating half the Spanish Royal family, you know. And I'm__"

"So," Christian cut in, "Bette, did you know this Valkeyre Te Kanawa character?"

"Valkeyre, why?"

"Oh, *dahling*, haven't you heard? She's dead. Did a Tommy Cooper and keeled over on stage. Frightful shame."

"So you didn't know him?" Christian repeated.

"Not really," said Bette.

"Do you know what he died of, Rob?"

"An overdose of some kind I should imagine. The poor creature's had two that I know of. Why are you so interested?"

"Oh, nothing, just another angle on the story here."

"*Dahling*, the 'story' today is simple: Pied Piper of Tat lures thousands of men into park in South London. Give it up, you're stuck making very light entertainment with dreary old me. Your days of cutting edge documentaries were over the day you flashed Moira Stewart at a Christmas party."

"I did not flash Moira Stewart! It was a complete misunderstanding and I__"

"Rufus, *dahling*," Bo waved over at a couple who had just arrived, "loved the play."

"Is that who I think it is, Christian?" said Bette.

"If you think it's an ageing actor in a play for which they virtually can't give away tickets," said Bo, "then yes, it is."

"Not him, the flouncy queen with him."

"That's 'Sir' flouncy queen, to you," said Christian.

"I'd better go say hello, *dahlings*."

"Yeah, I should get back to the stage," said Bette. "See your crew in an hour, Christian...?"

Christian nodded half-heartedly and walked off in a sulk.

Bette sashayed out towards the picket fence and her flirtatious hunk; a quick wink would recharge her battery. Unfortunately, his replacement swung open the gate without so much as a smile. His tattooed knuckles of 'love' and 'hat'- the 'e' from 'hate' missing along with the finger upon which it was once tattooed – had little of the well-groomed style of his predecessor. Bette felt the straps of her shoes dig into her wounds. She could feel the day turning.

CHAPTER 30

In the name of the audience's mercy, Bette decided to cut Chlamydia's encores short. She had been about to take to the stage to get her off when someone tapped her on the shoulder.

"There's a change to the running order," said the assistant stage manager, whose gender Bette hadn't quite ascertained.

"Don't say 'running' order, Sam." Bette pointed to her sore feet. "Can't we call it the walking-at-a-sedate-and-comfortable-pace order?"

"Call it whatever you like, darlin', but once Chlamydia's finished you've to introduce Drucilla."

"Drucilla?"

"Yeah, she's only on for a couple of minutes. It's about her friend, Stella. We couldn't refuse under the circumstances."

Bette thought the rush of adrenaline might have dulled the pain in her ankles a little, but it didn't. Drucilla wasn't supposed to be anywhere near the stage today; Bette's alibi that she never came in contact with her all day was now compromised.

Drucilla came into view over Sam's shoulder. She was wearing a silver sequined jumpsuit and her wig had been spiked and metallic sprayed. She was like a glitterball with feet. The only flash of colour was scarlet lips and a red Hermes Berken strung ostentatiously over her left forearm.

"Well, I'd__" Bette was silenced by a bloodcurdling '*Gollllllllldfinguuurrrrrr*' from the stage. When the note eventually died Bette couldn't remember what she had been about to say; Chlamydia's voice would have had Martin Luther King forgetting what he had dreamt.

"I won't take up much of your time," said Drucilla, in a voice that sounded on the verge of tears. "I just want to say a few words about Stella. If that's okay?"

Sam smiled supportively at Drucilla and left her to Bette.

"How long do you need?" said Bette, trying to get a good look at Drucilla's lips.

Drucilla watched Sam disappear from view before answering. "Just introduce me, you streak of uric acid."

"Thought as much." In the shade of backstage, Bette couldn't tell if she had applied recently. "You didn't strike me as the grieving type."

"Keep out of my way I won't have to strike you at all."

Chlamydia was macheteing her way to the end of her song. If she tortured her audience any longer the organisers would have been up in front of a jury at The Hague.

"You've got two minutes," said Bette. "And then I'm opening the trap door." Bette took to the stage.

Chlamydia didn't want to get off. Despite blood almost pouring from the ears of those nearest the front, the crowd were still egging her on for more.

"I have CDs available at_"

Bette ripped the mike from Chlamydia's hand.

"Let's hear some big love for London's 'big' voice," said Bette. Then, off mike, "Get off, you demented bitch."

The crowd booed at Bette as Chlamydia shuffled from the stage. Bette took it in her stride; this was traditionally what happened to any compere wherever Chlamydia performed.

Once she had the audience back under control, Bette ran through the rest of the afternoon's highlights in double quick time, keeping watch out of the corner of her eye in case Drucilla looked like she was about to apply anything to her lips.

They didn't so much as glance at each other as they passed on stage. Bette moved into the wings and out of sight of the stage to sit down and kick off her shoes; the pain was building and the straps now felt as if they were chewing through to the bone. Massaging her ankle, she spotted Drucilla's bag. It was under the chair next to her. Curiosity gnawed at her. Did she have the lipgloss with her? Was she going to keel over dead by the end of today? Was her plan already in action and it was all just a matter of hours...or less? She needed to know.

Checking no one was looking, and keeping an ear out for Drucilla's voice still droning on from the stage, Bette hooked the bag with her foot and pulled it out from under the chair. Careful not to leave any fingerprints, she unzipped the bag with a disposable hanky then lifted one of her shoes and poked it in to see what was inside. Amongst all the handbag crap was an asthma inhaler, hankies, her phone, various bits of makeup and...Bette had to do a double take; there were two huge wads of notes. Without thinking, she reached in and pulled one out; it must easily have been a couple of grand. *Who was the devious bitch paying off with this,* she wondered?

"Find anything interesting?" came Manthrax's unmistakably nasal voice.

Bette's blood ran cold. Manthrax was coming up the side steps to the stage, her tattooed arms crossed over her sleeveless dress, framing the words 'I don't do mingers' on the cleavage. She walked over and grabbed the wad of cash and the bag. "You skanky, thieving, bitch." She threw the cash into the bag.

"It's not what you think. I was just so moved by what Drucilla was saying about Stella. I needed a hanky." She waved the hanky she was holding.

Manthrax's overly pencilled eyebrows arched. She smiled. Bette tuned in to what Drucilla was saying for the first time. She was shamelessly plugging her night at The Tumble Dryer.

"You really are desperate scum, ain't ya?"

Bette's mouth opened in preparation for words. All that came out was a pathetic squeak. She could smell the faint odour of an oncoming avalanche of shit; if anything happened to Drucilla now, Manthrax was witness to Bette having gone through her bag.

"Cat got your tongue?" said Manthrax.

Bette grabbed her mike and headed for the stage barefoot. Drucilla passed her without acknowledgement. Bette had no time for any showbiz warm-up. She knew she couldn't let Drucilla out of her sight; she had to get the lipgloss back. If anything happened to her now, Bette would be the first one they suspected, and Manthrax would make damn sure of it.

"A big round of applause for..." Bette went blank; she could see Drucilla leaving with Manthrax. Manthrax was demonstrating how she found Bette rummaging in the bag and finding the wad of notes, "for...for...our next fabulous act." She gestured to a furious looking little potato-head man and exited the stage.

She checked her watch. She had twenty minutes before she needed to be back on stage. Malee was on next and Bette was supposed to be doing a costume change, but retrieving the lipgloss had to take priority. She pulled on her shoes and headed out into the park.

Ducking and weaving through the multitude of big hair and tacky drag, Bette came to a halt when she saw Drucilla stopping up ahead. Manthrax was nowhere to be seen. In an attempt to remain inconspicuous Bette joined the end of a huge queue for the portaloos.

Drucilla had stopped to speak to a quartet of trannies who had laid out a gingham spread and had unpacked two large picnic baskets: there was champagne, crystal glasses, china plates, crustless sandwiches and petit fours on a silver cake stand, each item precisely positioned in a ballet of manners and gentility. The scene could have been straight out of *Pride and Prejudice*, if it hadn't been for the bricklayers' hands dwarfing the delicate flutes of bubbly with which they toasted each other and Drucilla. Manthrax appeared beside her with a can of cider and Drucilla bid her farewells, handing back the crystal flute.

Bette's heartbeat thumped in her ears, almost drowning out the sound of the potato-head man's singing as she moved away from the toilet queue. *What the fuck am I going to do,* she asked herself? *Maybe, if I just keep following her, when I see her going to apply I can bump into her and knock the lipgloss out of her hand.* Bette knew it was a crap plan, a really crap plan, but it was all she had to stop herself from losing it and running up and ripping the bag from Drucilla's chubby fingers.

Various people were nodding hello and trying to catch Bette's eye as she followed Drucilla through the crowd. Ignoring them all, she kept her focus on the red bag. She watched as it weaved through the bustle of manmade fibres and cheap feather boas, keeping it firmly in sight as one badly made up face after another smiled past in a macabre clown's convention of cross-dressed eagerness. Gangs of friends minced about in the safety of their own costumed numbers, and within each group Bette noticed one or two peer pressured faces aglow with awkward forced-happiness. Then, outside the *Ladies Who Launch* tent, Bette saw Mandy, being embraced by Drucilla.

Bette watched from a distance as they were surrounded by a gaggle of drag queens. Drucilla introduced Mandy to each of them, getting him to hand out what appeared to be his business cards.

The sense of overwhelming betrayal hit Bette; it was a bitch slap to the heart. Her eyes hurt with the sting of tears demanding to be set free. She hadn't quite believed it up until now, but there he was: Judas at the all-you-can-eat-last-supper buffet. Bette's stomach churned as she was forced to watch.

Mandy bid his farewell to Drucilla when Manthrax appeared out of the tent. Drucilla and Manthrax moved on. Mandy spotted Bette and beamed a smile. He bounded over.

"You were right about coming here today," he said, "I'm having the best day."

"Got yourself some new friends, too, I see."

His arm was grabbed before he had a chance to reply.

"This is the bonna homie Drucilla's been telling us all about, Davina," said a drag queen in an excruciatingly over-affected manner. "What he can't do with fur fabric just isn't worth knowing." She said this to another drag queen whom Bette vaguely recognised as a regular on the amateur circuit.

Mandy blushed.

"It's Bette, isn't it?" said Davina. Bette nodded. Davina gave a tiny wave by rippling the fingers on her right hand. Bette wanted to punch her. "So this is the little genius who keeps you gorgeous. No wonder you've been keeping him all to yourself. He's adorable." Davina pinched Mandy's cheek.

"She's not been keeping me all to herself," said Mandy. "I don't know where I'd be without Bette."

"I've heard you can do with a sewing machine what Delia can do with plain flour and a muffin tray," said the one Bette recognised. "Here, that's my card. Call me. I've got some work for you and I'd__"

"Pushy bitch," said Davina. "I've got this bonna silk damask that's just itching to be made into something mega."

Bette thought it highly unlikely Davina had anything 'bonna'; otherwise why would she be standing in an outfit that could only be described as outsized tragic.

"Anyway," said Davina, "call us." They minced off.

Seeing Drucilla almost slipping from sight, Bette realised she didn't have time for little Judas.

"I was just coming down to see you," said Mandy.

"Really? I'll see you down there, then." Bette turned on her heels and tore off in Drucilla's direction, leaving Mandy with a bemused expression.

Drucilla was heading towards the market place. Blood was now running down Bette's shins. She took off her shoes and threw them in the nearest bin.

Bette's throat was dry and crackling. Her eyes continued to sting. She had thought Mandy was someone she could trust. Raw with anger, betrayal, and the pain of bleeding feet, she kept after Drucilla, fuming at her ability to cause chaos. How much more was Drucilla going to take from her?

Weaving through the crowds, Bette had no idea what she was doing now. Her brain had given up looking for a plan, and to top it all she was going to have to go and introduce Malee shortly: Malee and her one hit wonder; Malee and her perfect figure; Malee and her beautiful bloody hair.

A drag queen, who looked like a six-year-old who'd found his mother's makeup bag, said hello. Bette ignored him and continued into the market place after Drucilla.

The market place was a myriad of stalls designed to tempt monies from the wannabe crossdresser, drag queen, gay man or collector of crap. The usual Camden Market, New Age garbage was here, alongside feather boas, dildos, basques and bangles. Drucilla stopped at a stall. Bette turned to the one nearest to her and pretended to shop. She lifted a wig block.

"That one's called the Monaco Mullet," said the 'girl' behind the Hair Apparent stall. "It's based on Princess Stephanie of Monaco. It's real human hair, from Thailand. And it has a certificate to prove the hair's not from any tsunami victims. There was a lot of those about a few years ago."

Bette hadn't even noticed what she was looking at; her eyes were trained on the red Berken three stalls down. Drucilla still hadn't reapplied lipgloss. "I was looking for something a little less butch."

Drucilla was paying for something on the Safe and Sound stall. From what Bette could make out from where she was, it sold personal alarms and pepper sprays.

"What about our Balmoral range?" said the assistant.

Drucilla was moving on.

"No thanks. I think I'll stick with my own."

Bette turned to follow Drucilla.

"Excuse me," said the sale's assistant, pointing at the wig block in Bette's hand. "Unless you're buying..."

Nodding a quick apology, and trying not to let the bag out of her sight, Bette turned to replace the wig block. Something squished between her toes and squelched across the sole of her bare foot. That was when it happened. That was when she saw red.

CHAPTER 31

Bette was almost tearing her hair out at the roots; she couldn't find her passport. She knew it was just a matter of time before the police came knocking at her door, and after what happened today, Manthrax would be all too eager to point an accusing finger when Drucilla eventually keeled over. Escape seemed the only option. Bette knew she couldn't cope with life in a high security prison. No access to good quality cleansers and moisturisers would be death row for her skin tone, and she had never forgotten what prison had done to Myra Hindley's hair; a couple of weeks without conditioning and straightening and she would be frizzing upwards and outwards like a 70's Motown star on rehab.

She lifted the joint from the ashtray and relit it. She had to decide where she was going; her wardrobe needed planning. Hiding out on the Brazilian drag circuit seemed a good option, or maybe Thailand.

"Oh flag down a spaceship and hitch a lift back to planet Earth," she screamed to the room. "You're a black drag queen, for Christ's sake. Hiding from Interpol in a Bangkok revue show ain't gonna work."

Her hand shook as she drew hard on the joint. The frightening choice before her was simple enough: if she wanted to evade imprisonment, she couldn't take her drag. But was it too great a sacrifice for liberty? How could she possibly choose?

The phone rang. She waited for the machine to take it.

"Ooooh, girlfriend," came Anaesthesia's voice, "I just left Brixton and you've pissed off some people today. What happened to you, girl? Did you really twat Drucilla with a wig block and try to steal her bag?" Bette sunk deeper into the sofa as she remembered the hollow pop of the polystyrene wig block as it smacked against Drucilla's head; the dog shit had pushed her over the edge. The cab driver who took her home after she ran from the park wasn't too pleased with it, either. "It was all goin' on today, girl. After you vanished someone dropped dead in the *Whips 'n' eyelashes* tent. I haven't found out who yet, but with any luck it might be Drucilla. Anyway, I'm out to meet a man off Gaydar. Says he's only twenty-six and has a swimmer's build. I've told him I'm ten years younger and carrying a few extra pounds, so wish me luck." Anaesthesia hung up.

Bette checked the time. It was just after 1am. She went through to the bedroom and took one last look at herself in the mirror before taking off the dress in which she'd run from the park. Was this the end of the line for Bette? Was it over? Was it all destroyed?

She stomped through to Bette's room and stared at the rows of dresses, the shelves of bags and shoes, the makeup, the years of her life that were to be abandoned if she had any chance of escaping prison. She sat down before the mirror and scooped a handful of crème. It was cold to the touch, a cold she knew would travel straight to her heart the moment it touched her face. She rubbed the crème in her fingers, wondering if she was destined to spend her time in Hell as part of a double act with Drucilla: *Captain Ahab and Tineal*. She stripped down to her underwear and prepared to take off her face for the last time.

Twenty minutes later and she was still sitting before the mirror, makeup remover now dripping through her fingers and her balls popping out either side of her g-string in a classic camel's hoof formation. Each time she had tried to lift her hand near her face she started to shake. She watched in the mirror as tears freed themselves from her eyes and ran down her cheeks; her makeup cushioned their sensation, allowing her not to accept them as hers. Through blurred eyes she stared in the mirror at the tears, hating and pitying them at the same time.

She let out a scream and swiped her arm across the dressing table. The instruments of Bette's creation were thrown across the room. Face powder filled the air in a Max Factor snow storm. The open tub of makeup remover splashed against the full-length mirror, splattering it as if a giant seagull had shit on it from above. She threw herself at one of the costume rails and tore a dress from its hanger. She gripped its material between her teeth, gnawing at a seam until a tear started. She gripped both sides of the tear and tried to rip the dress apart. Her hands, which were still covered in makeup remover, slipped from the sequins. She turned to the mess on the floor and dropped to her knees in search of scissors. She couldn't find any. She screamed again and grabbed what was closest, throwing herself at the dress and stabbing it with a makeup brush and an eyeliner pencil until they snapped in her hands.

She collapsed onto the floor beside the dress and wept.

A familiar sound stopped her mid-wail as she came up for her third breath of snotty, inconsolable sobbing. She turned on her knees and scrambled through the carnage on the floor for the source of the sound.

"Spencer," came the tinny voice from her mobile, "Spence, what's going on…Spencer…SPENCE…BETTE!"

Bette grabbed the ravaged dress, smearing what was left of it with white crème before lifting the phone. "Hello." She wiped her nose on her arm.

"Girl, you okay?" said Anaesthesia. "What's all the screaming about? I thought I was listening to you being murdered."

"Sorry, Anaesthesia…I'm…I…I was watching a Farrah Fawsett movie."

"Oooh, which one?"

"Er…I think it's…*Who will love my crippled children while my drunken husband beats me*…or something."

"I like that one."

Bette brushed some perfume bottles aside and sat on the floor. "Did my phone call you again?"

"Looks like it, girl. S'okay, though, I've just left a shag's place. Twenty-six and a swimmer's build: I don't think so. She was forty-two with an eating disorder. Twenty-six was her waist. I'd have snapped that twig in two if I'd jumped on it. So what happened to you today? And why haven't you called me? I was sick with worry…I thought I was missing out on this season's big gossip."

"It's a long story. I'm not feeling very well…" Bette paused. She needed to know. She needed to know before she went completely mad; if Bette was to be wiped from her face for the last time, if she was to vanish from the mirror totally, she needed to hear the news of Drucilla's demise through Bette's ears; if this was to be her last pleasure, she wanted to savour it. "So do you know who died at the park?"

"Carmen Monoxide told me. She called me just as I was going into the shag's place. You'll never guess. When Carmen told me you could have knocked me down with an unfunny barb… Poor Shirley Brassey."

"Shirley?" Bette was confused. "Shirley's dead?"

"No, Shirley's not dead."

"Then what has she got to do with it?"

"She's got alopecia."

Bette struggled to keep hold of the conversation. "What's that got to do with someone dying?"

"You know Troy, the little muscle mary from the Tumble Dryer, donkey dick and mosquito brain?"

"Yeah, I know him."

"He had some kind of fit up on a podium. Went arse over stilly and broke his neck. If I've said it once, girl, I've said it a hundred times: stillies are dangerous in the hands of amateurs."

"So what's that got to do with Shirley?"

"On the way down he hit Shirley and tore her wig straight off. The whole world knows about her alopecia now."

Unsure whether she felt relieved or disappointed, Bette persevered. "So what about Drucilla? Do you know if she called the police?" Bette expected Drucilla to accuse her of trying to steal the cash.

"She's makin' all sorts of noise about you having assaulted her and trying to rob her. But she said nothing about any cash. And she didn't call the police."

"But she's okay?"

"It was a polystyrene wig block you hit her with, not a crowbar. She's fine. More than fine, I'd say."

"Huh?"

"As you legged it from the park, she legged it for the stage and offered her services to do the compering job you left."

The phone almost slipped from Bette's hand. "What!?"

"What were they supposed to do, girl? You'd vanished and she offered. You've done yourself no favours. And her and Malee got interviewed by some film crew who were looking for you."

Bette's heart sank; she had turned into a pathological career self-harmer.

"You still there, girl?"

Bette nodded despondently and then grunted at the phone.

"So tell me, girl, what happened to you? Was it a bad E? 'Cos I had one of those a couple of weeks ago. After I threw up I had to take a vallium. I was convinced I was Vivian Leigh. Tara was burning and I was__"

"I've got to go, Anaesthesia. Farrah's husband's just arrived home."

"Oh, don't, you'll have me bawlin'. We'll speak tomorrow."

Bette switched off the phone. She stood up and grabbed a towel from a shelf and wiped her hands. Knowing Drucilla couldn't have gone all day without reapplying, the lipgloss must have got lost when they were fighting over the bag; a lot of its contents did get scattered on the grass.

She turned to the mirror. She was a mess. A cocktail of face powders covered her from head to toe, robbing her hair of its normal lustre and making her look as if she had been aged for a low-budget, B movie. She shook her hair and sat down. The face in the mirror was dishevelled and war torn, but Bette smiled at it like a parent who had just saved their child from running into the road. Drucilla had nearly destroyed her. She had nearly extinguished Bette altogether; it had been moments away.

She shook her hair again. What did she think Spencer could have done without her? What life could he have had when the only thing *he* could put down on a CV was 'walk perfectly in six inch heels'? His only skill *is* Bette. Going on the run in flats would never have worked.

The air in the room was thick with cosmetic powder; it was as dry as a SAGA orgy. A drink was called for.

The JD in the kitchen offered little in the way of refreshment. The pitiful vapour in the bottle mocked her need for alcohol. Unprepared to abandon the idea of a drink just yet, Bette opened cupboard doors looking for the stash of miniatures she'd handbagged from the drink's promotion. She found them. Quite a stock, actually.

It took three miniatures before she stopped exhaling powder. *This must be how Catherine Zeta Jones feels after she's blown her hubby*, she thought. She opened a fourth and poured this one into a glass. She sipped slowly.

The throbbing in her temples, which had started in the park, eased as she opened the fifth miniature. She smiled; she never thought she would be happy to hear Drucilla was alive. She realised her future and everything she had ever worked for had been gambled on half-deranged plans to commit murder. What had she been thinking? What had she been doing? She wasn't going to allow herself to go down that road again, no sir. She knocked back her drink. Next time it would be done right, and she wanted to see it when it did.

CHAPTER 32

Spencer opened his eyes. The room was dark. He could just make out the subdued sparkle of a face powder-dusted dress hanging on the back of the bedroom door. He switched on the bedside light and pulled back the duvet. He needed to pee. He swung himself out of bed and stumbled past the chest of drawers, momentarily questioning why it had makeup removers and cosmetics on it before remembering the mess in Bette's room; it had been easier to transfer stuff through here.

He made his way to the loo, switching lights on as he went. After his piss he watched the pink disinfectant spiralling round the bowl and imagined it to be his own little tornado that had come to whisk him off to Oz.

He stopped at the breakfast bar on the way back to the bedroom. The empty remains of ten packs of cigarettes were scattered across its surface. The bold face letters across the torn packs announced that 'SMOKING KILLS'. He checked the time. He had twenty minutes before the off-licence shut and he knew he was going to need a drink when he woke up properly.

The sound of the post snapping through the letterbox woke Spencer with a start. It was the second morning he had found himself naked on the sofa, and day three of his let's-kill-off-the-liver tour. He pushed an empty bottle of JD along the sofa, distancing himself physically if not psychologically. A cigarette paper detached from his cheek and fluttered to the floor as he grunted and stood to face the mirror above the fireplace. He was a Cabbage Patch doll: his face was puffy with piggy eyes and his hair looked like it had been styled by a three-year-old on an inadequate dose of Ritalin.

"You win, Ike," he said to the mirror. "Keep the name." He

grabbed the bottle and checked for residue.

He went to the kitchen, leaving the decision of whether he would have coffee or alcohol until he got there.

Saucepans sat in rows on the kitchen worktops. Each was filled with the soggy contents of counterfeit Marlboros. Behind them stood a half-pint glass, quarter full of a yellowish liquid resembling that of 'morning after' urine.

The kettle needed filling. He lifted a bottle of JD and poured its content remains into a mug and returned to the sofa.

He was beginning to loathe himself with the kind of passion he had once reserved for the Young Conservatives. He couldn't face the world yet, not after his humiliating performance at the weekend, and he couldn't trust himself to go any further than the off-licence, not while his kitchen was an Al Qaeda cookery school. He had tried, and failed, to convince himself he was nothing more than a victim of the information superhighway, corrupted by easy access to too much information that wasn't safe for the public domain. Once upon a time it was only pinch-faced doctors with dark, socialite pasts in Agatha Christie novels who had access to lethal toxins, but nowadays it seemed anyone with an Internet connection and a forty a day habit could brew enough poison to wipe out everyone in the library and have enough left over for the guests in the drawing room. Some things should be on a need-to-know basis. A point proven by the fact he now knew nicotine poison was second only to that of cyanide and how to make it at home.

He spun the empty bottle that was sitting next to him on the sofa. It came to a halt pointing towards the hallway just as the intercom buzzed. He ignored it. It buzzed again. He didn't care if they got repetitive strain injury from pressing the button; he wasn't answering. After a few more attempts, it stopped.

He finished the mug of JD and was contemplating going to bed when the front door banged.

"I know you're in there, *dahling*." The door banged again. "I've brought myself a packed lunch, so I can sit here for hours until you open up."

Panic exploded in Spencer's head. He burst into frenzied

activity. Empty bottles were shoved behind speakers and under furniture, dirty glasses were stacked into cupboards, ashtrays were emptied, the tobacco mush in the saucepans was tossed into the waste disposal. He stopped. If he switched on the waste disposal the noise would give him away for sure, but he would be rid of the stuff, and he knew that was the right thing to do. He switched it on. The mush vanished.

"*Dahling*, I can hear you in there."

He ran to the bedroom and pulled on joggers and a tee shirt.

"If you have a man in there, *dahling*, I'm going to blab about your gold membership to the Dianna Ross fan club."

Still contemplating trying to sit it out, Spencer crept along the hall towards the front door. He stopped in front of the hall mirror for some reassurance that he didn't look like the maitre'd of a crack kitchen. The reflection told him it was an unrealistic job aspiration. His nerve broke as he heard a creak and he threw himself onto the floor. He crouched against the door with his head below the letterbox just as it opened.

"*Dahling*, open the door. I shouldn't be on my knees at my age. I get flashbacks to the early 80's and a best forgotten week on Fire Island."

Spencer held his breath.

"*Daaahling*, you really should run a brush through your hair. It's like a draught excluder."

Spencer reached up to feel his hair sticking vertically from his scalp.

Rob blew at it through the letterbox. "And some conditioner wouldn't go amiss."

"I can't see anyone, Rob. I look like shit and I feel worse."

"Open the door, now!" Rob's fingers stuck through the letterbox and grabbed a clump of hair. "Open it or I take out my nail scissors."

Spencer grasped his hair and reached up to unlock the door. "It's open, you mad bitch. Now let go."

The hair was released at the same time as the door thumped Spencer on the head. Rob pushed in.

"This is not a good look," Rob said, towering over Spencer's humiliated shell. With his Barbie lunchbox tucked under his Versace shirted arm, he strode past into the flat.

Spencer pulled himself from the floor and followed.

"Unless what I'm smelling is *Rancid Pit* by Lancôme, it might be efficacious to open a window and jump in the shower."

Rob's immaculate appearance and hint of expensive scent were oppressive.

"Rob, I'm not well. I'm not up for visitors."

"Yes, well," Rob sat his lunchbox on the coffee table, "visitors come when invited and leave when they're asked. I'm a friend, *dahling*, we come when least expected and stay until the injunction takes effect." He walked over to a speaker and pulled an empty bottle from behind it. "And if I'm not mistaken, if I moved your armchair I'd find more."

Spencer's eyes darted around the room; did Rob have hidden cameras?

Rob's eyebrow twitched and slumped. "*Dahling*, you're talking to someone who used to suck the alcohol out of a deodorant stick in an emergency. They used to frisk me at AA meetings for hip flasks. I know the signs. And they all point to the coastal town of Pisshead-on-Sea."

"Rob, I really am ill." Spencer was beginning to believe himself.

"I'm sure you are. And I'm equally sure if I sniffed that Winnie the Pooh mug there," he pointed at the empty mug, "I wouldn't smell Dowe Egbert's."

"I'll be okay in a few days."

"You'll be in need of a new liver in a few days." Rob seemed to be trying to form an expression his face was incapable of granting; one side of his face juddered up as the other spasmed to the side.

"What's with the face?"

Rob's expression reigned back into neutral. "We can talk once you've run a brush through your hair and smartened yourself up a bit." He pointed towards the bathroom.

Without the energy to fight, Spencer obeyed.

He didn't feel or look a whole lot better after the shower;

an agonising headache was almost blurring his vision and his hair had gone a day over the ability to fix it with a simple wash.

"Come along, *dahling*," Rob called from the other room, "we don't have all day. We need to be there by four."

Spencer snapped out of his unZen-like state of pulling and tugging at his hair and ran from the bathroom. "Where?"

"Stella's memorial."

The brush dropped from Spencer's hair. "I can't."

"You jolly well can. If you want to get the weekend's debacle behind you it's better to face the enemy now."

Spencer couldn't decide what was worse: attending the funeral of someone he murdered, or facing the public after going psycho-bitch. He remembered the pop of the wig block and decided facing Drucilla was worse.

"I can't. It'll be humiliating."

"Of course it'll be humiliating. What do you expect after that appalling behaviour? But it's the right thing to do and you're going to do it. I could just as easily have run from Madonna's hotel suit when she came back from taking a call and caught me sniffing her chair, but I didn't. I continued as a true pro and did the interview. Besides, if you play your cards right and brazen it out it'll be put down to celebrity eccentricity and your public will adore you for it. Queens love nothing more than a doolally tap diva. Come along, it's character building."

"Yeah, well, this character building thing, I think I'd like to re-examine my blue prints. I think I'm suffering from some design defects."

"Trust me. Not showing will just make things worse. Drucilla will make enough mileage from the weekend without you doing a no-show today. She's already making a thing about not having the police on you as being a favour to Norman Daniels. Don't give her any more ammunition."

Spencer knew there was little point expending energy arguing with Rob; he was probably going to need it all for later. "So what do we wear to something like this?"

"Well, when the late, great Regina Fong died," Rob genuflected, "it was a basic and respectful black all round...Sirena Mckellan did a beautiful speech at that memorial. It brought a tear to my eye with the working tear duct. You see, the higher up the drag tree one is, the less respectful it is to steal the limelight from the deceased."

"So are we wearing black?"

"Good Lord, no," Rob's voice rang with incredulity. "It was Stella, not Judy. She had no class in life and it seems she wanted to go out that way. Drucilla announced at the park...I believe you introduced her..." Bette cringed, "that the service was to be held at the Tumble Dryer and it was a dress up affair. Personally I think it's all rather tacky, but it's her funeral."

"So what are you wearing?"

"I'm wearing a divine little taupe, tasselled number. I bought the most fabulous shoes for it when I was in Milan." Rob's enthusiasm for the new shoes only registered in his voice; his face sagged expressionless.

"Have you had your face looked at?"

Rob pulled a smile together. "Let's have a little pact today, shall we? I won't ask why you attacked Drucilla with a lump of polystyrene and tried to steal her handbag like a mad crack whore, and you don't draw attention to my toxin filled face sliding off my skull."

Spencer nodded.

Rob picked up his lunchbox and tucked it back under his arm. "I'll be back for you in a couple of hours."

"I'd better start on my hair, then."

Rob looked him up and down. "I said a *couple* of hours, *dahling*. Wear a hat."

Bette got made-up in the bedroom. She decided to go for basic black by donning the same outfit she had worn to Dolce's funeral. It also had the added advantage of having been in the bedroom when everything else got covered in face powder.

With a brief let-up in the hangover proving little more than a tease, Bette pulled on her dark glasses and went to the kitchen for some paracetamol.

The clickity clack of her heels across the kitchen floor had a reassuring sound. She felt grounded again. Knocking back the paracetamols, she spotted something tucked away beside the breadbin: the quarter full glass of nicotine poison.

Bette lifted the glass and stared in at its contents. If she didn't finish the job it would be like Germaine Greer only burning one cup of her bra. She swilled the liquid around in the glass. It left a yellowish syrup sticking to the sides. This was divine providence; she saw the perfect opportunity. It had all the elements she needed.

She opened the breadbin and pulled out a half full bottle of Drambuie. She then took a funnel from a drawer and decanted the nicotine into the Drambuie.

With some minor alterations, Bette thought this could be even better than her original plan. The tributes and eulogies would no doubt be delivered from the stage, which meant everyone would move away from the bar. She tipped the bottle back and forth a few times to mix the contents. Once everyone was rapt in mournful insincerity, she could swap the poisoned bottle for the one Drucilla keeps behind the bar. Then, with Bo attracting her usual attention, they would move as far away from the bar as possible and wait. Once Drucilla has done her piece, she would no doubt return to the bar for a drink. The barman would pour her a Drambuie and in the inevitable screeching confusion that would follow her keeling over, Bette would swap the bottles back. With nothing in the bottle, the finger would point to someone having poisoned her glass. Plenty people would witness Bette being nowhere near when the drink was poured. This was perfect. It couldn't fail.

CHAPTER 33

"If she could have got this many people to come see one of her shows when she was alive she might not have been such a miserable bitch," said Bette, who was horrified at the amount of people who had turned up at the Tumble Dryer.

"Yes," said Bo, "people are so supportive once you're dead."

Bette scanned the bar and dancefloor. It was packed. The quiet gathering of mourning sycophants that Bette had expected was a cross between a pantomime dames' convention and a sink estate protest march. How was she going to swap the Drambuie in this? The shoulder bag with the bottle suddenly felt heavy. "I don't get it. No one liked her. Who are all these people?"

"It is a rather surprising turnout. Maybe she owed them all money."

"Shall we get some drinks?" Bette was anxious to get a place near the bar so she could reappraise her plan.

"Just mineral water for us both, I think." Bo's face stammered a warning look.

"You need to get that seen to."

"*Dahling*, I'm fine. It's just settling."

Bette raised her eyebrow in a playful impression. "Really, *daaahling*?"

Bo attempted a frown, which ended up in a gurn, and pointed to the bar.

The end of the bar where Bette needed to be was being staked out by Drucilla and her cronies. Bette decided to keep a distance from her for the time being and pushed her way up to the bar and ordered two mineral waters. Something about Drucilla's furtive glances, even at a distance, seemed ill at ease.

Bo was deep in conversation with a Jackie Stallone clone in

a fur coat when Bette arrived back with the drinks.

"Bette, *dahling*, I want you to meet an old friend of mine, Lady Tena."

A wrinkled, bejewelled hand, the likes of which was last seen as Nefertari's tomb was opened, slowly appeared from the fur sleeve. "Charmed, I'm sure."

"Tena, this is my dearest sister, Bette Noir."

Bette shook the crepe paper hand, wondering if this was how Liz Taylor felt. "Pleased to meet you. And F.Y.I. I'm *luuuuvin'* the coat."

Lady Tena pursed her collagen, which was probably the only part of her face that could still move, and pulled her collar up around her neck. "Play your cards right, honey, and I'll let you try it on later. You look like a gal who should wear fur."

Bette loved her instantly.

"We must do lunch while you're in town, *dahling*. Otherwise we only ever get to see each other at funerals."

Lady Tena sighed. "This reminds me of the eighties." She gestured to the crowd. "Queens packing into funerals and memorials, hoping they're getting left the drag or the dildos." She turned to Bette. "You should have seen the butt plugs that came with this coat."

Bette stroked a fur sleeve covetously. "So long as it didn't stipulate in the will that I had to wear them at the same time, I could handle it."

Lady Tena nodded in Drucilla's direction. "Have you been over to offer your condolences yet?"

"Condolences!" Bette swished her hair at Bo in mock indignation. "I'm here under protest."

"Under protest," said Lady Tena, an expression almost registering on her face. "I'm here under false pretences: I was told it was Drucilla's funeral."

Bette couldn't think of another human being she had admired so much, so quickly.

"I need a drink before I go near her," said Lady Tena. "You still on Mother Nature's Babycham, Bo?"

"Yes, *dahling*, I'm still on the sparkling mineral water."

Tena nodded. "Just us then, Bette."

Lady Tena turned and sidled through the crowd to the bar. Bette watched as people stole a discreet stroke of the fur, each mouthing '*it's real*' to the person next to them.

"How do you two know each other?" said Bette, as a woman with a bleached mullet thrust a pen and a beer mat at Bo.

"We ran a club together in Bangkok for a while. It was just after Tena's sex change in the 70's." Bo signed the mat.

"You never told me you lived in Bangkok."

"We didn't really *live* there. We were deported after four months. Shame really - the club was just starting to take off."

Over the years, Bette had come to realise that getting to know Bo was like peeling an onion...with tweezers. "What did you do to get deported?"

"Neither of us is entirely sure. The charges were all in Thai, and we were frightfully drunk. But whatever it was, you weren't allowed to do it to, or with, an American serviceman and a robed monk within, or near, the grounds of a Royal Palace. Tena's father was rather high up in the Foreign Office so some strings were pulled and the whole thing was hushed up. I still can't bear to wear orange."

"I think I'm losing my drag-dar, Bo. I would have sworn Tena was a man."

"She is, *dahling*." Bo signed an autograph for a short avuncular man with his young 'nephew'. "She had it all put back about twenty years ago. Of course, I've not seen her since April Ashley's seventieth birthday bash, so who knows what's down there at the moment." Bo smiled and patted the man on his bald patch for him to move on.

"Here we go." Tena handed Bette two empty glasses. Then, in a move that reminded Bette of the Great Spondulli, Tena reached into her coat and produced a bottle of champagne. "I hate the domestic plonk you get in these places, so I always bring my own." She popped the cork with the ease of someone who has done this daily for decades and filled their glasses.

Bette simply adored Tena.

"Shall we?" said Bo, frowning at the champagne then pointing in Drucilla's direction.

Bette and Tena glanced at each other, and without a word or a flicker of body language knocked back their drinks. Tena refilled the glasses and gestured for Bo to lead the way.

Clutching her glass in one hand and the strap of her bag in the other, Bette focused on the back of Bo's dress and tried to ignore the nods and unsubtle points she was getting as they got closer to Drucilla. She tried convincing herself they were pointing at Bo or Tena but, as they drew closer, she saw someone miming her attack with the wig block.

Sherry and Manthrax stood either side of Drucilla. In cheap, dark suits it was the first time Bette had ever seen them in mufti. They were living proof that the gay 'good taste' gene, the one so venerated by styleless fag hags in need of semen, was a recessive one.

"*Bags* to the wall, girls," said Drucilla, clutching a tacky fake Fendi to her mourning marquee of a dress. "I'm surprised you could show your face here, Bette. I hope they've upped your medication for the day?"

"And...we're off," Tena said, before Bette could respond.

"Lady Tena, how are you?" Drucilla smirked at her henchmen. "Didn't I attend your funeral a couple of years ago, or are they just burying the body parts as they fall off?"

"Drucilla, *honey*," Tena's tone said everything her face couldn't, "always a joy to see you. And are these two gentlemen your Green Peace bodyguards? Very wise. I wondered why they were frisking us for harpoons when we came in."

Drucilla ignored Tena as her eyes drilled into Bette. "I've decided not to press charges on *you*. But if I so much as see you looking at me funny I'll tear you a new skinny, black ass."

"Now, now, now," Bo stepped forward, "we're all here to pay our respects." Bo pecked Drucilla on each cheek. "I'm deeply sorry for the loss of your dear friend. Having lost many friends of my own over the years, I know it's something that never gets any easier. You and Stella were so very close. We were all very fond of her. She was a great talent, original and inspirational and I know she will be sadly missed in the industry. Now, if there's anything I can do, you have to but ask." A stunned silence fell upon everyone in earshot as Bo stood rubbing Drucilla's acrylic-clad shoulder.

"I...well...thanks...I..." stammered Drucilla.

"'Scuse me gents," said a cute, spiky-haired blond in a dark suit and tie, "we need to get started, if that's okay?"

Drucilla nodded to Sherry and Manthrax and they all left in the direction of the stage.

Lady Tena stepped in front of Bo. "In a Swiss clinic right now there's a jar with a face in it that is registering horror."

"Unless the reason you kissed her is because you've got meningitis," said Bette, "I think we need an explanation."

"*Dahlings*, there's a time and a place. A little decorum, please." Bo sipped her drink and took a seat at the corner of the bar. "Girls, do either of you know how to send a dog mad?"

Bette and Tena shook their heads.

"You rap it on the nose and give it a chocolate. Drucilla will be chasing her tail all day after that."

Once again, Bette realised she had so much still to learn from Bo.

When the sound system hummed into life, people started to move away from the bar and down towards the dancefloor and the stage. Bette glanced over the bar to where Drucilla's bottle of Drambuie sat. It was still there, perched next to one of the glasswashers. She couldn't see how full it was, though; the bottle in her bag had to be roughly the same. If need be she would empty some in the loo to get it right.

"Shall we stay here?" said Bette.

"Suits me, honey." Tena plonked the bottle of champagne onto the bar.

Bo nodded.

The tributes started with a drag artist called Steve Cross, a representative of Bette's most loathed genre of drag: the ones who consider themselves such consummate *artistes* they don't need a stage name...or a leg wax. Steve read *Over the Rainbow*, in the form of a poem, dabbing his forehead with his bra pad now and again in an attempt to illicit inappropriate laughter. A ripple of applause broke out once he was finished.

"She played a victim of homophobic abuse in *Casualty* once," said Bo.

Tom, one of the barmen, nodded hello to Bette as he lifted the bar hatch to go collect glasses.

Bette smiled back and moved herself next to the open hatch. She could see the bottle clearer now. The one behind the bar and the one in her bag were about the same. She clutched the strap of her bag in relief. With only one person behind the bar now, she had an idea.

"Can I try on your coat, Lady Tena?"

"Bette, *really*." Bo's face twitched with disapproval. "Stella's brother is about to do *How Green is My Valley*."

"Knock yourself out, babe," said Tena, allowing the coat to slip from her shoulders like overcooked chicken from the bone.

Bo tutted and turned her attention back to the stage.

Bette swung the coat over her shoulders, keeping her arms out of the sleeves so she could open her bag without being seen. The coat's weighty mass engulfed her in sumptuous luxury. Bette hugged the fur to her skin. In principle, she hated everything the coat stood for, but with it wrapped around her the lives of a few hundred minks seemed a small price to pay for the ecstasy that caressed every pore of her exposed flesh.

The over inflated airbeds that passed as Tena's lips pursed into a smile. "Suits you, honey."

Bette shamelessly inhaled the scent of mink corpse. "Any advice on how to get one of my own?"

"Honey," Tena stood back and gave Bette the once over, "just keep doin' what ya do…and learn how to read cardiographs. Is it your first mink?"

Bette whimpered an affirmative as the collar embraced her neck seductively and its satin lining stroked her legs in an almost unbearable foreplay of sexual couture. Suddenly the late Anna Nicole-Smith didn't seem so dumb.

Tearing herself back to the job at hand, Bette moved on to

the next step of her amended plan. "Bo, Bo, what do you think?"

Bo's face juddered in a dyslexic semaphore of expressions as she spun round to face Bette. "I think you are both simply disgraceful."

Bette pushed it. "Do you think ermine's more my colour?"

Bo snatched her glass from the bar. "I'm moving closer to the stage so I can hear better."

Perfect, thought Bette. Bo moved down into the crowd away from the bar. Tena shrugged her bony shoulders.

Bette pulled on her gloves and moved into position at the open bar hatch. She unclipped her bag and under cover of the coat took out the poisoned bottle. She stage whispered to the remaining barman. "Tim...what do you think?" Once she had the barman's attention she stepped through the bar hatch. She twirled her back to him, snatching Drucilla's bottle of Drambuie as the coat fanned out and slipped it unnoticed into her bag. "It's fabulous, isn't it?" she said over her shoulder, before doing another full spin and depositing the poisoned bottle in place. The barman smiled and gave a thumbs-up. Bette clipped her bag shut and turned to Lady Tena. "I feel like Jim Carey in *The Mask*. Take this away from me." Bette reluctantly dropped the coat from her shoulders and draped it back over Tena's.

"Well done, honey," said Lady Tena, slipping her arms back into the fur. "The first time I tried one on I burst into tears when I had to give it back...You've got class, babe."

Bette offered a coy smile and gripped the strap of her bag. "We should probably go after Bo."

Tena nodded and refilled their glasses.

A quick glance back at the Drambuie and Bette led the way down to the dancefloor and over to Bo. She was marooned amidst a gaggle of adoring fans, of whom none came higher than her cleavage.

"You're just in time to hear Drucilla," said Bo, grabbing Bette's arm and pulling herself away from the fans.

"Whoopee," whispered Lady Tena. "I'd just hated to have missed that."

Drucilla came on stage, looking suitably mournful, and

proceeded to product place her clubs throughout the eulogy.

"Really," whispered Bo, "this is quite disgraceful." The side of Bo's face was twitching uncontrollably. She didn't seem to notice.

"Bo, are you__" Bette's concern was stopped mid-sentence by Drucilla's closing line."

"I'd now like to hand you over to D.C. Heinz. Please give him your fullest attention."

Bette could feel a pulse in her tongue as Drucilla turned the microphone over to the cute blonde from earlier. She could feel her eyes bulge into a panicking stare as Drucilla left the stage and headed across the perimeter of the dancefloor towards the bar.

"As many of you may already know," began D.C. Heinz, "we are treating the murder of Mr Briggs__"

"Stella!" someone shouted from the dancefloor.

"…Mr Briggs," D.C. Heinz persevered, "as very serious." Bette could see Drucilla at the other side of the dancefloor. She had stopped to speak to Manthrax and Sherry. "…And in light of the events over the weekend that resulted in the deaths of Mr Marchant__"

"Valkeyre," someone shouted.

D.C. Heinz ignored the interruption. "…and Mr Troy Cropper. We are urging caution until such times as we can ascertain if the deaths were connected."

Bette craned to see if Drucilla had moved. She was still talking to Sherry and Manthrax. A smile caught Bette's eye as she glanced nervously towards the bar. It was Mildew, shining bright in a dark grey, shell suit and black baseball cap. This, Bette surmised, was the chav equivalent of a formal black tie. He flicked Bette the finger.

"We are very interested to speak to anyone who may have spoken to Mr Cropper before his death on Saturday afternoon," D.C. Heinz was saying. "Any information can be given in the strictest confidence…"

Drucilla was moving towards the bar again. Bette could feel every muscle in her body tense. Drucilla dropping dead in front of the police had not been part of the plan.

Bo grabbed Bette's arm. "Pay attention. *Thissh isssh* important. *Lissshen* to what'*ssh* being *ssshaid*."

Bette's knuckles began to hurt as her grip on the bag strap tightened. Drucilla was only feet away from bar.

"…we don't want to cause any undue concern…" continued D.C. Heinz's sombre tones from the stage, "until such times as we…" Drucilla was at the bar. Bette could hardly hear D.C. Heinz for the rushing of blood in her ears. The barman was heading towards Drucilla, asking what measure she wanted by moving his thumb and forefinger apart. "…Your cooperation in this matter will be much appreciated." Drucilla signalled to the barman that she wanted a large one. The barman lifted the poisoned bottle and a glass. "…Thank you for your time."

Bette's attention was pulled back to the stage when the microphone clunked and whined as D.C. Heinz switched it off. Bette turned back in time to see the barman handing Drucilla a very large Drambuie.

"Oh, my Lord," exclaimed Bo, letting go of Bette's arm. "There'*ssh* a drag *sssherial* killer on the *loosshe*." All around the dancefloor the crowd was leaping to the same conclusion.

"Just as well I'm only in town for a few days," said Lady Tena. "No man with a lippy in his handbag and a feather boa in his closet is safe."

Drucilla sat on a stool at the end of the bar and whispered something into Manthrax's ear. Bette felt her knees start to shake. There was nothing she could do now.

"You okay, Bo?" said Lady Tena. "You're looking a bit lop sided."

"You know, *dahling*, I am feeling rather odd."

Bette couldn't tear her eyes away from the bar. Drucilla was lifting the drink to her lips. Bette held her breath. If she had the dose right it would take under a minute for the poison to take effect. Once it was down her throat there was no saving her.

D.C. Heinz approached Drucilla and handed her what appeared to be his card. She sat the glass down and put the card in her bag. The bar started to fill. Bette lost her line of sight.

"Bo, I think you should sit down..." said Lady Tena.

Bette craned to see Drucilla. People were moving from the dancefloor, making it impossible to see the far end of the bar without moving closer.

"Bo...are you okay?" said Lady Tena.

A path cleared in the crowd as Drucilla was shaking D.C. Heinz's hand. Her glass was still on the bar.

Something crashed behind Bette and a glass shattered on the dancefloor. Bette turned to see Lady Tena paralyzed in horror; Bo was lying shaking on the floor, her eyes white as they rolled back into her head.

Screams erupted from all around them. Someone's wig flew into the air as people scrambled to throw themselves as far away from Bo as possible.

"The serial killer, the serial killer!" someone screamed.

In a desperate attempt to get as far away from ground zero as possible, the panicking exodus ran for the exits as if chased by axe-wielding hairdressers. Bette dropped to her knees at Bo's side. Bo's neck was swelling and her face was turning bright red. Bette ripped open Bo's dress so she could breathe.

"Tena, phone an ambulance!" Bette screamed, cursing herself for leaving her phone behind.

"I...I...I don't use them. Mobiles, I mean."

Bette jumped to her feet and threw herself into the hysterical mob, aiming for the phone at the end of the bar. As she threw a screaming screamer out of the way, her eyes met Drucilla's over the heads of the throng. She stared at Bette in unmistakable terror and ran.

Bette leapt forward. Not designed for gymnastics, her stiletto heel snapped as she hit the floor. She catapulted backwards, cracking her skull on the floor in front of Mildew's Reebok's. Evidently figuring no one would notice in the chaos, Mildew kicked Bette in the head and grabbed the drink nearest to him and knocked it back. He turned and ran for the exit.

Bette's bag was torn from her shoulder as it caught around someone's foot. She grabbed the bag before it disappeared, and pulled. A wig flew in one direction as a body flew in the other. Someone stepped on Bette as she tried to get up. She hit the floor again, getting a mouthful of well-seasoned nightclub carpet in the process. She propelled herself from the floor, aiming for the end of the bar, headbutting someone in the chest as they got in the way.

She grabbed the phone and dialled 999. Looking back she could see D.C. Heinz crouched on the floor next to Bo.

"Ambulance, please," she panted into the phone.

People were climbing over each other to escape. With everyone's attention on their exit, Bette removed the bottle from her bag and quickly swapped them over. As she was put through to another operator, her voice was drowned out by the sound of more screams. Bette looked up to see a shell-suited body lying still in the doorway.

CHAPTER 34

Spencer prepared himself for bad news as he marched along the art-strewn corridors towards Rob's hospital room. He had visited the hospital every day for the past week and a half, and over the weekend Rob's face had finally reduced to that of a snoutless Vietnamese pig: tiny eyes looking out from a discoloured and swollen head. But today Rob had summoned Spencer at a very specific time.

He stopped outside the room and took a deep breath. He tapped on the door.

"Come in, *dahling*."

The fragrance of cut flowers assaulted Spencer as he opened the door. Not since Princess Diana's funeral had the decapitation of so many blooms been down to one person.

Mandy smiled sheepishly from beside Rob's bed. "Hi."

Spencer offered a reluctant nod.

Rob patted the bed. "Come sit next to me, *dahling*."

Spencer sat as far away from Mandy as he could and shot Rob a censorious look.

"I made a scrapbook of what the press have been saying about Bo," said Mandy, gesturing towards a large open book on the bed. "I like this one the best." He pointed to a clipping from the Evening Standard. The headline, 'Cult TV star hideously deformed in experimental cosmetic treatment', stood out above a picture of Rob looking like the Elephant Man.

"Why would you think *that* was good?" said Spencer.

"It says he's a cult TV star," Mandy said. "And later in the piece it says he's 'one of the channel's highest rated stars'. Oh…I think they must have got your age wrong, though."

Rob picked imaginary fluff from his bed spread. "They're always getting that wrong." He took the book and passed it to Spencer. "Let's see what the gay press had to say about me, *dahling*. Surely they were more generous."

Spencer flicked through then frowned at Mandy before reading it out. "The good news is they down-played your condition."

"Ooh, goody." Rob pulled himself up on his pillows. "What did they say?"

"'Drag serial killer on the loose: memorial service massacre at the Tumble Dryer. TV star rushed to hospital'."

Rob scratched one of the three chins that now bulged from around his neck and smiled. "At least they're not calling me hideous."

Mandy cringed.

"Have the doctors said anything more about when you can come out?" said Spencer.

"*Dahling*, according to the Standard I *came out* before Oscar Wilde."

"You're looking a lot better," said Mandy. "I can see your eyes under the swelling now."

"*Dahling*, I know you mean well, but you're a long way off being able run self-esteem seminars."

"Yeah," said Spencer, "why don't you go along to oncology and tell everyone not to worry because blind men love lumpy tits?"

Mandy shrunk under Spencer's remark and cowered like a badly house-trained puppy. "I think I'll go see if I can get a vase for the flowers Lesley Ash sent you. Do you want a drink of anything when I'm out, Spencer?"

Spencer didn't look up from the scrapbook. "I'm fine."

Mandy shuffled round the flowers and out the door.

"Okay, what's wrong with you?" Rob said as the door closed. "You're being thoroughly beastly and Mandy says you won't return his calls."

"What do you mean?"

"Oh don't be coy. That boy worships you and you're acting as if he's a VAT inspector. What's the problem?"

"He knows."

"I have news for you, *dahling*, he doesn't."

"Don't let him take you in, too. Behind that bumbling façade there's a treacherous little bitch."

"Are we talking about the same person?"

"Trust me, Rob." Spencer wasn't in the mood to debate Mandy's deceit, and he couldn't tell Rob he had overheard Drucilla's conversation whilst hiding in a cupboard waiting to poison her. "He's not to be trusted."

"This is to do with the job Drucilla offered him, isn't it?"

"He told you about that, then?"

"Yes. And he told me he turned it down."

"Is *that* what he told you?"

"Yes. And I think you were simply beastly stopping him from taking it."

"I have it on good authority that he's taken the job. And after everything Drucilla has tried to do to me, do you think that's an act of loyalty?"

"I think you're a little obsessed with her at the moment, that's all."

"Obsessed! Why does everyone keep saying that? She's trying to ruin me. No one seems to get it: if the club doesn't work, I'm fucked. Bette Noir Inc. is going under."

"*Dahling*, would life without Bette be so awful?"

The question took Spencer by surprise. "That's okay for you to say. You're at the top of your tree. You have it all."

Rob's cartoon sized head tilted to one side. "Is that what you think?"

"Well, isn't it? You're on the invitation list for every A-list cocktail party and soirée, and according to the papers you're 'a cult TV star'." Spencer gestured to the room's rainforest of flora. "Everybody loves you." He plucked some cards from nearby bouquets. "'Chins up, *dahling*, Elton', 'Get well soon, Paris.'"

Rob slammed his hand on the bed. "Look at the cards and tell me if you find a single one addressed to Rob. You'll find none. This is all for Bo. Not me."

"But you are Bo."

"NO, I'M NOT! And you're not Bette. Don't let yourself get

lost under it all like me. Most of the people who sent these flowers don't even know my real name. Whenever I turn up out of drag to one of those A-list soirees that you seem to rate so highly, the look of crippling disappointment on the host's face could qualify them for disabled parking. Rob doesn't get invited anywhere. And anywhere I do go all people want to talk about is Bo. I live my life in someone else's Jimmy Choo's. I'd love to be free of Bo, but I'm too old to do a Paul O'Grady. I'll probably need to have Bo's name on the order of service at my funeral if I want anyone to turn up."

Spencer had never seen Rob like this. He had never even considered the possibility that Rob could be anything other than gloriously happy. He had everything; everything Spencer ever aspired to be, that is. "You're talking nonsense, Rob. I'd swap places with you in a New York minute."

"Really? Just take a good look at me," Rob raised his hands in the air, "and learn from what you see. I'm a laughing stock. When I put the radio on earlier I heard some still-breastfeeding presenter making jokes about me, and he was right: I'm the gay scene's very own Joan Rivers, chasing youth as if it was something I could catch. I'm pathetic. As the years wear on the makeup gets thicker and the surgery gets more '*experimental*'. Bo's a character, and like Marge bloody Simpson she can't get older, for as soon as she does I'm finished. Bo's not a career anymore, *dahling*: she's a jailer. I'm imprisoned in a wardrobe, for Christ's sake."

"Oh get real, Rob. You've had an amazing career. One to be proud of. People would kill to have the career you have. Trust me." Spencer was painfully aware of the irony in his statement. "You know what you sound like? Those millionaires who say money doesn't make you happy and that they were better off when they had nothing. Thing is, you never see those people giving it all away so they have nothing again, do you? Money and fame maybe can't buy you love, but it seems you can get a shit load of self-pity for your buck. This is such Robbie Williams bullshit. If you're that unhappy, give it up and let someone else step into your shoes."

"You think it's that easy, do you? If only it were. You have to know when to get out. If you don't spot it, you're stuck there, condemned by the laws of diminishing returns. You see it all the time with soap stars that've had a good run in a series. They leave at what they think is their peak, thinking they'll be inundated with offers because they were bigger than the role they played. But then nothing comes, and they're out there, in the wilderness, knowing they can't go back, knowing it's all over. Those are the ones you see in panto, still billboarded under the name they played in *Eastenders* twenty years ago so people will know who they are. I'm no one without Bo and I don't know if I can be that. I'm stuck behind the mask. I'm stuck behind a frock and a wig for the rest of my days, terrified to step out from behind it because all that's under it is a sad old, lonely queen."

"Lonely...? But you've got...what's-his-name, the ATM. He seems to really like you."

"*Dahling*, I may be getting on, but I'm neither deluded nor demented yet. I think it's fairly safe to say Sharyar wouldn't look at me twice if it weren't for Bo." Rob reached out and took Spencer's hand. "Don't get stuck behind your mask. Look around you, *dahling*, open your eyes. Everyone is hiding behind something and terrified to step out from behind it. Look at the gay scene. The bars and clubs are bursting at the seams with people hiding from themselves; hiding behind drugs, alcohol, steroids, sex - whatever your mask, they're masks nonetheless. Take the Internet: people write profiles of themselves that take inches from their waists and add them to their cocks. Years drop off as they create their very own picture in the cyber attic. At least I'm honest, I suppose."

"What do you mean?"

"Well, I at least go under the real knife. Photoshop is for those who're too scared to have the surgery." Rob squeezed Spencer's hand. "I've trodden on a lot of toes over the years to get where I am. I've lost too many friends in the pursuit of Bo's career, and all I've really learnt is that the most important thing in life is relationships: the people you love."

"Rob, you're worrying me now. Are you okay?"

Rob said nothing for a few moments then pulled his hand away. "I'm fine, *dahling*. It's just seeing your life flash before your eyes and not recognising the person in it was a bit of a shock." He pulled himself up in the bed. "I want you to speak to Mandy. I simply insist you sort things out. If I shirk off this mortal coil and you two aren't speaking I'll have you banned from my funeral." He smiled and straightened himself. "So any news about what happened at the Tumble Dryer?"

Spencer would have welcomed any change of subject but that. "It was murder. Someone poisoned Mildew's drink. They said he died almost instantly." This was a fact Spencer didn't question.

"Do they have any suspects?"

"Don't know. It was Mildew. There must be hundreds."

"I don't think the poison was for him."

Spencer almost swallowed his tongue. "Why?"

"The serial killer, he only goes for drag queens. Unless the killer counts chav as drag, it must have been for someone else."

"The one at the park, Troy, he wasn't a drag queen."

"Ahh," Rob raised his finger, "but he was *in* drag."

Spencer pulled another card from some flowers. They were from Jonathan Ross. "So who do you think it is? We must have seen them that day."

"Who knows, but I'm sure the psychological profile will be of some balding tranny with a P45 from Esteé Lauder. I'll wager it's some sad creature who's been refused the op on the grounds of psychological instability. I can just picture her, huge hands and an entire wardrobe of floral patterns."

Spencer stroked the soft, fabric conditioned sheets on Rob's bed. "You really think so?"

"Absolutely, *dahling*. Let's face it, murdering someone while Lilly Law is on the cabaret line-up is a bit *blue collar*. Whoever it is can't be very bright."

Spencer bit his tongue, literally. Was this what people were thinking? Had he become just another loony psycho? He opened the scrapbook and flicked through its pages again. "They have you down here as one of his intended victims."

"I prefer that to the Standard's version of silly-old-queen-in-bloatox-allergy-scare."

"So what's happening with your show?"

"They're running *The Best of Bo*. But if it doesn't get better soon I'm going to have to change my name to Belle Paulsey and do a radio phone-in show."

Spencer looked into Rob's piggy eyes. "Are you going to be okay?"

"They think so. They say it's done some damage to my liver and kidneys, but I think that was done years ago." He mimed knocking back a very large drink. "To be honest, I'm quite enjoying the rest. There's a divine little Italian nurse who simply adores my show. He's coming to give me a bed bath soon. You pay extra, but he's worth every penny."

"Is there anything I can do?"

"Yes. You can talk to Mandy. Whatever it is that's bothering you can be worked out. Besides, who are you going to get to make you dresses if you're not speaking?"

"Mandy won't have time to make anyone else's dresses for a while. I told you, he's going to be working for Drucilla."

"For Heaven's sake, he's not. Why won't you believe that?"

The door opened and a dark-haired, chisel-jawed, sparkling-eyed, worth-every-penny nurse popped his head round. "Shall I come back later, Rob?"

"No, *dahling*, my friend's just leaving." Rob turned to Spencer. "Go speak to Mandy. I'll see you tomorrow."

Knowing he was as wanted in the room as a virulent strain of MRSA, Spencer blew a kiss and left. He came face-to-face with Mandy, who was clutching a vase.

"I wouldn't go in there right now," said Spencer.

"Salvatore?"

Spencer nodded.

Mandy put the vase on a chair and shuffled uncomfortably. "What's wrong, Spencer? Why are you so angry with me? What have I done?" Mandy's lip quivered.

Spencer looked at him for any outward signs of the change that had overcome him. Other than his newfound acting ability, he seemed the same. Spencer wanted to tell him what he'd heard, but he knew it wouldn't make any odds. Not now. Mandy had always been the one person he thought he could trust with his life. He was the one person he could have told about all this and not been judged.

"I've got to go, Mandy."

Mandy's eyes were welling up. "Please, Spencer. I don't know what I've done."

"*Really*." Spencer's tone had no hint of a question.

"Really."

Spencer wanted to believe him more than anything in the world right now, but he knew he was lying. "I'll call you later."

Spencer wiped a tear from his eye as he headed off down the corridor towards the lifts. He almost collided with a woman and a cute blonde number. It took Spencer a moment before he recognised the blonde. The woman spoke.

"Spencer Hobbs?" she said.

Spencer nodded. He was afraid if he opened his mouth to speak his heart would drop out; it had just jumped to the back of his throat.

"D.C. Peabody and D.C. Heinz," she said, flashing her warrant card. "We'd like a word."

CHAPTER 35

Spencer woke screaming. He sat bolt upright in bed and switched on the lamp. His eyes darted about the bedroom, desperate for reassurance it was only a dream. He relaxed as he spotted two dresses hanging on the outside of the wardrobe door.

Since the police interview two days ago the dreams had got worse. This time he had dreamt he was locked up with Phil Spector in a cell with thousands of wigs.

He was drenched in sweat. Cold, wet tendrils of hair clung to his face and shoulders. He prodded the pillow. It squelched with perspiration. He shook his hair. Splashes of sweat rained against the bedside lamp. He turned the pillow before taking a slug from a glass of Jack Daniels on the bedside table and picked up a half-smoked joint from the ashtray. He lit the joint and inhaled greedily. Smoke penetrated deep into his lungs. He held it there, allowing nicotine and cannabis to warm him from the inside. He took another draw before fully exhaling the last and watched as smoke filled the air with a comforting blue haze.

He hadn't been able to stop thinking about the moment he had the warrant card flashed at him; the police officer couldn't have had a more anaphylactic reaction from him if she had hit him in the bollocks with a Taser gun. Despite all that, however, his interview had gone well. They had been there to see Rob; Spencer had just been a bonus that saved them a journey. Thanks to Bo's 'incident' it seemed Spencer had a perfect alibi. Everyone had seen them on the opposite side of the club and the poisoned bottle had been rushed off the premises in a flashing blue ambulance light when Bette accompanied Bo to the hospital.

He took another draw from the joint.

The thing Spencer was having difficulty understanding

was why the police were seeing Troy and Valkeyre's deaths as suspicious. The police had questioned Spencer about Mildew, Norman Daniels, Mad Mickey, Valkeyre and Stella, but as far as he knew, Valkeyre had been an overdose and Troy had broken his neck in a fatal stillie accident. What the Hell was going on?

He drew on the last of the spliff and stubbed it out.

Things had just got worse last night with a phone call from Norman Daniels. Drucilla had clearly wasted no time in making mileage out of it all. She had suggested to Daniels that it might be a good idea to close Opus Gay for a couple of months - just until the killer was caught. Bette's club, according to Drucilla's counsel, was 'a potential target for a drag serial killer' and that 'the club had been damaged by enough bad publicity for one year'. Spencer couldn't afford for that to happen. You couldn't do that to a club in its first few months; it would never get back off the ground. And even if it could, he knew Drucilla would have Manthrax in there the moment Bette was gone. He had pleaded with Norman Daniels, saying a policy of business-as-usual was going to be best for the club for the time being. Daniels seemed to swallow it, for now, but Spencer knew Drucilla wouldn't let it rest there.

He curled up and tried to picture the scrummy DC Heinz. D.C. Heinz, or Aaron as he had insisted on being called, had programmed his number into Spencer's phone - he still wasn't getting on with the new phone - with instructions to call him if he had any information or saw anything suspicious. When he handed the phone back, Spencer thought he got a bit of a vibe from him as their hands touched. It wasn't quite a let's-ditch-the-skirt-in-the-sensible-shoes-and-go-find-a-cubicle sort of vibe, but there was something. He was tempted to call his number just to say hi, but he thought that would have been as subtle as a skid mark on a wedding dress and as sensible as standing in a puddle of water and sticking a fork into a toaster.

Feeling Bette's voice building under his scalp he pulled the duvet over his head. *You're damned if you do and you're damned if you don't*, she kept repeating. *Drucilla will get you if you don't get rid of her. Once she's dead it'll be over. Once she's gone, Daniels will back off. The police have no idea what's going on. No one suspects you.* Spencer punched the bed. He grabbed the glass from the bedside table and slugged back the remains of the JD.

In an attempt to drown out Bette's voice he turned his thoughts to the pile of bank letters sitting on the hall table. He hadn't opened any for weeks now: he didn't need to; numbers were down everywhere because of his own 'serial killer' publicity, so he had doubled the size of his magazine ads and sent Bernice and her flyer team out as often as Bernice could organise it. This wasn't how he had imagined club promoting was going to be. It was more to do with bills and backstabbing than it was with socialising and networking. *You're damned if you don't,* came Bette's voice again.

He looked at the alarm clock. Beauty came from within, he reminded himself, from within bottles, jars and compacts, and with a journalist coming to interview him in a couple of hours he was going to have to get up and get a face on.

The journalist and photographer were from a new magazine called *Pecs and the City*. They were coming to do a piece on Bette and Opus Gay. Spencer wanted to cry; he knew he had to hand the day over, once again, to Bette.

Bette unwrapped a chocolate liqueur from its foil and popped it into her mouth. It was from the last box of the chocolates she had bulk purchased to give out free at the club, and if they weren't so vile she would have sat down and eaten the lot. She took a shiny new chisel from its plastic sheath and held the blade against the gold lame of her dress as the chocolate's liquid centre burst onto her tongue. She opened the fridge door. Several attempts to get the cat out by defrosting the fridge had failed; Lucy had been popping in more often than usual. Bette suspected it was to get away from the demon seed felines next door, but each time she arrived it meant switching the fridge back on and Gabbana becoming more embedded in the building wall of ice. She opened the freezer compartment door.

Gripping the handle of the chisel, she cleaved into the ice. She needed something to take her mind off the cancelled interview with *Pecs and the City* and this seemed as good a distraction as any.

With the words 'reliable source' running over and over again in her head, Bette slammed into the ice. Gouging at it in a cathartic frenzy, she had no doubt in her mind who the 'reliable source' at the Tumble Dryer was. Drucilla was 'leaking' to everyone who would listen that Opus Gay was being cancelled.

With building momentum she swung the chisel several times. Chips of ice skidded across the floor as she hacked her way through, each slash tensing her bicep in a most unladylike fashion. Drucilla would have known *Pecs and the City* would have dropped Bette at the merest whiff of a disaster in their first edition. In these uncertain times they'd have seen that as a terrifying omen. Understandably.

A block of ice came free and shattered on the floor as the chisel broke through and hit Gabbana between the eyes (eye, really, one was already missing). Bette stopped to peer into the mouth of the compartment. Gabbana was almost unrecognisable. She took a deep breath and continued.

Bette couldn't understand why the police weren't interested in her. If there was someone who loathed Drucilla more, she wanted to meet them.

Another block of ice came clattering to the floor. She kicked it out of the way and readjusted her grip on the chisel before hacking at the ice with renewed vigour.

She suspected the numbers at the club were going to be down because of the serial killer rumours, but if the punters got any hint of the club closing they'd abandon it like a sink estate toddler whose parent had won a free trip to Spain.

The chisel hacked into Gabbana's side. Bette had to twist the blade to get it back out. She picked up pace. The chisel slipped and hit the side of the compartment, scarring the enamel. She readjusted her grip again and continued her attack with a determined fury.

More ice hit the floor. She sat the chisel down and squeezed both hands into the freezer compartment. She tugged at Gabbana's remains. He didn't budge. She pushed her arm in deeper to get a better grip and bracing herself with a knee against the side of the fridge she prepared to rip the cat free.

Her hands came across something, something she had

forgotten all about. She pulled out the small frozen tub she had bought from the magician's suppliers and sat it on the worktop. She closed the fridge door.

The Great Spondulli had used this stuff to make his own pyrotechnics and luminous effects. Like so many of the things he used for visual effect it was highly toxic.

She unwrapped another chocolate. It was then she had the idea. She stared at the little tub of phosphorous and savoured the possibility. It was just so…delicious.

Sometime later Bette removed her protective cycling mask and put the five chocolates, which now each contained a small piece of phosphorous in with their liqueur, into a Tuperware container and sealed it shut. She put the container into the fridge and sat the foil wrappers to one side, intending to rewrap the chocolates when their seals had cooled.

Once the kitchen had been carefully cleaned, Bette went through to the bedroom to remove her makeup. Courtesy of the futile wardrobe drama she had put herself through for the *Pecs and the City* interview, a selection of dresses lay on the bed. She looked at them through nostalgic eyes for a moment; she was most likely going to have to make do without a new one for quite some time, what with Mandy being a backstabbing, two-faced, betraying slimeball ho, and with her about to unleash a torrent of serial killer publicity, she might have to spend some serious money on advertising for next month. But something about this felt right. She knew deep down this was going to do the job.

CHAPTER 36

00.20 The Tumble Dryer

The hateful determination that coursed through Bette was building like cholesterol in a fat man's arteries. She knew she was heading towards a vengeance induced coronary if she didn't complete her task. It had taken over her every waking thought, but tonight she knew it would be over; after tonight she would be able to sleep the sleep of the...well, not quite the just, but she'd be able to sleep without the sound of her grinding teeth as a lullaby.

She sashayed up to the ticket booth. "Any sign of unwelcome guests?" She tried not to stare at the new piercing on Bernice's cheek. The cheek was swollen and red, making her look like she was trying to swallow a giant gobstopper.

Bernice shook her head.

Bette stepped aside as half-drowned shipwreck victims trickled through the Tumble Dryer's doors. Bette realised her punters were going to be staying away in their droves tonight: light drizzle was manageable, the occasional downpour was avoidable, but the potential for full-blown thunderbolts and lightening was very, very frightening to the clubbing elite. Those few steps from door to cab and cab to door could destroy aesthetic perfection in the same way a tidal wave does to a Maldivian beach.

Bette peered out the club's glass doors to see cabs filled to the brim, circling the block in a snowed-in airport formation. Portholes wiped into the steamy windows gave the briefest glimpse of the weather's hostages as they drove past.

Two huge golf umbrellas arrived at the doors with two equally huge candy floss pink, hair doo's beneath them. Giggling and screeching, the two drag queens thrust themselves at the doormen. Both doormen turned the colour of the vibrant hair doo's as 'mercy his hands are big' and 'if you're putting your hands near me I'll be expecting a phone number' were shrieked at them.

Bette nodded and moved aside as their brollies dripped their way up to the booth. She smiled and handed them a drink's token each before heading into the main club.

Music hit her in the stomach as she pushed through the doors. At first thinking the place was filled with steam from wet customers, Bette was relieved when she heard the familiar rush of a nearby smoke machine.

The numbers for the night were down, but miraculously, not too much. Bette congratulated herself on her choice of PA. In a grateful turnaround of demographic, the club was around a quarter lesbian. They had all come to see the dyke-rock band, *Thin Lezzy*. This, as Bette told herself proudly, was true 'fusion' clubbing.

Cruella De Pill, shaking an empty lusherette tray, minced over to Bette. "WHERE'S MANDY?" said Cruella. "I DIDN'T GET ANY CHOCOLATES AND I'M OUT OF GLOWSTICKS - I DON'T KNOW WHAT THEY'RE DOING WITH THEM. AND I COULD DO WITH A LOO BREAK."

"MANDY'S NOT WORKING TONIGHT AND WE'RE OUT OF CHOCOLATES," Bette snapped. "I'LL GET YOU SOME GLOW STICKS BEFORE I INTRODUCE THIN LEZZY, BUT GO EASY ON THEM. THEY COST MONEY. AND FOR CHRIST'S SAKE LAY OFF THE VODKA AND COKE AND YOU WON'T NEED TO GO PISS AS MUCH."

Cruella looked suitably chastised. "SO WHERE'S THE GEORGEOUS DANNY ON SECURITY? I SWEAR SOME FOLKS COME HERE JUST TO GET FRISKED BY HIM."

Somewhere, underneath the metric tonnage of foul mood, Bette missed Danny, too. "NORMAN DANIELS GOT RID OF THE OLD SECURITY COMPANY LAST WEEK. HE BLAMED THEM FOR NOT KEEPING THE DEALERS OUT."

Cruella rolled her eyes. "HE NEEDS TO TAKE A FISTFULL OF CHILL PILLS. EVERYWHERE'S GOT A PROBLEM. A MATE OF MINE WORKS AT BALL BUSTERS AND THEY

DON'T KNOW HOW THE FUCK ITS GETTING IN. AND YOU CAN'T GET IN THAT PLACE WITH SO MUCH AS A PILL. AND FYI, THERE'S TWO PEOPLE DEALING BLU IN HERE."

"WHAT!!? WHO?"

"ONE'S SAM, THE DINKY LITTLE MUSCLE MARY WITH THE GORILLA TATTOO ON HIS BACK."

"IS HE ONE OF MICKEY'S GUYS?"

"I DON'T THINK SO. I THOUGHT HE WAS AN ESCORT. SHOWS WHAT I KNOW. I CAN'T KEEP UP WITH WHAT THEY'RE SELLING FROM ONE WEEK TO THE NEXT. IT COULD BE AMWAY PRODUCTS AND I WOULDN'T KNOW THESE DAYS."

"DON'T SAY ANYTHING TO SECURITY. I'LL SORT THIS." Bette headed for the stage. She had dodged three calls from Mad Mickey earlier in the day. Had he just ordered his boys to set up shop regardless? If so, had she given away what little negotiating room she had with him, and the customary freebies that come with such an endorsement?

As she got to the side door to the stage, someone dropped out of a whirling Dervish, disco spin in front of her.

"HI, BETTE," said Jerry, an attractive thirty-something, muscle mary who seemed to have no life whatsoever outside clubbing and gyms. Bette saw Jerry and those like him as the ravens to her Tower of London. "GREAT NIGHT."

"THANKS, SWEETHEART. YOU SEEN DRUCILLA?"

"NO ONE HAS, BABE. NO ONE'S SEEN HER SINCE THE MEMORIAL SERVICE."

After introducing Thin Lezzy, Bette went to her dressing room and opened her makeup case. She took out a plastic bag of chocolates, inside which was a smaller plastic bag containing the poisoned chocolates. Realising the overkill she only brought three: one would be enough, two to be sure, three for backup. She had left the other two at home. But it was all pointless without Drucilla. Maybe she was lying low because of *the feather boa constrictor*, which was the name the tabloids were giving to the suspected killer. Bette thought that would be an ironic knee in the groin too far.

Bette sat the chocolates to one side and opened another box of glow sticks. Her hands were shaking. If it weren't for the fact her sack, crack, legs, chest and arms had been waxed to perfection yesterday morning, hairs would have been prickling all over her body with tension and anticipation.

She looked at the rows of airline sick bags on the floor. Thin Lezzy had provided forty of them as goodie bags. They were to be given out in the VIP lounge. The bags contained a free copy of their new CD; a *Barf to the beat* wristband; a pack of rainbow flag, dental dams and some promotional material about their tour. Bette was also going to put a VIP flyer for Opus Gay and a couple of chocolates in each of them – Drucilla's bag getting the 'special flavoured' ones. Her intention was to give them out late in the VIP lounge; Drucilla always ended her night there. The poison would take up to two hours to take effect, by which time Drucilla would be off the premises.

She prodded the bag of chocolates. If Drucilla didn't turn up, however, she would have to get rid of them; they weren't safe to keep around.

She squealed and jumped as she heard a knock at the door. She threw the bag of chocolates into the box of glowsticks.

"Bette, it's Mandy."

Bette could feel her face pucker. "Can I help you?"

"I saw you coming back here and wondered if you needed any help. Some of the Lusherettes need their trays filled."

Bette tore open the door. "How did you get in?"

"I paid. I just thought you must have forgot to put me on the guest list. I know how busy you've been."

"I'm managing fine without you, thanks." Bette grabbed an armful of glow sticks. "Now if you don't mind, I'm busy."

She pushed past, dropping half the glow sticks. She left them where they fell and marched along the corridor.

00.45 Stoke Newington

Lucy had hoped a box of chocolates and some late night trash TV would take her mind off her court appearance next week. It hadn't. She left the last chocolate in the box - she was deeply suspicious of anyone who liked hazelnut clusters - and got up to go to bed. Hirohito stirred from his end of the sofa. He glared at Lucy with disdain and stretched before using the sofa's armrest as a scratching post. Lucy threw the empty box of chocolates at him; her entire lounge furniture now looked as if it had been rescued from a wood chipper. Hirohito hissed and ripped at a cushion before jumping off.

After brushing her teeth and getting undressed, Lucy pulled on her giant 'If you think this is sexy, wait till you see my BIG pants' tee-shirt and went back through to the living room to switch off and unplug the TV. Leaving its noise on till she had officially given up on the day was always the last thing she did. It was a ritual she'd been doing since her divorce. She flicked the TV off at the plug. For the first time in years she felt the need for a hug. She reassured herself it was just a hug she needed and not a man; she was proud of her 'impenetrable independence', even if the man who had described her as such had not done so as a compliment. Not that there were any men on the horizon; they all seemed to get scared off once they discovered what she did for a living. A fact that usually amused her, but with her company's future in the balance it didn't seem quite so comical.

Once in bed she listened to the rain. Despite its tropical fury she could still hear Chairman Meow hissing from the hallway. She checked the water pistol on the bedside table was full before turning to Hilary Clinton's biography; for the past week it had proved to be a better sedative than warm milk and Rohipnol. She decided she wasn't up for it tonight so left Hilary beside the pistol. Before switching off the light she took a moment to look at her baseball bat next to the bed. She was going to call him Bill.

01.18 The Tumble Dryer

Mandy could feel his gaping wound of Bette's rejection sutchreing as Gerald disappeared through the crowd of sweaty bodies towards the bar. Mandy's heart leapt as Gerald looked back and smiled.

Gerald wasn't the most breathtaking beauty down whose throat Mandy had thrust his tongue, but he was the first man in ages to have propositioned Mandy. Rob's advice about playing it cooler had come to mind and he had let Gerald go to the bar on his own. Mandy felt ill at ease with this tactic; too many men over the years had made a quick getaway under the ruse of a trip to the bar or the toilet.

Thin Lezzy's lead singer, Anna Wrexia, who Mandy thought was a lot more 'hefty' than her name suggested, was introducing their new single, *Barf to the beat*. The club began to swirl around Mandy like a French perfume advert. He was high, and he hadn't touched a pill. This would never have happened if he had been working. He was glad Gerald had talked to him when he did; it had stopped him running after Bette and further humiliating himself.

Mandy jumped as someone tapped on his shoulder.

"WHO'S THE MEAT MUFFIN?" said Mary Poppers, her lusherette tray smacking Mandy as he turned to face her.

"HIS NAME'S GERALD." Mandy rubbed his cheek.

"NICE ARMS."

Mandy nodded like a toy dog in the back window of a car.

"YOU CHECKED OUT THE MINI-BAR PRIVELAGES YET?" Mary cupped her hand at crotch level.

"NO," Mandy lied.

Mary arched back and leered down her awning-sized cleavage in playful disbelief. "HONEY, IT'S BAD MANNERS NOT TO." She looked over her shoulder then rummaged in her waistband. She pulled out a small purse, opened it and took out a tiny piece of paper. "HERE. SPLIT THAT BETWEEN THE TWO OF YOU."

Mandy took the piece of paper and slipped it into his wallet. "IS THAT WHAT I THINK IT IS?"

Mary nodded. "FAB ACID."

"I'VE NEVER DONE ACID BEFORE."

"I HAD THE BEST SEX ON A QUARTER OF ONE OF THOSE. IT WAS MEGA. I'D BEEN GOING AT IT FOR TWELVE HOURS BEFORE I REALISED I WAS ON MY OWN." She nodded down at her almost empty tray. "I'M OUT OF CONDOMS AND GLOWSTICKS."

Mandy looked into the lusherette tray. "NO ONE'S GOT ANY CHOCOLATES. WHERE DID YOU GET THOSE?"

"DON'T TELL BETTE, BUT I TOOK A LOAD HOME WITH ME LAST MONTH. BUT THEY'RE VILE, SO I BROUGHT THEM BACK."

"I'M NOT WORKING TONIGHT. YOU'LL HAVE TO ASK BETTE." Mandy pointed to Bette over at the bar.

"I'M GOING NOWHERE NEAR *HER*. SHE'S IN A STROP THAT CAN BE SEEN FROM SPACE. CAN'T YOU GET ME THE GLOWSTICKS AND RUBBERS? I'D GO MYSELF, BUT THESE NEW HEELS ARE KILLIN' ME ON THE STAIRS." She nodded to her platforms, which seemed more precarious than usual.

"I DON'T THINK BETTE WANTS ME BACKSTAGE." Mandy felt a gnawing pain at the thought of his damaged friendship. Try as he would, he could neither work out what he had done nor make up for it.

"PLEASE, MANDY."

Fearful rejecting someone's cry for help might jinx his night-to-be with Gerald, Mandy relented. "OKAY. BUT WAIT THERE AND TELL GERALD WHERE I'VE GONE?"

"DO YOU WANT ME TO CHECK OUT THE…?" Mary cupped her hand again.

Mandy grinned, and then stopped. "NO!"

Security stopped Mandy as he got to the backstage door. "BIN TOLD I CAN'T LET YOU IN, MATE. STAFF ONLY."

"HE'S WITH ME," came Anaesthesia's voice from behind Mandy. She was wrestling with a large box of records. "GIMME A HAND, GIRL."

Mandy took the box from Anaesthesia and went through

the door that was now being held open. He struggled along the backstage corridor with the box of records, Anaesthesia following behind him.

"You okay, Anaesthesia?" Mandy thought even her afro looked limp.

"No, girl, I'm not feeling too great. I called Bette earlier to tell her I wasn't well enough to work tonight. I've been throwing up all day. But she threw an eppi, so I ended up swapping with Tony T and doing his earlier set. I've had to have a bucket up in the bloody DJ booth with me... Talking of Bette, where is she?"

"Don't worry, she's at the bar talking to that guy from X Factor," Mandy waited for Anaesthesia to open Bette's dressing room door then swung the box into the room and sat it next to one of Bette's makeup cases, "and then she'll be on stage when Thin Lezzy finish."

"Thank God," said Anaesthesia. "I don't fancy bumping into her again in the mood she's in."

"So why are you leaving your records here?" Mandy pulled open the box of glowsticks.

"The car. I had to bring this lot in by cab. Bette said she would take them home with her, but I got the feeling the favour involved me giving her my soul in return."

"What's the matter with her at the moment?"

"I dunno. Stress, I guess."

"So what's wrong with your car?" Mandy pulled condoms and lube from the box and stuffed them into the baggy, side pockets of his cargo pants.

"Had my tyres slashed. And I don't think it's a coincidence it happened the day after I told Drucilla to go fuck herself."

"How come?"

"She asked me to go work for her again."

"Me too." Mandy lifted some glowsticks. "I told her no, of course. How'd you let her down?"

"I didn't."

"You what!?" Mandy dropped some glowsticks.

"I didn't say I would go work for her, but I know what she's like if she doesn't get her way. She asked me at The Dryer's calendar shoot and I told her Bette was paying me silly money. I thought if I asked for too much money she'd back off."

"Did she?"

"No. She said she was willing to pay the money. I've been avoiding her ever since. I had to tell her the other night when I saw her. Hence the slashed tyres last night, I guess."

"Can you see any chocolates?"

Anaesthesia glanced around the room. "Nope."

Mandy pulled two more handfuls of glowsticks from the box. A bag of chocolates dropped out, spilling its contents across the floor along with another small bag containing three separate chocolates. He scooped them up into their bag and handed the small bag to Anaesthesia. "I think this is all the chocolates that are left. You want these ones?"

Anaesthesia took the bag and tore it open. "One'll do." She threw the others into the bag in Mandy's hand.

Mandy stuffed the bag of chocolates into the other pocket of his cargo pants. "Come on, let's get out of here. You know you're going to have to tell Bette what Drucilla's offered you."

"Can't you do it for me, girl?" Anaesthesia unwrapped the chocolate liqueur and popped it into her mouth.

"She's not speaking to me for some reason."

"Lucky you."

As the door opened to the dancefloor and music rushed Mandy, he hugged the glow sticks to his chest and smiled; whatever Bette was annoyed with him about would be forgotten when Anaesthesia told her about Drucilla. They'd be best mates again by the end of the weekend.

"THESE CHOCOLATES TASTE AWFUL, GIRL."

CHAPTER 37

02.00 The Tumble Dryer

Mandy reeled at his own stupidity. He thought he should at least by now be able to recognise the subtle signs of when a man was bullshitting him: his lips were moving.

"I THINK HE WAS TELLING THE TRUTH, MANDY," said Mary Poppers. "HIS FRIEND LOOKED LIKE DEATH. I RECKON HE'D BEEN DOING BLU."

Mandy was speechless; he was getting ditched courtesy of the old 'my friend's not feeling well and I'm going to have to take him home' routine. Mandy had heard them all: 'I've got work in the morning'; 'I'm not feeling too good'; 'I've recently been abducted by aliens and all my orifices have been sealed by probes'. And this one didn't even have the decency to do it in person.

"DON'T LOOK SO SAD, MANDY," said Mary. "HE LEFT YOU THIS." Mary shook a piece of paper. "HE SAID HE WAS REALLY SORRY AND WANTS YOU TO CALL."

Mandy looked at the piece of paper and just knew the number would be for a Chinese takeaway somewhere.

"IF YOU MOVE YOU CAN PROBABLY STILL CATCH THEM AT THE COAT CHECK," said Mary.

"WHAT'S THE POINT?" Mandy put the glowsticks onto Mary's tray and took the piece of paper.

"I FEEL REALLY BAD AT HAVING ASKED YOU TO GO GET ALL THIS CRAP NOW."

Mandy shrugged. "DON'T, HE'D JUST HAVE BOLTED AT SOME POINT. AT LEAST THIS WAY I DIDN'T HAVE TO BUY HIM A DRINK." Mandy fought to pull a smile. "I THINK I'LL GO HOME. I'VE HAD ENOUGH."

After getting his jacket from the coatcheck Mandy had hoped against the odds that he might bump into Gerald and his 'sick friend', but they were nowhere to be seen. They were most likely on their way to another club.

"Where you off to, mate?" asked the cab controller.

"A party in Soho," said Mandy, digging out a chocolate liqueur from the bag he had forgotten to give to Mary.

02.15 The Tumble Dryer

With Thin Lezzy back in their dressing rooms, Bette decided on a costume change to alter her mood; she fancied something scarlet. She closed her dressing room door and took a deep breath, inhaling the calm of couture whilst exhaling the tension of bloodlust. Having been told by several people Drucilla hadn't been seen for days, Bette was beginning to wonder if the old boot was going to turn up.

Anaesthesia's record box was sitting next to the box of glowsticks. A chocolate was on the floor beside it. Bette let out a shriek. She dropped to her knees and tore through the glowsticks. The world went into slow motion; nothing she did seemed to be at the speed her limbs demanded. Glowsticks scattered everywhere. Dresses were thrown from rails. Boxes were upturned. Chairs were thrown across the room. She stopped; the chocolates were definitely gone.

She could hardly breathe. She grabbed her coat and searched through its pockets for her phone. There was no signal. She waved the phone from side to side. Nothing. She tore from the room and ran down the corridor for one of the backstage fire exits, checking for a signal as she went. She thumped the fire door open and jumped onto the metal grille of the staircase. The rain drenched her instantly. She teetered and grabbed the rail as a heel went through the metal lattice. It stuck. She kicked her foot forward, ripping the shoe deliberately from the ensnared heel. Blinking from the rain battering her face, she could just make out the phone had a signal. She called Anaesthesia. It went straight through to voicemail.

Half hopping, half running, she made her way back to the dressing room and kicked off her shoes. She caught her reflection in the mirror as she pulled on a pair of trainers; she looked like she had gone through a carwash in an open top. She grabbed her car keys.

With her feet liberated by trainers, she hitched up her dress and sprinted back along the corridor.

02.35 Soho

Mandy hadn't intended on going to the party. He hated parties, especially on his own, but he figured tonight couldn't get any worse, and it might be good for business; these guys had money and with his curtains backdropping the evening's event he might get some work out of it. He checked if he had business cards.

The cab dropped him off right in front of the building and had driven away before Mandy realised the change he had told the driver to keep was six rather than one pound.

He ran to the apartment block's front door and pressed the top button of the video intercom.

He was soaked to the skin by the time a voice came from the panel. "Hi."

"Hi, it's Mandy." He smiled at the camera lens.

"Who?"

"Mandy." There was silence from the intercom. "I did your curtains. Have I got the wrong night for the party?"

"TONY!" shrieked the voice from the intercom.

A few moments later another voice came on. "Hi, Mandy, come up." The door buzzed open.

Mandy skidded as he stepped onto the wet, polished marble of the hallway. *Not that posh*, he thought, *if this had been McDonald's there would be a yellow plastic 'Hazard' sign on the floor by now.* The lift doors opened. The penthouse didn't have a number, just a gold 'P'. The button lit around his finger as he pressed.

The mirrored interior of the lift reflected dozens of Mandy back at him. None of them looked happy. What was he doing here, he thought? This was so out of his league. He told himself he'd just have a quick drink and go, then he realised he hadn't brought a bottle. He wondered if this was the kind of party you brought a bottle to. Probably not. It was probably catered. He wondered about the reaction he'd just got.

He reached into his pocket to find the invitation. To get to it he had to pull out a handful of the condoms and lube he had got for Mary. Suddenly the lift doors opened directly into the penthouse.

"Hi, Mandy," said Tony, who was wearing nothing but a pair of leather chaps and a red jockstrap. "Don't worry about those." He pointed at the condoms. "We've got plenty here."

02.42 The Tumble Dryer

Bette had to know if Anaesthesia was still in the club. She told the security guard at the backstage door next to the dancefloor to lift her onto his shoulders. He was reluctant at first, seeing Bette's rain sodden dress, but something in her eyes told him she meant business.

She spotted Anaesthesia's hair on the other side of the dancefloor. She was next to someone dancing with his arms in the air as if trying to attract the attention of an overhead rescue plane. Bette climbed down and propelled herself through the crowd.

Hitting the middle of the dancefloor the music dropped tempo. A wave of amyl nitrate engulfed her sinuses; on all sides, drag queens were shoving bottles of poppers up their noses in anticipation of the music's let-it-all-go crescendo. She had seconds before the air became thick with sweaty feather boas and unshaved armpits. Brandishing her nails in a scratch-to-kill formation, Bette cleaved a path to the edge of the dancefloor. She had been within feet of Anaesthesia when the music let rip. Anaesthesia disappeared as the dancefloor erupted with a mass of limbs trying to escape their torsos.

A lit cigarette narrowly missed Bette's face; it was being brandished by a *fag dancer* (the fag dancer was one of Bette's pet hates and if the cigarette ban had done anything, it was to get rid of them). She stabbed her nails into the back of the fag dancer's neck and shoved him face first into the cleavage of a giantess drag queen. The drag queen shrieked with delight and thrust him deeper into her bosom. Bette ploughed on, leaving the fag dancer fighting for air.

Anaesthesia had moved. Bette spun on her trainers and scanned for any signs of her. She was over near the bar. Bette turned her weapons of manicure destruction in her direction, aimed and shoved through. Clubbers yelped and squealed as she stormed past, her nails lacerating anything that stood in her way.

02.49 Soho

Tony took Mandy through to a small room and handed him a plastic bag. "Just put your clothes in this and leave the bag over there with the rest." He pointed to rows of other bags. Dozens of them. He leaned against the door and smiled. "I wasn't sure you'd come."

"I...er...well, I..." Mandy had never felt so awkward; nightmares of turning up to school with no trousers on had nothing on this. He had thought the 'dress code: jocks and cockrings' on the invitation was just a joke. "I just...it was...I..."

"Come on." Tony pointed at the plastic bag and winked. "Let's get you undressed and I'll show you around."

Mandy wanted to scream and run. He wanted to curl up and die. He'd never taken his clothes off in front of someone with the lights on. He undressed in the dark at home.

Tony moved closer and took the lapels of Mandy's jacket, gently slipping it from his shoulders. He took the plastic bag and slipped the jacket inside. He then unbuttoned the top of Mandy's shirt. Mandy stopped him.

"Look, I think I...I...it's just I...when you...the day I...well I didn't...know you...it was just...I...I'm not really..."

"Tony!" the shrill, clipped tone of Guy, Tony's partner, startled them both. Guy appeared at the door wearing nothing but a cockring. "Can I have a word?"

Tony winked and handed Mandy the plastic bag before leaving the room to speak to Guy. Mandy moved over to the window, checking to see if it had a fire escape he could climb out of. No such luck. He looked at the bag in his hand and wondered: would it be so awful to go see what was going on? He is a consenting adult, and after all, he'd never been to a sex party before; this kind of thing just didn't happen to him. He'd never even had a threesome. He might never get the chance again - *the chance to humiliate myself like this again, more like,* he thought. He redid the button on his shirt.

"I thought we'd agreed to discuss who was being invited?" came Guy's hissing whisper from the hallway. Mandy tiptoed closer. "I don't remember agreeing to the fat seamstress."

Mandy felt the blow as a physical assault. Guy couldn't have wounded him more if he had punched him in the mouth. He bit his lip in an attempt to distract his senses from the sting of tears biting his eyes. What had he been thinking? What was this emotional masochism he had got himself into? How many more horrible rejections could he cram into one night?

"Get over yourself," Tony whispered. "I like him. If you had your way the place would be full of vapid hookers and dickless muscle marys. We've paid for half a dozen escorts to be here tonight just so you can have your twink factor. I like a bit of character and personality."

Mandy smiled. It wasn't much of a compliment, but over the years he had learned to take them from wherever they came.

"Oh fine. Go lube up his '*personality*', then."

Mandy snatched his jacket out of the plastic bag and was pulling it on when Tony came back into the room.

"Oh," said Tony, looking at the plastic bag on the floor, "you heard that, huh?"

"Look, Tony, this was a mistake. I need to go...I'm sorry."

"You're sorry. My bitch boyfriend should be the one who's saying sorry."

"I'd better go."

"No, Mandy, please stay. Guy's just off his tits on blu. He becomes a bit of a cow on the stuff and everyone who knows him knows to just ignore him when he's like this." Tony came over and removed Mandy's jacket again. He threw it onto the floor and pulled Mandy towards him. Before he knew what was happening, Tony's tongue was in Mandy's mouth. It was nice, forceful but gentle, with a faint hint of...cock, probably.

By the time Tony pulled away from Mandy's face, Mandy's shirt was undone; Tony was a fast mover. He slapped Mandy's belly.

"I like a man with some meat on him," Tony said.

Mandy felt himself blush.

Tony pulled off Mandy's shirt and dropped it into the bag. "Come on, stay for a while. Please." He tweaked Mandy's nipple and smiled. "I really appreciate the work you did for us the other week." He smiled again. "I love a man who's good with his hands." He stroked Mandy's forearm. "I'm going to get you a beer. When I come back I want to see that kit off." Tony winked and left.

Mandy wanted to die. It was going to be more of a scene to leave now. He sat on a chair and unbuttoned his trousers, relieved he was wearing his good pants. He had no idea what he was doing. He had no idea how these things worked or the politics of them. Were people just going to be hammering at it and he was expected to just jump in, or did you sit around like at a school dance and wait until someone asked you? What if no one wanted to have sex with him? Rejected wholesale at an orgy would be the ultimate humiliation. He took out his wallet and found the acid tab Mary Poppers had given him. He swallowed it.

The bag of chocolates fell from his pocket as he pulled off his trousers. One fell onto the floor. Tony picked it up as he arrived with a beer. The lights in the room flickered.

"We've had problems with the electrics since we moved in a few weeks ago," said Tony, unpeeling the chocolate from its foil wrapper. "They would choose tonight to play up. I don't think the storm's helping, though." He popped the chocolate into his mouth.

02.53 The Tumble Dryer

By the time she caught up with Anaesthesia, Bette was holding back tears. She would never forgive herself if she had hurt Anaesthesia.

"WHA'S UP, GIRLFRIEND?" Anaesthesia took her forefinger and pushed Bette back a few inches before giving her dripping aesthetic the once over. "IS THERE A WET TEE-SHIRT COMPETITION NO ONE TOLD ME ABOUT?"

"Did you eat any of the chocolates?" wheezed Bette.

"WHAT?" said Anaesthesia.

"The chocolates from the dressing room, what did you do with them? Did you eat any?"

"WHAT? I CAN'T HEAR YOU?"

Bette sucked in air. "DID YOU EAT ANY OF THE CHOCOLATES FROM THE DRESSING ROOM?"

"JUST THE ONE. BUT I THREW IT UP. MY STOMACH'S BAD, GIRL. I'M GOING HOME."

Bette grabbed Anaesthesia's shoulder. "WHERE ARE THE REST OF THE CHOCOLATES?"

"MANDY WAS GETTING THEM FOR MARY POPPERS. I DON'T KNOW WHAT THE BIG DEAL IS. THEY'RE VILE."

Bette pecked Anaesthesia on the cheek. "GO HOME AND GET SOME REST."

CHAPTER 38

03.01 Soho

Mandy kept his underwear on as Tony showed him round. There must have been over forty naked men scattered throughout the large apartment; several of the more 'complex' huddles of sexual activity in the upstairs bedrooms could have been four couples or four double-jointed singles, so an exact headcount was difficult. It was, however, a tabloid paparazzo's wet dream; Mandy had to consciously stop himself from pointing at some of the well-known faces. One of whom he had only ever seen being interviewed by Jeremy Paxman.

Once the tour was over, Tony slipped Mandy a Viagra and with a wink and a slap on the ass told him he would be back for him later, leaving him to 'chill' in the lounge. The lounge, as Mandy had been told, was a no sex area due to, ironically, the cream shag-pile carpet.

Mandy sat on one of the three sofas. The sofas, which were covered with throws for the night, curved around a sculpted glass table that screamed money inaudibly beneath its wail of bad taste. Eight other men sat round making post and pre-coital small-talk, occasionally helping themselves to the contents of a large glass bowl of jelly beans that sat in the middle of the table. Tony had emptied Mandy's bag of chocolates into it.

The lights flickered and the music juddered as a crack of thunder detonated outside. The mass of blackout curtains hid any flash of lightening. Mandy felt a flush of pride in his work.

Sitting across from Mandy was a particularly beautiful man. He sat on his own, arms outstretched behind him across the sofa, legs apart displaying an impressive cock and a well-toned six-pack. Judging by his casual disinterest in those around him, Mandy assumed he was an escort. Mandy smiled at him nervously. The man reached over to the bowl and took a chocolate. He offered a cold, dismissive smile in return. As he unwrapped the chocolate's foil, he dropped his eyes to Mandy's waist where his gaze lingered disapprovingly.

Mandy looked down at his belly. Overwhelmed by self-consciousness, he felt fat. He felt ugly. He felt someone behind him massaging his neck.

03.13 The Tumble Dryer

Running up the back stairs to the remaining staff toilet, Bette was sucking in air like a child's goldfish on a kitchen floor. She thundered through the door, and froze. This season's prison fashions flashed before her eyes as she saw Mary's platform boots sticking out from under a cubicle door. The boots were still. No sound came from the cubicle.

"MARY," Bette screamed, throwing herself at the cubicle door. The door popped open as the force of her body slammed against it. "MARY, ARE YOU__"

Mary looked round from her kneeling position, letting her companion's dick slip from between her lips.

"Hi," said Mary, wiping her chin.

Bette tore her eyes away from the man's crotch and in doing so spotted Mary's lusherette tray under the wash hand basins.

"I expect you downstairs in five minutes." Bette pulled the cubicle door shut and turned to the lusherette tray. She rummaged through until she came across the chocolates. "Have you given any of these chocolates away?"

A full-mouthed 'no' mumbled from the cubicle. Bette almost shrieked with relief; she'd got all of the chocolates back.

03.25 Stoke Newington

Despite the fact the crack of thunder had woken Lucy with a

jolt and torn her from the arms of Brad Pitt, she lay still for a moment, savouring the first rush of adrenaline she'd experienced under a duvet in over a year. She glanced indecisively at the top drawer of her bedside table; its contents had new batteries, but years of her grandmother's paranoia that all electrical appliances had to be turned off during a thunderstorm through fear they might attract lightening came flooding back. She turned over and tried to get back to Brad.

She struggled to find the 'resume play' button in her subconscious before being jarred by a squeal from under the bed. She tried to ignore it; Brad was pulling on his clothes. More squeals were followed by the familiar thumping of Hirohito and Chairman Meow fighting. Lightning flashed. The commotion beneath her got louder. She sighed and reached to the bedside table for the water pistol.

She grabbed the pistol. Another roar of thunder made her jump, causing her to drop the gun. Now wishing it was an AK47, she leant over the side of the bed to retrieve it. As she stretched out, the cats charged from their place of hiding. They pounced on her hand in a coordinated attack. One dug its teeth into her trigger finger and the other clawed its way up her arm and along her nightshirt into her hair, embedding its claws into her scalp.

Lucy screamed and leapt from the bed. Dangling in mid-air, Hirohito locked his teeth around her finger as Chairman Meow fought with her hair for a better purchase on flesh. His claws dug deeper into her scalp. A trickle of blood ran past her eye. She shook and flicked her hand. Hirohito hit the floor with a thud and darted back under the bed.

With the sensation of claw on cranial bone flooding her senses, Lucy grabbed Chairman Meow with both hands. She gritted her teeth in readiness and wrenched at the cat, ripping claws, hair and flesh from her scalp in the process. She tore open a wardrobe door and threw Chairman Meow inside. She slammed the door shut and locked it.

Hirohito's hissing from under the bed could be heard over the rain. Lucy moved over to the baseball bat and grasped it with both hands. She prodded it towards the hissing; if there was to be any hope of a safe night's sleep she had to get them out of the room. A flash of lightning allowed a brief glimpse of Hirohito. His eyes shone and his back was arched. He spat and clawed at the bat.

A crack of thunder shook the windows and the wardrobe erupted into a waste-disposal-unit-chewing-cutlery frenzy. Lucy had a horrifying realisation: her new Donna Karen was in there, and she hadn't worn it yet. In desperation she swung the bat at the wardrobe to give it a warning thud. Hirohito, in an unfortunate act of timing, took the opportunity of the bat retreating to pounce on it and graft himself to its shaft. The unintentional momentum that propelled the rather startled Hirohito towards the wardrobe was enough to leave a cat shaped dent in the door. The wardrobe went quiet and Hirohito slid off the end of the bat, hitting the floor with a bony clunk.

"Fuck," said Lucy, tapping Hirohito with the bat in an unnecessary confirmation of terminal status, "they'll never let me be a lesbian now."

Lucy knew there was no time to mourn. There was nothing she could do about Hirohito, but there might still be time to save her wardrobe. Suspecting another crack of thunder would have Chairman Meow shredding like a corporate accountant, she knew she had to get him out of there. Fast.

She raced to the kitchen and got a pair of oven gloves. She pulled them on and returned to the bedroom. Another flash of lightening told her she only had seconds. She threw open the wardrobe door and ripped Chairman Meow from her little red dress - foregoing the moment to acknowledge the irony. Brandishing him at arms' length she headed for the spare room, intending on shutting him in there until he calmed or his claws wore down.

Chairman Meow wrestled in the oven-mitted grasp, almost dislocating limbs in his feverish attempts to escape. Thunder rumbled through the flat as Lucy came face-to-face with the spare room's closed door. Weighing up the options, she decided to crouch down and try to open the door with her chin.

As her chin bore down on the door handle, Chairman

Meow's teeth pierced through the glove and into Lucy's already wounded finger. The cat exploded from her grasp. It spun in the air, limbs and torso twisting and turning like a Rubik's cube trying to find what went where, before ably defying the myth that cats always land on their feet.

In a flash the cat flipped round into predatory stance. They paused for a moment, sizing each other up as they caught their breath, each apparently as impressed by the other's fortitude.

Lucy could feel blood soaking the oven glove from inside. A line had to be drawn, she told herself. She'd fed them, she'd pampered them, she'd even bought them jewellery. And what did she get in return? They were cold, unaffectionate and demanding, and spent most of their time playing with themselves. If she wanted this crap she'd get married again.

Chairman Meow pounced.

Sensing this was to the death, Lucy abandoned any attempt to subdue and met him mid-air with her foot. He catapulted backwards through the open kitchen door and landed on top of the stainless steel, waste bin. The last Lucy saw of him was the look of shock on his face as the swing-top rotated, depositing him inside. She ran and pulled the door closed. Moments later there was a crash. He was free, and now he had access to knives.

Lucy mopped blood from her forehead with the oven glove and returned to the bedroom. Hirohito lay twisted on the floor, a smear of blood on the wardrobe above him. She wondered if maybe it was time to think about having a dog instead, if only for their more robust constitution.

The wardrobe's open door exposed the horror of Chairman Meow's tantrum. Lucy needed a drink; she was shaking and bleeding and the only alcohol was in the kitchen. A quick glance at the bedside clock told her Spencer wouldn't be home for hours. She pulled on a pair of jeans and got his spare keys.

03.40 The Tumble Dryer

With the chocolates flushed down the toilet, Bette could turn her attention to getting the goody bags up to the VIP room. Spending a while up there with a few celebs might be just what her mood needed. Sitting in front of the mirror, she thought the makeup was repairable, but her favourite shoes, on the other hand, were a write-off. Despite the fact her hair was frizzing for England, she smiled at the mirror; she had a big red hat to match her fabulous red dress. She was not going to be beaten.

Straightening her red dress she came to the conclusion that murder wasn't as simple as it looked in the movies. With no sign of Drucilla and having nearly killed two of her friends, she was coming to the conclusion that maybe she wasn't cut out for the homicide business. She got her hat from its hat box.

03.51 Soho

Ice dropped into Mandy's glass from the dispenser on the front of a large American-styled fridge.

"He's a total bitch," said the stocky, shaven-headed man who, after administering a much needed neck rub to release tension, had taken Mandy upstairs and rogered him silly. "Tony was all over me earlier and the look I got from Guy could have killed houseplants. I mean, let's face it, he's no oil painting."

Mandy was struggling with the concept of small talk whilst standing in nothing but his underwear – which he'd rescued from the floor and pulled back on the moment they had finished - and was aware of gazing rather too intently into the man's eyes to stop himself from staring at his cock; it was a distraction: it was a fat one, juicy and uncircumcised, and Mandy wanted more. "Tony said it's because he's on blu. It can get some people like that, apparently."

"Bullshit! The man's just a bitch." He stared at Mandy for a moment. "I know you from somewhere. We've met before."

"I don't think so. Although, I might just not recognise you with your clothes off." Mandy couldn't believe himself; he was joking with someone at an orgy. He felt so fabulously cosmopolitan. He caught himself staring at the cock again and looked away.

"It'll come to me in a bit. I never forget a face."

"There you are," Tony said from the kitchen doorway. "I've been looking for you." He came in and took Mandy by the hand. "Come with me." Mandy snatched another quick look at the fat cock before letting himself be led upstairs by Tony.

03.55 Stoke Newington

Once in Spencer's flat, Lucy tended to her scratches and torn flesh with some TCP and antiseptic cream. She missed Dolce and Gabbana; over the years they had never so much as hissed at her.

She went into the kitchen and poured herself a vodka. She was shaking. She darted glances about the room, oddly aware of being alone; being alone in someone else's flat seeking comfort from someone whom she knew wasn't there. She wrapped her arms around herself and held tight. A fog of melancholy rolled in over her senses. She gripped herself tighter. For some strange reason she felt as if she was going to cry.

After a few minutes she released herself from her own embrace and went to the fridge for some coke for her vodka. A Tupperware box with a couple of chocolates sat right at the front. She took the chocolates out and poured the coke into her glass.

CHAPTER 39

04.00 The Tumble Dryer

Bette sat in the Lint Tray making desert wind sounds and imagining tumble weed rolling by as the latest Cafe Del Mar sounds droned insipidly in the background. This was disastrous; there wasn't so much as a hanger-on or an ex-reality TV contestant in there. If the freeloaders were abandoning the place she was done for. She threw off her hat, letting her frizz dart for freedom. It sprang from her scalp in open defiance of aesthetic then drooped to the sides of her face, further framing her catastrophe. The many smoked-glass mirrors that dotted the VIP room, allowing the visiting celebrity to remind themselves with an effortless glance just how fabulous they looked, taunted Bette; they busied the room with her solitary reflection, allowing dozens of her to be seen at various angles of despair. She poured herself a large glass of champagne from the bottle she had brought with her. She did it in two slugs.

Bette lifted her champagne bottle and left.

She moved past security as he was arguing with some slurring, barely standing man who was demanding entry into the VIP area on the grounds he was a TV personality. Bette vaguely recognised him. She thought he might have been killed-off in some soap opera while back.

04.24 Stoke Newington

Lucy's head was spinning. She wanted to throw up again. She struggled with her grasp on reality. Was she really lying in bed next door dying of blood loss in her sleep, or was she having a nervous breakdown? Her sister always said this would happen if she didn't get a man. Lucy had always assumed it was men that would send her loopy, not their absence.

Her stomach wrenched again and she ran back to the loo.

04.48 Soho

Mandy was back in the lounge, gripping the sofa below him for security as his first ever acid trip tore through his synapses in an overwhelming rush of surreality. Things hadn't gone well with him and Tony upstairs, and Mandy had the feeling he was now outstaying his welcome; a fact that wouldn't have bothered him so much if he could only stand to put his clothes on to leave.

It had turned out Tony's interest in Mandy's manual dexterity wasn't limited to his ability to run up curtains. Mandy had seen people doing it in porn movies, and even then wasn't sure how it was physically possible. He thought much of it was down to CGI, and had never understood why anyone would want to stick their hand up someone's ass, anyway. Surprisingly enough it had been quite pleasant at first: warm, soft, inviting. Then he started to come up on the acid and it all got a bit James Herriot. Mandy had panicked; he knew nothing about animal husbandry.

"You okay?" said the man with the fat dick, who had just appeared at the table with an attaché case.

"I just need a minute," said Mandy, trying to sound casual. "Strong acid." He had no idea whether it was strong, weak or otherwise. He did know, however, that it would be the last he would ever do. The lights flickered throughout the apartment. At least he thought it was the lights; it could just as easily have been his vision.

The man nodded and passed Mandy a joint. He then sat his attaché case on the table. People started to gather.

"I reckon I've got where I know you from," said the man. "Do you work at The Tumble Dryer?"

"Sort of." Mandy imagined a cartoon frying pan smacking him on the side of the head at the mention of The Tumble Dryer. "I work at Opus Gay." He passed the joint back to him.

"I thought so. It's Mandy, isn't it? I'm Rick."

Mandy smiled and nodded, realising they'd exchanged bodily fluids before names. "So where have we met?"

Rick opened the attaché case. "At the club. I do some artwork for Bette."

The lights flickered again.

It came back to Mandy. Rick was the artist Bette got in to do the stage backdrops. He looked very different in clothes.

Rick passed the joint back to Mandy and turned to the queue that had been building next him. He started to dish out pills and powders to people who had somehow produced rolls of cash from naked bodies.

"You got any blu?" said the hooker from earlier, jostling to the front of the queue and almost hitting Rick in the eye with his dick.

"Plenty," said Rick, "so there's no need to push." He shoved the man's crotch from his face.

"I loved the work you did for the Cirque Du So Gay show," said Mandy. "And I know Bette loved it."

"I've just started. This is just a sideline." He nodded to the case. "I did the backdrop for tonight's Thin Lezzy set, too."

"Looked good."

Rick continued to dish out pills and powders, taking cash in wads and shoving it into the back of the attaché case. "Listen, Mandy, I'd appreciate if you didn't say anything to Bette about me doing this..." He pointed once again to the case. This is just temporary, till I get myself established."

Mandy smiled and nodded, hoping his silence might buy him some more of that fat dick. Rick smiled back and handed a bag of pills and a couple of wraps to someone.

Guy arrived behind Rick and sat on the back on the sofa. "So you two know each other, then?"

"We work for the same person," said Rick, winking at Mandy.

Mandy turned to face Guy. Guy's pupils were dilated to black discs and he had a manic, serial-killer-on-the-run twitch about him. The lights flickered again.

"I'm getting pissed off with this," said Guy. "It's been one thing after another since we moved in. The skylight in the kitchen is jammed, the alcove they cut into the bedroom wall for the plasma screen is too small," he started to gesticulate wildly, "half the recessed lighting in the dining room doesn't work, the decking for the second balcony still hasn't arrived and you might as well wait for irritable bowel syndrome than expect anything from the jacuzzi."

Mandy thought it a shame the lounge was a no-sex area: he would have loved someone to shove their dick in Guy's mouth to shut him up.

"Pass me a bottle of water, Mindy." Guy flapped his wrist at a bottle on the table.

Mandy lifted the bottle, which seemed to pulsate at his touch, and handed it to Guy.

"I'd like some more blu when you've got a minute..." he waved the bottle top in the air as if trying to catch Rick's name, "...Ray?"

Rick looked up from another transaction and nodded.

The lights flashed again.

"That's it," said Guy. "This is ridiculous. I've had enough. I can't cope with this flash, flash, flashing. I'm going to have to ask anyone who's epileptic to leave." He handed the water back to Mandy and stormed upstairs still waving the bottle top.

Mandy returned the bottle to the table. "I think he's had enough blu."

No one spoke.

"Nah," said Rick, after serving someone a couple of wraps, "he's okay. He just needs some K to even things out."

Mandy thought Rick's customer support package was second only to Microsoft. He stubbed out the joint.

"No, no, no," Guy screeched from upstairs, "battery-operated electrical toys only!"

The lights flickered and died, plunging the apartment into total darkness.

"Aaaaaarrrgh! It's a raid!" Guy screamed. "It's a raid!"

The rumble of bodies falling off beds and falling off each other thundered through the ceiling.

"Hide the drugs! Hide the drugs!" Guy continued.

There was a loud slap.

"It's the fuse box again, you hysterical queen," it sounded like Tony.

"You'd better have washed your hands, *missy*," said Guy.

Someone could be heard coming down the stairs. "Stay where you are, everyone." It was Guy.

Panic started to rise in Mandy's chest. He tried to concentrate on his breathing. He gripped the sofa. In the total darkness of the room the acid took flight: eddies of subtle colours began to build in his peripheral vision. They swirled and twisted, gathering momentum in larger and larger shapes and forms. In their midst something hid. He could feel it. He knew it was there. Something. Something everyone else couldn't sense. Something sinister. Hiding. Hiding in the darkness. It had been waiting. Waiting for the lights to go out. He breathed deep. Then, like a lightning storm on a distant horizon, small flashes of light stabbed in the corners of his vision, too sudden to turn and see, too quick to face and make out. He gripped the sofa tighter.

Someone started to wheeze at the table. People could be heard moving as the wheezing turned into a more desperate gasping. Whoever it was sucked at the air in a terrified rasp, wheezing as if the room had no oxygen. Something hit the attaché case. It could be heard tipping over with a clunk, followed by the sound of hundreds of pills scattering across the table's surface.

In what Mandy assumed was the blind scramble to save everything from rolling off the table and being eaten by the shag pile, someone knocked over the bottle of water. He could hear its contents glugging across the table. He gripped the sofa even tighter, his fingers almost tearing through the material down to the leather below. He could hear panicked breathing all around as people struggled in the darkness to save the pharmacy from being destroyed by the water. Three times he heard the dull, painful clunk of heads banging together.

What happened next Mandy couldn't be sure if he was tripping or actually seeing. From mid-air a streak of luminous ectoplasm streaked across the room, hitting a man square in the face and torso. Now glowing an unearthly green, the expression of horror on his face was plain to see. The man screamed.

The second blast of luminous green burst down in the opposite direction, this time spraying someone's legs and feet.

"Aw, fuck!" said the man with the luminous legs. "You just shit J-lube on me, you dirty bastard." The legs jumped back, leaving shimmering pools of *recto-plasm* on the shag-pile.

"It's puke! It's puke!" screamed the man with the glowing complexion. "He puked on me."

Trying to wipe the vomit from his face, the man moved back from the table as the glowing legs jumped past. For a bizarre moment Mandy saw the head and legs as being one person, and like some bad acid-trip-shadow-puppet-massacre they split apart and ran in different directions.

Another wretch ejaculated more luminous stomach contents across two of the sofas, lighting them up like Sellafield Christmas trees. The glowing legs could be seen running to the foot of the stairs, their route marked by radioactive splodges in their wake.

A resounding thud hit the table.

The lights came back on.

"Panic over," said Guy, bouncing into the room. "Everything's..." He stopped, eyes wide, and stared at the table. His mouth opened and closed in silence as if someone had at long last pressed mute on his remote control. Then, pointing at the carnage with a shaking hand, cold terror ripped from his throat. "Aaaaaarrrrrrgh! OH, MY GOD. Aaaarrrrrgh! NO. NO. NOT MY SHAG-PILE!"

Everyone froze. Even shit legs. Mandy had no idea what had just happened. Was everyone else now part of his acid trip? Why did people take this stuff? It was awful. He closed his eyes and kept them shut. He had heard of 'bad trips' and hoped this was just something, with determination, from which he could awaken unharmed. When he opened his eyes it was all still the same and Guy was still screaming.

Tony ran downstairs at a pelt, an erection bobbing up and down suggesting the blackout hadn't stopped his fun for long.

He ran straight over to the table. Rick lay face down.

"He's still breathing," said Tony. "Someone call an ambulance."

Guy stopped screaming. "Can't you just slap him, too?" He stomped towards Tony, cuffing someone who was trying to use a sofa throw to wipe puke from his arm. "We can't have an ambulance here: upstairs there's two magistrates, a High Court judge, a TV newsreader and a cabinet minister in a sling - who, by the way, you seem to be spending an awful lot of time with."

Mandy spotted a phone on a side table next to the sofa and grabbed it. His fingers hovered over the keys for a moment; he couldn't remember how many 9's he needed to press.

"You lot." Guy pointed to the crowd at the top of the stairs. "Get down here and start scrubbing. This had better not stain."

Rick spasmed on the carpet and went still.

CHAPTER 40

05.02 Stoke Newington

Lucy's head spun. Her stomach was now empty of everything but its lining. Lying on Spencer's sofa, she tried to reach the table for her glass. Her hand flopped to the floor and stayed there.

05.19 Soho

Mandy sat stunned, still struggling with the acid, pleading his limbs to move. It seemed the luminous vomit had not been part of any trip he was having. Everyone had seen it; this was real, trippy, scary and smelly, but real.

The paramedics had killed the atmosphere of the party somewhat and the guests had started leaving the moment Tony left in his car to go with the ambulance. Not since a splash had been heard outside in Michael Barrymore's pool had a place emptied so fast. Mandy wanted to leave, too, but he couldn't get off the sofa. He knew if he tried to get up he would either burst into tears or run from the building screaming like a loon, and still without any clothes on, that wasn't really an option.

05.23 The Tumble Dryer

Bette knocked back her first Jack Daniels of the night and waved goodbye to some stragglers as they pulled on their coats. She looked out at the empty dancefloor and sighed.

"I'm really sorry about tonight, Bette," said Mary Poppers. "It won't happen again."

Ordinarily Bette would have been furious, but she realised

if Mary hadn't been such a slapper there could have been dead bodies to account for. "It's fine, Mary. Don't worry about it."

"You look knackered."

"I am."

"Listen, why don't you get off early? Me and the rest of the girls can take down all the stuff."

Bette perked up. "Only if you don't mind."

Mary rubbed Bette's shoulder and smiled. "I'm thinkin' this way tomorrow you remember me doing a good job, not a blow job."

Bette smiled back then headed for the dressing room.

05.28 Soho

"I'll never live this down," said Guy, closing the door on the last of the guests and returning to Mandy, who'd at last managed to get himself together enough to pull clothes on. "I saw the looks they gave me…I knew some of them before their second course of steroids."

Mandy couldn't help think Guy's reaction to Tony's latest phone call, saying Rick had died, was a little lacking in compassion. Having taken nearly ten minutes, Mandy finished tying his laces. "I don't mind staying a bit longer, but__."

"That's very kind, Mindy, but I asked you to stay for a reason." Guy was tousling the carpet with his foot where they had been scrubbing. "I need you to do something for me."

"I'm not really in the mood now."

Guy stopped rubbing the carpet. "This cost £65 a square metre. Do I look like someone who's horny?"

"Sorry, it's just__"

"I can't believe this. We wanted a dealer to come over and stay in the kitchen. I didn't want the lardy pig joining in between setting up shop every couple of hours. It was such a bloody cheek. Typical of Tony, he can't resist a bit of flab."

Mandy wanted to slap him, but just getting up from the sofa was going to be an effort. "So what is it you want me for?"

"I need you to get rid of something for me."

"The body's gone."

Guy looked confused. "The what?"

"Rick...the ambulance."

"Oh, him. No, that's not what I meant." He went through to the kitchen and brought back Rick's attaché case. "I can't have this here." He sat it on the table. "Most of it was in bags. It can't stay here. What if...thingy." Guy shook his wrist.

"Rick."

"Yes, Rick. What if__"

"He dies." Mandy added coldly.

Guy frowned. "I was thinking about what happens if the police want to know why he was here. I don't want to be in the middle of another Operation Screwdriver."

"Spanner." Mandy looked down at his feet to see his laces untie themselves. He looked away.

"Screwdriver, Spanner, what's the difference? We'd never be invited to another of Elton's birthday parties again."

Mandy was humbled by Guy's altruism, much in the same way starving Africans must feel when they get to shake the ungloved hand of a visiting supermodel as she does a video short for Children in Need. "Why ask me?"

"You can take them back where they belong."

"What are you talking about?"

"Rick said you both work for Mickey."

"No he didn't."

"Yes he did. I distinctly remember him saying you both worked for Mickey."

"He said we worked for the same person."

"Oh, throw out my conditioner and split my hairs, why don't you. Just take the bloody case and get out of here."

"He meant my friend at The Tumble Dryer."

"Ah, your *friend*. I see. Nudge, nudge." Guy tapped the side of his nose. "I'm getting you. You see it's usually Tony who deals with all our drug requirements. It's him who 'deals' with the dealers."

Mandy's vision seemed to pulse as the lights in the room throbbed and changed colour. Guy was looking taller as he stared down at Mandy, who was feeling smaller by the second.

"I don't work for him."

"Look, just take it to Mickey." Guy threw three twenties onto the case. "The police could be here any minute."

"I can't."

Guy's face screwed up. "Well, I can't have these here." He pulled another two twenties from his pocket. "Here. Now will you take them back to Mickey, or do I tell him you've refused?"

"I don't know where Mickey is. I don't work for him. Can't you phone him and get him to send someone round for them?"

"I've tried, and there's no answer." Guy nodded impatiently at the case. "The police could be here any minute, for Christ's sake."

"Give me Mickey's number."

Guy read out the number. Mandy's fingers felt huge, the size of salamis. He mistyped the number several times before getting through to Mickey's voicemail.

"Happy now?" said Guy.

Mandy looked up at Guy. He was turning green and getting bigger. His eyes were fiery red and his fists were the size of footballs. He glowered at Mandy with murderous eyes.

Guy picked up the cash with one huge green hand and lifted the case with the other. He thrust them at Mandy. "Are you going to take these or not?" His voice seemed to boom.

Terrified, Mandy took the case and backed out of the room towards the lift doors; he wasn't going to turn his back on this psycho. Maybe it was him who killed Rick. He held his gaze until the lift's doors closed, replacing Guy's image with his own terrified reflection.

05.45 Tumble Dryer

Spencer heaved Bette's gear and Anaesthesia's records into the car. He needed the quiet of his flat to regroup his thoughts; he had almost killed one of his best friends tonight and the psychological repair of that was going to require alcohol and silence. And to top it all, he needed to apologise to Mandy for being such a bitch, again: Anaesthesia had told him about an offer Drucilla had made about working at the club. He had got it all wrong. Rob had been right: he had been treating Mandy appallingly. The whole thing with Drucilla had got out of hand. The club, his career, none of it was worth this.

He slipped behind the driver's seat and turned on the ignition, comforted by the fact at least no one got hurt.

05.57 Trafalgar Square

With the acid tripping unabated through his senses, Mandy wandered aimlessly through the streets before finding himself sitting on the steps of the National Gallery in Trafalgar Square. He hugged the case to his chest. A girl was throwing-up in the gutter a few feet away from him while her friends argued about someone called Tommy.

Mandy watched on as the stone seemed to yield beneath him. It was comforting, soft, even warm. He knew if he sat here long enough he would be absorbed into the building, becoming part of London's landscape. He didn't want to get up.

Around the square, red buses came and went in a vehicular ballet that had played for a hundred years. He wondered why red. Who had decided on red? It was such an angry colour. Why not purple or orange? Or lemon, that was a nice colour. Yes, lemon would have been a much nicer colour.

The girl who had been emptying her stomach stood up and wiped her mouth. After removing her hooped earrings she ran at one of the other girls. She grabbed her by the hair and spun her round, pulling her to the pavement before kicking her in the face. Her friends joined in and before long everyone had a clump of everyone else's hair. A bag hit the ground. Condoms and an empty half bottle of Bacardi fell out. Mandy hugged the case tighter.

Blood splattered up the steps as one of the girls fell near his feet. She was clutching a handful of someone's hair. She didn't seem to notice Mandy. Maybe he was invisible. That might be cool. Maybe the case had magical powers. If it did he could get past security and have a look round Posh and Becks' house, or he could sneak into Kentucky Fried Chicken and find out what the secret blend of herbs and spices was.

One of the girls fell backwards. The crack of her skull hitting the pavement resonated up the steps towards him. Someone screamed. Blood was pouring from the head of the girl who lay crumpled on the pavement; she wasn't moving.

Mandy felt the steps cold and hard beneath him. One of the girls screamed at him for help. She could see him. He ran.

CHAPTER 41

06.12 Stoke Newington

Spencer harrumphed the first of the bags and boxes up to his front door. He figured it would take four round trips to get all his and Anaesthesia's stuff upstairs. Once indoors he was going to have a long, hot soak. He could almost smell the bubbles. He just wanted to wash the night from his senses, cleanse his pores of its memory and make a decision about whether he wanted to keep Opus Gay. He didn't have the strength to fight Drucilla anymore; she was welcome to it.

06.21 Islington

"Don't go messin' me about, mate," said the cab driver. "If you change your mind again I'm gonna have to chuck you out. I've better things to do with my time than drive around in bloody circles with you all mornin'."

"Sorry," said Mandy, clutching the case to his chest from the back seat of a black cab. "I won't change my mind again."

"Okay, mate, but if you do, you're walkin'."

The driver's sighs echoed through the intercom as the cab turned. Mandy looked out the window at the quiet streets. The world just went on, oblivious to what he had seen tonight. This had been the worst night of his life and the only place on earth that felt safe right now was the inside of this cab. A terrifying thought occurred to him: What if the acid never wore off?

They stopped at a set of lights. The red light was an evil, red demon eye staring, unblinking, at Mandy.

06.26 Stoke Newington

Spencer was exhausted by the time he had heaved the last of Anaesthesia's records up to his front door. His key slid into the lock and turned with a satisfying click. It was great to be home, away from the dramas of the night. He wanted to lock the door and shut out the world.

He had pulled the first of the bags inside before he realised the light was on. He stopped, replaying what he had done as he left last night: he had definitely turned off the hall light.

With dread rising in his stomach, he prepared himself for a burgled flat. Expecting the worse, he tiptoed along the hall and peered round into the lounge. Lucy was face down on the sofa, a leg and arm dangling lifeless to the floor. Spencer froze. The night had overloaded his system: he couldn't move.

06.28 Soho

Guy had paced a furrow in the shag-pile like a motorway through green belt. He was furious at Rick. There was nothing worse than dealers who couldn't hold their own products; it was so unprofessional. He looked at the time. Tony would be on his way home by now. It would be too late to remind him to leave business cards for the relatives. Drug dealers were always good for expensive funerals; all that undeclared cash.

He stopped mid-furrow. He'd forgotten about his own drugs. Visions of armed police smashing through the door and stripping the apartment bare flashed before him. He got the turtle shell, drug box from the kitchen and emptied its contents into a plastic bag. He smiled as he saw the bag of blu. He had taken it from the attaché case before giving it to the fat seamstress. He reckoned there must be about a grand's worth there. After what had happened, no one would notice. And if they did, the seamstress would get the blame.

He pulled out the bag of blu and opened it. He dabbed in a finger and lifted a mound of powder to his nose.

"One for luck," he said, and snorted.

He closed the bag, deciding not to mention the 'free' blu to Tony until later; it wasn't that he'd disapprove, they owned five Rolex watches courtesy of dressed corpses in closed caskets, but he'd just fret.

Now where, he wondered, *can I hide the drugs?*

06.30 Stoke Newington

Breaking out of his paralysis, Spencer ran to the sofa where Lucy sprawled lifeless. Her face and arms were covered in cuts and scratches. He shook her foot. "Lucy."

Lucy shot up, wide-eyed and blinking, looking like a silent movie star expressing shock.

"What happened to you?" Spencer said.

Lucy scanned the room as if trying to place where she was. "Fuck...that's strong grass. One spliff wiped me."

"What happened to you?" Spencer sat next to her. Lucy moved away and lifted a glass of JD from the coffee table. "Lucy, please, talk to me. Who did this to you?"

Lucy blinked again and stared intently at Spencer before handing him her glass. "Top me up, hon, will you?"

"Never mind the bloody glass, what happened to you?"

Lucy shook the glass at him again. "A refill, please."

Spencer took the glass, but something in Lucy's tone suggested there was more.

"And don't forget the *ice*."

Dark, fetid dread rolled in around Spencer.

"Yes, I've been in the freezer," Lucy answered Spencer's telepathic question.

Spencer's mouth dropped open. Silence gushed out.

Eventually, Lucy spoke. "I thought I was going mad."

"I can explain..." He had absolutely no idea how he could explain a mutilated cat in his freezer.

"Well?"

Spencer's brain juddered to a halt. The imaginary scent of

Radox turned to burning flesh with a subtle hint of brimstone. "First tell me what happened to you."

Lucy's brow furrowed. "The kamikaze twins next door went for me. They attacked me. Chairman Meow is locked in the kitchen, probably building a cat tank from the tumble dryer and the electric knife, and Hirohito...well, let's just say you need to make room in your freezer for one more."

Okay, thought Spencer, *that wasn't the answer I expected.*

"Well?" said Lucy. "Why is Gabbana in your freezer?"

Spencer just stared at Lucy. It was as if time had frozen, and the chill was unbearable. *Say something, you plonker*, a voice screamed in his head. Still nothing. *For Christ's sake, say something*, the voice ordered.

A barely audible squeak came from the back of his throat.

Lucy took the glass and slugged the remnants. "WELL?"

He couldn't think for the sound of gears grinding in his head. He decided to throw his brain into neutral and let himself freewheel. "I found him in the road..." *You what!* screamed the voice in his head. "He must have been hit by a car..." Then, remembering the state Gabbana was in, "...or two. I didn't want you to see him like that...I thought it would be too upsetting."

"Upsetting! A leg fell into my bloody drink when I went to get ice. Short of dangling him on a string outside my bedroom window and whispering '*come into the light*', I don't see how it could have been more upsetting. I puked with bloody shock."

The intercom buzzed, making Spencer jump with a squeal.

"Who's that at this time?" said Lucy. "If it's some bit of cock, you can tell him to leave. I'm not finished with you yet."

Confused, Spencer went to the intercom. "Hello."

"I need to speak to you," came Mandy's voice.

Spencer buzzed him in and quickly brought in the records and other bags he had left outside his door. Mandy appeared seconds later carrying an attaché case.

"I'm sorry for having been such a troll to you, Mandy."

"I think I'm in trouble." Mandy didn't seem to notice the apology. "Real trouble. I didn't know where to go."

Spencer pointed him to the lounge. Lucy and Mandy stared at each other. "What are *you* doing here?" they chorused.

"I found my dead cat in *his* freezer." Lucy stabbed a finger in the air at Spencer.

"A dealer died at a sex party I was at and I've ended up with all his drugs." Mandy held the case up.

"Okay," said Lucy, "you win. You first."

"You were at a sex party?" said Spencer. "You got invited to a sex party?"

"Yes." He sat the case on the floor beside Lucy and sat down. "But let's prioritise here, did I mention the dead body and the caseful of drugs?"

Unaccustomed to sarcasm from Mandy, Spencer decided to let the comment ride. Then he spotted the two remaining poisoned chocolates sitting on the worktop. How had they got out the fridge?

"How did he die?" Spencer moved over to the chocolates.

"Yeah," said Lucy, pulling the case onto her lap, "tell us. Did he choke on another man's thingy?" She mimed a blowjob.

"It was weird. I'm still not sure what happened. I was tripping. Still am, a bit. He just started throwing up luminous puke and collapsed."

"Luminous puke?" Spencer picked up the chocolates. That would have been a side effect of phosphorous poisoning. But he was sure he got all the chocolates.

"Bright green."

"Spencer…" said Lucy.

"Had this guy been at the club with you?" said Spencer.

"No. I met him there. He was a dealer they got in for the night. It was Rick, the guy who does the stage backdrops."

"He definitely wasn't at the club?"

"No. Why?"

"Oh, nothing." Spencer took the chocolates over to the bin. "I didn't know Rick was a dealer."

"Spencer…" Lucy tried again.

"He only did it part time. He asked me not to say anything,

but I don't suppose it matters now. Can I have one of those?" He pointed at the chocolates. "I've had a bad taste in my mouth since I left Soho. I took some with me to the party but they got nabbed."

The mother of all alarm bells rang out in Spencer's head. He threw the chocolates in the bin. "They've gone off."

"Spencer!" Lucy thumped the table. She got his attention. "Take a look at this." She swung the now open case around so he could see inside.

"Wooow."

"There's more." She pulled the case's pocket open to reveal thousands of pounds in cash. "Can we keep it?" Spencer hadn't seen a glint in Lucy's eyes like this since she electrified the bins to stop drunks pissing on them.

"They're Mad Mickey's," said Mandy. "I've called him a few times but there's no answer. What if he comes looking for them? What if he comes looking for me?"

06.43 Soho

Guy stared at himself in the elevator's mirror. He thought he looked awful: bags under eyes that were little more than dark sockets and his Caribbean tan depleted by the night's stress.

"I'm hiding them down in the MG," he said into his phone. "Where are you?"

"I'm nearly home," said Tony. "Why are you putting drugs down in the MG?"

"What if the police arrived back here with you and wanted to search the place?"

"What would they be searching our place for?"

"Oh I don't know, Ms calm-and-bloody-collected, I've never had a dealer die in my flat before. I don't know what police procedure is for that sort of thing."

"So you're putting the case down in the car?"

"No, just our stuff. I gave the case to the lardy seamstress. He knows, or works for Mickey, or something."

Silence hissed from the other end of the phone, then: "You

did what! But Joe__"

The line went dead just as the elevator opened at the basement. Guy took one last look at himself in the mirror before getting out. He longed for the 80's; his skin had been tight, his hairline wasn't receding and gay men were dropping like flies; age and combination therapy: the enemy of the gay undertaker.

He headed along the corridor to the underground parking, feeling pleased for once with the level of crappy service the building offered: the security cameras were being repaired and were going to be offline until Tuesday. He would have had to think twice before doing this if they had been working.

The neon light above the MG's parking space flickered. Pulling his car keys from his pocket he heard the buzz of the street level doors opening. He hid the plastic bag under his shirt and waited to see whose car appeared. It was Tony.

Relieved to see him, Guy waved and moved over towards Tony's parking space. Tony didn't wave back.

"Huffy bitch," said Guy, but soon realised it wasn't one of Tony's 'moods'.

Tony was staring ahead, face expressionless and eyes bulging. A spray of glowing vomit hit the inside of the windscreen and Guy could just make out Tony slouching forward onto the wheel. Rooted to the spot, Guy screamed. The scream was drowned out by the roar of the engine. Tony's car sped towards its parking space.

The plastic bag flew out of Guy's hand as the bonnet of the Mercedes hit his chest. His face was next, denting the paintwork before he was thrown backwards against the wall. He felt bones crack and splinter as his head smacked against the concrete. Sandwiched between the car and the wall, he flopped forward onto the bonnet, the Merc disk impaling his gut. It rained blu around him.

Feeling his eyes roll back, Guy snorted one last line.

06.57 Stoke Newington

A couple of lines of coke courtesy of the attaché case later and

Spencer was feeling sick; Mandy had recanted the relevant facts of his evening in as much detail as he could remember, leaving Spencer in no doubt that the *feather boa constrictor* had struck again.

"You have to call Tony and Guy," said Spencer. "This is their responsibility. They can't just dump this on you." He had to sever this link before the police got involved. And he didn't want to tell Mickey to come and pick them up; he didn't want Mickey knowing his or Mandy's address.

Mandy took out his phone and called Tony and Guy's number. "It's going through to voicemail. It's going through to voicemail. What should I do? Should I try Mickey again?"

"Shhhh," said Spencer. "I need to think."

Spencer wanted to keep as far away from the scene of the crime as possible, and as far away from Mickey as possible, but he couldn't leave Mandy to do this on his own; he was getting all woman-on-the-verge-of-a-nervous-breakdown on him already and the only way this wasn't going to snap back at Spencer like a fat man on a bungee was if he took control.

"Take them back to the slappers in Soho," said Lucy. "It's their problem."

Without any other options, Spencer had to agree. "Lucy, can we take your car?" He didn't want anyone recognising his.

"I'm coming with you, then," said Lucy, chopping another three lines. "I wouldn't miss this for the world." She pulled three packets of ready-wrapped coke from the case. "And I'm taking my commission in advance." With a rolled-up note in her hand she dipped down and snorted a line with such vigour the Queen's picture pulled to look like Joan Rivers.

Mandy's eyes bulged like the rabbit that knew it was cosmetic fodder. Spencer just shrugged.

CHAPTER 42

"Just drive," said Spencer, spotting the police cars outside Tony and Guy's building. "Don't slow down, Lucy. Keep going."

Unfazed by Spencer's panic, Lucy drove on at a leisurely pace.

"Don't slow down," Mandy said from the back of the car. "Are you mad?"

"Shut up and press your noses against the windows like real Londoners," said Lucy. The car ambled along in second gear. "If we don't slow down and stare we'll look suspicious."

Spencer and Mandy did as they were told and stared out at the four police cars and the ambulance parked in front of the building. Spencer tried hard to focus on a smear on the window, denying the image of two body bags being lifted into the back of an ambulance.

"Who was in their flat when you left?" said Spencer.

"Just Guy," said Mandy, his lips unmoving in an apparent attempt to hide his answer from any long-sighted, lip-reading policemen who might be looking their way. "Tony was on his way back from the hospital. This might be nothing to do with them. It could just be a coincidence."

"Sure, it's a coincidence, hon." Lucy pulled the car into third gear. "And Harold Shipman just lived in an area with a *really* high septuagenarian suicide rate."

"What am I going to do," said Mandy. "What am I in the middle of? Is this some drug wars thing?"

Lucy turned off the street and parked.

"What you doing?" said Spencer.

"There's always a nosey neighbour hovering around stuff like this. Someone has to go see who was in those bags. I'll be back in a minute."

"Spencer, say something," said Mandy. "Stop her."

Spencer watched Lucy disappear in the rear view mirror and resorted to quiet prayer.

After a while Mandy spoke. "So why have you been so awful to me?"

Spencer turned to face him, but Mandy was looking down to the case at his feet. "I've not been myself lately. I thought you were lying to me and working with Drucilla. And before you say anything, I know – it was stupid and I deserve a slap for even thinking it. To be honest, I don't know what's been wrong with me. I'm beginning to think this whole club promoting thing isn't for me."

"Why is it you always take these things out on me?"

Spencer didn't know what to say, so they sat in silence again until Lucy returned.

"I got these so I could look like an early bird out for the papers." She deposited a pile of plastic wrapped broadsheets onto Spencer's lap and turned to face Mandy. "Did they live in the penthouse?"

Mandy nodded.

"Is there just the one penthouse?"

He nodded again.

"It was them."

Mandy whimpered.

Spencer was beginning to marvel at his own path of destruction.

"Just take them to this Mickey guy, then," said Lucy.

"We don't know where he lives," said Mandy.

"Did you leave a message on his voicemail?"

"No."

"Well this is good news."

"Not for the two in the recycling bags," said Spencer. "How is this good news?"

"We've just got ourselves a free party bag. And I don't mean *him*." She flicked her thumb at Mandy. "No one knows we've got the case. He didn't leave any message on the dealer's phone to say he had the stuff."

The cash would come in handy, thought Spencer, but the

look of horror on Mandy's face, which was draining of blood before their eyes, told him it wasn't an option.

"He'll find out, somehow," said Mandy. "And I don't want to be on his hit list."

"Well what do you want to do, Thelma?" Lucy grabbed the steering wheel and jarred it from side to side. "Shall we head for the nearest precipice?"

Spencer turned back to Mandy. "You said there were hookers at this party?"

"Yeah." Mandy was staring at the case again.

"Did you know any of them?"

"What are you trying to say?"

Spencer pulled Mandy's chin up to face him. "Focus, Mandy. I'm not saying you pay for hookers on the side. Did you know any of them?"

"One was called Augustine," Mandy said, after a fashion.

"Dark hair, big cock and a total prat?"

"That's him."

"He works for Francois," said Spencer. "He's always trying to get on the guest list for Opus Gay, and everywhere else for that matter. And I got Rick's number from Francois, too."

"So?" Mandy looked back to the case.

"Lucy, take us to Mandy's place."

Mandy's shoulders sank. "Why are we going there?"

"We need you to sober up and get something from your flat. Just in case."

"I've never been in a brothel before," said Lucy, as she parked near Francois' West End office a few hours later. "Do they let women into these places?"

"Yes," said Spencer. "They have cleaners."

Lucy's eyes narrowed to reproachful slits. "Why are we going into a whorehouse, anyway?"

"*You* are going nowhere. *I'm* going to see Francois."

"Aw, come on. I'm in shock after seeing Gabbana. I'm in mourning all over again. Seeing a bunch of men having their asses whipped might be just what I need."

"It's not squash courts. There's no spectators' gallery."

"Are you sure this will work?" said Mandy.

"Of course it will work." Spencer had no idea about anything right now, but he had to imply authority to keep his posse calm. Not since the Ant Hill Mob had there been a more unlikely crew. "Okay, we've gone through this. Mandy, you get ready. You know what to do if I'm not out in ten minutes." Spencer grabbed the case and headed along the street.

Next to a Prêt a Manger was a door discreetly marked 'S&T for Men'. Although standing for Stockard and Trimble, its commonly used nickname was Slap and Trickle. Spencer gripped the attaché case and went in.

The reception area was a mixture of Harley Street, dental clinic chic and nightclub VIP room seedy. Jay, the receptionist, whose name stood proud on his lapel badge over an impressive cleavage, sat upright at his desk.

"Good morning, sir," said Jay, a smile as fake as his tan stretching across his face.

Spencer offered a polite nod in return; his facial muscles were incapable of granting anything more frivolous at this point. Taking a deep breath, he knew if he had any hope of getting though this he was going to have to think like Bette. He flicked his hair.

"No, it's not," said Spencer. "Yes, there is. Yes, I would. Francois."

A confused glaze came over Jay's face as his brain juddered into action. From his days as receptionist here, Spencer knew the script all too well. He waited as Jay ran through it in his head: *Is this your first time here? Is there someone you have in mind? Would you like me to see if he's available? Could you give me a name, please?*

"I'm afraid he's not in this morning," said Jay, clearly perturbed by Spencer's pre-emption.

Spencer knew that was a lie. Sunday mornings were known as Francois' Delia Days: armed with a whisk and a calculator, Sunday was when he cooked his best books.

"I don't have time for this." Spencer leaned on the desk.

"Could you tell him...Bette Noir is here?"

"I said he isn't in."

"And if anybody cared what you had to say," Spencer stared at the name badge and paused, "...*Jay*, you wouldn't be working front of house in a brothel."

The professional smile disintegrated from Jay's face. "As I said, *sir*, he's not here. And if that's all you want, I'm going to have to ask you to leave."

The front door opened and a man in his mid-sixties wearing a powder blue safari suit walked in. *American tourist*, thought Spencer.

"That's the third time I've left here with crabs," said Spencer. "And when I asked for a butch, hairy top, you gave me a lesbian in a gorilla suit with a strap-on. When did she last have that suit cleaned?" The sound of traffic from outside was heard again. Spencer didn't need to look behind to see if the man was still there. He raised an eyebrow and smiled at Jay. "You want to check again if Francois's in?"

Jay snatched the receiver of his phone and pressed a button. "Someone called Bette *Nwah* is here to see you. I told him you weren't in, but__" Jay's expression went from bitter to twisted. "Oh...okay." He replaced the receiver. "Last door on the left." As if trying to get rid of a freshly picked bogey, he flicked his finger at one of the two doors opposite the desk. The door buzzed.

The sound of groaning and spanking as he went past the various private rooms on the way to Francois' office brought it all back. The time he spent here was not one upon which he liked to reminisce. He knocked on Francois' door.

"Come in."

Spencer held tight to the case and pushed the door.

Like Francois, the office was a pretentious, over-dressed affair. The walls were a burgundy chamois and centre stage, in front of the window, was a large expanse of desk. Francois was putting papers into a drawer. The door closed of its own accord behind Spencer.

"Brandy?" said Francois, strolling over to a grotesquely

veneered cabinet.

"No thanks."

Francois poured himself a drink and returned to the desk.

"It's really nice to see you, Spencer. I don't see enough of you these days." His tone had all the sincerity of an Oscar acceptance speech. "So to what do I owe the pleasure?"

"It's about the party you catered for in Soho last night."

"That's a shame." He missed his footing as he went to sit down. "I thought it might be something a bit more 'social'."

Spencer shivered. "Did you supply guys for the party in Soho last night?"

"We cater for a lot of functions on a Saturday evening. And they're *all* confidential."

"Okay, I'll narrow it down a little: this is the one where the dealer died."

"Died?"

"Mort, stiff, cadaver, dead, deceased, passed-on, pushing-up-the-pansies__"

"Okay, okay," Francois waved his hand in the air. "I get it." Francois' gin-rosy cheeks flushed. "The boys just told me he had been taken to hospital with an overdose."

Spencer thought that would have made sense. The hookers would have been first to grab their clutch bags and run at any sign of trouble. "Did you organise a dealer for them?"

"You know I don't have anything to do with drugs."

"Come on, I worked here, remember?"

Francois smiled. "Then you'll remember what a discreet operation I like to run and drugs are not part of it."

"No, but you always knew a man who did." Spencer lifted the case onto the desk. "This was the dealer's from last night. I take it he worked for Mickey. Can you get it back to him?"

A rapid fire of expressions tore across Francois' face, leaving Spencer at a loss what could possibly be going on in his head. Something wasn't right.

"How did you end up with that?"

"It's a long story. Suffice to say I'm doing you a favour."

Beads of sweat started popping out across Francois' brow. "This is nothing to do with me. I have nothing to do with this. You'll have to take it away."

"Come on, Francois. Can't you just send one of your guys over to Mickey's with it?"

Francois' brow started to gush. He picked up the phone. "Jay, get my lawyer on the phone." As he listened to what Jay had to say his dripping brows furrowed. "...I don't give a shit if it's Sunday. Get him out of bed or call him on the fucking golf course if you have to." He slammed the phone down and emptied his glass. "So how did you get the case?"

"A friend was at the party. He ended up with it after they couldn't get Mickey on the phone to come and collect it."

"He what?"

"They tried to get hold of Mickey to collect them. But listen, there's more to it." Spencer took a breath, maybe some more information might motivate him into giving Mickey's address. "I hope last night wasn't on account, because when we went past the place in Soho Tony and Guy were being taken out in body bags. You need to let Mickey know that__"

Francois picked up the phone again. "Jay, would you send in Gustav, please – *Ms Noir* is leaving."

"What? You bastard, Francois."

"Sorry, Spencer, it's nothing personal. Whatever you've got yourself involved in is nothing to do with me or my boys."

The door opened and a shaven-headed giant walked in. His massive arms, which bulged from his tee-shirt in defiance of its stitching, were covered in tattoos of daggers and blood dripping skulls, and from beneath his tee shirt the outline of two huge nipple rings the size of medieval doorknockers stood proud of an enormous, pumped chest.

CHAPTER 43

The behemoth looked Spencer up and down and waited for instructions.

"I'm afraid I'm going to have to insist you leave." Francois' hands were shaking. "I'd hate for things to get unpleasant." He offered a weak smile.

Spencer smiled back and turned to the giant. "Hi, Rose."

"Hi, *Ssspenccce*," lisped the mass of tattoos. "Had a fab time at the club *lasst* night. Thanks*s* for the gue*sst list*s*s*. I'm paying for it now, though." Rose pulled at his face. "I'm like a bag o' shite in a *gymsslip*." He glanced at Francois. "I hear you want *sssomeone* chucked out?"

"Never mind," snapped Francois, his eyes beaming hate across the room at Rose. "I thought I told you strong and *silent*? Not *ssssssssstrong* and *sssssssssilent*."

Sticking his nose in the air and slapping a hand on his hip, Rose turned for the door. "I get paid for blowjob*ss* and mild *ss*CP. If you want *bouncerss*, get *dykesss*." The door closed by itself behind him.

"I'm sure it was better in rehearsal," said Spencer.

"Just get out."

Spencer stared at the case. He had to get rid of it. It was a chaotic thread that could lead the police to his door and connect him with last night's events. He could strangle Mandy for this. "I'm not getting stuck with Mickey's drugs after all this shit. You know what he's like. Just tell me where he's operating out of these days and I'll take the case there." Spencer wasn't certain, but he thought he heard Francois whimper.

Francois pulled himself up from the chair and leant across the desk. "You don't want to fuck with me, Spencer."

"No one wants to fuck with you, Francois. That's why you run a brothel. You're the only person I know who gets tax relief on a hand job." He flicked his hair in a manner he recognised as all too 'Bette'.

The phone rang. Francois pulled back and snatched the receiver. "WHAT?" A tube map of spidery veins broke out on his face. "What...? Tell him...tell him I'll be with him in a minute." He put the phone down and stepped back from the desk. "Oh my God. Oh my God. This is all too rich for my blood. This has all gone too far. Too rich for my blood. Oh God. You have to get out of here, Spencer."

"What's the matter?"

"The police are in reception. They want to speak to me. This is too rich for my blood. It's way too rich for my blood. I can't cope with this." In rapid succession his eyes darted several times from the case to the door. "It's all gone too far. Too far for me. Didn't want involved. I said I didn't want involved." He grabbed a pen and notepad and started to scribble. Once finished he tore off the page and thrust it at Spencer. "Take the case there. Go out the back way. Don't let the old bill see you. This is too much for me. That's it. I want nothing more to do with all this. Nothing. You tell him that. It's too much for me. People are dying. It's just money for fuck's sake."

Fascinated by the breakdown unfolding before him, Spencer took the piece of paper.

"You fucking deaf?" Sweat was gushing down Francois' face, causing him to blink wide and startled eyes. "I said the police are in reception."

Spencer pulled himself together as Francois started pushing him towards the door. Wiping sweat from his eyes, he pointed Spencer along the corridor to the fire exit.

Spencer and Mandy arrived back at the car at the same time. The engine was running. No sooner were the doors closed, Lucy pulled away from the kerb.

"So he wouldn't take the case, then?" said Mandy, as he pulled the front of his policeman's uniform and it came undone at the velcroed seems.

"I didn't really expect him to. I thought he'd play it like this, but we managed to get Mickey's address." Spencer waved the piece of paper.

Mandy was struggling to get out of the kiss-o-gram uniform. Spencer's heart missed a beat as the fake walkie-talkie crackled to life when the uniform hit the floor.

"It was in the pocket of one of the uniforms," said Mandy. "I used it to get out of the place on another call."

Now he gets savvy, thought Spencer.

"So where do the drugs need to go?" said Lucy.

"Wilfred Brimble House in Stockwell."

"That place is a bloody demilitarised zone. One of my shit packers lives there. He wears a bullet proof vest to put the rubbish out. When people apply for housing benefit there, under 'type of accommodation' they put *'lair'*."

"You don't need to take me, Lucy," Mandy said. "You two have done enough. I can deal with this from here."

Lucy shrugged. "It's either this or the *Eastenders* omnibus."

For a brief second Spencer was tempted to let Mandy take the case to Mickey, but it would have been like sending Little Red Riding Hood to deliver pizzas to the wolf. "I think it would be better if I went." Spencer dreaded the idea, but he couldn't let Mandy get involved with Mickey when all of this was technically his mess. He'd avoided Mickey this long; it was time to get him over and done with. Also, this way, Mickey still doesn't get to know where Spencer lived.

"I can't ask you to do this, Spence." Mandy was shaking, struggling to pull on his trousers - back to front.

"That's what friends are for." Spencer looked down at the case; he figured being arrested for drugs was the least of the crimes on his potential rap sheet. "Consider it payment in lieu of the beautiful shroud you're going to make me."

All three of them forced a feeble laugh.

The intercom system of Wilfred Brimble House had a table leg sticking out of it. Probably, Spencer thought, from the IKEA Fuukt range. He was going to have to go up unannounced.

Number 74 was on the sixth floor. Getting into the lift he could feel the building creak under the strain of renters and buyers living juxtaposition to one another. The owners of mortgages to properties no one would buy displayed their status with leaded-glass double glazing and reinforced front doors; whereas, by pissing in the lift, their neighbours had found a simpler way of demarking territory. Spencer held his breath and stood splay-legged on tiptoe as a pool of recycled Tennant's Super sloshed around at his trainers. The lift chundered from floor to floor as if powered by a bronchial pit pony in the basement. It juddered to a halt at the sixth floor and the doors opened with a grinding, metal-on-metal screech.

The corridor ahead of him had all the charm of a Turkish prison, but it was a delightful example of London's multi-cultural melting pot: it had graffiti in at least four languages, and Aziz seemed to 'rule' in two of them.

Number 74 had a Fort Knox configuration of locks. Spencer thought it might as well have a light above the door flashing 'DEALER', until he saw most of the other doors on the floor were the same. He rang the bell.

The pinpoint of light through the spy hole vanished; someone was watching him. The sound of the lift rattling back to the ground floor echoed along the corridor; it would never have been of use for a speedy escape, anyway.

Locks started to click and bolts clunked from the other side of the door. A final ker-chunk and the door started to open. An arm reached out and grabbed Spencer, pulling him into the flat and shoving him out of the way as the door closed behind him. The sweet scent of beeswax hit him just before the wall. He held tight to the case.

Still facing the wall, he could hear the sound of chubs and bolts being resecured, locking him in.

CHAPTER 44

Spencer could feel his pulse in his teeth. Nothing made sense: two stunning Art Deco wall lights lit the hallway and expensive parquet flooring stretched throughout what he could see of the flat. He felt as if he had been pulled through a chav wardrobe into gay Narnia. Once the last bolt had been pulled back into place, the man in the white track suit who had pulled Spencer through the door turned to face him. The shock of what Spencer saw had him sucking in air in a conscious attempt to keep himself breathing.

"What are you doing here?" said the man in the white track suit. His voice was familiar, chillingly recognisable, but the track-suited form of Drucilla out of drag - no wig, no makeup, no frock - was proving difficult to take in.

"I...I...I..." Spencer held up the case, his grip on it tightening as his grip on reality faltered. "...Francois told me to bring this here." His mind felt like a garment with a dangling thread, events pulling on it and unravelling his sanity row by row. "Whose place is this?"

"It's Stella's. I mean, was Stella's." Drucilla nodded for Spencer to go through to the lounge. "Are you okay, Spencer? Is it Mickey? Have you had trouble with Mickey?"

Spencer wasn't sure what disturbed him more: Drucilla using his first name or him offering concern. Like Vanessa Feltz at an all-you-can-eat buffet, Spencer struggled to take it all in. He stopped before a plasma TV that had the kind of screen usually found in multiplexes showing obscure French films. He then took a sharp intake of breath as he saw the sofa; he had formed puddles of drool outside Linge Roset's window when he first saw it. The manager had finally barred him from the store, citing Spencer's moaning, whimpering and stroking of the sofa's fabric was putting off customers.

"Is that Rick's?" Drucilla pointed at the case before sitting down on what Spencer remembered as being over five grand's worth of furniture.

Spencer nodded and scanned the room. Was he about to be ripped off? Had he been set-up by Francois? He gripped the case tight. "I take it you've heard about him, then?"

"Yes." The word came out of Drucilla in a wheeze.

"Have you heard about Tony and Guy?"

Drucilla's eyes widened. "What about them?"

"They're dead, too."

What happened next took Spencer by surprise; it was so out of character and unexpected that it was like seeing the Queen flashing her tits during the Christmas address: Drucilla looked down into his hands and started to sob.

"Oh God, Spencer," he bawled. "I'm so scared. I don't know what's going on. I think Mickey's trying to kill me." With his face in his hands, his entire body trembled. "He murdered Stella and now he wants to kill me." He pulled an asthma inhaler from his pocket. He struggled to keep his shaking hands under control at first and missed his mouth once before sucking greedily on the inhaler. "He's after me. He wants me dead." He wiped his nose on his sleeve. "I know you and I haven't exactly been close." He looked up at Spencer. Tears were escaping from bloodshot eyes. Spencer shrugged politely, thinking he'd had fungal nail infections whose company he'd preferred. "I'm really sorry you've got involved. Francois' a bastard for doing this to you. He should never have sent you here." He wiped tears from his eyes. "How did you end up with the case? Has Mickey harmed someone you know?"

"No, everyone's okay. So why would Mickey want to harm you?" He couldn't stop himself from asking.

"It's complicated. Thing is it's nothing to do with me."

"So you know what's in the case, then?"

"I imagine it's drugs."

Not for the first time in the last twenty four hours, Spencer was confused. "Okay, so what's going on? Why would Francois send me here with a case full of Mickey's drugs?"

"You don't want to know. It'd only put you in danger." Drucilla started to shake. Spencer had never seen anyone so scared. If dogs really could smell fear, they'd pick this scent up miles away. "Why do you think I've been hiding out here? I don't want to see anyone else get hurt. You have to believe me." He struggled to form what Spencer assumed was a comforting smile, but it collapsed under pressure of a quivering lip. "Just leave the case and forget all about this. It's the safest thing for you to do." He returned his inhaler to his pocket.

Bolstered by the security that the threat in question was actually himself, and determined he wasn't leaving thousands of pounds worth of Mickey's drugs with Drucilla, Spencer pressed on. "If you think Mickey's after you, why on Earth would you want me to leave you his drugs? Surely that's only going to make things worse? He'll definitely be coming after you."

"They're not Mickey's."

"Who the Hell's are they, then?"

"I'd tried to get him to stop. You know what I think about drugs. But Stella would never listen to me."

"You're losing me now."

"Stella did some dealing. That case is his. Rick worked for him, so did Troy and Mildew." He looked at Spencer. "You're in danger if Mickey finds out you brought that case here. You've heard how Mickey deals with competition. Look what he did to Tony and Guy, and they were just customers. Think what he'd do to you if he thought you were involved."

Spencer was having difficulty in picturing Stella as the drag world's Pablo Escobar. "Stella was a dealer? Stella...?"

"He was just another sad, vain, old drag queen with no pension plan. Let's face it, there's plenty of us about."

Spencer felt a twinge of resentment at the implication he was part of this demographic. "So what are you saying?"

Drucilla shrugged. "I reckon he just wanted to have a few quid in his pocket when the day came that no one would pay him to put on a trowel-full of slap anymore. Everywhere's cutting back and it's us older ones they cut back on first."

"I didn't mean that." Once again, Spencer took umbrage at being included in this collective. "Are you saying you think Mickey killed Stella?" The police interview was beginning to make sense now; no wonder they weren't interested in Spencer. "So why would he want to kill you?"

"I have no idea. Because I won't let his guys deal in my clubs. Because I was friends with Stella, maybe. I don't know. I really don't know. Thing is, I'd convinced Stella to give it up. I told him our friendship couldn't go on anymore whilst he was involved in this. I won't lie to you, Spencer, it was partly because I was afraid what it might do to my reputation if it got out, but it was mostly out of concern. That's why I wanted him to get a night at The Tumble Dryer. I wanted him to get another focus. I'm so sorry, Spencer. I know I've been such a bitch to you, but I was trying to save my friend. I knew it was the only thing that might save him. He had some really unpleasant business associates, but he had agreed to give it up if I could get him a night at The Dryer. I know I've given you a hard time. God, I've been vile, I know, but I figured someone like you could make a success of their club wherever they went. I mean, look at you, Opus Gay would be great wherever you took it. And unlike you, Stella didn't have any real experience to get a night somewhere else." He wiped away a tear. "But with my influence at The Dryer I thought I could get him in, and get him away from dealing. It was only a matter of time before something awful happened. You know what I'm talking about: you'd do whatever it took to help someone you cared about. I thought if I could just... I'm such a useless friend. I should have tried harder. I could have saved..." He started to sob again.

Confused by guilt and pity, Spencer found himself putting the case on the floor and sitting next to Drucilla so he could put his arm around him. Sobbing uncontrollably, he shook under Spencer's embrace. Spencer couldn't believe he had been so full of fear and hatred for him; it wasn't Drucilla he should have been afraid would cause his downfall, it was Bette. All Drucilla had been doing was trying to help a friend. Okay, he was capable of being a vile bitch in the process, but as Drucilla had tried to help a troubled friend, Spencer was nearly killing off his. If the Buddhists had it right, Spencer was coming back as a pubic louse for the next thousand years.

"It was horrible what Mickey did to Stella," Drucilla said. Spencer prayed he wasn't going to go into a graphic description of Stella asphyxiating in a soup of his own blackheads. "I only got the marks from the police chalk out of the parquet this morning." He pointed to a feint outline on the floor of a giant gingerbread man in a splayed disco point. Spencer cringed.

"Have you told the police you think it's Mickey?"

"I can't say anything to the police. And neither can you. I don't want to get on the wrong side of Stella's business associates. It's way too dangerous."

"You can't hide here forever." Spencer was shocked by the genuine concern in his voice.

"What do you suggest I do, paint a target on my back and wait?"

A target on your ass would be bigger, thought Spencer, instantly feeling bad for thinking it.

Drucilla wiped his eyes. "Who knows you're here?"

"No one," Spencer lied.

"So how did you end up with the case, then? Weren't you working at the club last night?"

"It's complicated. Mandy was at the party. Look, Druci___" Under the circumstances it didn't seem right calling Drucilla by his stage name, but it had just occurred to Spencer that he didn't know his real name; he'd never been interested enough to ask.

"It's Joe," he said, apparently sensing Spencer's dilemma. "My name's Joe." He smiled weakly. "I'm sorry Francois got you involved. He shouldn't have done this to you."

Spencer shrugged. It made sense why Francois hadn't said anything about whose address he had written down; believing the police were in reception, he couldn't risk mentioning Drucilla's name and being told where to stick the case.

"Okay, then, Joe, why don't you___" Spencer's phone rang. He let go Joe's shoulder before scrambling in his pocket for the phone. It was Mandy. He disconnected the call. Then something

occurred to him. "How long ago was it that Stella died?" Joe seemed to tense momentarily. "And surely Rick would have__"
The phone rang again. It was Mandy, again. "Let me get this." Spencer moved over to the window.

"Mickey's on his way up," Mandy yelped. "Mad Mickey's on his way up. We just saw him going into the building. Lucy and I saw him going into the building. He's got a baseball bat!"

"What?"

"Mad Mickey, he just went into the building. With a baseball bat!" Mandy's voice had the rising hysteria of a business class trolley dolly with a cabin full of rabbis and only two kosher meals in the galley.

"You sure?"

"Yes, it was definitely a baseball bat."

Spencer rolled his eyes. "I meant are you sure it's him?"

"Of course I'm sure it's him. Who else looks like that?"

Spencer gulped. "I'll call you back." He turned back to Joe. "Listen…I don't want you to get all…panicky, but I think Mickey's on his way up."

Joe stood up and wiped his nose on his sleeve. His expression sharpened. He looked Spencer up and down then turned and walked through to the kitchen.

"You okay?" said Spencer. "I think we should__"

Joe reappeared with a gun in his hand, its barrel pointing at Spencer with cold, calm accuracy. It being the first gun Spencer had ever seen, he was surprised at how big it was. It also being the first time one had been pointed at his face, he was likewise surprised by the sudden contraction of his bollocks and every sphincter in his body shutting with a bang.

"I should have known," Joe said. "You're in this with Mickey. You smoke me out and he comes to finish the job."

"It's not like that. Honest. I have no idea why Mickey's here. You're just being paranoid."

"I'm supposed to believe that, am I?"

The penny dropped. "You're Stella's nasty business associates. Aren't you?"

"It was worth a try, you dumb bitch. I told you that crap for the sympathy vote. I had to get the gear off you and scare the shit out of you so you'd keep your mouth shut. But it looks like I needn't have bothered. And if you're wondering how I managed the tears: a quick skoosh of the asthma inhaler in them and you could star in a Jacqueline Smith movie." He raised the gun. "I only have one thing to say to you__"

The three loud bangs came in quick succession. After the first, Spencer was already screaming his way to the floor. By the third he was crumpled on the parquet awaiting the inevitable agony of bullet wound death. It was the nelly shriek from Joe and the clunk of the gun hitting the floor that pulled Spencer from his tragic death scene. The gun hadn't been fired; the noise was someone thundering on the front door.

Equally freaked out of their pantyhose, Spencer and Joe stared at each other for a moment. Another hammering at the door broke the spell. Spencer threw himself across the polished floor at the gun. Joe kicked it away just in time and brought his foot down on Spencer's hand. Spencer screamed as his thumb went crack. He sunk his teeth deep into Joe's calf. Joe let out a castrato scream and swung his fist at Spencer's head. The sickening sensation of flesh tearing away from flesh churned Spencer's stomach as his teeth were ripped away from the leg.

The door banged again and Mickey could be heard screaming, "I know you're in there."

Spencer lunged for the gun again.

As his fingers touched its handle every breath of air was forced from his body and he felt his ribs go pop; Joe had thrown himself on top of him.

In a breathless, star-spangled haze, Spencer saw Joe calmly pick up the gun and limp towards the door. Then the room behind the stars went dark.

CHAPTER 45

Spencer's ribs screamed in agony; someone was lifting him onto the sofa.

"Spence, can you hear me? Spence, open your eyes."

Spencer didn't recognise the voice at first, but the giant hands and ease with which they deposited him onto the sofa told him it must be Mickey.

"Just leave the bitch alone and shut up." Spencer had no doubt who that was.

With his ribs squeaking on every exchange of air, Spencer opened his eyes. Mickey, who was clearly in the final weeks of his latest course of steroids, was sitting next to him. His head looked oddly small for the amount of muscle over which it presided. A tiny lycra vest, that bore only passing resemblance to a garment and had the look of a condom stretched over a road cone, strained to cover part of his torso. Joe stood before them, blood seeping through his tracksuit leg, his gun pointing at Mickey and his eyes sparkling with pure malevolence. A sliver of smile tore across his face.

"Nice of you to join us," he said.

"You okay, Spence?" said Mickey.

"I said shut it, you brainless troll." Joe took a step back and pointed the gun with both hands.

A twitch pulled at Mickey's upper lip as if an invisible nurse was stitching an invisible cut. "You'd better just fucking shoot me, 'cos I'm gonna rip you a new shitter."

"Don't think I won't. You don't need to worry about *if*. You should be sweating about where." He circled the gun in the direction of Mickey's crotch.

Mickey clenched his fists at his sides and sat back. Pain shot through Spencer's ribs with the movement of the sofa.

"I'm rather surprised at you two," Joe said. "I'd never have put you together as business bedmates."

"I don't know what the fuck you're talking about," said Mickey.

"Don't play dumb," said Joe. "How else could you have known where I was?"

Mickey smiled. "Francois was on the phone to me as soon as *he* left." He flicked his thumb at Spencer. "He told me you were hiding here. He also told me it was anonymous fucking tip-offs from you that was fingering me to the old bill. He told me fucking everything. He also told me that you and he was__"

"He what!?" Joe's smile evaporated in an instant.

"You heard."

Joe's mouth opened and closed in silence before words could form through his rage. "The twisted little fucker. I'll__"

"Could someone call me an ambulance," said Spencer. "I think my ribs are broken."

Mickey and Joe both cast a shut-the-fuck-up glare.

"Francois obviously thinks I won't have the balls to deal with you," Joe said. "The backstabbing, little shit thinks you're going to kill me and doesn't want left on the losing side."

Spencer could feel Mickey's muscles tensing through the sofa.

"More like he just doesn't want to be in business with a fucking psycho." Mickey's knuckles were glowing white.

"Guys," wheezed Spencer, "this is obviously a private conversation. Maybe it's best if I just leave and get some medical attention while you sort it out."

"Shut it!" Mickey and Joe chorused.

"I'm the psycho, am I?" said Joe. "It's not me who's been on the homicidal bender."

No, thought Spencer, *that'd be me*. His ribs crackled.

"I had fuck all to do with any of that," said Mickey. "And if I did, you'd be the first to be zipped up in an elephant fucking body bag. So what about Samuel and Valkeyre, you saying you had fuck all to do with that?"

"Of course I had nothing to do with that chav and your naff

queen. And you know it."

"Sure you fucking didn't. So it was just a coincidence you were the last fucking person to see Samuel alive?"

"What you talking about, you steroid-filled dipshit? I never saw Samuel."

"Really? So how come you were at the fucking hospital the day he died?"

"I was visiting Stella, you moron. The guy you poisoned. I never saw your naff chav..." Joe's eyes widened. "It was Samuel, wasn't it? He went in to finish him off at the hospital and fucked up by poisoning himself, didn't he? Didn't he?" The gun shook in his hand.

Mickey smiled again. "Samuel phoned me just before he was killed to say he'd just seen you."

Spencer could feel his ribs crackle like bubble wrap under his shirt. He was struggling to breathe. "Guys, I really need..."

The gun swung to point at Spencer. "Shut the fu__"

With nothing left on his body to tense, Mickey snapped, propelling the testosterone-fuelled jet pack of his body at Joe. Joe hadn't a chance. Mickey's solid mass hit him square in the stomach with a sickening thud, catapulting them both across the room into a parlour palm. Spencer heard the familiar sound of the gun hitting the floor.

Mickey wasted no time in setting about him. His feet and fists became a blur of hate and hormones.

Spencer could see the gun just a few inches from his feet, but pinned against the sofa by the pain of his broken ribs it might as well have been in the next county. Joe squealed as Mickey took a step back to get a better swing with his boot. He seemed oblivious to Spencer and the missing gun; he just kept piling in with his feet. Spencer knew if he didn't stop him he was going to kill Joe.

Spencer took a deep breath and tried to reach the gun with his foot. A juggernaut of pain broadsided him, blurring his vision. He couldn't give up.

In an attempt to reduce the pressure on his ribs he exhaled as much air as he could and tried to lean forward. His body refused;

he didn't move an inch. He tried to shout, but the wheezing rasp that came out had no chance of being heard over the sound of boot on bone and flesh.

Joe stopped pleading. Mickey went over and picked up the baseball bat. He swung it in the air a few times as if checking its balance before taking it to Joe's crumpled remains.

Mustering the memory of every bottle of poppers he had ever sniffed and every line of K he had ever snorted, Spencer willed himself through the pain barrier towards the gun. Half on, half off the sofa, he grasped the metal handle. A Domestos hi-colonic of pain coursed through his body as he squeezed the trigger. The gun cracked. The plasma screen took the bullet and exploded. Spencer was thrown upright in a torturous jolt.

The gun clattered to the floor once again.

Mickey stopped mid-swing.

"Please, Mickey," said Spencer, "you'll kill him."

Mickey looked round at the gun lying on the floor and picked it up before kicking out one last time. He dropped the bat at his feet.

Spencer was surprisingly relieved to hear Joe cough and splutter from under the palm. Seeing the gun in Mickey's hand, Spencer's ribs dulled. He knew he was still in excruciating pain, but it was being suppressed by his now dizzying levels of adrenaline. He sat forward. Mickey was examining the gun. Spencer pulled himself from the sofa and moved over to Joe on the floor.

"Let the fat fuck die," Mickey said.

Sickened by the swathe of violence in his own wake, Spencer crouched down next to Joe and helped him sit up. He was so completely covered in blood it was difficult to see where the wounds were.

"We need to get him an ambulance, Mickey."

"I don't think so." Mickey checked the gun's clip with familiar ease. "I need some answers first."

Joe coughed and wheezed and spat blood onto his leg.

"My place got raided this morning." Mickey prodded the gun playfully against the shattered plasma screen. Bits of glass fell away. "I was just getting back from a club and I saw them kicking my door in. This is very fucking bad for business. Very fucking bad." He kicked the baseball bat away from his feet. "Francois told me how you got stuck with this, Spence." He pointed the gun at the case. "But how come you never returned any of my fucking calls? I've been phoning you for weeks to try and tell you to watch your back from this evil fuck." He sneered at Joe.

"You what!?" Spencer let go of Joe, letting him fall back, banging his head against the wall. "But I thought you were trying to aks me if your guys could work Opus Gay."

Mickey laughed. "Get you, Mr Fucking Big Shot. I was doing you a fucking favour." He pointed the gun at Joe. "Trying to give you the heads up on *him*. Did you really think I needed fucking permission? I wanted to help you keep the place clean, and to make sure this fat fuck didn't slip his guys in when mine were keeping a low profile."

"You were trying to keep the place clean? I don't get it."

"Daniels' licence review. Christ, Spence, you any idea how many of my best customers worked in the city? You any idea how many fucking bankers I used to have on my books? I'm losing customers right left and fucking centre. What good would it do me if another club lost its licence? I'm losing venues all over the fucking shop. I'm a fucking businessman, Spence. I gotta look after my fucking market. I wouldn't touch blu because it was attracting too much fucking agro. But this greedy cunt..." he glared again at Joe, "he didn't give a fuck."

Spencer felt small and naive. "Mickey, I had no idea."

Joe squeezed Spencer's hand. "Inhaler, inhaler." He started to rummage in his pocket.

"Tell him to keep his hands where I can see them."

"It's just an inhaler," said Spencer. "He can't breathe."

Mickey knelt down in front of them and pointed the gun barrel at Joe. "Maybe I should just put the pig out of its fucking misery. If I'm gettin' blamed for these murders I might as well get some of the action."

"Please, Mickey, leave him alone." Spencer couldn't let this happen. He moved between Joe and the gun.

Joe struggled to pull a small brown cylinder to his mouth.

"Why do you give a shit about this poisonous fucker? He'd happily__"

From out of the corner of his eye Spencer saw Joe turn what he had thought to be an inhaler at Mickey. Pepper spray jetted into Mickey's eyes.

Mickey's scream, the two shots and Joe's sudden burst of energy all seemed to happen at once. Joe lunged at Mickey, knocking him backwards and hitting his head against the floor with a dull crack. Joe then threw himself himself onto Mickey's chest in his trademark body flop whilst wrenching the gun from his hand as he elbowed him in the face.

Joe moved away with the gun. Mickey thrashed and screamed at the burning in his eyes. The gun was now pointing at Mickey.

"Get up," Joe ordered. And then, to Spencer's surprise, he slipped to the side and crouched down next to Spencer.

Mickey, eyes closed and streaming, propelled himself at where Joe had been standing. The gun fired. Blood spattered across the walls. Mickey hit the floor.

Silence rushed in to fill the gap left by the shot. The world seemed to stop. A tossed coin would have suspended mid-air. A single breath would have remained on the lips.

The moment was broken by an ice cream van's tinny rendition of *The Magic Roundabout* six floors below. Joe stepped over the body and flopped onto the sofa. He pulled the real inhaler from his pocket.

Spencer couldn't move. He was slumped against the wall, his head bleeding from where he had smacked the solid concrete. His ribs didn't bother him anymore; he felt a bit of a drama queen having thought them so bad. He thought it was a shame about the shirt, however; the hole in the middle would spoil the hang. A leg of his jeans had suffered a similar fate.

Joe muttered something from across the room, but the close proximity to four gunshots in a confined space had Spencer's ears ringing like a Motorhead roadie's.

"What?"

Obviously suffering the same, Joe repeated: "MY TRACK SUIT'S RUINED." He pulled at the blood-soaked fabric.

Without the energy to point out that it was ruined the moment a Chinese sweatshop owner had decided to make it in XXXL, Spencer just watched as his blood stretched away from him. It traced its way along the grooves in the parquet, snaking towards Mickey's still body. A dark pool fed by them both began to form. It wasn't as red as the blood in the movies.

"So if it wasn't Mickey doing the killing, who was it?" Joe smiled a bloody smile, exposing a now-missing tooth. "It was you, wasn't it? Why didn't I see it...? Brilliant plan, really. You kill some of his guys, some of my guys, and then watch us kill each other. Now you've got a foothold in The Dryer it would leave you with a nicely lucrative business. You just didn't seem the type." He grimaced as he pulled material away from his bleeding leg. "So what was your plan? Smoke me out with that...," he pointed to the case, "and then get my whereabouts to Mickey after you've had his place busted? Might have worked if Francois hadn't beaten you to it. I'll bet you had intended being well away from here by the time Mickey arrived. So is your slapper mate, the dressmaker – what's his name, Mandy? - in on it? Did he do the three in Soho?"

So long as he didn't move, Spencer had little feeling in his body at all. He knew he was dying, and the only thing that really bothered him was that he would have to listen to Joe until it happened. He became aware of a piece of broken plant pot digging into his butt.

"CAT GOT YOUR TONGUE?" said Joe.

"You're going to get done for our murders." Spencer tried to keep movement to an absolute minimum.

"You think...? You see I think this is how it's all going to go: As soon as you've bled to death I'm gonna call the police and an ambulance. Once they get here and start thumping on the door, I'm going to take up position, all dramatic and unconscious-like, and just wait." He adjusted his position. "I'll tell the police I've been hiding away here because you've made threats to me about what you'd do if I didn't let your boys deal in my clubs. I knew

Stella was involved and had been caught in the crossfire of some feud between you and Mickey, and I didn't want to be next. But you tracked me down here and tried bribing me. I'm assuming your fingerprints are all over that case, and its contents..."

Spencer watched as the growing pool of blood in front of him reflected more and more of the broken television screen. Consciousness was slipping away and he had no desire to fight it.

"...attacked me the moment I opened the door. But it wasn't me Mickey was after." Joe snapped his fingers. "Pay attention. I don't want you to miss this. So then I'll tell the police that you and Mickey..."

Joe's voice seemed to fade into the background. The only thing stopping Spencer drifting off completely was the stabbing sensation of a shard of plant pot sticking into his rump. He tried to move his leg so it would fall away. He felt his phone drop from his back pocket. Spencer felt his eyes close.

"...but then you two fought. A gun was dropped. I grab it and shoot the TV." Joe was still droning on when Spencer came round. A macabre, bloody mouthed, girly smile was pulling across Joe's face and the pitch of his voice was rising into a mocking squeak. "*I was frightened of the gun and just wanted you to stop...*"

Spencer closed his eyes and tried to concentrate on moving his arm. It was flopped lifeless behind him and his hand was only a few inches away from the phone. He could just reach. He stretched his fingers towards it. He was wide awake now and trying not to scream from the pain.

"... And I'm sure the police will agree with me there." Joe straightened himself. "You know something, and this will stick in your craw a bit, but we have a lot in common, you and me."

Spencer couldn't let that go unchallenged. "Watch me die if you want, but don't expect me to listen to that bullshit." Spencer tried to grab the phone, but his thumb was twisted at a bizarre angle to the rest of his hand.

"I think you'll find we do. We're both ambitious, we're both willing to do whatever it takes to protect our future and we're both driven by our fear of that self-same future."

"Fear of your future, that's your excuse for selling drugs?"

"What's yours? Don't get all high and bloody mighty with me, sweetie. You're just the same. Why do you do it?"

"I don't. I just wanted to make a really amazing night out. It was nothing to do with drugs." Spencer spat blood onto his shirt.

"Cut the crap. We both know why we ended up in drugs: we know how clubbing works. We know the clubs are all just empty trimmings. They're just the walls the punters get wasted and laid behind. The real money is in what gets them wasted."

Spencer's eyes wanted to close. Was this to be his ironic fate, left to die listening to Joe's hateful drivel? He snapped; he knew he had nothing to lose. "It was never about drugs. It was always just about you. Don't you get it, you stupid fuck?" He tried to close his hand around the phone. Pain coursed through his body. "It wasn't about drugs. It was you. It was you I wanted to kill. I've been trying to kill you!" It felt great to say it out loud.

"What are you talking about?"

"It was only ever about you. Everything else was an accident, a big, crap, fucked-up accident. I just wanted you dead. You're an evil bitch and I hate that other people have died because of me. I hate myself for that, but my biggest regret is that I failed. My biggest regret is that you're still alive." He tried again to close his hand around the phone, but his fingers appeared to be incapable of even the simplest contraction.

Joe's face seemed to grind through the gears of expression before coming to a halt at confusion. "So this was all just about your stupid little club?"

"Yes, just my stupid little club. I just wanted to make a club that was fun for people to go to and that shits like you couldn't get a foothold in. Yes, I wanted it to reboot my career, but I also wanted it to be somewhere that people could go to and not need to take drugs to enjoy themselves."

Joe laughed. It was a cold, confident laugh. "You stupid, naive, twat. You have absolutely no idea how it all works, do you? The whole clubbing scene is a balance. And you and your stupid club are just part of it. New clubs and new drugs have to come along every few years to stop people feeling like they're in a rut. 'Cos as soon as they start feeling that they start looking at their lives and the amount of money they're spending on drugs and clubbing. Just look at what's happened to drugs over the past twenty-five years: first we had acid and coke; then along came ecstasy; big loved-up fun was had by all and then we got ketamine; then there was G, and we all know what a bloody mess that was; then we got MDMA, because basically there was none in the pills anymore; then we got crystal; then MDMA was remarketed as 'pure' MDMA, because the MDMA was being cut to fuck; and then we came to blu. Keep things moving to keep them interested, but it's really just sticking a new wheel in the same old hamster's cage."

"That's just cynical bullshit. It's just the crap you use to justify dealing." Spencer tried to channel his concentration into his hand.

Joe roared an aggressive belly laugh. "I don't need to justify anything. People go to amazing lengths not to see things as they are. And the gay scene, as always, leads the way. That's why they call it slamming, not intravenous drug use. That's why they call it bareback, not unprotected sex. No one wants to see the truth. We bully and oppress ourselves into a segregated state of body apartheid. Our magazines are filled with page after page of beautiful people now. Your ads for Opus Gay are full of them. Club promoters like you sell their clubs on a pitch of beauty and perfection. Six packs are presented as the norm and those who don't have them are made feel crap for not being good enough. And the ones with the six packs are just as miserable, constantly perforating their asses with steroid needles because there's always someone out there with bigger pecs and a better six pack. But a line and a pill and it all feels like a happy party - a chemical clown's smile that stops them feeling inadequate and insecure."

With every synapses of concentration he could muster, Spencer wrapped his hand around the phone one last time. He couldn't remember the combination of touch sensitive menus he had to go through to make a call, but he didn't care; it didn't matter. Gritting his teeth through the pain, he gripped the phone as tightly as he could bear and swung his arm over his body, aiming the phone at

Joe's head. It landed pitifully on the sofa beside him. He picked a piece of broken pot and threw that, too. It glanced off Joe's trainers, injuring little more than Spencer's pride.

Joe grinned a bloody grin. "You throw like a girl." He grimaced as he moved on the sofa. "So you had nothing to do with drugs. How pathetic. And how ironic that you end up making life easier all round for me. This couldn't have worked out better. I'm free of you and Mickey now. With one pull of that trigger I wiped out the competition, and with Opus Gay out of the way, I'll get Manthrax your night at the club."

Terminally exhausted after his burst of energy, Spencer just wanted it all to end now. "Why did you want my night at the club? What was so important about having another night at The Dryer? There's plenty clubs you can sell your crap in."

Joe laughed. "You stupid twat, you still don't get it. I don't want it to sell drugs in. Quite the opposite. We've got plenty venues for that. Why do you think I keep my nights drug free? It keeps my name clean and gives us somewhere to launder the cash through."

Spencer's eyelids were getting heavy. The room was getting smaller and darker. Then something occurred to him. "Anthony, the guy who had the night before me, it was you who had him killed, wasn't it?"

Jo smiled. "What a dipshit he was. He used his phone to record a conversation he'd had with Stella. He didn't want blu being sold in his club and was threatening to expose Stella to Norman Daniels if his boys didn't leave."

"That's why they only stole his phone."

Joe nodded. "That's what happens when you employ kids. They were just supposed to slap him about a bit and nab the phone and takings. They got a bit carried away. Stupid twat didn't have the takings on him and they didn't believe him." He pulled at his track suit leg again and grimaced. "All works out well in the end, though. I'm going to spin this and leave here the hero as you take the blame *postmously*."

Spencer saw the pool of blood spill out to where the police chalk had been on the floor and knew for sure he wasn't going to make it. "POSTHUMOUSLY, you illiterate, fat bitch."

Joe pulled himself up with a grunt and moved over to Spencer. Spencer calmly closed his eyes as the fist came towards him

CHAPTER 46

Spencer had never visited anyone in prison before and it struck him that the whole process seemed designed to humiliate the visitor. He weaved through the tables past shaven-headed psychopaths, trying not to make eye contact with anyone.

Bette sat on her own, looking demurely into her hands. She jumped to her feet on seeing him. Spencer froze. Bette threw open her arms to greet him, mouth agape and tongue writhing in prehensile anticipation.

Spencer panicked. This wasn't right. He ran for the door, the door with all the light coming from it, but the guards were pulling him back, back towards Bette. He struggled. Prisoners joined in, dragging him back, away from the light...

"And again. CLEAR!"

It was as if he was inside a giant marshmallow from which he had to eat his way out, but he wasn't hungry. Occasionally he could hear muffled voices through the marshmallow, but like being in bed on a cold morning when you're bursting for a pee, he just tried to ignore it and get back to being comfortable.

"...wouldn't let me go up. I wanted to go up after I saw Mickey, but Lucy said we should trust you and keep out of the way. We called the police as soon as we heard the shots. And when they brought you out...Oh, God, I'm so sorry, Spence. This is all my fault. If I hadn't gone to that stupid party. I'm such a useless idiot..."

"...idiot magistrate gave me three fines and eighty-four hours community service. You'd think I had force fed them the bloody cat shit. And do you know what they've got me doing…? Dog shit patrol in Abney Park. Who says the judicial system doesn't have a sense of irony? It was originally only going to be sixty hours community service, but the magistrate heard I had been giving out business cards in the waiting area and stuck the rest on. Got quite a few jobs from it. I'm thinking about leafleting divorce courts.

"Mrs Chapori's not been helping matters for you. She's given an interview to one of the tabloids and told them she knew you were a bad un and a dealer and that you used to lift your hand to your lovely girlfriend, Bette. I had to tell her that you and Bette were one in the same. I still don't think she gets it. The tabloids are just quoting her about the dealer bit, of course.

"The doctors aren't being very helpful to us here. They won't tell us anything about how you are. They say they'll only speak to next of kin. I told them I was your nearest thing to next of kin, but they wouldn't…"

"…wouldn't budge, so he's bought me this bask and suspenders to take with me. I tried them on the other night. I nearly pissed meself laughing. I was a honey-glazed ham with a frill."

"You sure you want to go through with it?"

"Yeah, gets me out the house. And he doesn't know it yet, but I've bought a riding crop…Should we change this one's bags?"

"Nah…he's okay."

"He's a drag queen. He looks a bit like that one that was at Tania's hen night."

"Was that the night with the tequila slammers?"

"Nah, you're thinking about the time…"

"…time I changed my Gaydar profile, girl. And you'll be pleased to know that I've taken down the picture of me on the beach at Gran Canaria doing my man-fanny pose from *Silence of the Lambs*. I still think is says I'm playful, but you're right: my hair was a mess. On my new profile I'm describing myself as 'flabulous'. It means overweight and carrying it with style. I think it captures me. I also think that…"

"...think that at my age, *dahling*, I should have known better than wear the pale blue. The veins on the back of my legs were not my idea of a coordinated accessory, so I'm booking myself in to have them done. The christening was lovely, despite the chosen names. I mean, for goodness sake, Peach Melba and Cranberry, you'd think the woman's ovaries were sponsored by Del Monte. But that's L.A. for you. Anyway, the talks went well. I might be doing five shows from there and...oh, I'll tell you when you're up and about.

"I'm not really sure what to do with these grapes. Rather silly of me bringing them. Fortnum and Mason's. Very nice.

"I have to say, I think you're better off in here at the moment. I shouldn't like to tell you what's being said about you out there. Character assassination, *dahling*, the last time I saw an assassination attempt like this there was a grassy knoll in the background. Drucilla's saying some absolutely frightful things about you. But F.Y.I. the policeman on duty outside your room is a dish. As police..."

"...police have been asking me all sorts of weird questions. Lucy told me to keep quiet about who was at the party. She said I would just make the whole media thing worse. I don't think they believe me. I told them I was too mashed. I also told them it was all my fault and that the case wasn't yours, but Drucilla has been saying you were a dealer. She says you killed people. She's lying to everyone and everyone is believing her. Oh, God, I wish I'd never gone to that party. You'd still be okay if I'd just... Please wake up, Spence. I can't cope with this. You're lying there because of me. I should never have let you go up there. Before I..."

"...before I knew it he was shaking it at me. Girlfriend, I could have died. He cornered me like a randy chihuahua. I mean, Jesus-for-a-child, it wasn't Beverly Hills. It was the cottage in John Lewis. I just rolled up my copy of Boyz and hit it. Ooooh did she scream.

"The papers are saying some fierce things about you. And Drucilla is coming out of all this like the turd that don't stink.

Did you really shoot Mickey? I know you've been having some *'anger management issues'* lately, girl, and Mickey did overdo the spandex theme, but was blowing his brains out really the best way to critique his fashion sense?

"Oh, before I forget, I don't know if anybody has told you about Bo, but her ATM has sold…"

"…sold a frightful story to the press, *dahling*. All about you supplying the goods for my drug-crazed sex parties. I've told all the papers that the last time I participated in an orgy the porn was on a cine projector, but no one is taking a blind bit of notice. It's all simply ghastly - the doorman of my building winked at me this morning.

"I'm a little annoyed with the doctors here, *dahling*. No one will tell us how you are, but the looks they give when we ask are most distressing. The police officer outside said things were bad. The way I see it, you never listened to anyone, anyway, so don't go listening to them now if you hear them saying anything bad. One doctor said that…"

"…said that you killed Mickey, and some other people. I've told everyone the drugs weren't yours and that it was my fault you ended up with them, but no one seems to listen. I keep telling them what happened. Gerald says this is typical of the police when this sort of thing breaks out between dealers. He says the police like to just leave the dealers to it and kill each other off. I was really annoyed with him and told him this was nothing to do with you and that whatever dealers were involved in the murders it wasn't you.

"Oh, Gerald's a guy I'm seeing, by the way. I met him that night at the…the last night at the club. We didn't hook up till a few days later…well, obviously…I went to that party…and…I…well…I…you know what happened. He's a really nice guy. He's a lawyer. He's been giving me advice on what to say. He agrees with Lucy and told me to keep quiet about who was at the party. He says they don't need to know and that it would just cause even more publicity than there already is. Which wouldn't help anyone. But imagine, me with a lawyer. He's single, drives a Renault Megane and has all his own teeth. I can't wait for you to meet him. He has the flattest stomach…"

"…stomach and spleen. The trauma to the cranium, caused by being thrown against a concrete wall by the force of the first bullet, caused the initial bleeding that may have brought about the condition of coma. The ribs, which caused abrasions to the lungs, fortunately didn't puncture. The above-the-knee amputation was a result of the second bullet shattering the kneecap. Collins, looking at the extensive damage to the leg, in a case like this…"

"…this nurse has more eyeliner on than I do. Admittedly, I'm not long finished dog shit patrol. What's the thing with camp Goths? Doesn't the NHS have a psych evaluation process? I mean, you'd think the ones with death and vampire fixations would get weeded out before getting a job in intensive care. Don't worry, hon, I'm sure he's great at his job. But if you feel yourself going, don't open your eyes for one final look. You don't want the last thing you see to be Maryland Manson.

"Listen, hon, you need to wake up now. You've got to be able to defend yourself about what's being said. They've got you down as some murderous drug dealer. Some fat drag queen has told the police that you killed all these people. And the police and everyone else is believing her. You've got to sort…"

"…sort things out with Norman Daniels. Gerald came to see him with me and got Daniels to agree to let me run Opus Gay for the next two months for you. He said that since all the advertising and acts were booked…"

"…booked in so I thought we could make a few quid this way… After all, what's a good agent for? I know you'll need money when you get better so I thought this way even lying here you could do some work. Don't worry, I've tidied your hair. I hope you don't mind me taking the pictures… Some of the…tabloids…are offering…good money…for a snap or two of you…lying here. The Old Bill outside means none of them can get near you…so the money's…good. I'll cut you in when…you wake up…"

"… wake up, girlfriend? There's fierce character crime being committed upon your good name out there. I had to slap a queen at the Candy Bar the other night. She called you a cold blooded murderer. She'd been pushing her luck all night, though: been giving my dress the evils.

"By the way, Mandy did you a blinder at the weekend. The club was a huge success. The girl's a natural. There were TV cameras outside the club filming people going in. Mandy was interviewed. Drucilla's furious.

"The current tale the tabloids are touting is that you and Mickey were in some tit-for-tat gangland killing thing. Apparently Mickey's posse killed someone on your team and you retaliated and then it all kicked off. They're saying Valkeyre, Stella, Troy, Mildew, somebody called Samuel, Rick and a couple of funeral directors in Soho got killed. You gotta love the irony of the two funeral directors. I said to the man from the *News of the World*, 'My friend Spencer could never pull off a crime like that. She couldn't pull off a wax strip without fainting. It's just not in the girl's nature.' Thing is, the police aren't contradicting the papers.

"Now, I've brought you in a copy of *Soap Weekly*. We don't want you falling behind. So, we'll start with Corrie: Ken Barlow's about to get some bad news…and, oh, you'll never guess who's…"

"…guess who's seeing someone. Lucy. I'll let her tell you herself how they met, but let's just say they're well matched.

"The club went brilliantly at the weekend. It was packed. I think the TV cameras helped get some interest. I did an interview with them. They've been trying to get an interview with Norman Daniels, but he asked if I'd do it. And the weirdest thing has happened with the licence review. You'll never guess.

"I don't want you to worry about Opus Gay. Everything's going great and I'm sure you'll be up and about for the next one, anyway…"

"...any way someone could get in here to take pictures. I'm sending a letter of complaint to the trust manager, *dahling*. With a policeman outside your door how did a photographer get in here? It must be one of the nurses or cleaners. The pictures are all over the tabloids. The upside, however, is the pictures could have been worse – fortunately I had my hairdresser, Jean Marc, come in and cut your hair the other day, so you were looking good. Thing is, in the picture I could have sworn you had a touch of lipgloss on.

"And not to let you hog all the limelight, the network has suspended me. My producer said it was nothing personal and he was sure everything will be back to normal after all these accusations of me being a drug-crazed sex addict are all cleared up. There's several anaemic looking rent boys - whom I've never seen in my life before - selling stories of their wild nights of kinky sex with me. I'd love to be capable of half the activities I'm supposed to have pursued with them. *Dahling*, until I saw a picture of it in the *Daily Mail*, I didn't even know what a speculum was. It's all so ghastly. They're giving me a right Angus Deytoning. And to top it all, last..."

"...last of my community service and I've met this really nice guy, Peter. I didn't want to tell you about it until I was sure he was going to be around when you came-too, but it looks like he's going to be a regular diner at chez Lucy. He was on dog shit patrol for having put half a ton of manure on his neighbour's roses. They shared a roof terrace. I like his style.

"Gawd, Spencer, have you any idea how much I hate making this bloody small talk? I...I don't know how much longer I can bear this. I hate seeing you like this. Wake up. Please. It's okay for you lying here in bed..."

"...bed and breakfast in Brighton. Not your usual B and B, *dahling*, that's been done to death by all the other retired drag and leather queens, but something a bit more specialised and up-market. I'm going to call it 'The Dressing-Up Box'. It's going to cater exclusively for trannies, drag queens, their partners and admirers. All the staff will be in drag; we'll run regular tutorials for makeup, deportment and etiquette; there'll be a fine dining club and occasional guest speakers. I'm also thinking about an executive suit with a fifty-two inch plasma screen in it. That's going to be called the TV room. All the rooms will be designed to enhance the dressing-up experience: big mirrors, ambient lighting, that sort of thing. I've set up my own production company and am having to move fast to squeeze in some free publicity. I'm doing a fly-on-the-wall docu on my downfall from the network to my rise as the country's most exotic landlady. I'll get the camera crew to follow me from hunting for the property to its fabulous opening night. The final scene of the documentary will have me taking my make-up off after the opening party – never to be put on again. I've had it with Bo, *dahling*. I'm retiring her forever and I can't tell you how good it feels to say it. I've also been thinking, why don't you come into business with me? Let's leave London behind. You wouldn't believe..."

"...believe a man could make me feel like that again. I'm telling you, hon, the things he can do with... God, I miss you, Spencer. I want to tell you all about Russell, properly. Even Mrs Chapori likes him. Wake up.

"Mandy's working like a thing possessed to keep the club going. It's tomorrow night. He's expecting TV cameras outside again. He's doing an amazing job..."

"...amazing job with the club, girl. Drucilla has been trying to get Opus Gay closed, but Mandy has the place packed. For some reason Norman Daniels is almost dry humping his leg. I don't know what that's all about. Drucilla is none too pleased. She's still saying Opus Gay is bad taste in view of it being run by a killer. You should have seen her face after Mandy did another interview with the news cameras outside the club the other night. Well, you can imagine. I'd like to slap that bitch's double chins right off her pugly face. One of these days..."

"...days since I last saw him. He seems to be busier still with your club. I left a message for him to knock my door when he was next up at your flat, but I've seen nothing of him. Anaesthesia says he did an amazing job doing Opus Gay again. Who would have thought he had it in him.

"Mrs Chapori still hasn't got the gist of what's happened. I'm a bit worried about the old bat. The police brought her back to the house the other day and knocked on my door to ask if I could go sit with her for a while. She had gone to report Bette as a missing person. She's afraid not having seen her for weeks that Spencer's drug gang had abducted her. She'd even emptied her Post Office savings account in case they wanted a ransom. She just won't accept Bette's not real. Anaesthesia's tried talking to her, but she's starting to get paranoid that we're all in on it somehow. She's had a burglar alarm fitted and is driving the whole building mad with it: she keeps forgetting the pin number to switch it off. Come on, hon, Mrs C really misses you. You gotta wake up so everyone in the building can get some sleep. She just won't believe..."

"...believe me I have no idea what they're talking about, *dahling*. I've had several texts on the way here all asking the same thing, 'have you heard?' Well heard what? I've tried calling Anaesthesia, but she's been engaged on her mobile and landline constantly for the past hour and a half. And as for Mandy, he isn't returning anyone's calls at the moment. I've not heard anything from him in weeks. As to what the mysterious news..."

"...news for you, girlfriend. I just spoke to Pavlova. Carmen Monoxide told her the barman she is seeing works there and he saw it all. He told her they arrived..."

"...arrived as I was packing some lambs hearts into our 'have a heart' gift boxes. I had to slap him to calm him down. Well, I probably didn't *have* to, but what am I supposed to do when some hysterical queen comes running at me? It was hardly even a tap. When he calmed down he told me..."

"...told me that Chlamydia spoke to Norman Daniels and he says it's true. Girlfriend, it's all been happening. I'm carryin' me a brolly just in case the birds start fallin' out the trees. I'd have clippered my afro to have seen it. The two muscle Marys went quietly, but Manthrax nutted one of the cops..."

"...cops were all over the place. Apparently six clubs were raided at the same time. What's going on? I've been trying to find out but Anaesthesia isn't speaking to me and I've not seen Mandy in weeks. I tried to call..."

"...call me old fashioned, *dahling*, but this wasn't an acceptable sideline for a drag queen in my days. We used to do pantos, seaside reviews and Terrence Higgins Trust benefits. This is all so vulgar. Apparently some non-entity called Devine Inspiration was arrested as she came into The Tumble Dryer with four hundred wraps of blu hidden about her person. I haven't heard what Drucilla has to say about it all, but I'm sure I'll hear tonight. It's Ursula Mufcross's birthday doo, and I know she's invited…Oh, and Anaesthesia isn't speaking to Lucy. Lucy apparently hit Anaesthesia round the head with a box of pigs' liver or something the other day. Anaesthesia says she's holding out for an apology. I told her I was holding out for a face cream that really does make the skin look younger, and that we'd both be wrinkled old hags before either happens. So you really must wake up now, *dahling*, you're..."

"...you're a bloody genius, hon. A bloody genius. Anaesthesia and Rob phoned me last night and told me that the vile drag queen who's been accusing you of murder is in jail. She's in Jail. You've brought down the entire gay scene's drug supply. You're in the clear. Every queen in London hates you, and you'll probably need an armed guard with you for the rest of your life to protect you from cold turkey clubbers, but you're in the clear. Come on, Spence, you gotta..."

"...you gotta move that black ass. Girlfriend, I always knew none of this shit was you. If you was gonna bump someone off it would have been the same old hooter the rest of us would have done: Drucilla. That mother's been long overdue... Bette...!? Bette...!? Aaaaaarrrrghhh...nurse...nurse...NURSE...! Ooh, lovin' what you're doing with the eyes...It's Bette, she blinked. I swear she blinked. Oops, I'll move, shall I...? Don't mind me... Oh, hello, another one...would 'excuse me' hurt...? Blue's so your colour. Have you ever thought of a hair tint...? There, she did it again. She blinked...it was me who did it...I brought her back from the brink. She followed my voice from the void... You know, I've often been told I have an angelic quality to my voice...Hold on. My headache's gone...My headache's gone...It's just gone...gone. I'm telling you, gone, as if it was never there. Oh-my-God. I can heal. I can heal...Oh-my-God, I can heal! Quick, quick, wheel me in some cripples before this goes ... Oh, dear. I'm going to have to sit down. I'm having a religious moment...I think I'm going to fai__"

Spencer felt himself being expelled from unconsciousness. It was like being torn from the womb and dragged under protest into an ice-cold world. There was a blur of people around him.

"Spencer, can you hear me?" someone asked.

He could feel his leg twitching as he struggled to reply; somehow he had been rewired and he didn't know what buttons in his head operated what parts of his body.

CHAPTER 47

The week following Spencer's return to consciousness saw a parade of well-wishers traipse past the end of his bed, but with a short-term memory as capacious as that of a guppy, as each person left they took with them the memory of their visit. The only reference as to how many people had been to see him was the ever-growing mountain of grapes.

For the first couple of days, speech was difficult: his mouth wanted to go in one direction and his tongue and words the other. Once he had remastered the art, he then spent the next two days sobbing; where his kneecap had been blown off by Mickey's bullet the lower part of his leg had been amputated, and the scar tissue across his chest meant even above-the-waist swimwear photoshoots were now out of the question.

"So I'm definitely not under arrest?" Spencer asked of a police officer whose name he couldn't remember if he had been given let alone what it was, and being of such strikingly bland features, Spencer knew he would forget him with similar ease.

"I believe D.C. Heinz went through this with you," said the officer.

Spencer's bed hummed and vibrated as he pushed the button to sit up. "D.C. who?"

"D.C. Heinz."

Spencer thought for a moment. "Blonde, bum like two prize winning melons in a lycra hammock and a smile that could give a nun an erection?"

"Yes…Officer Heinz is fair haired."

"He's been to see me?"

"Yes," the officer was beginning to sound impatient, "Officer Heinz was here a couple of days ago. But it was thought best if

I dealt with you from now on."

A sense of embarrassed dread percolated through Spencer's dulled senses. He could feel himself blush and didn't know why. "Let's just say I don't remember, shall we?" The officer's bland smile told Spencer everything he needed to re-file the memory under 'never think about this again'. "So where's Drucilla now?"

"Joe Braithwaite was arrested and charged with the murders. He has also been charged with possession with intent to supply."

Spencer's eye caught a framed picture sitting on the windowsill. It was of Anaesthesia, dressed like the black Madonna with a halo around her afro. Spencer had no idea what all that was about, but he looked forward to hearing the tale.

"Jesus Christ!" Spencer yelped, turning back to see the policeman he had forgotten was there. "Sorry, you were saying."

The officer's eyes rolled back momentarily before he continued. "Joe Braithwaite is now on remand__"

"You mean Drucilla?"

"Yes, Drucilla." He was definitely sounding irascible.

"So when did all this happen?"

The officer seemed to flush at the question. "A couple of weeks ago…while you were unconscious. We took the opportunity of allowing Mr Braithwaite to think we believed his story that you were the murderer and that the drugs were yours. And in the absence of a next of kin, we let it known that you might be in a worse condition than you actually were."

"So everyone thought I was virtually a gonner?"

"You were seriously injured."

"But you told everyone I wasn't going to make it."

"Joe Braithwaite had to believe there was little chance of you awakening and giving evidence against him. We needed him to resume his operation under the misconception he wasn't in the picture." The officer looked a little sheepish. "We took the precaution of posting someone outside your room just in case anyone decided a better guarantee of your silence was needed."

Like a fine wine on the pallet, Spencer rolled the information around his thoughts, savouring their implications. "So he's in jail?"

"On remand, yes."

Spencer couldn't be sure if he had been told all this before. Surely he would have remembered this feeling of elation? Could he really be in the clear?

"So where did you arrest him?" He needed a clearer picture of the moment. When the officer left he was going to have a nap picturing it.

"Everything came to fruition with simultaneous raids on Joe Braithwaite's home and several clubs across London. His organisation was quite extensive. That's why we needed him to believe he was free to operate: we wanted his whole network."

"How many people did you arrest?"

"Quite a number. The exact figure I don't have offhand. It consisted of several female impersonators__"

"If you're talking about Drucilla's cronies, they're *drag queens*. And tacky ones at that. *I'm* a female impersonator."

The expression that momentarily clouded the officer's face could only be described as '*whatever*'. "His *associates* brought large quantities of drugs into the clubs under cover of their elaborate attire."

"Of course. That's why we could never catch them getting the stuff into the club: drag queens were the only people who were never properly searched."

The officer continued. "The drugs were then distributed by one or two more informally dressed gentlemen." Spencer thought it strange how policemen could make the word 'gentlemen' sound like *scum-sucking-pond-life*. "Most of the workforce came via Francois Trimble's agency." He said Francois' name with the same loathsome disapproval a nun would say *feltching*. "As his various business concerns struggled to keep afloat, the runners and dealers were recruited from his payroll with him getting a finder's fee and a small cut of the business he sent their way. And with their more efficient mode of distribution cutting into Mickey Johnson's turf, Mickey Johnson retaliated by killing Mr Bryce as an example."

"You mean Stella?"

The officer nodded curtly. "Samuel Dobbs was then killed

in reprisal at St Bart's hospital." (Spencer still had no idea who Samuel Dobbs was.) "Video footage shows Joe Braithwaite going into the hospital dressed in...*professional* attire."

"Drag."

"Yes, drag. Joe Braithwaite had with him a bunch of flowers as he arrived at the hospital where he met Samuel Dobbs, and is seen shortly after leaving without the flowers."

Spencer was getting the picture. "Is this the day Stella died?"

"Yes." The officer clearly resented having to acknowledge Stella's pseudonym. "Samuel Dobbs' autopsy showed traces of rose stem and the same poison used to kill someone you'd know as Valkeyre. We think Troy Barrowclough, who had apparently started working as a dealer for Joe Braithwaite, had been given the task of killing...Valkeyre, whom he was working with at the time of the murder. We think he somehow managed to poison himself in the process."

"He wasn't very bright."

"So everyone we interviewed said."

The mystery Timberlands that came into Drucilla's dressing room when I was hiding, thought Spencer. *Valkeyre must have nicked the lipgloss. Bo had said she was a bit sticky fingered.* Spencer noticed the officer glancing uncomfortably at a newspaper sitting beside the bed. Its headline read, 'Pervy Politician in Police Cover-up'.

"So what about the party in Soho?" said Spencer.

The officer straightened his posture. "Two of the three murders in Soho were by the same method, and the third as an indirect result. Without a better idea of who was at the party, the exact nature of the events are proving difficult to piece together. We are treating the murders as part of the ongoing feud situation, however. A large quantity of the narcotic blu was found scattered over the body of one of the victims in Soho. We believe this to have been a symbolic gesture."

Spencer felt his eyes grow heavy. It was all so difficult to take in, but it seemed he was in the clear. "So what's going to happen to Drucilla?"

"Well, after his confession __"

"He confessed?"

A look of short-fused impatience scowled across the officer's face as if he had gone over this a hundred times. "Well...yes, of course he did."

Spencer's bed droned as he let it descend.

The officer's phone buzzed. A flash of relief brightened his face. He glanced at his phone's screen. "I'm afraid I'm going to have to make a move."

"Oh...okay, bye."

Spencer's brief joy of victory felt painfully short-lived; he couldn't escape the fact people had died. The officer was at the door when the bed stopped. "How'd you know it wasn't me?"

The officer's brow furrowed as he turned to face Spencer one last time. "Your call to D.C. Heinz. I'm afraid I really must go."

For a brief moment Spencer saw the room as a cartoon and above his head floated a giant, pulsing question mark.

CHAPTER 48

"Good to be home, hon?" said Lucy, pushing Spencer's wheelchair into the lounge where several half-hearted Christmas decorations had been slung round mirrors and pictures.

"Feels weird," said Spencer, tousling his uncomfortably short hair. "I honestly thought I'd never be back here."

Lucy steered him to a halt beside the coffee table. "Are you sure you wouldn't have been better staying in for another couple of days like the doctor suggested?"

"No way. I'd spent enough time sitting up in bed making the same small talk again and again. I couldn't cope with another day. But mostly I was dying for a spliff."

"And here's some I prepared earlier." Lucy made a flourished gesture to the half dozen ready-rolleds that sat beside a lighter in an orderly row next to the ashtray on the coffee table.

Spencer smiled.

Lucy sat on the sofa next to his chair. "So you still getting the phantom pains?"

Spencer looked down at the stub on his left leg where his knee once was. "Some nights I can feel my toes as if they're all still there. The worst thing is the phantom stiletto straps. I wake up sometimes with the pain of them digging in to an ankle that isn't there." He swung his right leg up and wiggled his toes in his sandal. He could feel an imaginary left leg do the same. "Anaesthesia says the upside is I never need pay for shoes again." He wiggled the missing toes on the missing foot on the missing lower leg. "They always display the right shoe in shop displays. She says she'll handbag me one every time she's in a shoe shop from now on. She's already got me three." He brought his leg back down. "So how's Mandy doing with my club? I hear he hasn't burnt it down."

"He's amazed us all. He was interviewed on just about every news channel for weeks. And he didn't fuck up once."

"Yeah, but he'll have to deal with Norman Daniels. And that takes a delicate touch. If I don't get back soon, Daniels' will have the club relegated to every thirteenth Tuesday. Have you seen Mandy lately?"

"Actually, I haven't."

Spencer leaned over and took a spliff. "He's phoned a few times, but he didn't come in to see me after I woke up."

"He's got a new man."

"He said. And what about *your* new man? I feel as if I've been away for..." Spencer struggled to do the maths.

"You have, hon." Lucy rubbed his leg.

Spencer lit the joint. "So what about you and your man? What's his name, Peter?"

"It's good. He can breathe through his ears, has a tongue like a length of stair carpet and hasn't once asked me to stick a finger up his ass. He's a keeper."

Spencer nodded in the direction of the kitchen. "Have you... you know, the cats?"

"Been gone for ages. If I have any more pets it's going to be chinchillas. I'll at least get a nice waistcoat out of it if they croak at that rate. I had to have Chairman Meow re-homed. He's probably shredding someone's three-piece suite as we speak."

Sensing Lucy's eyes burning into him, Spencer looked up from the joint he was savouring. "What?"

"Nothing, hon. I'm just pleased you're home. We thought you were never going to wake up." Lucy's voice trembled. "You know what they told us. It wasn't right the police tormenting us like that. They should have let us in on it. They should have told us you had called them and they knew you were innocent."

Spencer returned his attention to the spliff in an attempt to hide a wince; everyone thought he had called the police and cunningly taunted a confession from Drucilla for them to hear. It was too great an accolade to damage with the truth; it just didn't sound as heroic to say he'd been aiming the phone at Drucilla's head with the accuracy of a three-year-old girl and the crappy phone, which had been misdialling for weeks, just dialled the first name in his phonebook. That number had been Anaesthesia's up until D.C. Heinz had sent such conflicting signals by programming in his first name: Aaron. As a result, Drucilla's confession went through to a police officer's voicemail.

Lucy got up. "I'm going to have to move. I've got to go to the wholesaler's and pick up some more plastic dog turds. Will you be okay till I get back?"

He waved the spliff. "I'll probably be out like a light after this. What you up to this evening, you fancy watching a DVD?"

"I'm sorry, hon, I'm going out to dinner with Peter, but I'll make you something before I go."

Spencer smiled and offered his cheek for a departing peck.

Holding true to his prediction, Spencer fell asleep after a couple more puffs. He awoke in the wheelchair with a stiff neck and a string of drool leading down to his tee-shirt. A duvet of silence had engulfed the flat. He missed the constant bustle of the hospital; it had drowned out the accusing voices that had built in legion in his head since waking from his long sleep.

He wheeled over to the Hi-fi and pressed the radio button. No comforting lights came on; the room remained silent. He wheeled next to the socket on the skirting board, figuring Lucy's obsessive compulsion about unplugging electrical equipment was to blame. The plug lay on the floor. He tried to get the chair as close as possible and bent forward. It was no use. He was going to have to get out of the chair and onto his hands and knee. He left it and wheeled himself to the kitchen.

The idea of a cup of coffee provided little distraction. With everything that was once at waist height now at eye level and everything that was at eye level out of reach, the coffee was in no fear of making it into a cup unless he wanted to drink it whilst standing at the counter. Hopping, he had discovered in hospital, was not a good mode of transport for hot drinks.

He wheeled over to the phone and called Rob. The whole hotel thing was in full flow, apparently. Rob's PA answered; Rob was recording an interview for *Loose Women*. His PA said he'd get back to Spencer as soon as he was available.

He wheeled around the lounge a few times, as much to make noise as to clear his head, before feeling drawn towards the dressing room. Feeling like a character in a slasher movie heading into a dark forest with a flickering torch, he rolled down the corridor.

Starved of any olfactory stimulus other than NHS disinfectant for weeks, his head spun with the exhilarating scent of perfumes, cosmetics and shoe leather. Grateful someone had cleaned and tidied the place, he greedily inhaled the room's aromatic feast. He wheeled next to a row of dresses and ran his fingers through the sequins. He pulled his favourite Dexter Wong to his face and rubbed it against his cheek, recalling the exuberant applause its first outing had received. He grabbed the train of his BAHTI dress and kissed it, remembering how it once sparkled up on that massive bank of video screens. He whimpered as he stroked the arm of the Valentino he had rescued from a Hampstead charity shop and promised he would never leave it again. He sighed as he ran his fingers through the pale blue, sequined strips of the ice queen dress he had worn the night of Cirque du So Gay.

He moved over to his shoes and took his newest Manohlo's and cradled them in his arms. He put them back and ran his fingers over his jewellery boxes. His heart leapt as he saw his Gucci clutch and smiled at the memory of the movie premier for which he'd bought it. It was all still here. Safe.

At first he couldn't think why he thought it wouldn't be, until he looked at the dressing table. It wasn't the couture he was afraid of losing. It was Bette, and everything that came with her.

He pulled up alongside the dressing table. She'd been saved. As if rescued from the burning building of the situation, she had been saved. He lifted a brush and shook old powder from its bristles. He breathed in its scent. It was as if Bette had just left the room. Smiling with relief, he spun to face the full-length mirror. The reflection assaulted him with a cold and unexpected brutality.

He dropped the makeup brush and gripped the armrests of his wheelchair. He wanted to scream. He wanted to scream like a gay male choir watching a home birth video: the hair would take months to grow back, the broken nose had ruined facial symmetry, the missing leg part had devastated his prime asset and knowing there was enough scar tissue across his stomach to appear in 'Apocalypse Now: The Musical Review' he concluded his modelling career, similar to Paris Hilton's acting career, was a total bust.

A choking smog of fear engulfed him. He could feel his breathing get faster. The biting sensation of a phantom stiletto strap throbbed from a non-existent limb. Eyes wide and unblinking, he stared at the reflection. Unsure what he had expected, he was certain it wasn't this. He scrutinised what stared back at him for any signs of Bette and saw nothing. What was he going to do if he couldn't do Bette? Who was he without her? What was he without her? But then, staring into his own eyes in the mirror, the question he was most afraid of came to mind: Who had he been as her?

He continued to stare at the reflection. He knew he had done awful things in the name of Bette's career; awful things that would haunt him for the rest of his life. He wheeled closer to the mirror and its disturbing reflection. Who was the demon lurking behind the costume and ambition? Was it Bette, or was it Spencer? Was Bette just a Stanislavskian creation that ran away from him, taking flight and form of its own, or was Spencer an awful person who was incapable of admitting to what he was, a coward hiding behind a facade of costume and camp? Was he a monster or an unbalanced victim? How could he go on from here? He had no right to expect anything from the world after what he had done. But what did he have to offer the world now, anyway? What could possibly be out there for him now he had gone from glam to mutant drag?

A claxon sounded in his head announcing the every-man-for-himself evacuation of his mental acuity as a tidal wave of panic was spotted on the horizon. He threw his thoughts into the nearest lifeboat: the club. According to everything he had been hearing, Opus Gay was going from strength to strength. He took a deep breath. Being no stranger to reinvention, if he played this right Bette could be reborn as the greatest of the gay scene's survivors. He breathed deep again. He could re-promote her as the beauty who had stared Death in the face and given him makeover tips before sending him on his way. He sucked in another breath. He could do some charity work for the anti-gun lobby, and maybe something for the Elton John Foundation; Elton always loved a bit of tragedy and camp. He breathed in through his nose and exhaled deep from his mouth. She'd need to get Mandy onto some new dresses: something that made the most of her good leg. He'd Heather Mills-McCartney his way out of this if he had to. Another breath. This might all work out. The gay press were queuing up for interviews. He could make that work to the club's advantage. He knew she could turn this all around. She could...

Spencer pulled himself back from the mirror. He scanned the room. Did he want this again? Did he want to go back to being something he wasn't?

The doorbell rang. He exhaled slowly before wheeling himself to see who it was. After a bit of a struggle with the logistics he swung open the door to find Mandy.

"Welcome home," Mandy said, waving a bouquet of flowers.

Spencer couldn't believe what was standing before him. Mandy had lost weight, his hair wasn't bleached, and if Spencer wasn't mistaken those were G-Star jeans he was wearing.

"I had no idea your hair was brown," said Spencer. He pushed the door closed and spun his chair round, whereupon Mandy deposited the flowers and a plastic folder into his lap and wheeled him into the lounge.

"It was time for a change," said Mandy. "I wanted rid of the old me."

Spencer thought that a strange statement and had been about to say something when he noticed Mandy's shoes. "Are those Prada?"

Mandy nodded. "They were a present. They're killing my feet, and I'm not sure I like them." Mandy pulled Spencer to a halt at exactly the same spot Lucy had parked him.

"You look different," said Spencer, in an understatement that could have sat comfortably at a dinner table alongside 'the Iraq war turned out a bit messy' and 'the BNP aren't very fond of minorities'.

"Thanks." Mandy took the flowers to the kitchen and placed them in the sink. "I've been dressing like a bag lady for too long."

"I didn't think you looked like a bag lady."

Mandy came back and sat beside Spencer's chair. "Of course you did. Why wouldn't you? I did."

For some time now, Spencer knew his grip on reality had been tenuous at best...but this; if Anaesthesia arrived with her hair in a number two crop, wearing a pair of DM's and a Ben Sherman tee-shirt, he'd know he was dreaming and still in a coma.

"So how you feeling?"

Shocked, stunned and looking over my shoulder for the television cameras, thought Spencer. "Okay, I suppose."

Mandy looked at the leg. "When did they say you'd be up and about?"

"I get fitted with a prosthetic next week, and then I've got months of physio."

"What about the..." He waved his hand back and forth across Spencer's stomach.

"It's not too bad. So tell me about Gerald."

"You'll meet him shortly. He's coming to pick me up in ten minutes."

"Oh...aren't you staying for a while? I thought we could catch up properly."

Mandy shuffled uncomfortably. "Yeah, well...we've got a party over in Islington I have to go to. Condoleeza's bridal shower."

"Oh..."

"She's bought a six foot ice sculpture of a naked man. Apparently you pour vodka into his mouth and it comes out his dick chilled."

"Sounds fun."

"To be honest, I'm still a bit fragile from last night."

"Last night?"

"It was the opening of Victoria Embankment's new play, *Boy, I ain't No Lady*. The aftershow party didn't finish until seven this morning."

"I think I had invites to that."

"You did. I didn't think you'd want them to go to waste, so Gerald and I used them."

"Oh…"

"Norman says to send his best wishes, by the way."

"Norman?"

"Norman Daniels. It was his tenth wedding anniversary at the weekend. He hired one of those party boats on the Thames. You'll never guess who got up and sang."

"You got invited?"

"I did his wife's dress."

"But he invited you?"

"Yes. And he's told Gerald and I we can use his villa in Greece if we want."

"He's got a villa in Greece?"

"Lesbos, ironically."

Spencer shook his head; he wanted to wake up now.

Mandy took the plastic folder from Spencer's lap. Spencer had forgotten it was there.

"There's some things here I need you to sign. Club business."

"How's the club going? I heard it's been doing great."

"It has. We had television cameras outside for the last two." He passed some papers and a pen to Spencer. "And with Drucilla's night closed, Norman says Opus Gay can go twice a month. The first of the new nights starts on New Year's Eve."

"What, a second night? Did you say New Year's Eve? You're kidding. That's only a couple of weeks away. This is fabulous. This is…you're amazing, Mandy… I don't know what to say… This is the best news… I had a bit of a panic earlier, but this is great because I've__"

Mandy interrupted. "I paid off all the bills from before you went into hospital." He pointed at the papers. "And I need you to have a look at this." He passed some papers that were stapled together.

Spencer sat the papers on his lap and took Mandy's hand. "I can't thank you enough for all this. I could have been ruined without you. I don't deserve you as a friend, Mandy."

Mandy pulled his hand away. "I'm a little pushed for time."

"Oh…okay. I was just going to say…" Spencer paused, his attention seized by the papers on his lap. "What the fuck's this?" He shook the papers.

"Yeah, we need to talk about that."

"Damn right we do."

"Gerald will be here soon. If you need any translation of the legal jargon he'd be the one to ask. He drew it up."

"Have you lost the plot? I'm not signing this."

"I think you are."

Pain stabbed at Spencer's stomach as he pulled himself straight in his chair. "What's the matter with you?"

"I think you'll find it fair. The monies for the last two Opus Gay have been deposited into your account. Minus the bills, of course."

"Are you out of your mind? I'm not signing the club over to you."

"As I said, I've paid all the *outstanding bills*."

'Outstanding bills', the words screamed at Spencer; it was in that file he had put all the stuff on poisons he copied from the Internet. "Why should I?" The question was more reaction than any desire to know.

"I saw the file. I know what you did. I know it was you."

Spencer heard an involuntary squeak come from the back of his throat. Not feeling his lips touching, he assumed his face had frozen in a dropped-jaw configuration. He was paralyzed from the brain down.

"I read those notes. Phosphorous poisoning! It was me who took the poison to that party, wasn't it?"

"Mandy, I never meant for__"

"So was it true, were you really a dealer?"

"No, I…" Spencer didn't know where to go. If Mandy had seen the file there was no point in lying. He had to tell the truth. "I was trying to kill Drucilla. I know how mad that sounds, and I know how wrong it all was, but she was trying to ruin me. And it turns out she really was the mad, vicious cow I always said she was. You gotta admit that."

"Mercury, phosphorous, cyanide, what the Hell were you thinking?"

"I wasn't thinking. I was out of control. She was out to get me and I was turning into a paranoid basket case. No one believed she was trying to ruin me. Even you didn't."

"Maybe, but you don't go trying to kill someone. And why all those other people?"

Spencer made an involuntary shrug. "What can I say, I was a lousy killer."

"Do you think this is funny, Spencer? Maybe you can laugh, but I can't sleep at nights thinking about what you did."

"No. No, of course I don't think it's funny. I don't know what was wrong with me. It was like I lost myself somewhere along the way. It was like..." He stopped himself. He wanted to say it was like Bette had taken over his life, but he knew how crazy that sounded.

Mandy stared directly into Spencer's eyes. "I can't believe I blindly defended you when everyone else was bitching behind your back. No one at the club or anywhere else would speak out for you. Then it turns out I took your poison to that party. People died because of me. You know I thought about killing myself. I couldn't cope with knowing what we'd done."

"I'm so sorry, Mandy. You don't deserve this."

"Too right I don't. I've been worried sick. I didn't know what to think. I didn't know what to do. I couldn't believe what I was reading when I saw all that stuff. I wanted to go to the police."

"Why didn't you?"

"I nearly did. But you know what? I was afraid. I was afraid my shitty luck would end up with me being done for murder and you just walking free. I was afraid no one would believe I was that stupid not to know what was going on, or that I'd be forever known as the sidekick of a serial killer."

"I know there's nothing I can say to change things. I know I've no right to aks for your forgiveness, but taking the club... it's all I have."

"And you wouldn't have it at all if it wasn't for me. Drucilla was all lined up to take over your night. She was just waiting for the bad publicity to die down and Opus Gay was history. Meantime her and Daniels were only too happy for me to go out in front of the cameras and defend you, looking like a complete idiot. And, as it turns out, an accessory." He leaned forward. "But it didn't work that way, did it? The harsh publicity didn't kill the club: it made it. By some weird twist everybody loved it. It put the place on the map. And to top it all, Daniels now owes his licence to me."

"What...? Why?"

"Turns out one of the people at *that* party was the magistrate presiding over The Dryer's licence review. Let's just say I'm keeping my mouth shut about more than what *you* got up to."

"Look, Mandy, I can't defend myself. I was a complete loon. I don't know what was going on in my head. You saw what Drucilla was like with me. She was trying to send me round the bend. Turns out she succeeded. I left skid marks as I went screeching round the bend on two wheels."

"I don't care. I can't listen to you." He pointed at the papers on Spencer's lap. "Read the agreement."

Spencer threw the papers onto the floor. "If I wasn't in this wheelchair I'd__"

"But ya are in a wheelchair, Blanche, but ya are."

Spencer slumped back in the chair; it was going to take him a minute to recover from walking into a Baby Jane line. Especially from Mandy.

"I don't want this to be unpleasant, Spencer, but I know there's no other way it can be. This is too painful for me. I don't want to ever have to see you again." He gathered up the papers and placed them back on Spencer's lap. "I suggest you have a read through before Gerald gets here. He thinks it's your idea. I thought, under the circumstances, it was best if we keep it between us. I told him you wanted out of the clubbing business, in view of…" He pointed to Spencer's leg. "Norman Daniels will give you a call to verify it all at some point and I'll be expecting you to be sensible on the phone with him, too."

"I won't sign."

"Yes you will. And do you know why? Because it's the right thing to do."

"I've tried to be a good friend, Mandy. All I__"

"A good friend? I was fed up being your doormat. I'd had enough. You and everyone else have treated me like crap for years. How many more times did you think I'd listen to you saying sorry for being a bitch before I couldn't take any more? I've never been anything but a joke and a skivvy to you."

"That's not true."

"Really?" There was a pain in Mandy's voice that had Spencer wishing he hadn't pushed this. "It's strange how so many people have said to me recently that they'd given their number to you to pass on to me about work. Strange because you've never given me any numbers. But I'll tell you what was even stranger, finding all my business cards stored away in the back of your desk. Hundreds of them. Unopened boxes of them. Cards you told me you had been giving out to people."

"You were always saying how busy you were. I didn't want you to get overworked."

"Bull. You just wanted to make sure my time was spent making stuff for you." He slapped the papers back on Spencer's lap. Spencer flinched.

"Your friendship means everything to me, Mandy. You have to believe me." As the words came out of Spencer's mouth he realised he meant it; nothing was worth losing Mandy's friendship. "I've fucked up so much lately and screwed up everything in my life, but__"

"Too little too late. All I ever wanted was..." Mandy paused. He seemed to be rethinking whatever he had been about to say. "I just wanted to be a good friend. Over the years I'd got used to the gay scene treating me like shit, but I could cope with being a complete nobody with everyone else so long as I was a somebody with you."

"I..." Spencer stopped; he knew there was nothing he could say that would make any difference at this point. He wanted to rub his eyes; painfully dry, they were refusing him the luxury of self-pitying tears. He had missed Mandy's friendship throughout all of this, but seeing how much he had hurt him was almost too much to bear.

Spencer read the contract. Mandy was taking Opus Gay and all its associated rights; everything Spencer had worked for, everything he had strived and sacrificed for, everything he had...well, killed for. He read down to the line that awaited his signature. It was a tiny little line that when used would mean an end to it all; the club would be out of his life. Forever. A calm descended on him. He took a deep breath. Suddenly it didn't seem such a bad idea; something about it really did seem the right thing to do. His missing foot itched.

"You're absolutely right. I've been the worst kind of friend. You're welcome to the club. You deserve it. You deserve a great partner and you deserve a better friend than I was." He stared at the empty place where he would soon scribble his signature and wanted a pen...now. "You know, of everything I've lost in the past few months, losing your friendship will be the most painful." He looked up, directly at Mandy, but Mandy refused to look him in the eye. "If you've ever believed anything I've said to you, please believe that."

They sat without speaking and waited for Gerald. Gerald witnessed the signatures. Spencer thought him a bit plain, but he had a warm smile. He claimed to have been a big fan of Bette's. Spencer felt his use of past tense insensitive, but appropriate under the circumstances. They left with Mandy saying he would call later, but Spencer knew they would never speak again.

Spencer sat in silence once they had gone, overwhelmed by heartache and relief. He reached for one of Lucy's ready-rolleds, hoping it would once again knock him out and remove him from the pain.

His hand stopped before it reached a joint. He stared at them sitting side by side on the table and knew there and then what he had to do.

With tears begging to be released from dry eyes, he went

through to Bette's room and sat for a while amidst the couture and cosmetic that had once been everything to him. He had no idea what life had in store for him now, he had no idea what came next, but whatever it was, he knew he had to face it honestly as Spencer Hobbs. He wheeled over to the rails and began to take everything down; dresses went into plastic bags, shoes went into boxes, jewellery went into cases and Bette got packed away. Forever.